TIMEKEEPING in DEADWOOD

"That face you're making tells me you're not raring to follow Zelda inside."

"Think murky hallways and musty smells, and then add a boogeyman lying in wait."

He smirked. "But you're a big, bad Executioner."

"True, but I'm allergic to monsters."

"Since when?"

"Since I moved to Deadwood last year. If I get too close to one now, I break into a sweat, my throat closes up, my chest tightens, and then my knees weaken under a tank-sized sense of impending doom."

Doc focused back on the school. "Allergy or not, we can't leave if she's in there alone."

ALSO BY ANN CHARLES

DEADWOOD MYSTERY SERIES

TIMEREAPING IN DEADWOOD

BOOK 13

ANN CHARLES

ILLUSTRATED BY C.S. KUNKLE

For Becky Binder

Thank you for being so damned awesome.
You are full of sunshine and laughter.
Here's to many more hilarious and spooky times together!

―――――――――――――

TimeReaping in Deadwood
Copyright © 2023 by Ann Charles
Prescott AZ, USA

Cover Art by C.S. Kunkle
Cover Design by B Biddles
Editing by Eilis Flynn
Formatting by B Biddles

Library of Congress Control Number: 2023916094
E-book ISBN-:13: 978-1-940364-92-6
Print ISBN-:13: 978-1-940364-91-9

Dear Reader,

I've often said that one of my favorite things about writing the Deadwood Mystery series is having access to buildings and places that are usually closed to the public. This opportunity comes from wonderful "locals" who love history and who enjoy seeing some of the magnificent, older buildings in their town celebrated in print.

In this story, we return to Lead and the place I called the "old middle school" in book 12, *Never Say Sever in Deadwood*. In truth, this building was officially part of the Central School facility, which was built in 1913. During its lifetime as a school, it served the city of Lead as its sole elementary school with a brief stint as a temporary hospital when it was appropriated to house patients during the 1918 Spanish flu epidemic. At the end of the 1999–2000 school year, the school was closed after having been in continual use for 85 years.

It passed from private owner to private owner, eventually ending up in the capable and industrious hands of architect Robb Schlimgen. Robb is lovingly renovating the old school into beautiful private apartments, breathing new life into the entire complex. His affection for the place is obvious, judging by the amount of blood and sweat he and his helpers have poured into it and the quality of their workmanship.

On a side note, Robb is a charismatic, soft-spoken guy who is quick to laugh and doesn't mind when we jokingly call him "Demon Guardian." He is, after all, the nonfiction version of Dominick Masterson from the Deadwood Mystery series (and the Deadwood Undertaker series).

Anyway, Sam and I have had the privilege of touring the school complex multiple times with Robb, taking plenty of pictures so that I could accurately incorporate some of the interior scenes into the story. I think the effort has been worth it, and the setting feels more real to those who know the school inside and out. Many thanks to Robb (and Mary, his apartment manager and helper) for playing tour guide, and to Becky Binder for paving the way for our tours.

I hope you enjoy this newest chapter of Violet Parker's wild world! As the series evolves, so does she (along with the colorful characters in her life), making her series even more of a blast to write.

"Go away, the old buildings said. There is no place for you here. You are not wanted. We have secrets." ~Harper Lee, Author

Ann Charles
www.anncharles.com

ACKNOWLEDGMENTS

Thank you to the following fabulous members of *Homo sapiens* for your help with another trip through the pages with Violet Parker:

My husband, Sam Lucky, and our kids, Beaker and Chicken Noodle. I love you three to the moon and back!

Robb Schlimgen, the "Demon Guardian" of the old school in Lead, for giving us top-to-bottom tours of the place and lots of laughs in the process.

Violet's First Draft team: Mary Ida Kunkle, Becky Binder, Kristy McCaffrey, Marcia Britton, Paul Franklin, Diane Garland, Michelle Davis, Vicki Huskey, Lucinda Nelson, Stephanie Kunkle, and Wendy Gildersleeve. You guys give me motivation to keep typing!

C.S. Kunkle for turning my imp cover dreams into reality and for drawing such fantastic cover art and illustrations.

Sam Lucky, Violet's graphic artist/cover designer/formatter, for making this book look amazing inside and out.

Eilis Flynn, editor extraordinaire, for your superb eagle eyes. You keep me working on my grammar skills.

Violet's WorldKeeper, Diane Garland, for helping keep this series consistent and answering my random questions along the way.

Michelle Davis and Mark Davis for coming up with great promo items to share with Violet's fans.

Becky Binder for stepping in as our sales rockstar and opening doors for our books throughout Deadwood and Lead.

Wendy Gildersleeve for your help behind the scenes with beta runs and promo team fun.

Violet's Beta Team for reading previous Deadwood books and giving feedback in such a short timeframe. You guys are the best!

Violet's Deadwood Deputies, readers, and friends for your continued support and reviews. Without you, I'd have no reason to spy on her life and we'd miss out on all of the fun.

And my brother, Clint, for being a great little brother who'd go with me inside the old mines around Galena without hesitation.

KEY: Character (Book # in which they appear)—Description

Violet Lynn Parker (1–13)—Heroine of the series, real estate agent
Willis "Old Man" Harvey (1–13)—Violet's sidekick and bodyguard
Dane "Doc" Nyce (1–13)—Violet's boyfriend, medium
Detective "Coop" Cooper (1–13)—Deadwood and Lead's detective
Zoe Parker (1–13)—Violet's aunt and mentor in life
Layne Parker (1–13)—Violet's nine-year-old son
Adelynn Parker (1–13)—Violet's nine-year-old daughter
Natalie Beals (1–13)—Violet's best friend since childhood
Jerry Russo (4–9,11–13)—Violet's boss, owner of Calamity Jane Realty
Mona Hollister (1–9,11–13)—Violet's coworker and mentor in realty
Ray Underhill (1–9,12,13)—Violet's ex-coworker and nemesis at work
Benjamin Underhill (1–9,11–13)—Violet's coworker
Jane Grimes (1–9,11–13)—Violet's previous boss
Cornelius Curion (3–13)—Violet's client; so-called ghost whisperer
Reid Martin (2–13)—Captain of the fire dept., Aunt Zoe's ex-lover
Oscar "Ox" Martin (12)—Reid's son
Jeff Wymonds (1–9,12)—Violet's ex-client; dad of Addy's best friend
Prudence (2–9,11–13)—Ghost residing at the Carhart/Britton house
Zelda Britton (2,4–9,11–13)—Owner of the Carhart house in Lead
Tiffany Sugarbell (1–9,11,12)—Rival Realtor; Doc's ex-girlfriend
Dominick Masterson (4,7–9,11–13)—Previous client of Violet's old boss, Jane, and well-known Lead businessman
Mr. Black (2–4,6,8,9,11–13)—Mysterious, pale-faced Timekeeper
Hildegard Zuckerman (12)—Friend of Mr. Black and Ms. Wolff
Ms. Wolff (5,8,9)—Previous resident of Apt. 4 in the Galena House
Rosy (6–9,12)—Camerawoman from TV series called *Paranormal Realty*
Hope & Blake Parker (9-10,12-13)—Violet's parents
Susan Parker (1–10,13)—Violet's evil sister; aka "the Bitch from Hell"
Quint Parker (1–3,7–10)—Violet's brother; Layne's hero
Freesia Tender (5–9,13)—Owner of the Galena House
Stone Hawke (5–9,11,13)—Coop's ex-partner on the force; detective called in to solve cases
Rex Conner (3–9,11)—Biological father of Violet's children
Eddie Mudder (3,6–9,13)—Owner of Mudder Bros Funeral Parlor

"Wolves don't lose sleep over the opinion of sheep."

~**Aristotle**

CHAPTER ONE

Τhis here crazy-ass notion of yours has me thinkin' ya got termites in your rafters," Ol' Man Harvey said, eyeing me over a shopping cart laden with jars of honey.

I lifted my chin. My idea wasn't crazy. I preferred to think of it as borderline brilliant with a sprinkling of mad genius dusting the top. "I believe the saying is something about a spoonful of honey catches more flies than a gallon of vinegar."

My plan was to follow that literally—except instead of flies, I had something slightly bigger in mind.

"Any cluckbucket knows that," Harvey blurted loud enough to snag the attention of a guy wearing snowmobile bibs down by the condiments.

"Shhh!" I scowled at Harvey, my self-appointed bodyguard, who'd insisted on tagging along during my lunch hour.

I grabbed two squeeze bottles of honey from the shelf before glancing in the other direction for more eavesdroppers. The Piggly Wiggly grocery store had a busy beehive lunchtime buzz going on, but Mr. Bibs was the only one paying attention to us at the moment. Thankfully, the same scowl I used on Harvey also nipped Mr. Bibs's curiosity in the bud and sent him on his way, mustard in hand.

I probably should have waited until after work to swing by the store, but it was my turn to cook supper tonight for my two kids, Aunt Zoe, my boyfriend, and anyone else who showed up in my aunt's kitchen at mealtime. Normally, I'd stick to my standard culinary masterpiece—take-out pizza, because the only joy I found in cooking was when someone else was doing it for me. However, tonight I thought I'd make an old favorite of my son's: fish stick nachos.

This also happened to be a meal that was hard to burn.

Back to Harvey, I whispered, "I'm trying to catch an imp here." I set the squeeze bottles in the cart and then reached for two more. "The more honey I have for bait, the better chance I have of snagging that little, pointy-eared bastard."

Harvey knew as well as I did about the imp's obsession with anything and everything honey related.

His bushy gray eyebrows wrinkled. "You sure settin' a trap is gonna work on that critter? The last time you tried to catch it, you screwed up and set it free."

I hadn't been trying to *catch* the imp that day. I'd been trying to bash it senseless with my purse before it could sink those long, sharp claws into anyone—namely, Harvey's nephew, Detective Cooper, whose shoulder the imp had taken a liking to moments before. It was my bad luck that a window had been behind the imp and my purse had batted the sucker right through the glass.

"Am I sure?" I handed the bottles to him, nodding toward the cart before snagging a couple more from the shelf. "Of course not. Most mornings I'm not sure I'd be able to hit the floor if I fell out of bed. But this honey trap is worth a try."

He expressed his opinion of my grand plan through his nose in the form of a rather rude snort.

I narrowed my eyes. "Do you have any better ideas, Mr. Snuffleupagus?" After he managed nothing more than a sputter, I handed over more honey. "That's what I thought. Now stop being a buzz-reaper and help me fill this cart with anything that has honey in the ingredients."

Between the two of us, we emptied the honey section lickety-split. Then we grabbed several bottles of honey mustard on our way to the candy aisle, where we loaded up on bags of honey-flavored taffy, a treat we knew from experience the imp liked.

"Bein' that you're the only one who can actually see the critter," Harvey said, tossing the last bag of taffy into the cart, "I'm thinkin' it'll be best to do our hunting at night."

"*Our* hunting? Since when did catching this thing become a team sport?"

The bastard might have been small, but in my line of work, deadly creatures came in all sorts of packages and usually involved a set of spiky teeth. My plan didn't include risking Harvey's hide. Detective Cooper would fill my backside with buckshot if his uncle ended up with bite marks ... or worse.

"Listen, Sparky, when it comes to huntin', you can't spit much past your chin."

"I can spit and hunt just fine, thank you very much."

Did I need to remind him by counting off all the *other* non-human beings that I'd taken care of on my own over the past six months?

Well, mostly on my own, at least part of the time.

Okay, partly on my own *some* of the time.

Fine, so I might not be the most savvy *Scharfrichter*, but currently I was the only killer in the area. No, wait. Make that the only Executioner who still had a heartbeat.

"I ain't talkin' about man-huntin' here." Harvey grinned wide enough for his two gold teeth to show. "And even on that charge you weren't able to hit the side of a barn with a shotgun."

"Says who?"

"Says your momma." He snickered at my growl. "Not until Doc Nyce came along. That boy took to you like a lean tick to a fat hound."

"Hold it right there, old man." I held up my hand, raising a finger. "First and foremost, you need to stop talking to my mom so much."

"She's the one who calls me. Not answerin' is downright unfriendly. And poor mannered to boot. When it comes to ladies, I was raised to cover puddles with my cape." He leaned closer and winked at me. "Especially those who are pretty as pie supper, like your momma."

I sighed, groaning about the nosy, flower-child relic who'd raised me, *and* who couldn't keep her bucket mouth closed.

Lifting another finger, I aimed it along with the first at Harvey, delivering a solid shoulder poke. "Second, what have I told you about using unflattering animal references when it comes to me?"

He rubbed his shoulder. "Listen, girl, there's no need to get your horns out about this."

"A fat hound, a heifer in heat, and ... what was it you called me the other night when Doc and I were washing dishes after supper?"

"You mean when you two lovebirds were steaming up the window over the sink?"

"That was because of the hot water."

He harrumphed, clearly not buying my excuse. "I merely said your stud was pawin' the ground and rarin' to 'christen the yak,' which happens to have been one of my pappy's favorite sayin's."

"That was it. A yak." I tried to poke his shoulder again, but he swatted my hand away this time. "No woman wants to be thought of as a yak. They're big and shaggy." And probably extra stinky.

"Them there are fine qualities. And don't forget 'sturdy,' which is what a man wants in a woman if he's thinkin' north of his belt buckle." He wiggled his eyebrows at me. "Along with more curves than a barrel full of eels."

I wrinkled my nose back. "Eels?"

A slender, older lady was coming our way down the aisle, decked out in a puffy pink coat and matching boots.

"Well well well. If it isn't Willis Harvey in the flesh," she said with a twinkle in her brown gaze as she pushed her cart up next to ours, eyeing Harvey like he was the yak to be christened this afternoon.

"Junie Coppermoon! Aren't you lookin' pretty as a new-laid egg in that there frilly bonnet."

It was a silver knit beanie hat with a pom-pom topper, not a bonnet. But who was I to correct Prince Charming while he was preparing to spread his cape out for yet another pretty damsel?

He leaned closer and sniffed near Junie's neck. "You smell sweet as a bowlful of candy, too."

That earned him a playful arm slap and flirty giggle.

He pointed his thumb in my direction. "You know Violet Parker, don't ya?" To me, he said, "Junie was the English teacher up at the high school for over forty years before she retired. She dabbled in theater directin' at the Homestake Opera House, too."

I smiled and nodded politely.

Junie smiled in return, only there was a slyness to it, reminding me of a coyote with a chicken feather grin. She looked me over, starting with my windblown blond curls, traveling south over my indigo wool trench coat, and ending at the toes of my suede ankle boots.

"Sure," she said. "I've heard a thing or two at the senior center about your girl here." She glanced down at our cart and then did a double take. "That's a lot of honey for someone our age, Willis!" She gave me a hard look. "It'll send his sugar through the roof."

"Oh, this honey ain't for eatin'," Harvey butted in. "Sparky and I plan to use the sweet stuff to put a certain li'l devil into hell," he said with an exaggerated wink in my direction.

He really needed to zip his lips about the imp in public, even when it came to vague hints.

Junie gasped. "Good Lord!" Her cheeks turned as pink as her coat. "You two should be careful playing those sorts of bawdy games. Willis isn't as young and limber as he used to be, Miss Parker. Someone could break a hip!"

Without another word, she and her cart sped off down the aisle.

"Break a hip?" I frowned after her. What had she meant by *bawdy* games? "Doing what?" I asked Harvey. "I planned to catch and kill the little bastard, not leg wrestle naked with it."

"She's talking 'bout doing the horizontal boogie."

I whirled on him, not liking the sight of his obvious cringe. "Why on earth would Junie think the honey would be used for sex?"

"Because 'putting the devil into hell' is old-school slang for makin' whoopee."

I clapped my hands over my burning cheeks. "She's going to run back to the senior center and tell everyone that we're using honey to … to … to …" I growled. "What were you thinking telling her that? I have a reputation I'm trying to build in this town as a five-star real estate agent."

"Five-star? That might be stretchin' the blanket a little too far, what with your saucy billboards and ghost-lovin' reputation."

"Fine. Three-point-nine stars."

"Sparky, quit your huffin' and think this through. Better Junie thinks we're usin' the honey for fun rather than catchin' an imp."

"Maybe." Although given the chance, I would rather have deterred Junie with a non-sexual ruse.

"Ain't no 'maybe' about it." His blue eyes narrowed. "Now, you never did tell me what your mop-up plan was with the imp."

"I'm thinking along the lines of a Hansel and Gretel sort of trick."

"Lure the li'l bugger where exactly? Back inside its rusty cage where we found it?"

I assumed he was referring to the Sugarloaf Building where the imp had been imprisoned in an old-fashioned stove for umpteen decades before I'd accidentally freed it.

"Actually, I was thinking of a more permanent ending to this particular fairy tale."

"You mean …" He mimicked slicing his throat.

I nodded. "According to Aunt Zoe, imps are bad juju."

And she would know, having dealt with an imp years ago that had been hiding in a derelict schoolhouse in Deadwood. Wreaking havoc around town, like what this newest troublemaker had been doing of late, didn't even scratch the surface when it came to an imp's potential.

"And if they sink their claws into you," I added in a lower voice, "they can be downright deadly."

Aunt Zoe had told me all about the imp she'd caught back then and burned up in her glass blowing furnace. At the time, it'd been latched onto her favorite fire hose jockey, aka Captain Reid Martin of the Deadwood Fire Department. The only way she'd been able to even see the creature was via a special warded mirror in her house that reflected *other* beings regardless of their shielding abilities. It was pure luck that she'd been able to catch the sucker, let alone get rid of it.

I didn't think I'd have it as easy as she had, especially because she'd been able to catch her imp by surprise. The taste of freedom after being caged so long would surely make *my* imp extra leery of traps. But I had to try something before it wrecked any other stores or vehicles around town.

I pushed the shopping cart to the freezer section, grabbing a big bag of frozen fish sticks before bee-lining over to the liquor section. The store had several bottles of mead in stock, which was something the imp had sought out before. I handed them to Harvey one by one.

"Does your stud know about this big notion to catch the imp?" he asked as he took the last bottle of mead.

"Not yet."

I had only come up with the idea while daydreaming at my desk this morning at Calamity Jane Realty. I hadn't wanted to bother Doc, since he was busy working onsite at a new client's place over in

Sturgis this afternoon.

By day, Doc dealt in numbers and figures as a financial planner. He saved the chatter about imps and ghosts and whatever *others* we stumbled upon until he was home at night. Actually, he dealt with a wild-haired blonde and her almost-ten-year-old fraternal twins at home, but worrisome creatures were often the main topics after my kids left the supper table, and wispy entities were sometimes the focus of our whispers as we climbed into bed.

Harvey hooked his thumbs in his rainbow suspenders. "What about Coop?"

"What about your nosy nephew?" That reminded me of a more pressing question I had. "Hey, is Detective Bossypants coming for supper tonight?" I needed to know how many mouths I was going to be feeding.

"Probably. Coop tends to show up wherever Natalie is these days, and she already told me you asked her to bring some beer to refill the fridge."

Natalie Beals was my best friend and partner in misdemeanors ever since getting cooties was one of our three biggest concerns in life. Unfortunately, she'd somewhat recently turned into a smitten kitten around Cooper, in spite of the law dog's prickly personality and her family's usual aversion to shiny badges and potential Miranda warnings.

"Are you actually cookin' somethin' tonight?" Harvey asked as I grabbed two bags of tortilla chips at the end of an aisle.

"I don't like the tone in that question." I pushed the cart toward the self-checkout machines. "If you want to know the answer, you'll have to come over for supper. And while you're eating, you can explain to my boyfriend why there will likely be a new sordid rumor spread around town about me and honey-flavored sex."

My "bodyguard" and I received plenty of stares as we scanned the contents of our cart. When an employee asked me why we needed so much honey, I explained that my son was using it for his science fair project this year. Harvey, on the other hand, wiggled his eyebrows, grinned, and announced loudly that he was on a special honey diet that would return his libido to what it was in his twenties.

Next time, I was going to order honey online and skip the humiliation that came from shopping with the blowhard.

My cell phone rang when I paused outside the grocery store to button up my coat. Meanwhile, Harvey pushed the cart toward my Honda SUV, not bothering to close his coat in spite of the winter gusts doing their best to turn us into big ice cubes.

I tugged the phone from my pocket. "It's Cornelius," I said as I caught up with Harvey. "Here." I handed him my key. "You unload while I talk."

He sniffed. "Put Corny on speakerphone so I can hear."

Since there was nobody else nearby to eavesdrop, I nodded and answered, "Hello?"

"Who is this?" Cornelius Curion whispered.

I moved the phone closer to my ear, having trouble hearing his voice over the high-pitched whine of a snowmobile passing by on the hillside drive next to us.

"You know who this is," I said. "You called me."

"What's our password in Morse code?"

"Beep-damn-beep, Cornelius." I didn't have time for games with the Abe Lincoln lookalike, who was temporarily living upstairs over Calamity Jane Realty while his hotel on Deadwood's Main Street was in the midst of major renovations.

"Ah ha! Violet it is. Although your brain could have been hacked by an evil entity bent on—"

"Cornelius!" This was not the time for him to wax on with one of his kooky-spooky theories. "Why did you call?"

"I'm perplexed about your clock."

The clock he was referring to was not really *mine*, but rather a unique Black Forest handcrafted piece that I'd been tasked to monitor for creepy otherworldly—or was it other realmly—travelers. Officially, I was supposed to be some sort of Timekeeper. What this new role entailed exactly, I had yet to learn, but I'd been instructed on what to watch for when it came to the clocks.

And what to worry about.

"What's with the clock?" He was babysitting it for me because I had young children with curious fingers. "Is it chiming? Or cuckooing? Wait, you can't actually hear either. Or can you now?"

Harvey stopped putting my cloth shopping bags in the SUV and moved closer, listening.

"Violet, I need you to look in a mirror," Cornelius said.

"Why?" What did that have to do with the clock?

"Because I want to know if your aura is silver today."

"What does a silver aura mean for Sparky?" Harvey asked loud enough for Cornelius to hear.

There was a pause from the other end of the line. "Violet, it appears we have an entity on the call with us."

"We sure do. And after the shenanigans the old smartass pulled in Piggly Wiggly, he's about to get his suspenders snapped really hard."

"Ah, Mr. Harvey is at your side. Good. He can check what color your aura is. Silver auras tend to signify erratic mental energy."

I huffed. "My aura is going to be black and blue, same as your nose really soon, if you don't hurry up and tell me what's going on with the freaking clock."

"Ahhh," Cornelius said, sounding unruffled by my threat. "I'm guessing your aura has turned brown now, indicating your need to get what you want immediately."

"He's right." Harvey eyed the air above my head with a wrinkled nose. "It's muddy brown, Corny. Sort of reminds me of peekin' into the hole of an outhouse crapper."

I snapped one of Harvey's suspenders before he could block me.

A frigid cold blast of wind made us both grimace.

"Cornelius!" Shivering, I tightened the neck of my wool coat. "Why did you call?"

"The clock's hands are moving."

That wasn't so odd, not even for these kind of particular watch-clocks. "Like ticking minute by minute?"

"No, like spinning. Picture a whirling plate on a stick balanced on the red nose of a clown."

I held my phone away and frowned at it. "Why would you choose that imagery, Cornelius? You know how I loathe clowns after being stuck in a pitch-black elevator with a possessed clown doll."

"I think you need to pay me a visit, Violet."

"Okay, but first tell me—"

"Now!" Cornelius interrupted and then hung up.

I pocketed my phone. "Shittle-de-diddle."

"Whad'ya think spinnin' clock hands mean?" Harvey asked, setting the last grocery bag in the back of my SUV.

"I don't know." I closed the back door and then cringed as another freezing cold blast rattled me from teeth to toes. "But with my bad luck these days, we should probably keep an eye out for evil flying monkeys."

CHAPTER TWO

Time was a tricky devil.

At least that was what I'd been told more than once over the last couple of months.

Normally, time was simply, well, *time*. But that was before I'd been forced to jump through hoops—or rather a time loop—and given this new role as a Timekeeper.

Initially, the job didn't seem like something requiring a rocket science degree, but that was where the "tricky devil" part came into play. It turned out that this gig was *very* complicated, especially when time wasn't really "time," and screwing up on the job had life-or-death consequences.

According to the other Timekeeper, who was supposed to start officially training me soon, the main duty of my new role at this point was as follows: Keep an eye on any clocks I was given, so that I'd know when trouble had come to town with my name at the top of its hit list.

Or should that be its shit list?

"And that is about as cryptic as having my fortune told to me by Elvis the chicken," I said aloud as I pulled into the parking lot behind the Calamity Jane Realty office.

"What're you chatterin' about over there, Sparky?" I had tried to drop Harvey off back at Aunt Zoe's along with the frozen fish sticks, but he'd wanted to ride along with me to Cornelius's place to check out the worrisome clock with his own eyes.

"My Timekeeping task."

"Yep. It sure has me buffaloed."

"You mean the rules of the clock-watching game?"

"Nah. I meant why you of all people would be chosen with somethin' that is apparently as tricky as pickin' fly shit out of black pepper."

"What are you trying to say?"

"For one thing, it's like you said back in the parkin' lot—Lady Luck isn't too fond of you. Hell, if you bought a graveyard, I bet people around here would stop dyin'."

"At least then Detective Hawke would stop trying to pin every crime on me just because of my tendency for stumbling upon dead folks."

Detective Stone Hawke, Cooper's temporary partner at the Deadwood police station, had a theory about me. It involved boiling cauldrons and flying broomsticks. In his overly suspicious pea-brain, I was the reason for every fishy death he came across—along with a few misdemeanors, too.

"The other problem with you keepin' an eye on any of these clocks is that your knees turn to puddin' around them."

I pulled into my parking spot. "Yours would too if the chiming or cuckooing meant that someone or *something* was here to hunt you down and kill you and your family."

"Ain't that only half the time, though? I thought you said the cuckoos also meant the troublemaker skedaddled."

"Right, but only if the hands of the clock aren't moving." Which took me back to wondering why the hands on the clock were spinning today.

I shut off the engine and stared up at Cornelius's apartment in the driver's side mirror. "What do you remember about the rules of the clocks, Harvey?"

"Mostly the cuckoo part." He unclicked his seatbelt. "When you were tellin' me the rest, it sounded like you had your tongue caught in your eyeteeth and couldn't see what you were sayin'."

I frowned in his direction. "My tongue was not caught in my eyeteeth."

"You sure about that?"

Not entirely. I unclicked my seatbelt, too, reaching for my purse. "Okay, we're going to make this quick. If you want to stay longer to chat with Cornelius, have at it, but I need to get back to work before my afternoon appointment arrives."

My fingers were crossed that the couple scheduled to ride

around town with me to look at some available houses weren't obsessed with ghosts like the last two so-called potential buyers.

Thanks to my boss's marketing efforts, my coworker, Ben Underhill, and I had recently become reality TV stars. The second episode of *Paranormal Realty* had aired last evening, and the office's main phone had been ringing nonstop all morning. It seemed that selling haunted houses was good for bringing in "lookers." Whether they actually turned into buyers was another story.

Ben had also taken several new clients out last week only to find out they just wanted him to play tour guide through some reportedly haunted locations.

Harvey and I climbed out of my SUV, hurrying through the cold wind across the parking lot. At the top of the stairs leading up to the second-story apartment, Cornelius's door stood open a crack.

I hesitated, listening.

I didn't hear any cuckooing or chiming coming from inside, so the *other* individual represented by the clock was not coming or going through one of the metaphysical gates here in the Black Hills. But I did pick up the faint sounds of an accordion and a guitar—polka music. Cornelius's favorite.

After knocking twice, I called through the crack, "Cornelius? It's Harvey and me. Can we come in?"

Silence.

Harvey and I exchanged wrinkled brows and shrugs.

Pushing open the door, I stepped inside. The entry hall smelled like fried eggs and potatoes, reminding my stomach that I'd forgotten to pick up a sandwich at the store in my hurry to grab the honey and run.

Harvey shut the door behind us while I stomped the slush off my boots on a mat that had the words: *Enter if you dare.*

I'd rather not dare today, but the clock was my responsibility, not Cornelius's. Same as with the imp, it was time I stopped lollygagging on the job.

I tugged off my gloves, pocketing them. Now, if I could only figure out how to use this Timekeeping gig to keep my family safe.

Pinning a "Timekeeper" nametag on my shirt didn't mean I was going to take the Hellhound clock home with me, not after that heart-stopping vision I'd had about my daughter touching it. As if the black smoke that had seeped out of the cuckoo door and wrapped around her little finger wasn't creepy enough, in place of the cuckoo bird had been a blond girl who'd looked a lot like Addy and had dripping blood ringing her neck. The memory alone still made my chest tighten.

"I'm going to go see a man about a mule," Harvey told me after wiping off his boots.

"Are you speaking literally?" With Harvey, I could never be certain. One time, he'd actually meant he needed to talk to Doc about a mule he'd inherited from some uncle.

"I'm speaking urinar-ily." He hustled toward the bathroom.

I found my favorite Abe Lincoln doppelganger sitting on the floor in his kitchen. His long skinny legs were wrapped pretzel style, his black hair covered by a multicolored, baggy beanie hat that looked like something my mother might have knitted. He just needed a vest with fringe and a peace sign necklace to finish the hippie-yoga look. At least he was fully clothed today. After finding him only partly dressed from the top down more than once, I didn't take apparel for granted when it came to Cornelius.

"There you are," I said, unbuttoning my coat. The temperature seemed to have gone up ten degrees since we entered the front door.

A glance at the stove found a frying pan with four tater tots left. I grabbed a couple and popped one in my mouth, cold but still tasty, while looking down at the five large cards laid out on the floor in front of Cornelius. They formed a plus sign. But the cards weren't playing cards. They were like small, colorful paintings, frames and all, that lured me to take a longer look.

"What are you doing?" I stuck the second tater tot in my mouth, tilting my head slightly to see what was on the cards better.

Cornelius continued to stare down at them while stroking his pointy goatee. "Do you see this?" He gestured toward the card at the top of the formation.

"Of course." It looked like a medieval tower, only made of gold with shining silver windows. I bent closer. The top of the tower was in the process of being struck by lightning, sending pieces flying everywhere. "It's pretty. Too bad about the lightning strike, though."

He stared up at me, wrinkles crisscrossing his forehead above his bright, cornflower blue eyes. "I don't think you see it, Violet."

"I don't need glasses. I can see the darn card."

Whew! It was really warm in here. I shrugged off my coat,

draping it over one of the kitchen chairs. He must have the heat cranked up today.

Oh, I knew what it was. Jerry had the real estate office below extra toasty to welcome new clients. The heat must be rising through the floor.

"Where is the clock?" It wasn't on the kitchen table where he'd had it the last time I'd stopped by. "I'm short on time this afternoon."

"Yes, you are. Alarmingly so. We should contact the Tall Medium and have him come immediately."

I fanned myself. Why couldn't Cornelius call Doc by his name— or rather his nickname, since "Dane Nyce" was Doc's real name? Just because Doc was a mental medium with the extra abilities of an …

Hold up! "What do you mean, I'm *alarmingly* short on time?"

"It is shown here in the cards."

I looked down at the cards again, noticing the Roman number XVI at the top of the one with the tower on it. "What is shown exactly?"

"Your hair-raising predicament."

Was he talking about the clock or the cards now?

Harvey joined us, wiping his hands on his pants. "Where do you keep your hand towels, Corny?"

"I don't." His focus held steady on the cards. "The towel rack is haunted."

Harvey snickered. "Did you say *haunted*?" Before he followed Cornelius any further down that particular rabbit hole, I held up my hand to stop him.

"Save it for later." I turned back to the odd duck on the floor. "Where is the clock?"

"Violet, this is not good."

Neither was me being late for the appointment my boss had set up with these new clients, especially since Jerry was the one taking calls, making appointments, and coaching me from the sidelines. Even a couple of decades after he'd retired from professional basketball, my boss still couldn't get over his case of acute sports-itis. Thankfully, his disease wasn't infectious and spending my workdays "in the game" with him didn't require me to wear a jockstrap, which I'd heard could chafe something fierce.

"I agree," I said, stealing the last two tater tots away from Harvey as he reached for them. "I don't think the clock hands are supposed to spin."

Tossing both tots in my mouth, I took a step toward the living room, trying to see if he'd moved the clock in there. Maybe he'd hung it on the wall like normal people, rather than store it in the basement, which I'd done before asking him to keep watch instead of me.

"I'm not talking about your current clock conundrum." Cornelius snagged my leg and tugged me back his way. "According to these cards, you might be traveling on a path toward a painful death."

"Those cards?" I pointed at the floor. "Don't tell me you've taken up fortune telling now."

"Hey, those are fancy tarot cards." Harvey nudged me aside to take a closer look at them. "You like the cross spread, huh?"

I did a double take at my bodyguard. "What do you know about tarot cards?"

"It's not 'what,' but 'who.'" He crossed his arms. "She went by the name Madam Mayhem and boy howdy did that woman stoke me up like a steam engine."

Oh, jeez. "Let me guess. She worked at a brothel in Winnemucca."

"Nah. Ely, Nevada, was where she and her crystal ball called home. Just a block down from the train station." He shuddered. "That woman could be downright scary with her jars of porcupine quills, chicken feet, and fish eyes."

"So, she was a—"

"Seer," Cornelius finished for me. "I met Madam Mayhem once at a haunting in Tonopah."

"Then you didn't actually sleep with the seer," I said to Harvey.

"There was no way I was closin' my eyes when Madam Mayhem was in a room with me."

"Holy *frijoles*!" I parroted one of my son's expressions. "For once you have a story about a woman from Nevada that doesn't involve sex."

"Oh, we played plenty of birthday-suit patty-cake. That woman was built like a brick outhouse, with curves coming out her ears. I just didn't stick around to sleep in the same room as her."

"Quite bodacious," Cornelius agreed. "Even her toes were shapely."

I sighed at the two of them. "What was the point of your story, Harvey?"

He scratched his jaw through his beard. "Huh. I'll be damned. I don't rightly remember."

"When I noticed the clock hands spinning," Cornelius said, bringing us back to the original reason we were standing in his kitchen, "I had an idea."

"To call me. I know."

"No. To ask the tarot cards about your situation."

"And that's why you're telling me I'm doomed to die a painful death."

"Possibly." He once again pointed at the card with the tower and lightning on it. "The Tower card appearing at the top of the spread doesn't necessarily mean you're doomed, but it's certainly a warning that big change is on the horizon, maybe even the potential for upcoming peril."

I wasn't sure if I believed him or not. "Big peril as in someone is going to hunt me down and kill me? Or just little peril, like I'm going to fall on my ass in the parking lot on my way to my car and bruise my tail bone?"

"Bruised tail bones are big peril." Harvey shrugged when I glared at him. "What? That's a real pain in the ass."

"The cards aren't entirely clear on the matter." Cornelius leaned back on his hands. "Remember, these are tarot cards. They merely suggest what is to come. They allow room to change course and alter the future. But the Tower card concerns me, especially since Mercury is in retrograde for a few more days."

Not as much as the clock situation concerned me, but I bided my time, waiting for him to wrap up his version of Madam Mayhem's prophecy. "Why?"

"The Tower can indicate something is going to fail catastrophically, especially when placed in this aspect with these other cards." His voice lowered. "Something that was erroneously thought to be true. Keep in mind that anything else that might have been built on this false belief will come to an end as well—an unexpected ending." He ended in a whisper that bordered on creepy. "One that might very well bring chaos with it."

I gulped. Me dying sooner rather than later would be classified as an "unexpected ending" in my book. And if I was taken out of action, who would be around to keep my family from suffering their unexpected end as well?

Harvey clapped his hands together extra loud in the small kitchen, making me jump in surprise. "Well, slap the dog and spit on the fire! Sounds to me like it's about time for the sky to start fallin', Chicken Little."

* * *

Several hours later, I sat at my desk watching the clock—not the timepiece over my head in Cornelius's apartment with a Hellhound carved into it. This clock was merely the digital version on my computer screen that told me it was almost time to lock the doors here at Calamity Jane Realty and head home for the night to throw together some fish stick nachos.

However, it was that dang Hellhound clock that needed my attention. True to what Cornelius had said on the phone, the hands on the clock face were spinning and spinning, and at a decent clip, too. There was no cuckooing or chiming to be heard, though.

What this meant was beyond me and my meager Timekeeping knowledge, but there was one individual I hoped would have an explanation—Mr. Black, who happened to be my counterpart in this Timekeeping profession. He also happened to be an *other* who excelled in stealth and mystery, stood tall enough to give me a cricked neck, and had skin as pale as the moon with thick tufts of pure white hair to top him off.

Actually, Mr. Black was more of my tutor than counterpart at this point. He'd been keeping track of the clock upstairs (and a hoard of others) along with my predecessor, for who knew how long. I certainly hadn't gotten that particular answer out of him yet.

Unfortunately, Eddie Mudder, the one human I'd been told to use as the messenger to reach Mr. Black, was out of town for a morticians' conference in Denver for a week according to his voicemail. So, now I had a problem in addition to the spinning clock hands—I needed to figure out how to reach Mr. Black.

I checked the time again. Twenty more minutes and I could close up shop, head home, and put the fish sticks in the oven.

Leaning back in my chair, I glanced around at the other four desks that made up a rough circle in Calamity Jane's front room.

Mona Hollister's desk was the closest. My flame-haired mentor had taken today off. She'd left her desk neat and tidy with not a pen or paper clip out of place. A pair of her rhinestone-studded reading glasses, her only personal effect, were neatly folded and sitting next to the small, raked Zen sandbox. No sweet hint of her jasmine perfume lingered in the air today. No clackity-clack of her fingernails on her laptop keyboard broke the late winter afternoon silence.

I sure hoped Mona was doing something fun on this frigid winter day. Something that didn't involve anything even close to fretting about honey-loving imps and hand-spinning clocks. Something to reward herself for the slew of "pending" sales she'd recently added to Calamity Jane's pipeline.

Jerry Russo's desk was on the other side of Mona's. My boss had left work over an hour ago, mentioning something about heading down to Rapid City to meet with old friends who were in town for a few days.

Initially, Jerry had set up shop in the big office located down the back hallway. But ever since my old boss, Jane, who happened to be Jerry's ex-wife, had returned a few months ago—make that his *dead* ex-wife had showed up in her ghostly form—Jerry had relocated out front with the rest of us. Around that time, he'd hired Cornelius to set up his slew of expensive ghost-monitoring equipment in that back office, which used to be Jane's before she was brutally murdered.

I sighed, stretching my neck from side to side. It was hard to believe Jane had been dead for over five months already. It seemed like just yesterday she was standing over at the whiteboard, updating the sales pending list.

I glanced toward the back hallway, wondering if her ghost was floating around with me here this afternoon. Not that I'd be able to see her if she was. Not unless she really wanted me to, like that one time.

There hadn't been any cryptic notes etched in Mona's Zen sand, or written on the whiteboard, or typed on my computer, as Jane had done in the past, so she must be off doing whatever ghosts did when they weren't trying to bother with the living.

Then again, maybe Jane was standing over me, wondering why

I wasn't trying to find more clients in one of those ghost-groupie chat rooms. If there was such a thing. Hey, maybe I should explore that option. After all, Cornelius had found his way to me via an online ad about a haunted hotel, which was now *his* haunted hotel, with the commission from the sale in my bank account.

I grabbed a pen and wrote a reminder note about my idea on a piece of scrap paper. With any luck, I'd score big like Ben, who sat at one of the remaining two desks. He'd taken a new client out this afternoon to check out a few homes in the area, too. However, unlike my afternoon clients, his appeared to be a legit buyer. Right now, as I sat and twiddled my thumbs, he was in the process of wining and dining her down at The Wild Pasque, one of Deadwood's fancier restaurants.

Setting down the pen, I rested my chin in my hands. My two yahoo clients had made it clear when I pulled up at the first stop on what soon became Spooky Parker's Ghost Tour that they weren't really here to buy. They just wanted to look, take selfies in front of the haunted houses, and pick my brain for ghost stories. I should have seen that coming when their first question before we'd even left the parking lot was if I would autograph their "Haunted Deadwood" posters from the Deadwood Visitors' Center.

Jerry would need to work harder on screening my calls now that the second *Paranormal Realty* episode had aired. Otherwise, I was going to start charging tour guide rates to make up for a lack of commissions.

I eyed the last desk in the circle, now empty because the horse's ass who used to work here overstepped Jerry's rule about not screwing over fellow teammates—namely me.

Ray Underhill's obsession with getting me shit-canned had backfired. I shook my head, thinking of the last time I'd seen Ray. He'd stormed into the office when I was working alone, same as this afternoon. Only instead of his usual swagger, he'd been all wide-eyed and paranoid about someone following him, claiming his compromised predicament was all my fault.

The asshole never could take credit for his own screw-ups.

I stared out the window at Sherman Street, mostly empty, lit by streetlights. I didn't doubt that someone or something could be waiting out there in the dark for him. Or me, too. But I didn't believe that my monsters were in cahoots with his demons.

I picked up my cell phone to call Doc, wanting to talk to him about honey-loving imps, haunted houses, and that creepy Hellhound clock, but then I set the phone back on my desk, facedown this time. He'd be home with me soon enough. I'd wait until he was …

My cell phone rang.

Maybe Doc had picked up on my thoughts, him being a mental medium and all. That would be a first for us.

I flipped the phone over.

Shit.

Cooper's name showed on the screen.

I cringed. Why was he calling? My past experience with the detective had me hesitating, what with his tendency to try to bite my ear off through the phone.

It rang again.

And then again while my finger hovered over the button to accept the call.

It could be he was simply calling to ask what time supper was. Or to confirm that Natalie would be coming.

Or it could be he'd found another dead body and somehow it was connected to me. That had happened too many times over the last six months, and frankly, I wasn't in the mood to look at anything dead tonight. I had a feeling that a grisly murder scene and fish stick nachos wouldn't go well together.

The phone rang a fourth time.

However, if this were a call about a dead body, I had a firm alibi for most of today. And all of last night, too. My finger lowered toward the screen to take the call.

But what if the caller was really Detective Hawke, using Cooper's phone to try to fool me into answering? The bonehead had used that trick before.

No, I was not falling for that again.

Another ring.

It could be Natalie, though. She might be with Cooper, borrowing his cell phone because her battery was dead. Or she'd forgotten her phone back at her apartment in the Galena House. Or maybe …

Whoever was calling from Cooper's phone hung up halfway through the sixth ring.

Good! Now I'd see if a voice message was left, and then I'd decide if and when I'd call back.

I watched my phone, waiting.

After hearing Cornelius's warning about that Tower tarot card, I needed to keep my head low and watch out for whatever crap-blizzard might be coming my way. Not that I believed a set of tarot cards in the hands of one oddball could really predict my future, but it didn't hurt to be wary.

The bells over the front door jingle-clanged.

"Parker!" Cooper's voice made me yelp and jump up.

The detective glared at me from across the room. His blond hair was sticking up on end, bristly-looking, same as the rest of him from his scowl down to his clenched fists.

Crud. What had I done now?

I glared back just because. "Must you always enter my world snarling and barking, law dog?"

"Only when you don't answer your damned phone."

"I was busy," I defended. Kind of. Busy thinking, anyway.

"Bullshit. I stood across the street watching you being *not* busy while not answering my call."

My cheeks warmed. "If you were standing over there watching me, why didn't you just come over in the first place and save me the hassle of trying to lie to you?"

"Because unlike you, I *am* busy."

"Busy harassing innocent women," I finished for him.

His steel-gray eyes narrowed. "No, Parker. I'm busy dealing with one of your messes."

Double crud. What now?

"This is about the Tower card, isn't it?" I asked, falling back into my seat.

His scowl slipped for a moment, replaced by a what-the-hell stare. "What Tower card?"

"Cornelius asked the tarot gods, or universe, or whatever, something about my immediate future and pulled the Tower card, so big peril and chaos are about to ensue."

He let out a loud bark of laughter, only there was no mirth in it, just frustration. "Hell, Parker. Chaos is your middle name." He yanked open the front door and pointed outside. "Now get your ass in my rig."

"Why? I didn't do anything."

"Yes, you did. You let that damned imp go free, and now it's an even bigger pain in my ass than you!"

CHAPTER THREE

I t had started snowing by the time I pulled in behind Cooper's police cruiser up in Lead.

He didn't wait for me to join him out in the freezing wind and pelting snow. Instead, he rounded the front of my SUV and planted himself in my passenger seat, smelling minty cool—a mix of his cologne and the cold outside air. He pulled the door shut and closed us in together.

I cringed and shifted as far away from him as I could get. A rattlesnake slithering into my sleeping bag would be more cozy. "What are you doing?" I asked while letting my Honda idle to keep us warm.

"I need to fill you in on what's going on here, which I'd have done on the drive up if you weren't so damned pig-headed about riding along with me."

It wasn't a matter of being stubborn, it was more that I didn't want to be chewed on all the way to Lead and back for freeing the damned imp in the first place.

I shrugged. "I told you, I'm allergic to police vehicles." I'd ridden in the back of them too many times already in my almost thirty-six years.

"That's just plain dumb and stupid, Parker."

"It's partly your fault."

"Ah, shucks. If I hadn't left my tiny violin at home I could've played you a sob song."

By *home* he meant Doc's place, since Cooper was temporarily living there until I found him an acceptable house to buy in Deadwood. And by acceptable, it needed to be ghost-free, since

Cooper suffered from the ability to see the walking dead. Not zombies, which I hoped were still only fiction. Instead, he could see any specters still hanging around. Unfortunately for him, though, he saw them in their time-of-death state, no matter how gruesome the situation had been.

"Maybe I didn't want to hang out at this crime scene any longer than necessary. You could be here for hours playing detective, and I have supper to make for several people."

He smirked. "Fish stick nachos is no five-course feast."

I narrowed my eyes. "Did you interrogate your uncle this afternoon about what was for supper, or did the big mouth call you?" Harvey had better not have mentioned anything about my honey-trap plans for the imp.

"I texted Nat. She asked me to bring dessert." He scowled. "What in the hell kind of dessert goes with fish stick nachos?"

I shrugged. "Chocolate goes with anything, according to my kids."

"Nat suggested something with tequila in it for the adults, since nachos are considered a Mexican dish around these parts."

"That, too."

I looked up at the 1930s-era, square two-story house with a small boxed-in porch that sat ten feet or so back from the curb next to where Cooper had parked. Light flooded through the windows nearest to us on the lower floor, adding a soft glow to the leaf-bare bushes and mounds of snow below, but I couldn't see any movement through the gauzy curtains. The porch windows were partially shuttered and blocked with stacks of stuff—a pile of blankets in one, a mountain of puzzle boxes in the other.

Parked in front of a single-car garage built partly into the hillside was a 1970s Chevy pickup painted with what looked like gray primer paint. Rusted-out holes peppered the front and back quarter panels. I flicked my headlights on high to see it more clearly. The passenger side appeared to be stuffed full, almost to the top of the cab, with fast-food wrappers, clothes, newspapers, and two boots that didn't belong together. The bed of the truck had multiple crates, plastic tubs, and partially wilted cardboard boxes all strapped down under a torn camouflage tarp.

From the looks of the pickup and the porch, I had a feeling the garage would be stuffed to its gills, too, with more boxes, tubs, crates, and other general junk.

"So what's the story here?" I asked. "And why are there no other police cars around?"

"A couple of hours ago, a call came into the Lead police station. The homeowner claimed someone had broken into the garage and caused a couple thousand dollars' worth of damage. After one of the officers came by to check it out, she gave me a call."

"Because you're a police detective for both Deadwood and Lead," I finished for him.

"No, Parker. She contacted me because I'd requested the Lead officers keep me posted on any more potential burglaries after your imp made that mess at Piggly Wiggly."

"It's not my imp."

Officially, the little bastard had been Dominick Masterson's prisoner, a spoil that he'd taken from one of his subjects whom he'd killed for being a traitor. At least that was what Dominick had told me recently.

But why keep a troublemaking imp? That had been one of my questions at the time. Then I'd learned that an imp can bring prosperity to its keeper when properly trained. However, judging from the way this bastard was tearing up the town, I didn't think its dead owner had spent much time teaching it how to roll over or play fetch.

"Anyway," Cooper continued, "the officer had taken a few pictures and collected the necessary information to make an official report."

"Which the owner needs for insurance purposes," I figured out loud.

"She stopped in at the Deadwood police station and left them for me, but I was busy all day, which is why I didn't call you sooner so that you'd have plenty of time to hurry home, tie on a frilly apron, and bake those prize-winning fish sticks."

I didn't like his tone any more than I had his uncle's earlier when leaving the grocery store. "Don't knock my cooking until you try it."

"Making nachos is not really cooking, is it?"

"Says the guy who brings takeout for supper when it's his turn to make the meal."

"Some of us can accept our limitations in the kitchen with more grace than others."

I decided to be the bigger person and move on rather than give him another black eye. "Busy doing what?"

"Huh?"

"You said you were away from the station all day because you were busy. What were you busy doing?"

I only asked because I wondered if it were anything to do with several cases Detective Hawke was actively trying to pin on me.

"That's police business, Parker."

And we were back to the usual wall Cooper liked to keep between us. "Whatever."

I focused on the house, wondering if the person at home knew we were sitting out here. I had yet to see anyone look out the downstairs windows.

"Okay," I said. "So what makes you think this is another imp case and not just some local hoodlums looking to pull off a B&E so they could pinch a few tools?"

"That's not how cops talk, Parker." He extracted some photos from the pocket inside his coat and held them out for me to take along with a flashlight. "You really need to stop watching so much television."

"Shut up." I snatched the pictures and the light, shining the beam down on them one by one.

The first showed several aluminum trash cans that had been knocked over and partly crushed. Around the beat-up cans were what looked like finger-sized, short sticks tossed onto the ground, along with some torn boxes and plastic bags.

"It looks like a bunch of raccoons went to town on the trash cans."

Cooper pointed at the short sticks. "Those are chicken wing bones."

The second picture showed a standup freezer inside what appeared to be a partially packed garage. I glanced up at the house. *That* garage. Only the freezer was not standing in the photo. It lay on its side with the door missing. Several more boxes similar to the ones next to the trash cans in the first picture had spilled out onto a cracked concrete floor. Some of the boxes were crushed, others torn open.

I held the picture closer, making out the word "Wings" on a couple of the boxes. "There must have been a chicken wing sale at

Piggly Wiggly," I said, counting nine boxes total.

Wing bones lay scattered here and there, same as with the trash outside. The rest of the freezer contents appeared to have been left in the packaging, just scattered.

The final picture was of the slightly crooked, wooden garage door. I'd bet it was original to when the house was built, requiring manual opening. In the bottom right corner, several of the boards had been broken and torn free.

Hold on a minute.

I leaned closer to the photo. There were a few bite marks and several visible scratches around the broken boards.

I looked over at Cooper. "What makes you think this is the imp's doing? It could be just some hungry raccoons."

"The freezer door was torn off the hinges."

"Oh." I stared back at the picture of the freezer. "But chicken wings?"

"They're honey BBQ chicken wings."

"Honey." I winced. "That little shit."

He pointed at the garage door picture. "Do you see that mark scratched into the wood?"

I peered closer. "Kind of."

"It's a symbol," he said, sounding sure about it.

"How do you know? It looks like scratches."

"I checked it out with a magnifying glass." He grabbed the door handle. "Come on, I'll show you." He paused in the midst of climbing out. "Bring your phone. Nyce and Zoe should take a look at this. Maybe they'll be able to figure out what it means."

He shut the door as I killed the engine. I pocketed my phone and hurried out into the cold dark after him. I caught up at the garage door, squatting down next to him. He lit the door with a more powerful flashlight that he'd stopped by his rig to grab. The symbol was lower to the ground, certainly at imp level.

I pulled out my phone and snapped several pictures. "That looks like a ward. Do you think the imp left it or was it here before as some kind of marker for the imp to find?" I stood, still looking down at it.

"Both good questions."

I feigned surprise with an exaggerated gasp. "Did you just compliment me, Detective?"

"Not on purpose," he shot back.

"Well, I'm still going to write about your accidental kindness in my journal tonight and dot every 'i' with a smiley face." I focused on the ward. "Did it go in the house, too?"

"No, only the garage, and the owner doesn't think anything is missing besides his chicken wings."

I frowned at the ward, trying to make sense of the weird symbol. "Why would it leave a ward here?"

He shrugged. "Maybe Zoe will have a good theory to explain it. She's dealt with an imp in the past."

I wasn't surprised Cooper remembered that tale. His mind was a steel trap, especially when it came to all the times I'd screwed up and left him stuck with another crime scene to explain.

"Do you think there are any other wards inside the garage?"

"I went through all of the crime scene photos." He frowned. "There's a lot of shit packed into this place."

"Judging by the cab of that Chevy, I'm not surprised."

"This door was the only place I noticed a symbol like this." He clicked off the flashlight. "I don't think the Lead police officer noticed it, though, or she would have mentioned it in her report."

Well, the symbol wasn't very big. Not much larger than a regular playing card. And unless the cop had seen wards before, like Cooper and I had, or actually made wards, like Aunt Zoe, it could easily go unnoticed.

Cooper followed me back to my Honda.

"How long until I need to be at your aunt's place?" he asked as I climbed in behind the steering wheel.

"Supper will be ready in an hour." That should be enough time to put everything together. "I'll show Aunt Zoe the pictures when I get home. Maybe she'll have some ideas about this symbol by the time you get there."

Before he could say anything else, my phone rang. I checked out the screen and cursed, sending the call to voicemail.

"Nice, Parker. Kiss your mother with that mouth?"

"Don't start in about how much you like my mom better than me, Cooper." He'd only met her a couple of times and yet he now let her call him "Coop," a nickname used only by his inner circle of friends.

"What can I say?" He grinned. "Hope signed me up for a whiskey of the month club."

"She's just bribing you so that you don't arrest me anymore."

He chuckled. "She said you'd say that."

I rolled my eyes.

"And do that, too."

My phone started ringing again from the same caller—Dominick Masterson. Apparently, he wasn't going to be easily put off this evening. "It's Masterson."

That sobered Cooper. "Why is he calling you now?"

"I don't know. Probably to tell me something that will make the Tower card's prediction worse."

"Take the call on speaker," he bossed, reminding me of his uncle earlier at the store.

I accepted the call, putting it on speaker as ordered. "Hello, Dominick."

"Where is my *lidérc?*" He practically bit me through the phone. The casual cockiness and fake charm that he usually hid behind were nowhere to be found.

Cooper's gaze locked on mine, tension lines ringing his eyes.

"I'm not sure why you're calling *me* about this." I gave an award-winning performance, as if I weren't the one who'd snuck into the Sugarloaf Building earlier this month and happily sent that smoky Hungarian devil back to the hell from which it came.

But Masterson didn't know that and would never find out if I could help it. The *lidérc* had been another one of his caged pets, same as the imp. Only where the imp caused mayhem and messes, the *lidérc* attached to a human and drained them of energy, leaving nothing more than a worn-out carcass before moving on to its next victim. Capturing that smoky son of a bitch had nearly been the end of me. There was no way I could leave it hanging around to menace anyone else in the future.

"I'm calling you, *Scharfrichter,* because you are the last one who saw it."

"Says who?"

"Says I."

"Hmm. If I remember right, you saw it after I did when you collected the heirloom mirror I'd used to trap it so you could return my property to me."

"I didn't actually see the *lidérc* that night."

"But surely someone with your impressive abilities and keen

intellect must have sensed it was there."

I sort of meant that. After all, Masterson was no mere *other*. He was old. How old I had no idea, but he'd been around for a long, long time. Ancient even, like a crusty vampire, but he was no bloodsucker. Although to look at him, I'd put him in his early forties, and as handsome as he was dangerous.

"No, *Scharfrichter*. I trusted you had returned it as promised in exchange for your aunt."

"I did return it and you confirmed it. Deal fulfilled, so don't even start making threats about wooing Aunt Zoe again."

"Fine. It was there, but where is it now?"

"How should I know?" I sounded convincing even to my own ears, although Cooper didn't look impressed with my performance judging by that scowl lining his whole face. "I did my job, Dominick. That devil liked to disappear through walls. Maybe your wards didn't hold it when it was on the other side of the wall."

Silence came through the line for several seconds. Then, "If I find out you had anything to do with its disappearance—"

"Think about it, Dominick. Why on earth would I want to let that thing out again? It would come for me and my family, given a breath of a chance."

"Perhaps you executed it." His tone was all taunt.

I guffawed—a little too loudly based on Cooper's head shake. "Like I even have a clue how to do that."

"You've proven to be a fast learner."

"Not that fast." I sighed with a healthy dose of drama. "I have to go now, Dominick. When you find your *lidérc*, do me a favor and get rid of that menace for good."

I hung up before he could reply.

"Do you think he'll figure out what we did?" Cooper asked, still frowning at my phone.

"I hope not. Because if he does, he'll come for my throat."

* * *

As if the Hellhound clock's glitch, the potential-chaos Tower card, and the imp's freezer destruction weren't enough knuckle-chewing problems this afternoon, I arrived home to find my mother's red Prius parked in the driveway.

"This can't be good," I whispered, staring at the flower-edged PEACE, LOVE, AND HIPPIE-NESS bumper sticker slapped on the back bumper.

My mother wasn't the sort of parent who just showed up on a whim, especially on a cold, middle-of-the-winter afternoon. So, either my father had decided it would be fun to drive his wife up through the hills from Rapid City on a Monday to visit unannounced, or Mom had something to say that was serious enough to elicit her stepping out of her comfort zone.

Wait! Aunt Zoe's pickup was missing in action.

Shit, was this an emergency visit of some sort? It wasn't like my mom to come up to Deadwood without calling first to see if she could bring us something.

I grabbed my purse and stepped out into the cold, my heart pounding hard enough to make me a little winded as I climbed the front porch steps. I hesitated as I opened the door, listening, trying to catch a hint of what I was walking into by sound alone.

The living room was quiet, so the television must be off. There were no signs of life coming through the kitchen archway.

Something thudded overhead.

I closed the door and slipped off my boots, leaving them along with my purse on the nearby rug as I tiptoed over to the bottom of the stairs.

At the top of the steps two sets of eyes stared down at me. One set belonged to Bogart, our vegetarian cat, who was in a lewd pose while in the process of licking clean one of her back legs. If Harvey were here, he'd probably say he knew a red-light lady who preferred to greet her clients with that pose and go on to tell me cringy details about her other curvy attributes and bedroom skills.

Bogart blinked at me and returned to cleaning her fur.

Next to her, the owner of the other set of eyes clucked in greeting. Elvis the chicken angled her head to one side and then the other while looking down at me. Then she clucked again and turned her focus to the cat's upstretched leg, leaning closer to pluck something from Bogart's fur.

"You two are like monkeys," I told them. "Distracted by cleaning each other while you're supposed to be standing guard."

They ignored me and kept grooming.

Several more thuds came from behind the two watch pets, followed by a screech.

I hurried up the stairs, earning a squawk from Elvis as I stepped over the cleaning clowns.

My bedroom sat empty, but there was a polka-dotted wrapped gift sitting on the bed. I didn't detour to check out the present, heading down the hall instead.

Aunt Zoe had said she'd pick the kids up after school today, but if her pickup wasn't in the drive …

I paused at Addy's room, which was a mess with clothes and partly finished, pet-oriented projects scattered throughout. A half-built addition for Elvis's cage sat on the floor next to her bed. A bonnet for Bogart that she was in the process of embroidering with tiny cats was currently tied onto a stuffed mountain lion that sat on a stool in front of her sticker-covered mirror. The Duke, Addy's gerbil—or was it a hamster, I could never remember the difference—anyway, the little guy poked his head out of the paper towel tube play gym she'd taped together in his tank. After wiggling his whiskers at me, he backed out of view.

Nothing out of the ordinary here—well, except for the three-pronged spear leaning against her closet door. What was Layne's trident doing in Addy's room? He usually had strict rules when it came to his sister touching his weapons.

My gaze shifted to the unicorn school backpack sitting in the middle of Addy's twin bed. Someone had brought the kids home from school. Now to solve the other two mysteries: Aunt Zoe's current location and Mom's reason for being here.

A squeal of laughter lured me toward Layne's closed bedroom door. I didn't bother knocking.

"Layne?" I said, opening the door.

The door hit something midway, blocking it.

"Mom!" Addy's voice came from under a dinosaur comforter stretched across the room from the end of Layne's bed to his closet, where it was tied to the door handle. "Don't come in! You're going to mess up our fort."

Layne's head popped up from the adjacent side of the blanket fort. His blond hair was ruffled, his cheeks pink. "Is supper ready?"

"No, I just got home." I leaned against the door jamb, relieved all was normal on the home front.

Then I realized Layne and Addy were actually playing together and not fighting. Maybe not completely "normal," but I'd take this timeout between boxing rounds.

"Are you going to start supper now?" Layne pressed, as if he hadn't eaten in a week.

"Pretty soon," I said, wanting to find my mother and get the lowdown on where Aunt Zoe was first. "Have either of you two seen Grammy Hope?"

A third head bobbed up from under the tent. Her blond hair matched mine in color but was wavy where mine was all crazy curls.

"How was work, Violet?" my mother asked, smiling. Although her smile was a little too wide, bringing back the tickle of unease I'd experienced upon seeing her car in the drive.

"Work was good," I said slowly, carefully feeling my way through the conversation. "What's going on, Mom?"

As in, why was she here?

Addy emerged fully from under the blanket and climbed on the bed, bouncing up and down. "Grammy is staying the night. She's going to bunk with me!"

A bark came from under the blanket fort. Rooster the dog bounded out and stood next to the bed, barking up at Addy as she bounced.

"Addy, get down," I said, chastising along with Rooster. "Even your dog knows you aren't supposed to jump on the bed."

"Fine, Mother." Addy jumped off onto the floor next to Rooster, grabbing his front paws and lifting them to her shoulder so they could dance together in a circle. "Grammy is going to stay," she sang. "She's going to make cookies with us after supper."

"Oh, really?" I returned to my mother, but she'd disappeared under the fort. "Is there a particular reason why?"

"Because making cookies is what grammies do," Mom said from under the blanket. "I can't believe your momma doesn't know that," she whispered loudly, making both kids giggle.

Crossing my arms, I glared at where her head made a lump under the fort. "I meant, *why* are you spending the night?"

"We can chat later, Violet. Right now, we have a fort to defend from the evil dragon king."

I ignored her dismissiveness. "Dad is okay?"

"Your father is fine and his buns are as sexy as ever. Hubba hubba."

Addy giggled again.

I groaned. "Mother, I told you not to talk about your love life around me."

Her head emerged, her eyes sparkling with mirth. "Lighten up, Violet baby. I would've thought having a hot doctor around would have loosened your goose some."

"How would Doc loosen Mom's goose?" Addy asked. "We only have a chicken."

"Never mind," I told my child, hitting my mom with a zip-it scowl.

She laughed as if she had no cares in the world and disappeared under the blanket again. Lucky her. "Your dad is going to have a late poker night with his buddies, and I didn't want to hang out at home alone. So I came to see my little darlings with evil plans to spoil and tickle them."

Squeals of laughter erupted from under the blanket fort.

"Did you two get your homework done?" I asked, still loitering in the doorway, watching lumps move around under the comforter.

"They did, Violet," Mom answered in their place. "Now be a doll and go make supper for us. We're starving and can't wait to eat your fishy plate of carbohydrates."

Whatever! I started to walk away.

"Oh, Violet?"

I paused. "What?"

"Your aunt had to run down to Spearfish for some glass supplies. She said she should be home in time for supper, though, and to let her know if you need her to pick up anything at the store."

"Got it."

"Oh, and don't open that gift on your bed. It's not for you."

I glanced toward my bedroom. "Why is it on my bed then?"

"Because I want it to be a surprise."

"For Doc?"

"No, silly girl." My kids snorted at her tone. "It's an early birthday gift for Cornelius."

I didn't realize Cornelius's birthday was coming up soon. Then again, I wasn't much of a calendar keeper, unlike my mother, apparently.

"Is he coming to supper?" Knowing my mother, she'd called and invited Cornelius without talking to me first.

"Well, I invited him, but when he found out that fish sticks are on the menu, he said that he doesn't eat cube-shaped food. Something about it clogging his throat chakra, which makes it impossible for him to communicate with dead people."

I froze, wondering if Cornelius had told my mother about his and my multiple séances involving various ghosts.

"Did he really say 'dead people'?" I asked, trying to sound cynical, adding a fake laugh to throw her off even more. "That guy sure loves to mess with you. Remember how he talked about coffin flies the first time you met?"

"I think he actually believes in ghosts." She poked her head out from under the comforter, giving me a motherly glare. "And don't you go being a party pooper by playing skeptic. If he imagines he can talk to the dead, leave him be. He's not harming you any."

Actually, Cornelius was more of a spirit collector than a specter speaker. Or as Prudence, my ghostly Executioner colleague, liked to call him, a "spirit miser." During a recent possession attempt by Prudence, Cornelius had turned the tables on her, and she'd found herself on the other side of what she described as a door in his mind, behind which he kept terrors locked away. Apparently, this locked room was the result of a protective meditation technique his grandmother, a renowned seer from Louisiana, had taught him at a young age when she realized he was a magnet for wispy folks.

Doc liked to refer to Cornelius as a pied piper of ghosts, but in truth none of us understood what all he could do when it came to the paranormal world. Cornelius himself didn't even seem to realize the depths of his abilities. However, since moving to town and hanging out with Doc and me, he was quickly learning via the old trial by fire methodology.

After bowing out of Layne's bedroom under my mother's glare, I announced I was going to start supper and escaped to my room.

Twenty minutes later, I'd changed into an old sweatshirt and some yoga pants, secured my hair in a ponytail, and had fish sticks heating in the oven. Cornelius's lunch choice had spurred me to throw in a tray full of tater tots, too, for some additional carbohydrates to make my mother wrinkle her nose even more.

My mother often lived a metaphoric life that mimicked her name—Hope. As in she hoped I'd start eating healthier and exercising to be more like her, a long-legged flower child left over from the days of free love and sunshine. For years, she'd also hoped I'd find a good man to help me raise my kids, and she was over the moon that Doc had come along and gotten snared in my man-net.

I was in the process of texting Doc to warn him that my mother was here for the night, so he should expect to receive an extra helping of fawning drizzled with doting throughout the evening, when I heard the front door open.

I stepped into the dining room, hoping to see Doc taking off his coat. Or Harvey. Or Cooper, Natalie, Aunt Zoe, or Cornelius.

But it wasn't any of them.

It was my sister, Susan.

Aka Satan's concubine.

As in the three-decade-old pain in my ass who was supposed to be in the Caribbean somewhere trying to fix a domestic mess involving bigamy, my stolen identity, and some rich, old, ruthless dead guy who'd left the kids and me—actually, Susan pretending to be me—a ton of cash in his will.

My hackles not only rose at the sight of her, but also climbed on top of each other like a squad of cheerleaders forming a pyramid.

That Tower card concerns me ... Cornelius's voice replayed in my head. *Something that was erroneously thought to be true* ... *An unexpected ending* ... *One that might very well bring chaos with it.*

Hell's bells and Mercury in retrograde!

So, if Susan wasn't down in paradise fixing her mess, what unexpected ending was coming my way and how long until this chaos shit hit the fan?

CHAPTER FOUR

Susan stood on this side of the threshold, unwinding a green cashmere scarf from around her long, graceful neck.

The scarf reminded me of a snake, which reminded me of Medusa from Greek mythology, who didn't have much on my sister when it came to spite. They both had started out beautiful, but these days Susan had only one or two fewer snakes mixed in with her long, brown hair. However, she usually made up for the shortage of venom with her forked tongue and deadly bite.

"What are you doing here, Susan?"

A light bulb shined bright in my head. Ah ha! That was why Mom was here. She'd known her younger daughter was going to be paying me a visit tonight and must have come up to Deadwood to play referee.

"Did Mom tell you the good news?" Susan draped her scarf on the back of one of the dining room chairs.

"That you're moving to one of Saturn's many moons?"

She smirked. "I see your lousy sense of humor hasn't improved since I've been gone."

"I guess you should have stayed away longer." An eternity would have been about long enough.

"I didn't want you to start missing me."

She unbuttoned her long, black coat, revealing a sapphire-colored, velvet plunge jumpsuit. And by plunge, I meant a deep dive nearly to her navel, sharing with the world plenty of tanned skin with hints of curves and no bikini top lines.

"Criminy, Susan! Did you get your fashion sense from a 1970s porn flick?" I grabbed her scarf and tossed it back to her. "Put that back on. I have children, remember?"

"And a boyfriend. Or have you screwed up that relationship already?" She looked down her pert nose at me. "Judging from your choice of outfits tonight, you're one sad box of chocolates away from sinking into a peanut-butter fudge ice cream depression."

My gaze narrowed like a gunslinger's at high noon. Them there were fighting words. "You're the one who screwed up several of my relationships."

Or rather screwed around *with* those philandering ex-assholes.

"Blah blah blah." Susan twirled her finger in the air as if she didn't give a flipping care. "You really need to move on, Violet. Quit living in the past and release all of that pent-up aggression and negative energy."

That sounded like a chapter straight out of our mother's book of life on how to live a Hippie-Zen existence with a flower-filled soul.

But Susan wasn't done running her blabber mouth yet. "You should focus on fixing some of your current hangups, like your ongoing lack of fashion sense for your stout body type, and your apparent aspirations to spend your mid-life years as a wild-haired old hag."

I gritted my teeth. Mom was right to come play referee. At this rate, I was going to tackle the stick-insect and knuckle-rub a pack's worth of chewed gum into her hair before the fish sticks finished baking in the oven.

She draped the scarf around her neck, covering most of her exposed cleavage. "There. Happy?"

"No. You're still here."

"Trust me, *big* sis." She sniffed, glancing toward the kitchen. "You need me right now."

I sighed. "Yeah, I need you like a pair of inflamed hemorrhoids."

She opened her mouth, most likely to shoot another insult back, but I held up my hands, stopping her. "You know what, Susan, this never-ending battle between you and me has grown quite tedious. I'm done."

As in I was done with her bullshit. Done with our petty game of name calling. Done with the insecurities that came with seeing her. Done. Done. Done.

I had an imp to catch and a hand-spinning clock to figure out.

Maybe even a bounty hunter or two to dodge and kill. I had no oomph left to spare for this spite-filled crusade that had dragged on and on since she was old enough to start purposely breaking my toys.

I turned to head back to the kitchen.

"Oh, Violet," Mom called from the top of the stairs, stopping me mid-step. "I forgot to tell you that your sister was coming."

I thought of my mother's too-wide smile from earlier. "Forgot," I repeated. "Right."

I had a feeling it was more like she'd avoided warning me until it was too late to bar the door.

The stairs creaked as Mom eased down a couple of steps. "Susan, did you tell her?"

"Tell me what?" I looked at my sister, cringing in advance about whatever bomb she was about to drop on my head this time.

"Not yet," Susan told her, avoiding my stare.

On second thought, I probably didn't want to know. I headed for the kitchen.

"What's for supper?" I heard her ask Mom as I walked away. "Something smells fried."

"Fish stick nachos."

"Are you serious?" The disgusted tone in Susan's voice was loud and clear.

"Nobody asked you to eat with us," I called over my shoulder.

"Mom did." Susan followed me into the kitchen.

Our mother didn't join us, which had alarm bells clanging in my head.

"I need to talk to you, Vi, before anyone else comes."

Apparently, Susan wasn't going to delay the suspense about why she was gracing my doorstep out of the blue.

"I don't think that's a good idea," I told her, grabbing an oven mitt from the drawer.

According to Cornelius, Mercury being retrograde meant anything communication-wise could go sideways, so talking with Susan would surely lead to things being thrown at the wall. Or at her.

"Just hear me out," she insisted, leaning against the counter as I checked on the sticks and tots in the oven.

"If I do, will you leave?"

She hesitated and then nodded once.

I tossed aside the mitt and crossed my arms. "Okay, let 'er rip."

"I know I fucked up bigtime when I pretended to be you in St. Barts."

Yes, she had. It had been the cherry on the top of three decades of her vindictive shit piled on top of more of her jealous crap.

"And while I'm still working on cleaning up that mess, there's nothing more that can be done there right now, so I came back here to help you."

I took a cautious step backward, feeling like she was trying to roll a big Trojan horse through my kingdom's gate. "Help me how?"

Susan's version of helping was usually cockeyed at best. For example, she claimed her reason for screwing around with Rex Conner, the man who'd accidentally fathered my kids, was to show how unfit of a life partner he'd be for me. In short, she'd sacrificed her naked body on my behalf. Never mind that she'd supposedly fallen in love with the philandering jerk and wanted him for herself by that point.

"Well." She brushed some lint from her velvet sleeve. "I think I've established how good I am at falsification."

"You mean lying."

She shrugged. "Call it what you will."

"As the Greeks liked to say, a fig is a fig."

"Quit getting caught up on the small stuff." She waved me off. "Anyway, while I was away, I kept thinking about Rex."

"Of course you did." Had she ever stopped obsessing about him—the one fly who'd escaped her spider web?

"Mom had told me on the phone that he's been up here harassing you," she explained.

Mom had? Huh. I didn't realize my mother had been tuned into my life that much of late.

Did our mother have any idea that I was also dealing with supernatural troublemakers and fighting for my life? Dad did, but that was because this *Scharfrichter* gene came down through his family line. For whatever reason, it'd skipped Aunt Zoe, his sister, and landed square inside of me.

Although Aunt Zoe wasn't free of responsibility. It was her job to act as my *magistra*, or teacher. She also had to keep track of my deeds for future generations of Executioners, starting with my daughter, who was already emitting the worrisome "glow" of a killer according to a couple of seemingly trustworthy *others* I knew.

"What about Rex?" I asked, wanting to get this little talk about our shared ex-lover over with before Doc got home. "Let me guess." I tried to check my sarcasm, but my filter seemed to be temporarily out of order. "You're going to sacrifice your body to him *again* to save me. What a hero!"

Her cheeks darkened. "No. He's made it clear that I am not the one he wants. You are."

I scoffed. "Rex has only ever loved Rex. That hasn't changed over the last decade. Hell, he probably came out of the womb hugging himself."

"Yeah, I think I finally get that." She sighed. "I've humiliated myself enough when it comes to him. You were smarter than me to oust him from your life early on."

Holy shit! That might have been a compliment. First Cooper, now Susan. If Detective Hawke called to add one from him, I just might faint.

To be honest, though, I wasn't sure that intelligence was at the helm on my decision to walk away from Rex at that time, more like rage. Catching him in the act of having sex with my sister in my own bed had a way of terminating any thoughts of a potential future with the father of my unborn children.

But enough about the past.

"So, how is it you think you can help me with Rex? It seems like he's been trying to avoid you since returning to this neck of the woods."

"I have some ideas."

The glint in her perfectly lined eyes made me hesitate even more. I had a feeling it was more like she'd been doing some sinister plan hatching.

"I don't think this is a good idea, Susan." Whatever she was thinking.

"What do you have to lose?"

I glanced toward the dining room, listening for any sounds or signs of my kids, before whispering, "He has threatened to tell my kids he's the sperm donor if I don't stop messing with him, and whatever you're planning will probably fall into the 'messing with' category."

Officially, it was Natalie who'd been messing with Rex mostly, such as prying pieces off his expensive car and sending him flowers that spurred his allergies. However, I hadn't been willing to play along with his lie about having a family—as in me and the kids—that would have given him the promotion he'd wanted up at the science lab in Lead. That made me enemy number one in his book.

"I thought he signed papers before they were born that basically erased himself from their lives."

"He did." Thanks to our parents' lawyer.

Her lips tightened. "So, this is all in an effort to blackmail you back into his bed?"

"I don't think it's about sex, Susan." It was some other kind of power play. Or maybe just punishment for me not doing his bidding to help his career.

"Please, Violet. While I may like to give you trouble about your excessive curviness, I'm not ignorant of how male tastes vary when it comes to body types. Take Doc, for example."

I bristled again. "Leave Doc out of this."

"Relax. I'm not interested in competing for his attention."

"With our history, you expect me to take you at your word?"

She stared at me. "No, but like you, I'm finding this feud between us to be boring. There is no fun in taking from you anymore."

I sneered at her. "There never was, you spoiled tart."

Her eyes narrowed at my interruption, but she continued. "And in spite of what you think of me, I do love our mother and recognize that she has reached her limit on patience with my behavior. Same with your father."

"*Our* father," I corrected.

Even though Susan was not my father's biological child, Dad had adopted her at birth. He'd taken the place of her real father, who'd wanted nothing to do with her after a one-night stand during our parents' separation.

"Fine, our father." She shrugged. "I had a lot of time to think about things while I was in St. Barts. I could have fun focusing my energy on something other than messing with your perfect little life."

I thought of the price on my head, along with the creepy crazy shit I had to deal with of late. "Trust me, it's far from perfect."

"It looks good from where I'm standing. Two kids, a decent career, a nice guy in your bed who wants more than just sex."

Talking about my life with Susan made me antsy, like I was

helping line up her cannon, so I turned the spotlight back on her. "So, what then?" I canceled the bake timer two seconds before it buzzed and shut off the oven. "Are you thinking about pursuing your old dream of owning an art gallery?"

"No. That ship has sailed." She toyed with the ends of her scarf. "I was thinking more along the lines of screwing over assholes who use their money and power to try to hurt others. Like Hooch did."

Hooch was the old dead guy she'd used my name to marry down in paradise.

A strangled laugh came from my throat. "You have dreams of becoming Robin Hood now?"

She smiled, but it had no heart in it. "Something like that."

"So instead of trying to snare Rex for romantic purposes, you'd … " I trailed off, wanting her to finish for me so I could hear it straight from her lips, in case I needed her admission later in a living room, court-of-law situation with our parents playing jury.

"I'd drive him away once and for all."

"Would this include some shady business?"

"Possibly. You need someone who doesn't have to toe the legal line since you're a mother."

"Have you forgotten about Natalie?"

Her upper lip wrinkled. "Of course not, but Mom says she's dating a cop now. I would think that would curtail her illegal activities."

Yeah, I would have, too. But Natalie was not one to change her stripes just because her boyfriend slept with a badge on the nightstand.

"I'm not hindered by any law-abiding attachments," Susan continued.

I'd certainly learned that from experience over the years.

"And with my help, you could leave your dirty work to me while you continue trying to build this wholesome reputation in the community. We both know dirty work is what I do best."

Wholesome? I choked back a laugh. I hadn't earned the nickname Spooky Parker the Paranormal Realtor by organizing bake sales at the elementary school.

She needed to talk to Detective Hawke—he'd give her all the seedy details of my past brushes with the law, whether true or not. The asshole had been rifling through my past lately, having clandestine meetings with my old cohorts and new enemies for who knew what reason, undoubtedly trying to find some new means to pin one of the many crimes I didn't commit on me. If only I could be a fly on the wall and figure out what his game plan was …

I frowned at my sister. The woman who could possibly give the ol' femme fatale, Mata Hari, a run for her money.

Would it work? Susan spying for me? Could I trust her to worm her way into Detective Hawke's inner circle and find out what his next step was, so I could dodge the handcuffs he had all oiled and ready? Or would she turn on me and give me that cold-hearted smile as they locked me behind bars?

Addy came rushing into the kitchen with Rooster the dog following close behind. "Mom, can Grammy and I start making the cookies now?"

"Not yet." I pointed at the mutt. "What have I told you about bringing Rooster into the kitchen?"

"How am I supposed to let him out the back door to go potty if he can't walk through the kitchen?" She ran to the door and called for Rooster, opening it.

Elvis the chicken came running from the dining room, slipping out the door after Rooster before Addy could get it closed.

"There, see." She turned, her gaze settling on her aunt. "Are you staying for supper, too?"

Susan looked at me and mouthed one word: *Natalie?*

I nodded and smiled for real.

Natalie was the ace up my sleeve. My sister was afraid of her, and not just because my best friend had made a voodoo doll with Susan's actual hair somewhat recently and threatened to hold it over a lighter. Natalie had a history of making my nemesis pay for her misdeeds one way or another, and usually there was some form of pain involved.

"No, sugarbean," Susan told Addy. "I have to run. I just wanted to talk to your mom for a minute."

Addy's eyes narrowed. "Are you two fighting again?"

"I think we're done fighting for a while," Susan said, looking at me with raised eyebrows.

"Maybe," I answered, still suspicious in spite of her claim of calling a truce.

"Think about my offer," she said over Addy's head.

I just stared back. As tempting as it would be to use my sister's so-called powers for my own good, I didn't trust this new and enlightened Susan. After spending three decades getting stabbed in the back, I'd be a fool to not expect another shiv between my ribs if I let my guard down too soon.

Susan held out her hand to Addy. "How about you see me out?"

"Sure! But don't you need to say good-bye to Grammy?"

"You do it for me. She likes your hugs better."

Susan left the room with Addy bouncing after her, asking her aunt if she were flying away to "her island" again soon. I didn't care to hear Susan's answer, so I grabbed the Betty Boop cookie jar off the kitchen table and escaped to the laundry room to sort dirty clothes while pondering my sister's suggestion over a cookie or two.

After throwing a load of whites in the washer, I grabbed my cell phone and sent Doc a text message: *Maybe you should have an impromptu poker night with the guys at your place tonight and skip my lousy attempt at cooking.*

Even though Susan had left, my mother was still here. Doc had been extra busy lately with work. He might not want to spend an evening with Mom praising him left and right because she was so giddy that he hadn't dumped her daughter yet.

According to my mother, she'd spent years and years waiting for her middle child to find a guy—any guy, but especially one who had an ounce of decency in him. Poor Doc was centered in her sights now, and I feared she was spending her days at home polishing the old family shotgun in preparation to force him to marry me if he decided to make a run for it.

My cell phone pinged back as I returned to the kitchen to set the table.

Too late, Killer, he replied. *Is that Hope's car in the drive?*

He must be out front already. Damn.

We were all in for another night of my mother's buttering him up with high hopes of securing an engagement ring for her daughter.

I sighed, texting: *Yep. Mom is spending the night.*

Cool, he sent back.

Cool, huh? Then again, Doc's mom had died when he was just a kid. Maybe he actually enjoyed my mother's smothering. As a bonus for me, she would be too busy with him and everyone else to pay me and my quandary about Susan's visit much mind.

I heard the front door open as I started setting the table, followed by the creaking of certain stair steps. I had plates, silverware, and glasses placed all around the table by the time he joined me wearing a pair of faded jeans and black shirt with the long sleeves pushed up to his elbows. He must have stopped by our bedroom to change out of his work clothes.

"Hey, Tiger." He joined me at the counter where I was filling glasses with Aunt Zoe's lemonade for the kids. He dropped a kiss on my temple, smelling like a spicy version of home-sweet-home to me. "What's going on?"

I set the pitcher down, wrapped my arms around his neck, and gave him a good and *im*proper hug, pressing all of my soft parts against his hard ones. Then I nuzzled his short beard before pulling back and smiling up at him. "I need you to make me forget about my afternoon."

His grin was downright devilish. "I'm your huckleberry, Boots. But your mom might be shocked when she walks in on us."

"Maybe not." I wrinkled my nose. "I think she's writing a book about how to talk openly about sex in front of adult children. Or at least practicing writing a book. I swear, if she mentions again how sexy my father is, I'm going to get some of Addy's pink tiger-striped duct tape and seal her mouth closed."

He dipped down for another kiss, this time hitting me square on the lips.

"Mmm." He pulled back. "How come you taste like butterscotch?"

I shrugged. "I might have snacked on one of Aunt Zoe's butterscotch crunch cookies." Or maybe three.

He looked at the cookie jar. "Did you save any for me?"

"A broken one and some crumbs." What could I say? The sight of my sister required some therapeutic cookie inhalation. "But don't worry, Mom and Addy are going to make cookies later, so you can have fresh ones out of the oven."

"Good. Now, tell me what's going on."

"You mean with my mom being here?"

"I mean earlier. Cornelius texted me, saying something about a clock spinning and the Tower card."

"Right, that damned card." I returned the pitcher of lemonade to the fridge. "Nothing new, really. Just a prediction about some big peril and chaos about to ensue." I stuck to the short version.

His frown deepened as he set the kids' lemonade glasses down on the table. "Those are always hovering on the horizon around here these days." He returned to the cupboard and grabbed another glass, filling it with water. "Does that prediction have anything to do with the voicemail Harvey left me about a honey trap?"

Crippity-crap, a girl couldn't keep a secret around these parts to save her life.

"No. That's a different matter." Then I thought about the imp's latest break-in. "Well, sort of different. How was your day?" I asked, trying to maintain some semblance of normalcy in our life.

He took a long drink of water before answering. "Boring compared to yours from the sounds of it."

I sent him a flippant grin. "All part of the glamorous life of a ghost tour guide who's trying to be a real estate agent."

He set his glass down. "More ghost tours, huh?" As I passed him on the way to the pantry, he caught my hand and tugged me closer. "Your boss needs to screen your calls better."

I didn't need much urging to return to his arms, resting my forehead on his upper chest. "Maybe Cornelius and I should go into business with our own version of *Paranormal Realty*. You could be our special guest, Mr. Oracle."

Doc's mental medium abilities were only the tip of the iceberg. New skills seemed to be popping up weekly now that he'd stopped fighting his sixth sense and opened the mental door to whatever lay in wait.

He squeezed me closer, resting his chin on the top of my head. "I missed you today."

"Excellent. My love potion is still working."

His fingers trailed down my spine. "I want to know about this honey trap idea."

I pulled back a little and looked up at him, giving him a flirty wink. "You can torture it out of me later."

"Deal. Now kiss me again before everyone gets here."

I started to go up on my toes when the back door opened.

"Hoo-wee," Harvey said, shutting out the cold. "Looks like I made it just in time for the yak show."

I flipped off Harvey and stole a kiss from Doc before heading to the pantry to grab a bag of tortilla chips.

"Is that Hope's Prius in the driveway?" Harvey asked, peering into the dining room.

"Yep. Mom is spending the night."

"Where's your dad?" Doc asked.

"Playing poker with the guys."

Harvey rubbed his hands together. "Oh boy, this could be an exciting supper after all."

I pointed a pair of tongs at him. "Don't be flirting with my mom tonight."

He pointed back at me. "Don't be a party pooper."

Sheesh, he and Mom must be using the same insult handbook.

"Are you going to have enough fish sticks for everyone?" Doc asked, peeking into the opened oven door.

I tugged on my earlobe, doing the math. "I probably should have bought two bags. But then again, Mom only likes her fish fresh, so she'll probably just have some salad, and I'm not that hungry."

Doc's dark eyebrows lowered. "How many cookies did you really eat before I got here?"

I held up my right hand. "I plead the Fifth."

The back door opened again. Aunt Zoe hurried inside, along with a rush of cold air.

"Is Susan here yet?" she asked, tugging off her gloves and stocking cap.

Her long silver-streaked hair was tied back in a braid. Her old flannel shirt and cargo pants were dusty with soot from working out in her glass workshop behind the house.

"She came and went," I said, hip-bumping Doc aside so I could pull the tray of fish sticks from the oven.

I could feel Doc's gaze on me. "Your sister is back?"

"Unfortunately." I grabbed the tray of tots, too. "Harvey, will you call for the kids and Mom, please?"

"What do you mean 'came and went'?" Aunt Zoe pressed, joining me at the stove. "Your mom said Susan had something important to talk to you about."

Doc leaned back against the counter, his arms crossed. "That explains the cookies before supper."

"You mean I missed seein' you and your sister hissin' and clawin' at each other?" Harvey asked, his thumbs looped into his suspenders.

I shook my head. "There was no clawing."

"But there was hissing?" Aunt Zoe asked.

"Initially." I grabbed a plate and threw some chips on it. "But then we both decided we were tired of fighting and called a cease-fire."

Silence filled the room.

Harvey was the first to break it. "You're shittin' me."

I sprinkled shredded cheese on the chips. "Nope."

"After only three decades of feuding." Aunt Zoe washed her hands in the sink. "This calls for a round of victory drinks."

"I didn't technically win, though." I glanced Doc's way. He was still watching me closely. "I just lowered my guns first and told her I was done with all of her bullshit."

"Done with whose bullshit?" Natalie's voice came from the archway leading to the dining room.

I hadn't heard her come in, but then again I was a bit distracted. I glanced her way as she set a couple of six-packs of a local craft beer on the counter. She looked fresh from the farm in a pair of green overalls, pink cheeks, and her brunette hair split into two braids. Something made her look younger tonight. Happier. Maybe it was just the braids. Or maybe it was a certain detective keeping her company most nights.

"Susan's bullshit," Aunt Zoe told her, getting out the sour cream and salsa from the fridge. "She was here earlier and Violet finally put an end to the war."

Natalie did a double take. "I don't believe it. That was thirty years in the making."

I shrugged, popping the plate of chips and cheese into the microwave. "It was time to let it all go and move on with my life." I tapped a half minute and hit start. "She agreed and said she'd lost her taste for the fight, too."

Harvey scratched his cheek through his beard. "Are you sure this wasn't one of your *other* critters pretendin' to be your sister?"

"Or maybe one of Prudence's tricks," Natalie added.

"It was definitely Susan, and she's moving on to other projects." I scooped up several fish sticks with the spatula, waiting for the microwave to ding.

"Where's Coop?" Aunt Zoe asked as she set the bowl of coleslaw Harvey had made earlier on the table.

"He's running a little late," Natalie answered. "He mentioned something about Detective Hawke giving him more paperwork headaches."

What was Detective Hawke up to now? Did it have to do with me? Susan's offer to do my dirty work jumped back into my thoughts. I had to admit, having someone work a side angle to find out what Hawke was up to certainly tempted me.

Doc watched me put the plate of fish stick nachos together while sipping on one of the beers Natalie had handed him. I could tell he was seeing through my attempts at levity tonight. He would undoubtedly be running his own private interrogation later. I just hoped there'd be rewards for my honesty. Doc's rewards usually made my back arch and nether regions tingle.

"Is supper ready?" Layne asked, sliding into the kitchen in his socks. "Oh, hey Doc! Did you get that book on Maya gods?"

My son had an obsession lately with the Maya people, partly because his uncle Quint, my brother, who was one of Layne's favorite people on the planet, was heading down that way soon for a photojournalist job. But Layne also loved anything mythological, especially if it came with colorful lore surrounding it. Doc shared a fascination of non-earthly creatures with Layne, so I wasn't surprised there was a new book coming and figured I'd be hearing all about the Maya Underworld soon from both of them.

"It will be here later this week," Doc told Layne, sharing a fist-bump.

I pointed at the table. "Have a seat, kid." As I set the plate in front of Layne, I added, "I hope you washed your hands."

He sighed as if I were being pedantic. "Of course, Mom. You think Grammy would let me come down to eat otherwise?"

I ignored his sarcastic question. "Where's your sister?"

"She's right behind me," my mom said, joining us.

A roar of "Hellos" and greeting hugs followed at the sight of my mother.

I hadn't noticed Mom's outfit before because she'd been in the blanket fort, so the sight of her sunflower-covered corduroy jumper dress over her green sweater leggings made me shake my head. My mother—a flower child through and through. All she needed tonight was a bumblebee buzzing around her.

No sooner had I thought that, Addy's bouncing little body came flying into the kitchen. After giving Doc and Natalie a hug, she sat halfway onto her chair. "Hey, Mom?"

"What?" I asked, taking the plate of nachos for Addy that Doc handed to me.

"What dirty work does Aunt Susan want to do for you?"

I paused with her plate in mid-air.

The rest of the room paused with me, except for Layne, who was busy crunching on a mouthful of tortilla chips. And my mother, who was humming to herself over by the sink as she mixed up a bowlful of salad.

What the hell? Addy must have heard the last bit of Susan's and my conversation before she joined us in the kitchen. How much else had she heard? Lord, I hoped she hadn't heard anything about Rex.

My heart pounded as I stared down at Addy, who was too busy scooting her chair closer to notice she held center stage at the moment.

"Uhhh," was all my mind could come up with for an answer to her question about Susan's dirty-work offer.

"Is she going to help clean the house or something?"

Maybe *something*. That was if I went along with Susan's idea. I could feel all eyes from the rest of the room on me as I weighed my answer. "We'll see."

"I'm sure glad you two aren't gonna be fighting anymore."

"Why is that?" Aunt Zoe asked, beating me to the question.

If Addy had big plans about Susan and me skipping through flower-filled fields together, she was going to need to have a few things clarified. No fighting equaled no contact, in my book.

"Because maybe she can help you next time."

Oh, fudge nuggets, she must have heard Susan's talk about Rex.

Natalie leaned over the table toward Addy. "Help your mom how?"

"With the tower," Addy said, as if we all should know what she was talking about.

Harvey and I exchanged frowns. Surely Cornelius hadn't called my mother and mentioned that damned Tower card in passing. Mom would know better than to scare my kids with creepy prophecies, wouldn't she?

"What tower are you talking about?" Layne managed between crunching on chips.

Addy shrugged, taking the plate out of my hands. "The one that fell on Mom in my dream last night."

My mouth went dry. The image on the Tower card flashed through my thoughts, followed by Cornelius's whispered warning.

Addy's dreams were growing more and more connected to my life lately, from monsters trying to kill me to me being stuck in the dark—both true. And both were situations Addy had no way of knowing about outside of her dreams.

I cleared my throat, trying to loosen the grip of fear squeezing it tightly. "Addy, what did your dream have to do with Susan?"

She scooped up a piece of a fish stick with her cheese-covered chip. "She was there with you, silly."

CHAPTER FIVE

Two hours later, I was busy soothing my anxieties with a warm, sugary snickerdoodle cookie. It was not my first one, and probably wouldn't be my last this evening. I might even sneak a few upstairs to hide under my pillow for middle of the night worries that were sure to come after Addy's comment about that stupid falling tower dream. At least I'd have something to chew on besides my knuckles.

The supper dishes had been cleaned and dried and put away. So had the kids—only put into their beds by their grandmother after their baths instead of the cupboard. My mom had volunteered to tell each of them a story about me as a kid, and had led the two jumping-beans up the stairs, along with Rooster, while I cringed at what tall tales she would share. My childhood wasn't exactly an adventurous romp on par with Peter Pan and Wendy. It'd been more like a comedy-drama peppered with humiliating anecdotes.

With Mom and the kids out of the room, that left Aunt Zoe, Doc, Natalie, Cooper, and me to rehash the problems of the day and search for solutions.

Harvey had left shortly after supper, claiming to have a big date planned with a feisty widow who enjoyed "a cold night under a hot man." Those were his words, not mine. He'd grabbed a bottle of honey from the pantry on his way out, leaving us with a wink and a parting comment about starting some new honey-lovin' rumors down at the senior center. The images his words brought to mind had me thinking I could use a honey-cleansing lobotomy.

"Maybe it's just a coincidence." I shoved the last of the cookie in my mouth.

"There is no such thing as a coincidence, Killer. Especially in your world. Everything is connected." Doc pushed back from the table. "Anyone want another drink?"

I raised my hand, along with Natalie.

"I'm good," Aunt Zoe said, writing something on the pad of paper she'd grabbed right after Mom and the kids had headed upstairs.

Lifting his beer bottle, Cooper passed on Doc's offer with a slight head shake before taking a sip.

Natalie lowered her hand as Doc collected our glasses. "It would be nice to think of Addy's dream as simply little-kid brain fluff, you know." She frowned across the table at me. "But the girl tends to hit the nail on the head when it comes to … to …" She glanced at Doc, who was pouring a shot of Blanco tequila into each of our glasses. "Doc, what's the supernatural term for prophetic dreams? Is it some sort of telepathic thing?"

"No. Telepathic dreaming would be if Addy and Violet were communicating somehow through their dreams, sending messages or feelings back and forth." He squeezed some lime into each glass and then rinsed his hands under the kitchen faucet. "To date, Addy's dreams have only been one-sided," he added while filling the glasses the rest of the way with sparkling water.

"I remember reading something once about clairvoyant dreaming," Aunt Zoe said, looking up from her notes. "I believe it was defined as dreaming about something that is actually happening while you're sleeping."

"Correct." Doc swung by the freezer to add a few ice cubes to each glass before returning to the table to hand off our drinks. "Addy experienced clairvoyant dreaming that night she dreamed about Violet being stuck in the dark."

That was the time when Cornelius and I had gone into the dark realm with Doc's help and battled a creepy, pissed-off demon who went by the name Kyrkozz. I'd survived that experience with the help of some good old dynamite, but ended up lost in the dark because of it.

I took a sip from my glass, focusing for a moment on the refreshing mix of tequila, lime, and bubbly water mingling with the last of the cookie's sweetness still on my tongue, rather than fretting about Addy's dreams.

"Ranch Water" was the official name of this tequila drink concoction according to Cooper, who'd arrived late for supper with the makings for it in hand instead of dessert after receiving a message from Natalie about Mom's cookie-making plans. Apparently, it was a drink that some great-uncle of his from West Texas had introduced long ago at a family reunion.

I savored another sip of it. The drink was pretty basic, but had a cool kick that probably hit the spot after a hot, dry, dusty summer day. Or a warm afternoon at the beach, which was where I wanted to be at the moment rather than in the thick of a Black Hills freezing winter dealing with a strange clock and a troublemaking imp.

"It sounds like precognitive dreaming," Cooper said.

I gaped at him, along with everyone else. I couldn't help it. The word "precognitive" coming from the guy who'd been a stubborn mule with hooves firmly dug into the ground when it came to anything in the paranormal world took me by surprise.

Cooper shrugged. "What? Close your traps. Nat gave me a book on supernatural shit."

She grinned over the rim of her glass. "You said you didn't have time to read that crap—quote unquote."

"I don't, usually. But I couldn't sleep one night and there wasn't anything good on TV, so I skimmed it."

"You're right," Doc told him, settling into the chair next to me. "Precognitive dreaming is when you dream about something in the future, which fits Addy's situation."

"So, like a foreshadowing of something definite?" Natalie asked. "Or just a probable future?"

"A *possible* one," Doc clarified. "Something that may happen. Or may not."

"But definitely no mere coincidence," I said under my breath. Damn.

I knew that a parent was supposed to have pride in their child's expanding mind and be excited for their future potential, but Addy blossoming into a *Scharfrichter* was a mother's nightmare. A *precognitive* nightmare.

Of course, Addy could be trained in various fighting methods, as Doc had been doing for months now, teaching her how to swing just right and dodge when needed. But in my experience, death was very good at throwing curve balls. Addy could strike out at staying alive her first time up to bat. I needed to shield her as long as I could, giving her enough time to develop her skills—both mental and physical. But how, when this supernatural shit kept rolling in one deadly storm after another?

Aunt Zoe scribbled some more, her pencil loud in the silence weighing heavy in the kitchen. I knew without reading her writing that she was taking notes to add to the volumes of our family history, which told of previous *Scharfrichter* lives over many, many generations.

Aunt Zoe had been handed down the task of keeping track of my successes and failures; detailing everything from what my foes looked like, methods they used to try to kill me, and any accessories they had along with what weapons I used to execute them and how their bodies decomposed at death.

Unlike humans, *others* didn't slowly decompose over the days and months following their demise. Sometimes they quickly melted into black goo and sank into the earth. Other times they exploded almost instantly in a bright flash, and their ashes drifted away in the wind— or coated me and anyone close by.

In addition to fulfilling her *magistra* record-keeping duty, Aunt Zoe's notes could help us if we needed to go back and figure out some new moves—offense or defense—when the next troublemaker came to town.

"So, Addy is showing some sixth-sense abilities, same as her mother," Aunt Zoe said, looking at me while it was obvious her mind was on what she planned to write next.

"Yeah, but I don't have psychic dreams." My extra skills were more physical, like strength, speed, and stamina. Abilities that helped me fight when needed.

Doc clinked his glass against mine. "Do you remember any dreams like this from when you were her age?"

"No. I had regular little-girl dreams."

Cooper lifted his bottle of beer. "All about frilly dresses, pink ponies, baby dolls, and lollipops?"

A scoff of laughter came from the woman sitting next to him. "More like Catwoman gloves with razor-sharp claws, neighborhood treasure hunts, and three-scoop Coke floats." Natalie aimed a perplexed frown at Cooper. "What is wrong with you, old man? Did someone head-butt you back a century in time?"

Aunt Zoe smiled at me and then Doc. "I don't think much has changed in Nat's version of Violet's dreamland."

Doc leaned closer, his smolder cranked up high. "Tell me more about those Catwoman gloves, Boots."

I reached under the table, scratching my nails up his jean-covered thigh. "How about I give you a demonstration later, *mon amour*."

Cooper bumped the table hard enough to slosh my drink over the rim. "Parker, don't you dare start speaking French to him. We don't need another public display of sappy shit with that Tish and Gomez act." He focused on Doc. "So, what does Addy's dream mean for Parker and her sister?"

Doc shrugged. "Danger ahead. Same as usual."

"Jesus." Cooper glowered in my direction. "Is it too much to ask for a month free of your version of Armageddon?"

"I wish!" I sopped up the splash of spilled drink with my shirt sleeve. "Maybe you could help us out, Cooper, by finding a way to send Detective Hawke back to Rapid City for a few months."

Once again, Susan's offer to help me with some of my problems flitted through my thoughts. It would sure be nice to have Hawke off my tail for a while, if not for good. The temptation to find out what Susan thought she could do for me when it came to that big boorish gumshoe grew from a seed to a seedling. Maybe she could … no. Never mind.

"That's not going to happen anytime soon, Parker. So you'll have to come up with another plan." He sipped his beer, eyeing me as he set the bottle back on the table. "You could start by trying to help me catch your damned imp."

"I told you, it's not *my* imp." I rested my elbows on the table, leaning my chin on my linked fingers. "And I'm working on that."

Aunt Zoe tapped her pencil on the table a few times. "Are you going to tell us about your honey-trap idea that Harvey mentioned?"

Harvey was going to get a sweaty sock shoved into his blow hole if he didn't stop telling my secrets.

"I wasn't planning on it." Or bringing up Masterson's call about that damned *lidérc*, either. A side glance at Doc ran smack-dab into a solid glare. I winced slightly. "But I guess now is as good of time as any."

"It's a bad idea." Cooper cut me off out of the gate.

"You haven't even heard what my idea involves."

"I don't have to. You have a history of bad ideas. I'm just trying to stop you before this blows up in *my* face, as well as yours."

I clenched my hands. "It's not going to blow up in anyone's face, Detective Gloomy Von Grumpybear."

Well, anyone other than me, possibly. And maybe Doc, if he insisted on joining me in the hunt. Probably Harvey, also, since there'd be no keeping him away. Natalie, too.

Cooper looked at my best friend. "Is Parker's head filled with cartoon characters?"

She grinned back. "Actually, that was one of my nicknames for *you* back before you seduced me into submission."

He pointed his bottle at her. "You seduced me, Beals. I used to be a simple, poor, innocent guy trying to solve crimes for the good people of Deadwood and Lead."

Covering my mouth, I coughed out a "Bullshit."

Doc nudged me under the table with his knee. "Tell us your plan, Killer."

"I'm going to set a trap with honey as the bait. Easy peasy."

"Set the trap where?" Doc asked.

"Like with a box, a stick, and a string?" Natalie threw out before I could answer him.

"And do what with the imp if you manage to catch it?" Aunt Zoe jumped in next.

"This is worse than a bad idea." Cooper finished the last gulp of his beer. "Not quite as bad as thinking about catching a *lidérc* with only a mirror, but a close second."

I crossed my arms. "Cooper, you're just being contradictory tonight because I didn't answer your phone call earlier." I looked around at each of them. "See, this is why I didn't want to tell you guys yet. I'm still in the process of figuring out where and how to set the trap. I've only made it as far as deciding to do it and picking up some bait at the store."

"You should let Harvey help you," Natalie said. "He's an ace at setting traps out at his ranch."

"Those are illegal traps," Cooper reminded her.

And bad luck. Several months ago Harvey had found part of a human scalp with the ear still attached in one of the traps he'd set for whatever was prowling around his barn. Cooper and his police pals still hadn't figured out who was missing an ear. It seemed like someone with only one ear would be easy enough to find, but not in the Black Hills, apparently. Not these days, anyway.

Cooper pointed his empty beer bottle at me. "Uncle Willis will get you thrown back in jail if you two aren't careful."

"I didn't plan on having anyone help me with hunting or trapping the imp."

Doc stiffened visibly. "I thought you and I had come to an understanding about this partnership of ours."

"You're busy with work lately."

"Not that busy."

"And this imp stuff seems below your skillset."

Besides being a mental medium, Doc was some kind of Oracle that came from an ancient lineage. We were still finding out what exactly that role entailed, but according to Mr. Black, Doc's abilities to see in the dark realm and open doors there were sought after by many nefarious beings seeking power.

Criminy. This all sounded so nuts. A year ago I was a single mom working at a car dealership trying to make ends meet. Now this was my normal life—ghosts, monsters, and deadly dreams.

I met Doc's gaze. Correction, this was *our* not-so-normal life, and I was over the moon about having someone to pick me up when I stumbled and hold me tight when I was scared.

"Killer, anything having to do with you is my top priority. Period." He looked at Cooper. "You mentioned something earlier in the dining room about a symbol that might be a ward?"

Cooper's steely eyes landed on me. "Did you show him and Zoe the picture?"

"Not yet." I pulled out my phone and showed first Doc, then my aunt, explaining where Cooper had found the weird symbol and demonstrating how big it was with my hands.

Aunt Zoe handed back my phone. "Send me that picture, will you? I want to recreate it in my notes."

I nodded and did so right then before focusing on Cooper. "Did you have a chance to look at the previous imp crime scene pictures to check for others like this?"

When we'd parted earlier up in Lead, he'd mentioned heading back to the station to do that very thing while I came home to make supper.

"There were no other symbols or wards or whatever in the pictures on file, but that doesn't mean they aren't there somewhere."

"We should go back and check," Natalie said.

"Not 'we,' Nat," Cooper said. "Me and maybe Zoe."

She held out both hands, palms up. "You think I can't see, Coop? My vision is 20/20, you know."

"I think you need to be careful around anything to do with cases assigned to me. Hawke is already suspicious enough of Parker and me working together. If he catches wind of you hanging out at any of the crime scenes he's trying to pin on Parker, it's going to make her look even more guilty."

She huffed. "And him catching Zoe at one of these crime scenes won't have the same effect?"

"She has a point," I said, suspecting that his wanting Natalie to not be a part of any of this was more him just being overprotective than logical.

"Possibly," he conceded. "But Hawke isn't interested in pursuing Zoe romantically."

I doubted Detective Hawke wanted much to do with romance where Natalie was concerned either, just sex. Her tight curves and full lips had that sort of pull on the male species around these parts.

"Why does that make a difference?" I asked, curious if jealousy was taking part in any of Cooper's reasoning, too.

"Because Natalie lives right above Hawke and keeps listening in on his conversations, which is not officially illegal, but benefits us when it comes to keeping ahead of his crusade to put you behind bars." He returned to Natalie. "Hawke already knows you're Parker's pal, but his goal to get you into bed is overshadowing his common sense. Let's not rock that boat."

Frankly, I was amazed that Detective Hawke hadn't figured out that Cooper and Natalie were an item. All the signs were there if he paid attention when they were in the same vicinity, in spite of them still trying to keep their relationship a secret. The stolen glances, the provocative light touching, the way Cooper had trouble focusing when she was in sight, and the flirting Natalie couldn't hold back when he was within earshot.

I scoffed to myself. Some great detective Hawke was if he couldn't see any of that. It was probably those thick, black caterpillar-like eyebrows blocking his vision.

"If Hawke has any more reasons to suspect that you're helping Parker, he's going to get cagey around you," Cooper told Natalie. "Worse, he could start seeing you as a suspect. Considering your multiple near-brushes with the law, that could get sticky."

"My police record isn't that bad," she defended.

Cooper raised one eyebrow. "Officially, that's true. You've charmed your way out of multiple infractions."

"Name one."

"Destruction of property."

"What property?"

"One Jaguar belonging to a certain ex-boyfriend of Parker's. I remember seeing some windshield wipers one night at the Purple Door that had been snipped clean off."

I grimaced at Natalie. He had her there, even though she'd worked her magic on Cooper during a game of pool, and in the end, he too had let her off with a warning in return for an unofficial date at the shooting range.

He was right—Natalie was good at dodging the law. That skill was part of her DNA.

She lifted her chin. "You have proof of this, Detective? Fingerprints? The vandalized wiper blades? The crime scene weapon?" She shot a grin my way. "Hell, have you even considered that Susan might have been behind the clipped wipers? She was back in town by then, I think."

"I'll give you plenty of proof later, woman," Cooper said, reaching under the table and doing something that made Natalie cry out, laugh, and then loop her arm around his neck and pull him over for a loud kiss on his cheek.

Doc turned to me. "So, what dirty work was Susan offering to do for you before Addy showed up?"

"Oh, yeah," Natalie said, settling back into her chair. She picked up her glass. "Spill, Vi. I want to hear all about the Bloody Red Queen's change of heart."

"Hold on." I hopped up, made a quick search of the dining room to see if any little ears had wandered downstairs to listen in again, and then returned to rehash Susan's visit with them. When I finished, the four of them were silent for several beats.

"Well?" I prompted. "What do you guys think?"

"You can't trust her as far as you can throw her," Natalie said, "and we both know that while you might be one helluva slugger with a bat, your throwing arm is crap at best."

"My throwing arm is not that bad."

"Maybe back in high school, but now …" She made a thumbs-down gesture while blowing a raspberry. "Look at what you did to Doc's bedroom window with that rock."

I cringed slightly. Okay, I'd give her that one.

Doc chuckled. "That was a good night, Boots. Worth the sacrifice of a window."

My cheeks warmed, remembering exactly what happened after he'd let me in his patio door, and how many times it'd been repeated before I hurried home early the next morning.

"Another bad idea." Cooper weighed in with his two cents. "You'll both wind up in jail."

Aunt Zoe leaned back in her chair, arms crossed. "I wonder just what tricks Susan thinks she can get away with." To the others, she added, "The girl has been slick as a watermelon seed since she could stand on her own two feet."

"All the more reason for you to walk away from her offer," Doc said.

Natalie's gaze narrowed. "And how do you know she doesn't plan to double-cross you just to get you thrown behind bars so she can try to steal your man again?"

Been there, lived that. Sort of.

I rested my hand on Doc's arm. "I'm not going to take Susan up on her offer. It's too much of a risk all around, and I can't trust her. Not after so many years of betrayal."

Sorry, Mom, I thought, glancing at the ceiling. I'm sure a happy reunion would make my mother's hipster heart twirl through fields of flowers, but it just wasn't going to happen.

I yawned. The relaxing effect of my drink mixed with a full stomach was making my eyelids heavy, and my head, too. I leaned into Doc's shoulder, deciding to share my worries about the spinning clock with Aunt Zoe and the rest when the sun came back up.

"It's getting late," Natalie said to Cooper, standing up. "You ready to drive me home, Hot Cop?"

He looked up at her. "Yours or mine?"

"That depends on how tired you are." She trailed her fingers along his shoulder before grabbing his empty bottle and her glass, taking both over to the sink.

"Not that tired." He was out of his chair and back from the dining room with his car keys and her coat in hand by the time she'd finished washing her glass. "Zoe, I'll get in touch with you tomorrow about visiting the imp's previous crime scenes to look for more of those symbols."

She nodded, setting her pencil on the table. "I'll be in my workshop all day."

"Is it okay if I leave my truck out front all night?" Natalie asked her.

"Of course." Aunt Zoe smiled, her gaze bouncing back and forth between Natalie and Cooper. But her smile had a melancholy air to it, her brow slightly furrowed. "Take care of my favorite detective."

Natalie gave her a saucy wink. "I'll do my best."

Cooper pulled on his coat. "I'll see you in the morning, Nyce."

They must be planning to work out together at the Rec Center. Or maybe Cooper was just dropping off Doc's mail from home and staying for some coffee.

"The earlier the better," Doc told him. "I have a client coming in mid-morning, but I have research to do online before they show up."

That was good to hear about Doc being in his office all day. I didn't like it when he was too far away to come running quickly when I needed him these days. Maybe he could take five and visit Cornelius's place to have a look at the clock with me—if the spinning situation hadn't changed by then.

"Parker," Cooper said while helping Natalie with her coat. "Thanks for supper. It tasted better than it sounded."

"Aww." I looked up at Doc. "Cooper is being nice to me. Isn't that sweet?"

That earned a chuckle from Doc. "Maybe he'll bring you a teddy bear next time he comes over."

Cooper growled, scowling down at Natalie. "See? I tried, but they had to go and make it weird."

Giggling, she tugged on his hand. "Come on, law dog. I'll let you bite me tonight as a reward for being a good boy."

"Deal." He glanced back at me. "Try not to kill anything tomorrow, Parker."

"I'll see them out and lock up," Doc said, following in their wake.

Aunt Zoe sighed. Again, I heard a tinge of sadness in it.

"Are you okay tonight?" I asked, searching her face for the answer.

"I'm just tired."

I could see the truth in that by the lines around her eyes. But I was pretty sure this was more than only exhaustion.

"Nothing else weighing you down?" Like maybe missing a certain fire captain, who hadn't been by for supper in over a week.

"Nope." She stood and moved to the sink, staring out the kitchen window into the dark backyard. "I'm going to go take care of a few things in my workshop and shut everything down, then come in and get some sleep."

That was my cue to drop the investigation and walk away. If I wasn't so tired myself, I might have ignored her prompt and brought up Reid's name, but my bed was calling to me. Maybe in the morning I could get Aunt Zoe to crack about what was up with her.

"Sleep tight, kiddo," she said, dropping a kiss on my forehead before heading out the back door.

After a quick trip to the basement to make sure Elvis the chicken was secured in her roost for the night, I went searching for Doc. He wasn't in the dining room or living room. I heard the floor creak overhead and followed the sound upstairs into my bedroom, where I found him sitting on the edge of the bed.

"Shut the door," he said quietly, his poker face leaving me guessing as to why he wanted a private audience.

I did as told, leaning back against the solid wood. "What's wrong, Doc?"

"I talked to Cornelius this afternoon."

"About the spinning clock hands. I know." Doc had asked about that problem when he'd gotten home earlier this evening. "I'm going to try to get hold of Mr. Black somehow, even though Eddie Mudder is out of town for the week. I was thinking I could call Eddie and leave a message, saying it's important." When Doc sat there frowning at me without comment, I added, "I was also thinking that since you're going to be working at your office tomorrow, you and I could set up a time with Cornelius to go take a look at the clock in person."

"Okay," he said, and nothing else.

I took a step toward him, still sensing tension. "That's it?"

"About the clock situation? Yeah. That's it." He patted the bed next to him. "Come here."

I crossed the distance, easing down next to him. "Why do I have the feeling an anvil is about to fall on my head?"

He leaned forward, resting his elbows on his knees, fingers linked. "Tomorrow, Cooper and I are going to visit the basement in Cornelius's hotel." He turned his head, his eyes meeting mine. "You know what that means, right?"

My chest tightened. I did, and I didn't like the idea of him trying to reach out to Wilda Hessler's changeling ghost pal one iota.

"That's a bad idea, Doc."

He smirked. "You sound like Cooper."

"Why do you want to risk that parasite attaching to you? And of all people to go with you, why Cooper? Why not Cornelius? Or me?" Not that I wanted to go down in that basement again with that freaky-deaky changeling circling nearby, not even a little, but I would if he twisted my arm. "Cooper might be able to see ghosts, but he won't be able to help if it tries to possess you, which we both know it will. And the fact that Cornelius and I heard it trying to mimic your voice last time I was there means it's sure to come for you." I was talking faster and faster, but I couldn't slow the runaway train of panic in my head. "It must know that if it can possess you as a source of power, it will be able to wreak all kinds of havoc doing Lord only knows what to whom, and I can't handle something happening to you right now because I need you to help keep my kids safe, and—"

"Violet, stop." He grabbed my hand, wrapping it in his warm palms. "I love you."

I took a deep breath, trying to calm down. "I'm afraid of that thing," I whispered.

"You know as well as anyone, *Scharfrichter*, that you can't let fear dictate your actions."

"It's too risky, Doc. We don't know what it wants or how to keep it from getting what it wants if it tries to take it without asking."

"There's only one way we're going to find out."

I shook my head. "I can't kill ghosts, Doc. Only beings I can see and touch." Mostly. The *lidérc* had required brains as well as brawn to catch and execute.

"I know you can't." He lifted my hand to his lips, kissing my knuckles. "But maybe I can."

CHAPTER SIX

Tuesday, January 29th

I'd made it as far as brushing my teeth the next morning before shit hit the fan, starting with a single phone call.

Doc was long gone by that time, meeting Cooper early over at the Old Prospector Hotel. The kids were on their way to school thanks to my mom, who was planning to drop them off and then head back home to Rapid City. Aunt Zoe was outside in her workshop already, heating up her glass furnace. She'd taken Rooster and Elvis with her for company. That left me alone, slowly getting ready for work, crossing my fingers that my nine-thirty appointment would actually be interested in buying one of the houses on my list, not just investigating it for ghosts.

When my phone rang, showing Harvey on the other end of the line, I hesitated. If he was going to give me the blow-by-blow of his hot date last night in colorful, cringe-worthy detail—something he'd done to me not once, but several times before—I'd take a rain check. But I knew Harvey too well. He would hunt me down if I didn't answer.

I spit out enough of my toothpaste to talk. "What's going on, Harvey?"

"I caught your imp," he whispered.

"It's not my ..." My mind finally registered what he'd said. "You have the imp?"

"Did I stutter, girl?"

"In your custody?"

"Bull's-eye."

"At this very moment?"

"Are you hard of hearin' this morning, Sparky?"

Well, he was whispering. "This isn't some trick to get me to come rescue you again from a heavily fornicated blue-haired babe, is it?"

"Not this time."

"Good, because I had to wash my eyeballs out with soap aft—"

He huffed. "Girl, quit beatin' your gums and get your ass up here, pronto! I'm not sure how long I can keep this li'l sucker trapped."

"Trapped where? How did you do it?"

"I'll give you the tell-all when you're standin' here. Now get a move on, like your tail feathers are on fire."

He rattled off an address in Lead that sounded vaguely familiar before hanging up on me.

I gaped at my reflection in the mirror for a couple of blinks and then frowned back down at my phone. Had Harvey really caught the imp? Just like that? No long, drawn-out hunt? How in the hell …

My phone pinged.

A text popped up on the screen. It was from Harvey: *Bring more honey!*

That kicked me into gear. Luckily, I'd already put on my makeup and corralled my hair into a tidy bun, so it was simply a matter of grabbing my purse and a few bottles of honey, and then hitting the road.

A couple of blocks away from the address Harvey had given me, I found myself on the same street as the house where I'd met Cooper last evening. Ahh, so that was why the other address had sounded familiar.

I rolled slowly by the scene of the crime, thinking of the now-defunct freezer that had been full of honey BBQ chicken wings until the imp came along. Was it a coincidence Harvey had caught the wing-stealer close by? Probably not. As Doc had said last night, there was no such thing as a coincidence in my life anymore.

The house and garage looked more rundown in the sunlight. The garage roof clearly sagged from the weight of snow and decades of weathering. At least the mess around the trash cans had been cleaned up, making the place look less hoarder-like.

I found Harvey's white pickup farther down the street in the driveway of a cute, mid-century carriage-style house built over a narrow two-bay garage. I parked along the curb, wanting to give plenty of room around his vehicle in case things went sideways in some way that I hadn't thought of at this point.

Harvey waved me over before I'd even opened my door. I grabbed one of the bottles of honey and stepped out into the cold wind, shivering as I hurried up the drive.

"That's a pretty coat, princess," I teased as I joined him, handing him the honey. "Looks really nice with those red flannel pajama pants." The coat's puffy pink fabric reminded me of the one that Junie Coppermoon had been wearing yesterday at the store—a lot, actually. I leaned closer, sniffing. He smelled sweet, like cupcakes. So had Junie yesterday. "Whose coat is that?"

Had the retired English teacher been his hot date last night? Was that why he'd grabbed some honey on his way out? Had Harvey and his "putting the devil into hell" metaphor wooed Junie right in front of my eyes? I doubted there were many other women in town who owned a pink coat like that.

Wait! Hadn't she assumed Harvey and I were an item? That meant she knowingly stole him right out from under me. Wow! Blatant cattery at work. I'd heard before that teachers could be a rowdy bunch outside of the classroom. It appeared pink-loving Junie was cut from the same cloth.

Harvey shushed me. "That ain't important right now," he whispered, pointing at the extended cab of his pickup. "What are we gonna do about that?"

"About what?" I whispered back, looking around to see if we had eavesdroppers this morning. The coast seemed clear.

"Your sleepin' imp."

I tiptoed closer to the front passenger-side window, trying to peer inside, but there was something on the glass. It looked like a glaze coating that had been smeared by a dog's tongue. Harvey's fat, old yellow Labrador retriever, Red, must have been riding in the front seat lately.

"Don't bump the truck," he warned. "You'll wake the li'l bastard up and then we'll be in big trouble."

I held up my hands. "Calm down. I'm not touching it."

I side-stepped to the backseat window, which was clear enough, giving me a view of Red's dog-hair-covered blanket Harvey kept back there. His favorite shotgun, Bessie, which he never left home without these days, must be tucked away under the seat again, because there was no sight of it. Nor the imp, for that matter.

I returned to the front of the cab, trying to see through the messy glass. There was something on the seat that looked like a piece of a rope. Or was it a stethoscope? No, it must be rope. Otherwise, the seat looked empty, but down by the foot well it was too shadowy to see anything in the morning light. I needed a flashlight.

A few steps and I was back at Harvey's side. "What is that stuff all over the window?" I said under my breath.

"Honey."

"Red smeared honey on the glass?"

I could try to peek in through the windshield, but I knew from experience that I was too short to see much without standing on the pickup's running board. If the imp really was in there, I didn't want to rock the vehicle.

"No, the imp did."

I turned to him. "Why would it do that with something it loves to eat?"

Harvey sucked air through his teeth. "Well, that part wasn't entirely the imp's doin'. It got a tad messy in there last night when we were playin' around and the top popped off the honey bottle." He held up the bottle of honey I'd given to him, pretending to remove the top.

"You mean ..." I stopped, trying to collar my imagination before it took off in an R-rated direction I didn't want to follow.

Harvey shrugged. "Junie wanted a honey-lovin', hands-on demonstration."

Junie, huh? I knew it! After all, pink was a color of burning passion and lust, and she'd been draped in it from the neck down. "In your pickup?"

"What can I say? We were feelin' young and frisky."

Great goober peanuts! "It got down to ten below freezing last night."

He grinned. "Not in that cab it didn't. Not with all that friction."

I shuddered, focusing back on the pickup. "What makes you so sure the imp is in there? You can't even see the thing." To date, I was the only one who could see it, unfortunately, which was why I figured I should be hunting it alone.

"I was eatin' one of Junie's chocolate banana bran muffins, checkin' on my rig through the window." He pointed toward the big picture window above the garage.

"Why? Were you worried one of Junie's other boyfriends would show up?"

"Nah, Junie's dance card is always empty. She likes to pick her tango partners on the fly. Says spontaneity keeps her juices flowin'."

I sighed. I should've known better than to ask that.

"Anyhoo, I was checkin' because we'd left the truck windows cracked last night to air it out after we were finished. It got purty darn steamy in there, if you know what I mean." He winked and elbowed me.

At this point, I wished all of the pennies in my kids' piggy banks that I *didn't* know what he meant.

"That's when I noticed the driver's side door was open." At my wrinkled brow, he added, "I forgot to lock up after I hustled inside after her. With Junie's bare-apple bottom peeking out at me from the back of her hospital gown, I was lucky to remember how to put one foot in front of the other."

"What hospital …" I stopped myself. Good night, nurse! It was a stethoscope on the front seat. "You know what. Never mind. Keep telling your imp tale, old man."

"I grabbed Junie's coat quick since all of my clothes are in the washer thanks to our honey shenanigans—that stuff will get in every nook, cranny, and crack, I swear."

I grimaced. "You know, fewer details here would be fine with me."

"Where's the fun in not kissin' and tellin'?"

I waved for him to continue.

"When I got down here, I could hear something shufflin' around in the cab. Figured I'd forgotten to fully shut the door and a curious raccoon or maybe even a possum figured out how to get in there. Either way, I eased on up to the open driver's side door and peeked inside. That's when I saw it lickin' the window there."

"You couldn't actually see the imp, though, right?"

He shook his head. "I could see the results of its lickin'. It was the kookiest thing. That's when I remembered Junie's honey buns. Her backside got sticky, ya see, and she rubbed against the window real good when she climbed—"

I covered his mouth with my gloved hand. "I get the picture. What happened after you saw the window being licked?"

"I shut the door and locked it." He held up his keys. "I'd hunched down first, though, so it couldn't see me, figurin' it would think the wind shut it and not realize it'd been trapped on purpose. Trapped critters can get mighty spooked."

I knew that confined panic all too well, having been trapped myself by hunters more than once.

"That's when I called you."

That explained his whispering earlier on the phone.

I eased closer to his rig again, watching for any sign of movement, seeing none. "So, unless it slipped out through the window crack, the imp should be in there somewhere."

"Bingo-bango." He took my hand and placed the bottle of honey in it. "Now that I've trapped it for you, how are ya gonna get it outta there?"

I looked over at my Honda, thinking about what I had in the back of it since we couldn't easily access anything in Harvey's rig. A few cloth grocery bags and a blanket for starters. Since it was winter, I also had a small folding shovel, a bit of kitty litter and road salt for icy patches, an ice scraper, a flare, and a tire iron lug wrench.

"We could trap it in one of my bigger grocery bags."

Harvey's eyes narrowed. "Doesn't that critter have claws and teeth?"

Oh, yeah. "What if one of us bags it really quick and the other clobbers it with a tire iron?"

He tugged on his beard, his lips pursed. "You gonna be able to stomach doin' that?"

"I'm an Executioner, remember?"

"Yeah, but this ain't no regular critter, like a mouse or snake or mole. It's bigger for one thing, more like a well-fed tomcat accordin' to Zoe. Might be able to fight back some, too. Seems like you hesitated when it came to snuffin' out those *Nachzehrer* uglies."

"That was because they used to be humans at one time." I cringed at the thought alone of the *Nachzehrers*. "Listen, we're not going to bludgeon the imp to death right here and now, just give it a good clunk to knock it out so we can get it out of your rig."

"Where exactly is it in my truck?"

"Hold on." I rounded the back of his rig. The driver's window was a tad clearer than the passenger's glass, but either Red or the imp had done some licking on this side, too.

I peeked in through the glass, checking the floorboards. There it was, partway hidden under the passenger's seat. I could see a pointy ear sticking out. I watched it for a few seconds to make sure it didn't move. It sure looked to be sleeping. For now.

I waved Harvey over. "It's under the seat on the other side," I mouthed, pointing as if he could see it.

"If you say so." He jammed his hands in Junie's coat pockets as a cool blast ruffled our collars. "It's going to be hairy gettin' it out from under there, considerin' those claws and teeth you talked about."

"If I reach over the console from this side, I think I can grab it and bag it quick. You should be able to see its shape in the bag. Once I have it, you open the other door and clonk it on the head."

"How will I know which end is its head if it's in a bag?"

I glared at him.

"Okay, okay." He raised his hands. "I'm just tryin' to think about this from all angles before we wind up over our heads in imp."

I was already over my head with all my troubles these days, not only those due to the imp. "I'm going to go grab the stuff from my SUV." I glanced up at the house. "Do we need to worry about Junie showing up?"

"Nah, she's good and whipped. Probably sleep until noon. I gave her a good run last night. Up and down the stairs, around and around the dining room table." He wiggled his bushy eyebrows. "She likes to play tag in our birthday suits."

I scowled at him. "You know, a simple 'No' would have sufficed." I walked away, shaking my head, ignoring the sound of his snickers.

A minute later, I was back, bag in hand. I'd grabbed the biggest of the three I had. It was made of a thicker fabric, almost canvas-like. I handed off the tire iron to the dirty bird, double-checking that the imp hadn't moved while Harvey rounded the other side and got into position.

From the pine tree next to the garage, a blue jay screeched down at us. I couldn't tell if it was cheering us on or yelling at us for interrupting its morning routine. I shushed it and focused on the situation at hand.

Harvey gave a thumbs-up. I nodded back. He popped the automatic locks. I waited, watching to see if the imp woke. After several seconds, it still hadn't moved.

I eased the door open, and then stepped up on the rail, bag out and ready. My heart pounded in my ears as I climbed into the cab, angling around the steering wheel, one knee planted on the seat, the other leg on the floorboard keeping me balanced. The cab smelled musty and sweet, with an underlying odor of dog. I wrinkled my nose and leaned over the console, resting my weight on my right elbow, and flexed the gloved fingers of my left hand—ready to grasp.

I'd have one chance at this. Grab the imp and shove it in the bag. Twist the top tight. Then hold it up for Harvey to knock the little shit out. No problem. I hoped.

I took a steadying breath, slowly reaching down toward the floorboards.

I glanced up at Harvey's fuzzy shape on the other side of the glass to make sure he was ready. When I looked back down, the imp was crouched on the floorboard staring up at me with its red beady eyes.

It hissed.

I cried out in surprise.

It lunged for my face, claws first.

I swung my left arm, knocking the imp into the door. It bounced off of the door panel, coming back for round 2 in a blink.

I jerked back, slamming my elbow into the steering wheel. The jarring pain barely had time to register before the imp was on me, slashing, grunting, scratching, snarling.

I fought back with my eyes half-closed, smacking, yowling, punching, shrieking.

It pulled my hair.

I yanked on its ear until it let go.

It chomped on my forearm.

I slammed it into the dashboard, shaking it loose.

It rammed its head into my cheek.

My face throbbing, I pinned it by the throat against the steering wheel. "Hold still, you little prick!"

The horn honked loud in the still morning, echoing down the hillside. Oops!

"Fuck, *Scharfrichter*!" it gurgled.

I blinked in surprise when its words registered. Where had it learned that language?

My hesitation gave it enough time to wiggle free, landing a kick to my chin in the process.

I caught it by the tail as it dove for the open driver's side door, yanking it inside and tossing it over into the back of the cab.

It hit the back window with a thud and landed facedown on the dog blanket. The imp pushed up onto its haunches, shaking its head. Then it turned to look at me again, its lips pulling back to show tiny sharp needle-like teeth.

Shit! We needed to go to Plan B.

What was Plan B?

Oh yeah—retreat!

I scrambled backward, falling out of the rig in my haste to get the hell out of what had turned into a down and dirty cage fight. Harvey was there to catch me, slamming the door as soon as I was clear.

It thudded against the window several times. I scrambled upright, stepping farther back as the imp threw itself against the glass again and again. I could hear its grunts and growls clearly through the crack at the top of the window.

"What do we do now?" Harvey asked. "Bessie's under the back seat, so I can't shoot it."

"That's probably a good thing," I said between heavy breaths. I could only imagine how loud a gunshot would echo on a crisp winter morning.

"You okay, Sparky?" I could hear a tinge of laughter in his voice under the concern. "It sorta looked like you were being attacked by a swarm of bees from my side of the blurry glass."

My face ached and stung along with my elbow, I was tasting blood, and that was only what was registering at the moment. "That bastard could give a wolverine a run for its money."

"Well, I don't know if I'd go *that* far."

I shot him a glare. "Fine, you go in there and catch it then, big bad hunter."

Another thud against the glass made his whole truck rock. He grimaced, taking a step back. "I'll save that job for our local *Scharfrichter*, thank you very much."

"Wimp." I huffed, wiping my cheek. My glove came away with a streak of blood on it.

The imp was growing more and more wild inside the cab, growling and screeching, bouncing around like a bingo ball. Things started flying as I watched. Strips and pieces of fabric hit the windows, and then white bits of fluff.

"That son of a bitch is tearing up my seats," Harvey cried, pounding on the outside of the glass. "Knock it off, dammit!"

The imp did the opposite, slashing at the roof, biting on the headrests, snarling and keening.

"We have to get it out of there, Sparky!"

"I know! I know! Shit!" I pressed my nose against the driver's side window, pounding on it. "Stop it!"

Then I remembered the bottle of honey I'd brought. Opening it, I held it up to the top of the window. I squeezed the bottle enough for the honey to come out and drip down the glass on the other side.

The imp froze, staring at me around the headrest its jaws were currently locked onto. Its nostrils twitched. And then twitched again.

"That's it," I spoke in a soothing voice. "Come to momma, you ugly terror."

It hopped down onto the front seat and then rose on its back legs, sniffing the drip of honey, then licking it.

Its red eyes locked onto mine. "More," it demanded in a gargled growl.

I squirted another squeeze of honey down the window.

It licked it up, tapping its claw on the glass for more.

I squeezed again, frowning back at Harvey as it licked up the honey. "Maybe if you keep feeding it, I can open the door and catch it."

"You left the bag inside."

"I have more in the back of my SUV, remember?"

Harvey squinted. "I don't know if we should try goin' head to head with that critter again. You should look in the mirror before makin' any rash decisions."

"If we're going to catch this thing," I started, but then the honey bottle was knocked out of my hands.

I looked back and the imp had all of its fingers reaching out through the crack, its claws gripping the edge of the glass. Its nose was moving back and forth along the opening, sniffing the air.

"What's it doin' now?" Harvey asked, bending to pick up the half-empty bottle.

"I don't know. Looks like it's smelling the air."

Its claws clinked against the glass as it shifted side to side. "No cages!" it snarled, its hind feet now up on the windowsill, claws digging into the vinyl there. "No cages! No cages! No cages!"

"Can you hear what it's saying?" I asked Harvey.

"Yep. I think we need to figure out how to get him out of there and fast, before he eats my steerin' wheel."

The sound of an engine rumbling closer made the imp pause its chanting. It looked over its shoulder. I followed its gaze. Through the back window of Harvey's truck, I watched as a Deadwood Police vehicle skirched into the drive.

"Oh, crap," I muttered. What were the chances of Detective Crankypants driving past by happenstance?

Cooper was out of his door and rushing our way before the engine fully settled to a stop. "What do you mean, you have it trapped?" he barked at his uncle.

It appeared I wasn't the only one Harvey had called this morning.

When Cooper saw me, he skidded to a halt in his tracks. His steely eyes widened, his mouth falling open. "What in the hell happened to Parker?"

A loud crack rang out next to me.

I jumped toward Harvey, bumping into him as another crack echoed into the trees.

I turned to find the imp pulling the window inward, its back legs pushing while its fingers tugged.

"Holy hopped-up horny toads," Harvey growled, steadying me. "That critter is breakin' my window!"

No sooner were his words out than they came true. The window shattered and crumbled.

The imp hopped up on the windowsill, gave me one last snarl. "No cage!" It hissed and leapt to freedom.

"You gotta be kidding me," I said under my breath. I flipped the wily varmint off with both middle fingers as it vamoosed into the trees.

"What's going on out here?"

The voice came from above. I looked up to find Junie Coppermoon standing at the top of the porch steps in a furry pink robe and the same silver beanie with the pom-pom topper she'd had on in the store yesterday.

"Uhhh," I managed, frowning from Harvey to Cooper.

"Police business," Cooper blurted out.

Junie's gaze narrowed in on me before moving to the pickup and then back to Harvey, who was still holding the half-empty bottle of honey in his hands.

"Willis Harvey," she chastised. "You should know better." Her focus shifted to me. "And you need to seek therapy. He's almost old enough to be your grandfather!"

With a huff, she whirled around and went back into her house, slamming the front door in her wake.

Okay then.

My face hurt.

I grabbed the bottle of honey from Harvey. "I'm sorry about your pickup. I'll help pay for the damages."

Harvey frowned up at the porch. "The pickup is fixable. I'm more worried about Junie's ruffled feathers. I wouldn't mind pettin' them some more, if you get my gist." He patted my shoulder. "Go get cleaned up, Sparky. We'll try to catch that critter again later." He left us standing there, hustling up the porch steps after Junie.

Cooper crunched over the pieces of glass, whistling as he checked out the destruction inside the cab. "The next time you two try to catch this thing, you need to bring a professional along."

"What are you going to do, shoot it?"

"For starters." He turned back to me, cringing at what he saw. "Your face looks like the backend of bad luck, Parker."

"Thanks for the pep talk, Cooper." I shoved my hair out of my face, or tried to, but the wind had other plans. "Unless you have any other amazing words of wisdom, I have to go fix this." I pointed at my face. "And then take some clients out house shopping." I stalked away.

He followed me, catching up at my SUV. "I do have something to tell you. Two things, actually."

"What?" I said, yanking the door open.

"Cornelius wanted me to tell you that he drew a moon today."

I scoffed. "What does that even mean?"

"How the hell should I know? But he was insistent that you know."

"Fine. Message received." I was going to show Cornelius two pale half-moons of my own for sending such a cryptic message. "Anything else?"

"Yeah. Doc and I went down in the basement of Cornelius's hotel this morning."

That stopped me and all of my grumbling in a blink. The changeling! I'd forgotten all about it thanks to the imp. "Is Doc okay?"

"Nyce is fine. He's back at his office now."

"Did he hear or see anything?"

He shook his head. "Neither did I. And that has us worried."

"Why?"

He rubbed the back of his neck, looking worn around the edges in the morning light. "Because if it's not at the hotel anymore, where did it go and why did it leave?"

CHAPTER SEVEN

I drove straight home, raced into the house, and promptly tripped over the cat, who was cleaning herself right inside the front door.

"Dammit, Bogart!" I growled after I'd picked myself up off the floor. "Make better choices."

The dang cat had the nerve to hiss at me before she took off up the stairs. I limped after the furry boogerbutt, detouring to the bathroom, and added a bruised knee to my list of current ailments.

The sight of myself in the mirror inspired a shocked shriek. No wonder Cooper had been momentarily stunned when he saw me.

Half of my hair hung loose from the bun in curly knots that spiraled every which way. I tried to tuck some of it back up, but only made a bigger mess.

Then there was my face, which looked like I'd crawled through a thicket of brambles. The scratches from the imp's claws were going to be difficult to hide, even with a shitload of makeup. The cut that I'd brushed with my glove earlier now had a crusted streak of blood over the wound. More had oozed down my cheek and dried there. I leaned closer, gently touching the dark bruise forming under my eye from where the sucker had head butted me.

"Ain't this a real spankydandy way to start my day," I muttered, digging out the hydrogen peroxide and cotton balls from under the sink. I'd just finally gotten rid of the last black eye, dang it.

My boss was going to think I'd joined some top-secret fight club. Jerry would probably want to put me on billboards wearing boxing gloves around my neck and a slinky tank top, sporting a big championship belt along with a black eye and fire-engine red lipstick.

I could see the borderline bawdy taglines now: *Nobody knows the ropes like Violet Parker!* Or worse: *Visit Violet at Calamity Jane Realty for a knockout blow-by-blow!*

Growling under my breath, I started tending to my wounds along with my pride.

Who'd have figured such a small creature could do so much damage? I was going to have to put some serious thought into how I was going to catch that imp. The sharp-toothed little jerk had made its feelings clear on being jailed in a cage again. How long had Dominick had it locked away in that stove in the Sugarloaf Building, anyway? A decade? Two?

I was almost done covering what I could of the imp's pummeling when my phone rang. I glanced down at it, reminded instantly of a bigger problem than the imp waiting for me, and cursed before taking the call.

"Good morning, Cornelius. What news do you bring from the land of the spinning clock?"

There was a pause at the other end, then a humming sound. I knew that humming well from past séances.

"Speak, Cornelius, or I'm hanging up."

The humming stopped. "I believe I need to buy you a bouquet of gardenias, Violet." That made about as much sense as his earlier "moon" message.

"I prefer daisies."

"So I've heard, but what I'd be attempting to convey with these particular flowers is not temperance, so daisies wouldn't work."

I didn't have time for flower talk. "Did you mean to call my mother?" Hope-the-Hipster spoke "flower" as a second language, having won many blue ribbons at the county fair for her bouquets over the years.

"Not at all."

I really didn't have time for one of Cornelius's chats, but I took the bait anyway. "Why gardenias?"

"To encourage more sweetness from you via a hidden message."

"What message?" I asked between clenched teeth.

"A bouquet of gardenias, of course."

"You're making even less sense than usual today, Cornelius."

"That's because your vishuddha is likely misaligned."

"My what?"

He sighed as if I were extra thickheaded. "Exactly."

"I'm going to hang up if you don't start speaking my version of English now."

"Vishuddha is your throat chakra, which appears to be blocked. You should drink some hot water with lemon and raw honey in it to fix it."

I closed my eyes and counted to five. "Was there a reason for this call besides an update on my chakra?"

"Did the bristly detective deliver my message?"

"That you drew a moon? Yes, he did."

"I didn't draw *a* moon. I drew *the* Moon."

"The difference being?"

I checked the time on my phone. It had taken me a lot longer to fix the imp's damage to my face than I'd hoped, leaving not much time to stop by Doc's office before meeting my clients.

"A moon is a spherical object in the sky," he said.

"I might kill you before the next full moon if you don't get to your reason for calling soon."

"On second thought, I'll send you African marigolds. They'll convey your boorishness."

I huffed. "I'm not boorish, I just have to get to work to meet some clients and you're taking the horse-drawn carriage route to your point."

"Well, why didn't you declare your need for imperativeness upon answering?"

I counted to five again. "What do you mean about 'drawing the Moon'?"

"It's a tarot card in the major arcana that represents uncertainty and illusion, and this concerns me for you today."

"Why the concern for me?"

"Because when I asked what obstacles you might encounter, that was the final card I pulled."

"Were the other cards you drew as bad as the Moon?"

"Well, the Tower card came out again, this time in the present position."

"Lucky me." The Tower had spurred such not-lovely things for me yesterday. I couldn't wait to see what today brought besides my battle with the imp.

"Oddly, the Ace of Cups was in the position of matters that

might be helpful."

"And that's odd because the Ace of Cups means?"

"New starts. For example, a new relationship with someone who could bring happiness at home."

Was this about Susan? If I were to build a bridge over our past troubled waters, it would certainly make my mother happy.

I inspected my reflection. "Anything else?"

"Unfortunately, the Ten of Swords is one of your challenges."

The imp was a challenge, too, this morning, and the effects of our *tête-à-tête* were still evident on my face even after a double dose of foundation.

"That represents disappointment," Cornelius continued. "Such as failed plans."

Disappointment and failed plans? Check and check. I was beginning to think this tarot deck of Cornelius's had it out for me.

"So, you're calling to tell me I should expect a day full of uncertainty, failed plans, illusions, and new relationships that will probably end in chaos."

"More or less," he said.

"Do you have any positive words for me this morning on how to get through a day filled with these challenges?" Maybe he was better at pep talks than Cooper.

"Yesssss," he answered slowly. Too slowly. His tone sounded less than certain.

"I'm all ears."

"Lion's breath."

"Try again, Cornelius, and this time make sure your banjo is tuned right."

"It's a breathing technique where you inhale through your nose, then open your eyes and mouth wide. When you exhale, stick your tongue out and roar."

"Are you joking?"

"Oh, I never joke about malevolent spirits, toy poodles, or breathing," he answered.

"I know. I know." Actually, that breathing part was news to me. "Hey, are the clock hands still spinning?"

That's when I realized he'd hung up on me.

I cursed at my phone and then the ceiling. When I was finished "roaring" at both, I made a beeline out the door with ten minutes to get my ass to work before my clients were supposed to arrive.

* * *

After another frustrating morning of involuntary participation in paranormal investigations, and an afternoon wasted sitting at my desk while I combed through way too many work emails about Deadwood's ghostly housing market, earning a certificate from clown college seemed like a viable alternative. I already had the hair for the job, no wig required. And I knew the words to Smokey Robinson's recording of "The Tears of a Clown" by heart. I merely needed a big red nose and a tiny clown car.

I'd read somewhere a few years back that the upper crust of clowns made over six figures a year. Hell, if I could get the imp to go in with me, we could put on a physical comedy act that would certainly entertain a big top tent full of spectators. I had loads of experience juggling multiple catastrophes at once these days. After a few more tries, I might actually be good at it, too. Or just dead.

I sighed and returned to pondering my future in real estate while Mona clacked away on her keyboard and Ben researched a property online.

I'd completely missed seeing Jerry today, thankfully, since my makeup really wasn't covering my cuts and scratches and bruises, according to my coworkers. Apparently, Jerry had called into the office while I was out showing houses, and declared he had an afternoon appointment for which he hadn't given any further details.

Being secretive was odd for Jerry, but unlike Mona, I wasn't going to give that mystery much thought because I had enough uncertainties swirling in my head for the time being—like how I was going to catch that damned imp.

And why the Hellhound clock was acting so weird.

And what Detective Hawke's next move would be when it came to trying to lock me up behind bars.

And whether Susan was serious about helping me.

And if Cornelius's tarot card deck had any uplifting cards about my possible future.

And …

"Vi?" Mona's voice interrupted the circus music still playing in the background of my worries.

My focus switched from the sad clown face I'd drawn on the local listings sheet to her. She reminded me of a classic siren beauty today in her form-fitting emerald green cardigan and loose auburn hair. "Yeah?"

Above her bejeweled reading glasses, her eyebrows were wrinkled with concern. "Did you hear what Ben asked?"

"No, sorry," I said to Ben, who looked quite dapper himself in his gray sweater and black corduroy pants. "I was thinking about something else."

"I was wondering if Detective Cooper would be interested in buying a historical building rather than a house?"

Cooper, aka "Goldilocks," was a tough client. I'd shown him over twenty houses since he'd sold his place in Lead, and he'd come up with a reason to reject every single one, even those that fit his preferences to a T. I doubted he'd want to drop even more cash on an old building, but I could be wrong.

"I'll ask. What building are you talking about?"

Before Ben could answer, my cell phone rang. I checked it, saw Zelda Britton's name, and instantly shied away.

Zelda was a sweet, petite redhead who baked delicious, mouthwatering morsels of delight; however, the uppity ghost she lived with delivered repetitive eye-watering wallops of pain every damned time I was near her.

While Zelda may be responsible for the action of physically calling me, I had a feeling Prudence would be the one speaking when I answered. Especially with Cornelius pulling that damned Tower tarot card again this morning. "Chaos" was that haughty haint's middle name.

"Are you going to answer that?" Mona asked, "or just grimace at your phone like it's covered in cockroaches?"

After the beating I'd taken from the imp this morning to both my face and pride, I'd rather leap off the end of a plank into a sea filled with sharks.

"I'm considering letting it go to voicemail."

"Why?" Her lips thinned. "Is a particular 'problem' client bothering you again?"

Mona knew about Rex Conner. She was in the office with me the day my ex had shown up out of the blue and insisted on hiring me as his real estate agent. Jerry, who was clueless about my past (along with most everyone else in town), had thought me working with Rex was an excellent idea, what with my ex-shithead being so gung-ho to buy, buy, buy!

So, I'd been forced to play nice with Rex for months, or risk my kids learning that the man who'd refused to have anything to do with them from their inception was hanging around town. Soon after Mona had found out the truth about Rex's identity, she'd convinced Jerry to let her take over as his agent, saving me a trip to jail for attempted castration via blunt garden shears.

"Maybe you should get a restraining order, Violet." Ben knew about Rex, too, and had promised along with Mona to keep my ex's true identity a secret from Jerry. In my book, the fewer who knew the better.

"It's not Rex," I told them both, giving in and reaching for my phone. "It's Zelda Britton."

If it truly were Prudence on the other end of the line, there'd be no putting her off. Especially now that Zelda was happy to act as a possessed version of Pinocchio the puppet, dancing at the end of invisible strings to whatever song Prudence played.

"Isn't Zelda a friend of yours?" Ben asked.

I nodded, frowning at her name on my phone's screen. "I'm just not interested in stopping by Zelda's place today, and it's hard to say no to *her.*"

Mona's head tipped to the side, her eyes narrowing. I had a feeling she was going to be asking me more about my sudden aversion to Zelda later. In private.

"Hello?" I said warily.

"Violet," Zelda said in a tone higher than usual. Her breath rattled through the line in short bursts. "Do you think … you might be able … to come to Lead … umm … right away?"

What did Prudence want now? "I'm at work for another couple of hours. Can it wait?"

"Uhh, no … Not really. Prudence is being … rather insistent … at the moment."

Of course she was. Prudence knew only one way of operating— her way. Everyone else's wants and needs be damned, even though she was already dead. It wasn't like she had a ticking clock or anything. I glanced up at the ceiling separating me from Cornelius's apartment, where the Hellhound clock waited still.

"Petulant, even," Zelda added. Her breath was steadier now. "Yes, you are!" she snapped.

Was she talking to me?

"You won't listen to reason," she continued.

"Zelda, I didn't mean—" I started.

"I'm not talking to you, Violet." She sniffed. "Darn it, Prudence. I told you I don't feel comfortable going in that old school alone."

What old school? The only "old" school I knew about in Lead was the decaying middle school located a short distance behind the Historic Homestake Opera House, where I'd met Dominick Masterson earlier this month to talk about how to kill a *Nachzehrer*. While I was in there with him, I'd heard some hair-raising noises coming from the deep shadows down one of the hallways. Before I could check out the source—not that I'd wanted to, because what sane person would want to look for monsters in the dark?— Dominick had sidetracked me.

"I know you think you can keep me safe." Zelda was still talking to Prudence, I assumed. "But what if you can't?"

Great zookers! I didn't like the sound of this at all. I'd been around Prudence enough to know that if she was determined to go into that old school, she'd take the mental reins from Zelda and force the poor woman to go inside.

What was so darn important in the building that Prudence was willing to risk Zelda's safety, anyway?

"You keep forgetting that I'm only human," Zelda complained. "For all you know, your powers might be limited when we—"

"Zelda!" I snapped, earning raised brows from both Mona and Ben. I mouthed *sorry* to them and lowered my voice. "Where are you?"

Her answer made me groan. She was exactly where I'd dreaded—the old school. "I'll be there shortly. Tell your friend to chill."

I hung up and sighed. "I have to go to Lead to help Zelda with … " *A pain-in-the-ass, long-dead Executioner.* No, that wouldn't do. "With a situation," I finished, keeping it vague.

"You certainly seem to find yourself in the middle of the most interesting situations, Vi," Mona said, her fingernails once again clickity-clacking on her keyboard.

She didn't know the half of it. Well, actually she did know about half of my struggles—the least outrageous of the supernatural ones anyway, including ghosts and séances. Ben, on the other hand, only knew about the issues with Rex, and I hoped to keep it that way.

Two minutes later I rushed out of Calamity Jane Realty while still buttoning my coat, dodging piles of slush on my way across the parking lot. I'd reached the bumper of my SUV when I heard someone call my name.

I glanced around.

Doc stood outside the door of his office in a long-sleeved shirt and khakis, no coat or hat. He waved for me to come back.

I shook my head. "I can't," I hollered across the lot. "Zelda called. I have to get up to Lead right now." I figured he'd understand my hidden message in that explanation.

"Hold it right there, Killer!"

I'd figured right.

Doc jogged my way through the blasts of cold wind. I shivered on his behalf.

When he stopped in front of me, he did a double take. "Holy shit!" The lines on his forehead deepened. He reached toward my face, gently cupping my jaw as he inspected my battle scars. "What happened, sweetheart?"

"That stupid imp happened, that's what." I pulled slightly away, surprised he hadn't already heard about my prizefight with the imp from Harvey or Cooper. "Listen, as much as I'd love to share all of the humiliating details with you, I really need to get up to Lead before Prudence makes Zelda go into that spooky school where I'm pretty sure something not-very-nice is lurking."

Doc cursed. "I'm coming with you." He glanced back toward his office. "I just need to lock up."

"If you're coming only because you're worried about me scrapping with Prudence, I can assure you I'm in no condition to—"

"Violet." His tone didn't leave any room for argument. Neither did his hard stare. "We're a team."

I nodded. "Let's go then."

"I'll get my coat. Pick me up at the door."

A few minutes later, we were on our way to Lead with me still behind the wheel. As we left the parking lot, I filled Doc in on my morning adventure of running clients around to different houses that had starred on the *Paranormal Realty* TV show.

My retelling included a side note about a stop at Galena House, where Natalie was living for the winter while helping Freesia Tender, the owner, prep it for sale. Prep it even more, really, since it was already on the market. The listing was mine, so if I could secure a sale to any actual clients I was representing, I'd win doubly.

During the stop, Freesia had joined me and my clients, giving them a personal tour of the place. Her stint as a guide had allowed me the chance to escape and put my ear against the locked door to Ms. Wolff's old apartment, which still had crime scene tape hanging from one of the jambs.

Inside the apartment were many more Black Forest cuckoo clocks, similar to the one in Cornelius's abode. These were clocks that I really needed to have access to as a Timekeeper; at least that was my assumption, since I'd taken on Ms. Wolff's role when she died.

Unfortunately, Detective Hawke was staying in the apartment, claiming to be guarding the clocks until the case of Ms. Wolff's murder was solved. The irony being that the dufus was actually interfering with a process that could keep someone else from dying—namely me, since I had *other* bounty hunters on my ass now. Not to mention that I'd killed Ms. Wolff, but not by choice. She'd forced me to in order for her to be free of Timekeeper duties.

Criminy. How had my life gotten so complicated? Oh yeah, I'd moved to Deadwood so I could spend more time with my kids.

Anyway, I hadn't been able to hear any cuckooing going on inside the apartment, which I hoped was a good thing. If only I could shoehorn Hawke out of that place for good.

In the end, after spending a few hours with my ghost groupie clients throughout the morning, no offers had been bandied about for any properties. I wasn't surprised, really. There'd been too many selfies taken at each place for me to get bouncy about a sale.

"I'm not sure there is much value in the time we put into filming the TV show if nobody actually buys anything," I said, ending my rambling thoughts.

From the corner of my eye, I could see Doc watching me with his brow definitely lined. His focus had barely shifted since we'd left the lot, which explained my urge to blather even more, but I squelched it.

A glance in the mirror made me flinch. Ye gods! It was no wonder he couldn't take his eyes off me. I looked like my makeup had caught fire and someone had beat it out with a piece of barbed wire.

"So, tell me about your visit to Cornelius's hotel this morning." I changed topics, trying to shift his attention from my battered face. "Cooper mentioned that you didn't hear any sounds from the changeling or any other ghosts, which makes me wonder—"

"Why didn't you call earlier to tell me about your attempt to catch the imp?"

Okay, we'd talk about *that* then. "I didn't have time. It happened before I got to work."

"But you had enough time to go home and try to cover up your injuries with makeup. You could have called then."

"I knew you had a morning appointment. And I had an appointment, too." I pointed at my face. "Besides, I didn't want to distract you with this train wreck."

"How many times do I need to remind you that you're more important than my work, Violet?"

My heart swooned. "Trust me, if any of these injuries had been serious, I'd have come crying to you. It's all cosmetic." I glanced in the mirror again. Dang. My face was going to need more makeup before my kids saw it.

"Did the imp actually bite you anywhere, or just scratch the hell out of you?"

"It got in one bite, but it didn't break skin."

Which was probably thanks to the cashmere coat Doc had given me for Christmas. That coat had likely saved me from more scratches, too.

The bite had left a bruise on my forearm, though. I'd checked after I'd returned to work at lunch, rolling up my sweater sleeve while I hid in the bathroom and tried to patch up my makeup some more.

"I should have known better than to corner it in such a tight space." Hindsight was 20/20 and all that fiddle-faddle. "Especially since there was no room for me to take a good swing at it."

He leaned against the headrest, staring out the windshield as we wound our way up into Lead. "I want the details."

"Good, because you need to help me come up with a better plan to catch it next time."

"What was your plan this morning?"

I thought about trying to jazz up my answer, but in the end I told the truth. "Bag it and then hit it over the head with a tire iron."

He chuckled. "You're kidding, right?"

"No. Harvey's call caught me by surprise, so I didn't have time to analyze the whole situation and think about how we would relocate the imp from where he had it trapped in his truck. Next time, I might try the cat carrier Addy uses to take Elvis on trips."

"Back up and tell me everything, starting with how Harvey trapped the imp in his pickup in the first place."

I gave Doc the quick version of the whole mess. By the time I'd finished, we were almost at the old school and Doc's eyes were watery from amusement.

"There has to be a better way to catch it," Doc said, laughter in his tone. "A smarter way that won't result in you taking another beating."

"You sound like Cooper. He showed up after the fight was over and then proceeded to tell me what I'd done wrong. Talk about lousy pep talks."

Doc sobered. "I'm not trying to criticize your fighting skills, but you have about ten scratches on your face alone, not to mention the start of another black eye." He reached over and caught my hand, giving it a light squeeze. "I don't like seeing you hurt, *cara bella*."

"*Mon cher*." I lifted his hand to my lips, kissing his knuckles. "The main thing hurt is my pride." I let go of his hand and tapped the bruised area under my eye, wincing slightly. And maybe my cheek. "The rest is superficial."

"Has Zoe seen the results of your first attempt at imp wrangling?"

"Not yet. I'll have to come up with something to tell the kids, too." Thank God my mother had already gone home.

"We'll figure that out together."

Little hearts popped around my head at his words. I liked being a team. It was so much nicer than being a stressed-out single mother with no strong shoulders to lean on in times of crisis.

A minute later, I pulled into the snow-scattered parking lot of the dilapidated middle school. "Here we are," I said, trying to sound chipper.

The three-story brick building had the same haunted gloom as last time. From its boarded-up windows with paint-peeling frames, broken cornices, and cracked foundation, to the two sets of chained red double doors. The heavy gray clouds looming overhead added an unnerving, pants-peeing ambiance to the scene.

I rolled to a stop a short hop, skip, and jump from the entrance on the far side where I'd gone in on my previous visit. Upon closer inspection, only one of the red doors was chained today. The other was open slightly, letting some inner demon darkness leak out. Groovy doovy.

"Damn." Doc frowned at the crumbling building through the windshield. "This place reminds me of an abandoned state hospital in Vicksburg, Mississippi I once visited."

"Alone?" I asked.

"With the caretaker."

"Did you run into any ghosts there?"

"Yeah. A Confederate soldier with a hole in his guts from back when the hospital was serving the wounded during the Civil War, and a doctor who'd caught yellow fever in the late 1800s. I think the caretaker said the fever had killed a total of sixteen doctors in 1878."

"Two ghosts? That was all?"

"Well, we kept to the first floor. The caretaker was concerned about me being an insurance liability."

"Have you ever thought about returning and exploring further?"

He shook his head. "I found what I was looking for."

"Which was?"

"A long-lost memento I was paid to find." He looked around the lot. "Zelda's car isn't here."

What memento? I set that question aside for later when we weren't sitting ducks in an otherwise empty parking lot.

"I noticed."

"You think she might be in there anyway?" he asked.

I was afraid of that very notion. I stared at that open door, watching for movement in the slice of darkness behind it. "She could have parked somewhere nearby and walked here."

"That face you're making tells me you're not raring to follow Zelda inside."

"Think murky hallways and musty smells, and then add a boogeyman lying in wait."

He smirked. "But you're a big, bad Executioner."

"True, but I'm allergic to monsters."

"Since when?"

"Since I moved to Deadwood last year. If I get too close to one now, I break into a sweat, my throat closes up, my chest tightens, and then my knees weaken under a tank-sized sense of impending doom."

Doc focused back on the school. "Allergy or not, we can't leave if she's in there alone."

"Fucking Prudence and her infatuation with herself."

"Try calling Zelda."

I did and got no answer. "Damn." I shut off the engine, looking at my teammate. "Ready, Shaggy?"

Doc nodded. "I'll lead. You follow, Scooby."

I eased out into the cold, hunching into my scarf as I locked the doors. Doc rounded the front of the vehicle, holding his hand out for mine. He tugged me along as I slipped and slid across the broken asphalt and buckled concrete sidewalk toward the red doors.

"Maybe I should go back home and grab my snow boots."

He tightened his grip on my hand, his warmth seeping through my glove. "I'm right here with you, Killer."

"Why in the hell is Prudence so bent on going in this place?" I grumbled as we neared the cracked concrete steps. And how had she gotten the chain off the door? I checked out the base of the steps, finding no evidence of the second chain or the lock that had secured it. But I did see one of those tools used to break a vehicle window in case of emergency. It was hard to miss with its neon orange handle.

Doc stooped to pick it up and pointed it at the chained door. "Probably because of that."

I climbed the steps. A single word had been scratched into the metal:

DUZARX

I frowned back at Doc. "Is that supposed to be a warning or an official proclamation?"

"I guess we need to go inside and see." He looked about as happy to find out the answer as I was.

I hesitated, the urge to flee the scene burning clear to my feet. "According to Prudence, a *Duzarx* has eight eyes, several sets of razor-sharp teeth, and a lust for human flesh."

I distinctly remembered that description, along with a strong notion to do my best to never run into one. Certainly not inside a moldering, deserted school on a gloomy day.

"A *Duzarx*." Doc cursed under his breath. "Wait here." He released my hand and started toward my SUV.

I caught him by the sleeve before he'd made it two steps. "Where do you think you're going, Oracle?"

He frowned back at the open door and then me. "To get you something to kill it with, *Scharfrichter*."

CHAPTER EIGHT

Be afraid," Doc whispered, as I joined him inside the old school. "Be very afraid."

I slugged him lightly on the shoulder, whispering back, "New rule—no quoting scary movies in spooky places."

A musty whiff of dust, mold, and rot had me turtling lower into my scarf. If only I had a shell to hide in every time that shit went sideways in my life. On second thought, maybe that was a bad idea, because I'd probably never poke my head out again.

"*The Fly* isn't really that scary." Doc stepped farther into the wide hallway lined on one side with rusted metal lockers, most of which were dented and had seen their better days several decades ago. "It's more disturbing as a concept."

"I disagree." I pulled off my gloves. "The idea of my face falling off into the sink in bloody chunks gives me the heebie-jeebies." I cringed at the memory alone. "Isn't there a similar scene in *Poltergeist*?"

He glanced down at me. "Sort of. The guy pulls his skin off while looking in the mirror."

"Blech." I stuffed my gloves in my coat pockets. "Okay, it's time to talk about pink unicorns and rainbows."

I gripped the folding shovel Doc had brought from my rig. It was lightweight, but it could deliver a good wallop if needed, and at least a semi-decent stab. I sure hoped it wouldn't be put to the test, though.

Unfortunately, in my hurry to rush home to patch up after my imp tussle, I'd forgotten the tire iron at Junie Coppermoon's place. That meant Doc was stuck with the window breaker Zelda had left in front of the school along with my heavy-duty flashlight. After today, I was going to start carrying more hefty weapons in my SUV, Detective Hawke and his suspicions about me as a potential suspect for every crime committed in the northern Black Hills be damned.

"Where to, Killer?" Doc clicked on the flashlight.

"Your guess is as good as mine."

"Are you sensing any *others*?"

I thought about it for a second. "Well, at the moment, there are no hair-raising vibes prickling the back of my neck. There is a slight tingling sensation in my fingers, though, but that could be the cold."

I sniffed, testing the air for anything besides the stale odor of schooldays gone by. Nope, nothing out of the ordinary for an old, abandoned building. But yet … "I am feeling a strong urge to get the hell out of this crumbling pile of bricks and glass."

There was something more going on here than just the slow decay of the past. I'd sensed it the last time I stepped inside the building, too. Something ominous, hovering just out of reach. "I sort of feel like a chicken tiptoeing past an alligator that *looks* like it's sleeping."

"Yeah, those gators are tricky devils. So was the *lidérc*, but you won in the end, *Scharfrichter*."

"Barely, and only with help. How about you, Mr. Mental Medium? Picking up any smelly blips on your ghost radar?"

He sniffed, too, and then shook his head. "But the ghosts in this place might be wary."

"Yeah." I shivered from a mix of cold and nerves. "I get that. I'm right there with them."

I stared behind us at the entry doors. We'd left the unchained one partway open behind us, the same as it had been before we'd crossed the threshold. As I peered out through the gap at the gray sky, the door swayed inward and then back the other way, as if the school were alive and breathing. Well, considering the age of the building, it might be gasping, with lungs full of soot and dry rot.

"I sort of feel like we're in the belly of a decaying whale," I said to myself more than Doc.

"Think happier thoughts, Killer."

Dust particles churned in the light, creating a frenzy in midair at the boundary between fresh freedom and moldering imprisonment. I tugged my scarf higher, covering my mouth and nose, but not only because I could taste and smell the dust. A *Duzarx* might not be the lone toxin hiding in this place. There were drop-ceiling tiles overhead, many of which sagged severely thanks to leaks, or lay busted into pieces on the floor.

Doc shined the flashlight around, pushing back the shadows. "It's too bad Zelda didn't leave us a trail of breadcrumbs."

"Can you see any footprints? Prudence tends to drag her leg a little when she's possessing Zelda."

He squatted, directing the flashlight beam over the chipped tile flooring stretching into the gloom. "There are prints, but too many all mixed together."

"I'm not sure if that's a good thing or a bad thing."

"Me either." He stood up, aiming the beam forward.

On the right was the math classroom where I'd met Dominick almost two weeks ago. The splash of daylight shining out from the open doorway acted as a blind for whatever waited beyond. It was the "beyond" part that had me wanting to skip on out of here, because in that darkness was where I'd heard the scuffing sounds and swish-swish of something being dragged along the floor last time.

I hadn't explored the school outside of the math classroom when I was here to talk to Dominick. He'd been running the show, keeping Aunt Zoe, Harvey, and me corralled. Now Doc and I were free to roam, which I also wasn't sure about being a good thing or bad.

"Come on." Doc held out his arm, elbow crooked like a gentleman. "Let's go find Zelda and Prudence."

After one last glance at the exit, I latched onto him, holding tight as we neared the math classroom.

"You're cutting off the circulation to my hand," he whispered, moving the arm I had in a death grip.

"You've been around Cooper too long." I squeezed a bit harder. "You're starting to bellyache just like him."

His laugh came from low in his chest. "He'd shoot you for saying that."

"Not if I shot him first. Then I would carve my autograph on the bullet wound scar for him to remember me by."

"That's tough talk for a woman who recently admitted that she's afraid of dolls."

"*Clown* dolls, I said. That's a very different terror than regular dolls." I poked him in the ribs, making him grunt and cough-laugh. "And you'd be scared too, if you had been in the dark elevator with that half-burnt, possessed clown doll that day."

He gave me a sideways hug. "Don't you worry, bruiser, I'll protect you and your secret." He kissed me on the temple and added, "But it'll cost you a pound of naked flesh," before letting me go.

"Deal. How about we go home and I'll pay up right this minute?"

"Nice try, Boots." He stopped outside the math classroom, the flashlight not necessary thanks to the daylight coming through the partly boarded-up windows.

A longer look into the room found it in the same condition as before—a sad mess with mildewed textbooks strewn across the floor, along with pieces of rodent-chewed cardboard and chunks of plaster from the high ceiling. Wooden chairs sat empty while broken desks were shoved and piled in the corner.

"All clear," I whispered.

We moved on, creeping forward into the shadows. A few steps farther we came to a crossroads.

We had two options to our right from which to choose: a shadowy stairway leading up into the darkness beyond, or a long hallway with a pitch-black restroom entrance off one side and a couple of doorways farther down on the right, which I figured were more classrooms. One door was open. The upper panes of glass that had once graced the door lay shattered on the floor below it, sparkling in the flashlight beam.

Paint was peeling from the walls above the dented and graffiti-covered lockers that ran most of the length of the hall. At the end was a door with blackened window panes. Were they painted? It was hard to tell with only a flashlight beam. The windows next to the door were boarded up from the other side, casting deep shadows in the corner behind the open classroom door.

The hall appeared to turn and continue to the left—or ended at a recessed classroom. It was hard to be sure from our viewpoint, and I wasn't sure I wanted to find out.

I stared back at the shadow-filled corner behind the open

classroom door. There was just enough daylight leaking through the boards to make it look like something was crouched down there. Waiting? Hiding? Both? Was it an optical illusion? Or a *Duzarx* with its eight eyes watching us, waiting to lunge when we moved within grabbing distance?

My heart thudded in my ears, probably loud enough for Doc to hear the cowardly organ. "What's that at the end of the hall behind the open door?"

Doc took a couple of steps in that direction, stopping at the base of the stairwell that headed up into the shadows, and aimed the flashlight, illuminating the scene more. A sagging box had been plopped on top of another, both abutting a small teacher's desk tipped on its side.

I breathed a sigh of relief and loosened my sweaty grip on the shovel handle. Oh, how I wished I'd brought my mace.

Was Zelda carrying any weapons while sneaking around this place? Prudence probably had thought ahead and brought a whole arsenal along, something she'd be sure to brag about when she saw my silly shovel.

"I wonder if there's a gym to the left," Doc said, centering the light beam on the blackness where the hall turned. "Or an auditorium."

"I'm more worried about what's in this restroom." I pointed at the dark opening near us.

"Why?" He shifted the light to the entryway, which only drove the shadows deeper into the cave-like entrance. "You think something might be in there?"

"Yes, something vile."

"You mean the *Duzarx*? Or is that a stab at Prudence?"

I snorted. "I meant something else vile that has been living and thriving in those toilets for all these years."

Doc grinned down at me. "Now I'm worried, too. Maybe we should go the other way."

He swung his flashlight to the left side of the main hallway. We both eased forward, peeking through a set of double wooden doors that were missing several panes of glass. On the other side of the doors was a set of stairs leading down, down, down into a pitch-black world.

"What do you think is down there? A dungeon?" I took a baby

step closer, trying to see if there was any light at the bottom of the stairs.

There wasn't. Only darkness so thick I probably wouldn't be able to see my hand in front of my face. I sniffed the air, picking up a trace of something rotting and foul under the damp mustiness wafting up the steps. My whole body pulsed with get-up-and-go, thrumming in anticipation. There was definitely something down there. But I really didn't want to find out what. Not today. Not with the Tower card calling for chaos.

I moved closer to Doc, bumping into his arm. The beam of light shifted, sweeping past a doorway down below on the left side after the bottom step. For a split second, I thought I saw a pair of eyes staring back at me. Big eyes this time, not mouse-sized.

"Shit!" I grabbed Doc's arm and forced him to direct the beam steadily on the doorway.

"What are we looking at?" Doc took a couple more steps toward the lower stairs.

"I thought I saw someone standing in that doorway, but it's just an old US Army poster with Uncle Sam on it."

Doc skimmed the beam of light back and forth over the door. "I can see where you'd think that."

I huffed. "Jeez on crackers! This place has me jumping at my own shadow."

Some big bad Executioner I was today. My silly lily-livered heart was a black eye to all of my *Scharfrichter* predecessors.

"Don't beat yourself up, Killer. This place has multiple levels of schoolhouse horrors." He shined the light up the stairs heading to the second floor, angling his head to try to see farther. The boarded windows partway up tripled the creepiness factor.

"I'm not even sure what a *Duzarx* looks like." I glanced behind us down the hall we'd already traversed, making sure the front door was still open. "Let alone how I'm going to kill it."

The slice of daylight between the doors beckoned. Escape was merely a sprint away. I'd had to run farther to catch the ice cream truck more than once.

"Which way do you want to go?" Doc asked.

"I don't know." I sighed at my lack of desirable options. "What do you think is behind those?"

I pointed at a set of steel doors directly in front of us, both chained shut, same as the ones out front. Rust was slowly eating its way inward from the doors' outer corners, leaving ragged edges and splotches on the steel.

"Well." Doc spotlighted the steel doors. "A roomful of puppies and kittens would be a nice change of pace."

I smiled. "You've been hanging around Addy too much."

"What can I say? I have a soft spot for a girl who sings Elvis Presley's 'Can't Help Falling in Love' to her chicken." He shined the flashlight down the hallway to the right. "I vote we go this way first."

"Lead the way, Oracle."

He did with me trailing on his heels.

I hurried past the restroom without looking its way. Something about the room felt all wrong, and it wasn't the old toilets I'd joked about earlier. The sensation wasn't a physical reaction, more mental. Which reminded me …

"Cornelius drew the Tower card again for me this morning," I whispered as we neared the open classroom door right before the hall turned left. "He said it turned up in the present position. I seem to be stuck in the land of chaos."

Doc harrumphed. "We're going about this imp catching all wrong. We should have Cornelius draw tarot cards for it instead. Maybe if you wait until the imp gets the Tower card, you'd come out of your next battle with fewer scratches."

"Ha ha ha." I wrinkled my nose at him. "You're funny."

"I know. That's why you're nuts about me."

We paused at the classroom with the open door on our right. History had been the main subject in the classroom, according to the cracked placard on the wall. A quick peek into the heavily shadowed room with the flashlight found it mostly empty, except for some light fixtures dangling almost to the floor, broken chalkboard pieces, and a length of board with coat hooks still attached that had been ripped from the wall.

Oh, and a mouse, which sat frozen next to a wall radiator, staring back at us with glittery eyes.

"Want another pet?" Doc asked.

"I don't, but Elvis might. She's partial to rodents."

"To eat or play with?"

"Yes." I pushed the door closed, crunching on the broken glass as I stepped into the center of the hall.

It turned out the window panes in the door at the end were painted black. I scraped my nail over the glass. The paint was on the other side of it, same as the boards covering the windows next to the door.

The hall did continue left, but only for about ten feet. To one side was another bathroom entryway chockful of shadows. I skirted wide of the entrance, gripping Doc's arm again.

At the end of this short hall were double doors with glass panes in them. Unfortunately, the glass was all broken out and lay shattered on the floor. There were more boards nailed to the other side, blocking the view.

Doc reached for the handle of one door. Gymnasium or auditorium or another classroom, we would soon find out. The door started to open at his slight pull.

A tickle of unease spider-crawled its way up my spine, turning into a full-on bristle at the back of my neck.

No! I reached out and pushed the door quietly closed, leaning against it. The edge of one of the empty window panes dug into my shoulder blade. "There's something in there," I mouthed, barely hitting a whisper level.

Doc stared down at me, all traces of mirth gone from his face. "What do you want to do?" He matched my volume.

"Go home and get a bigger weapon."

His eyes narrowed. "Zelda could be in there, too."

"Fuck." My fingertips were tingling now. I couldn't leave without knowing for sure if Zelda was safe. Damn Prudence!

Doc squeezed my upper arm. "We can do this, Killer."

"But what if we can't?" I had no clue what I was facing with a *Duzarx*. For all I knew, it might spit a huge fireball at us. A folding shovel wasn't going to cut it.

"Then we'll get the hell out of here and come back with Harvey's cannon," he said.

I grinned in spite of the invisible hippo now sitting on my chest.

"You ready?" he asked, reaching for the door handle again.

"No." I took a breath. "Yes." Then again ... "Wait."

"What?"

"I forgot to tell you about the Moon." Maybe Doc should hear about the potential outcome for my day according to Cornelius's tarot cards before we go through the doors.

"You mean the blood moon?"

Huh? No, but … "What are you talking about?"

"The blood moon." When I continued to frown up at him, he added, "Don't you remember what Prudence said about having to kill the *Duzarx* before the next blood moon?"

"Yeah, but why are you bringing that up now?"

"Isn't that what you were going to tell me about?"

"No, I was going to tell you about the Moon."

He blinked and then frowned. "Like the cycles of it and how it affects the tides? Can't we save that for the drive home?"

I liked his optimism about our future potential. Maybe Doc should be reading the cards for me each morning.

I shook my head. "I mean the Moon tarot card that Cornelius drew from the deck for today's outcome."

Doc's forehead furrowed even deeper. "Does that have some significance for why you are stalling right now?"

"As a matter of fact, it does." I loosened my scarf. Had someone cranked up the heat in this place? "The Moon card has something to do with uncertainty and illusions."

"Fine. Got it." He rubbed his neck. "Are there any other words of wisdom from the great and powerful Cornelius that we need to heed before stepping through these doors?"

"Yeah. My vishda is blocked, and I need to breathe like a lion."

Doc did a double take. "Your what?"

"Vishduh. You know, my throat chakra."

"You mean 'vishuddha.' "

"Isn't that what I said?"

"No."

"Close enough."

He opened his mouth, then closed it, only to open it again. "What exactly does breathing like a lion entail?"

"Roaring, of course."

He snorted out a quiet laugh. And then another before he covered his mouth and turned away. A couple of deep breaths and he was facing me again. "Okay, Killer. Let's go in there and get to roaring."

I stepped away from the double doors, did a couple of shoulder stretches, and then a few jumping jacks while careful not to step on the bits of broken glass.

Doc watched me, his arms crossed.

"Are you ready now?" he asked when I finished cracking my knuckles.

"I think so." My body was humming anyway. It seemed to be ready for a fight even if my mind wasn't really in the mood for round 2. I reached for the door handle. "I'll pull it open and you light up the place."

He nodded. "On three."

"Yep." I gulped. How did one prepare mentally for an eight-eyed monster? I let go of the door handle. "Hold on. Which eye should I look into?"

He stared at me in the semi-darkness. "You're serious?"

"Yeah, there are eight to choose from."

"Go with the middle one."

I chewed on my lower lip. "I wish I had my mace."

"I'm going to start counting now, Violet."

"Maybe you should open the door so I can rush in swinging."

"Fine." He grasped the handle.

"And let's go in on five instead of three. Five gives me more time to gear up in my head, you know?"

"Sure." He took a deep breath. "One."

I grimaced at him. "What if it's not the *Duzarx*?"

"Two."

"Maybe we shouldn't look it in the eyes. Maybe that will make us go crazy or turn on each other."

He shook his head. "Three."

"There was a Ten of Swords as one of my challenges. Supposedly, that represents failed plans, like how my plan to catch the imp didn't work. Maybe we should come up with a different plan for this situation here."

His head tilted slightly, but he continued. "Four."

I gripped the shovel, holding it up like a bat. Okay, here went nothing.

Something clanged at the other end of the hall, out where we'd stood at a crossroads next to the stairwell.

Doc turned toward the sound.

I turned, too.

We eased to the end of the short hall and around the corner, the flashlight beam leading the way.

I gasped a little too loudly at the sight of a very tall, very stocky man with a shock of black hair and a long bushy beard who now stood frozen in the spotlight. He was dressed in denim coveralls that didn't quite reach the ankles of his work boots and heavy-duty welding gloves, all of which seemed to have seen better days three decades ago when they were probably first made. Great googly moogly! The big brute looked like he was one chainsaw short of a horror movie.

Shit!

There was something hanging from his hand, dragging on the floor, long and stringy, covered in polka dots.

I squinted. It was a scarf. Not polka dots—daisies!

I knew that scarf! It belonged to Zelda. Oh no!

My body pulsed from a wave of white-hot energy that made my palms burn.

What had the giant done to Zelda? He was big. Just like Prudence had said the *Duzarx* would be. Hadn't she? But he was six eyes short. That son of a bitch had better not have touched one hair on ...

Lion's breath, I heard Cornelius's voice above the rush of blood in my ears.

I inhaled long and deep in through my nose. Opening my eyes and mouth wide, I ran straight at the ogre, shovel out and ready to swing.

He raised his huge hands at me, fingers spread wide.

I stuck out my tongue and roared, letting the lion lead the way.

The brute screamed back.

Only it was more of a high-pitched shriek.

Filled with ... terror?

His hands were out to block me, his eyes wide with fright as he cringed. The scarf fell to the floor at his feet.

I slowed, cutting my roar short.

The guy was even bigger up close, and now he was whimpering and cringing.

My stomach clenched and then roiled, nausea making my mouth water.

"Violet?" A voice said from behind the brute.

Horse apples! I knew that voice.

Dominick Masterson crested the top of the stairs that led down into the complete darkness, stepping out from the shadows. In his black duster, hat, and cowboy boots, he looked like an Old West version of the devil—smoking hot and slick as hell.

I lowered the shovel right as Doc slid to a stop next to me. "It's Dominick," I whispered to him.

"I can see that, Tiger," he said loud and clear. "Or should I say, 'Lion'?"

My cheeks warmed, and it had nothing to do with the tingles and sparks of energy still lighting me up on the inside.

Masterson's presence explained my nausea, which was my internal warning system for his kind. I'd have preferred something snazzier, like an ancient elf-made blade that glowed when my enemies were near, but I'd come from a long line of *Scharfrichter* women, not hobbits. Queasiness was my secret weapon.

Dominick stepped around the broad-shouldered wall of muscles and beard, putting himself between us. Protecting the big guy? Could be. Or just taking command of the scene. It was hard to tell with Dominick. In my experience with him, his ego was usually the biggest monster in the room at any given moment.

"What a surprise it is to see you, *Schar* …" He paused, staring at me. "What happened to your face?"

He didn't need to know about my battle with his freaking imp. "I cut myself shaving."

Doc chuckled next to me.

Dominick's upper lip wrinkled at my blatant lie. Apparently his funny bone had been broken at some point during his long, long life. He should really get that fixed.

He made a point of sniffing the air near Doc. "You might want to be careful, *Scharfrichter*, when bringing your mate along to hunt. While I have always felt it a rare treat to stand in the presence of such a sage, there are some who would want to steal him for their own malevolent gain."

"Is that some kind of veiled threat, Dominick?" I puffed up my chest, still feeling lion-ish after that slightly embarrassing roar. Cornelius really had something there.

"Down, Killer," Doc said. "I think Mr. Masterson is just sharing a friendly warning. Isn't that right?"

"Of course." He brushed a spider web from his sleeve. "As the Dutch proverb goes, 'Who has only one eye must take care of it.' "

Behind Dominick, the big brute scuttled backward several feet, and then turned, stampeding down the stairs into the darkness.

When I moved to follow, Dominick blocked my path, his dark eyes hooded but hard, a challenge in their depths.

Doc caught me by the wrist, tugging me back his way.

"What are you doing here, *Scharfrichter*?" Dominick's gaze lingering on the shovel in my hand.

"I could ask the same of you," I replied, buying time. Cornelius's tarot cards hadn't warned me about everything, it turned out.

"I own this building," he said.

"I didn't see your vehicle in the lot," I shot back.

"I parked on the other side of the building along the street." He made a point of looking down the hallway from where we'd come and then at the flashlight in Doc's hand. "Were you searching for something in particular?"

I had a feeling he meant his precious *lidérc*, which made for a nice distraction, so I went along with it. "Yes, as a matter of fact I was."

Doc cleared his throat.

Dominick's brow raised. "And did you find it?"

"Not yet," I answered, glancing toward the exit doors. Both were closed now. Hmm.

Dominick must have seen the word Prudence had scratched into the door when he arrived. On the other hand, if he'd parked on the other side of the building, he might have entered through another door. So, someone else maybe closed the door and saw the word? Then again, it could have been simply a strong breeze that shut it.

"Why would you believe my *lidérc* would be hiding in this building?"

"When I was here last, I thought I heard something roaming the halls."

His mouth tightened. "Why would you not mention that then?"

"If you'll remember, you were busy telling me all about a certain other pest. As I told you then, I would decide what I would hunt and when. The *lidérc* would wait its turn."

"And have you eradicated that particular vermin?"

"With help, yes."

"Help, of course." Dominick's focus shifted to Doc. "Although catching a *Nachzehrer* does seem well below an Oracle's station." He turned back to me, one black eyebrow raised. "Tell me, how is your lovely aunt?"

"Happily living out her days in another man's arms."

Doc coughed, probably choking on my lie.

"Really, Violet." Dominick scoffed. "You could not be more obvious in that arena."

"Good, then you understand what I'm *not* saying."

His whole face hardened. "I will stick to our deal, but I really think I could offer Zoe far more."

"Yeah, well a mousetrap always offers plenty of free cheese, doesn't it?"

Doc smiled. "Well said, *Scharfrichter.*"

Dominick's nostrils flared. "If we're done here, I'll see you both out."

"No need." Doc thumbed behind us toward the front doors. "We can manage on our own." He bent and scooped up Zelda's scarf and then pulled me along.

"Violet," Dominick called as we reached the threshold. "I expect you will inform me of any other sightings of my lost pet."

"You betcha," I lied without a hitch.

The gray sky was a sight for sore eyes. I was happy to breathe fresh air again, even if it nearly froze my nose hairs together.

Once we were locked inside my SUV with the engine running, I noticed Zelda had sent me a text message. I read it and then growled. "You've got to be kidding me."

"What's wrong?"

"It's Zelda. She's at home." She must have dropped her scarf at some point during her visit, which was surprisingly careless of Prudence not to notice.

"How long ago did she send it?"

I checked. "Fifteen minutes ago. I didn't hear it, though. Weird."

"It's that place." He nodded at the school. "Concrete structures tend to block or absorb or even reflect RF waves. I sometimes have trouble with getting a signal in the locker room at the Rec Center for that reason."

"Damned Prudence. She could have gotten us killed going on her wild goose hunt."

"Probably not. You're tougher than you think." Doc combed his short beard with his fingers. "Why do you think Masterson was really there?"

I shifted into gear. "You're not buying that he periodically stops by the school solely because he owns it?"

"Not even a little."

"Yeah, me either."

"There's something in there." Doc turned back to look at the school as I drove away. "You were lit up like a slot machine when we were getting ready to go through those doors. I could see it in your eyes."

I was a hot mess the whole time we were in the damned building. "If the *Duzarx* is in there somewhere, could Dominick be hiding it?"

"It wouldn't be the first time Masterson has concealed a deadly creature."

I stopped at a cross street. "Do you think he has any other of his so-called pets in there?"

He shrugged. "Maybe he's keeping a zoo in various abandoned buildings throughout Lead, like the Sugarloaf Building and the school. It would be easy enough to do some research and test that theory."

"Research and test? I suppose that means you're going to want to go back in there."

"We probably should."

"Or not." I turned onto the main road heading back to Deadwood. "I'm not sure I want to run into that ogre again."

"He might be more scared of you than you of him."

"Not in the dark."

Doc stared out the window as we passed Gold Run Park in front of what little remained of the old Homestake Mine. "We need to find out what's behind those doors."

"Which ones? The chained steel ones or the double wooden doors at the end of the hall?"

"Both, and maybe check upstairs and down, too. I think I caught the scent of a ghost near the stairwell while you were talking to Masterson."

I sighed. "Why can't we just go on normal outings together like regular happy couples?"

My cell phone pinged. I handed it to Doc to read since I was driving.

"It's Eddie Mudder. He says: *Our pale friend says I'm supposed to tell you to use the key to open the clock for answers.*"

"The key?" I tapped my nails on the steering wheel, trying to remember where the key was that Mr. Black had given me months ago. Oh yeah, I'd given it to Aunt Zoe to keep safe, not wanting anything much to do with the clock at that time. I still didn't, but ignorance was no longer bliss. It was dangerous and tended to pile even more worry on my plate.

"I wonder what kind of answers might be inside the clock," I said, glancing Doc's way.

He reached out and squeezed my shoulder. "I guess we'll have to find out, Timekeeper."

CHAPTER NINE

ornelius's door was partway open when Doc and I arrived a short time later with the clock key in my pocket.

Aunt Zoe had asked plenty of questions when we'd stopped at home, starting with what had happened to my face and ending with why I needed the clock key. Before she'd hand over the key, I had to give her the short version of my blunder-filled day with the promise of more details later. Thankfully, Harvey had taken the kids to the grocery store with him to pick up supplies for supper, so they weren't there to see my injuries and bombard me with questions, too.

With a promise to be home in time to eat, Doc and I had taken off for Cornelius's place. I tried calling him on the way, but got his voicemail. Now here we were and his door was ajar.

"That's weird," I whispered, wondering if I should knock first or just go inside. I looked back at Doc, who was waiting two steps below the landing. "Something feels a little off about this."

One dark eyebrow lifted, almost touching the cuff of his black knit hat. "Most everything feels a little off when it comes to Cornelius. I think he prefers it that way."

"True." I decided to knock first in case he was sitting around naked for some mystical cleansing reason.

After a few seconds, I heard footfalls coming from the other side of the door.

"Cornelius, Doc and I need to …" I stalled out when Natalie opened the door wide.

Wearing a pair of paint-smeared jeans and a faded yellow Golddiggers High School shirt, she looked toolbelt primed and remodeling ready. But Jerry wasn't having any work done on this place that I had heard about, so why was she here?

She flinched at the sight of my face, then recovered with a quick grin. "Nice face, Edward Scissorhands. If you've come to sell us some wackadoo, go someplace else. We're all stocked up in here."

Oh, yeah? Two could play her game. "Knock knock, knucklehead."

She leaned against the door jamb, blocking the way. "Who's there?"

"Lettuce."

"Lettuce who?"

"Lettuce in, before I wackadoo you."

"That was pretty lame," Doc said from behind me.

"No comments from the cheap seats," I shot back at him. "What are you doing here?" I asked Natalie.

"I'm on fire watch." She stepped aside, out of the way, making room for me and Doc to join her inside the warm apartment.

Make that *really* warm apartment. Even warmer than yesterday.

A wave of heat made me pause in the entryway. Sheesh. I fanned my face. Someone needed to crack a window in this place. If not for the heat, then because of the sweet, tobacco-like fragrance thick in the air.

"What's that smell?" It sort of reminded me of a cigar, but I didn't remember seeing Cornelius with a stogie before.

Doc sniffed as he joined me in the entryway. "Chicory."

"Good guess, Tall Medium," Natalie said, using Cornelius's nickname for Doc. "Corny was burning incense when I arrived. He says it's good for removing obstacles. Do you think it would work on Coop when he's standing in the way of me helping Vi?"

"Probably not," I answered for Doc, noticing a slight haze in the air from the thick incense. "Your boyfriend gets extra snarly whenever I'm blowing smoke. Especially when I'm being wrongfully interrogated."

"Well, you do tend to add insult to injury when you're at the station," Doc said, a grin on his face.

"Like how?"

"Making his partner bark like a dog with a single word."

I lifted my chin. "That was Prudence's doing, not mine."

"And giving Coop a broken nose."

"That was off scene, not at the station, and he shouldn't have snuck up on me." I scowled at Doc. "Who are you siding with here, anyway? Me or Cooper?" When he hesitated, I added, "Let me rephrase that. Who do you want to spoon with under the covers tonight?"

Doc rubbed his beard, staring down at me through a half squint. "That depends on if you're wearing socks or not."

I laughed.

Natalie shrugged. "Coop does have warm feet and hands, and he always smells really good. I'd vote for him."

I scoffed. "I think you're biased, and I know better. Cooper is a porcupine with ice in his veins." I turned back to Doc. "I promise to wear socks."

"Then you win, Killer. I'm all yours."

When Doc started to close the door behind him, Natalie stuck her foot in the way and stopped him. "We need to leave it open."

"Why?" I asked, taking off my gloves and scarf. "So we don't melt or choke on incense smoke?"

"No. In case Corny catches on fire."

"What?" I tipped my head to the side. Had I heard her correctly? "Are you serious?"

"As a heart attack."

I pointed at her. "Don't jinx me with that. I'm having a bad-enough day already."

"Yeah, I can tell by your face." She turned to Doc. "Coop tells me you guys didn't get anywhere with the Hessler ghoulies. What's the plan now?"

That explained why she hadn't asked how my face had ended up the way it was. Cooper must have forewarned her that I'd had a run-in with the imp.

Doc unbuttoned his coat. "Coop wants to sit back on this and wait for them to make the first move."

The frown on his face gave me an inkling of his feelings regarding Cooper's idea, but I asked anyway. "What about you?"

"I'd like to go back with some extra-sensitive ears," he said.

Which I assumed meant Cornelius, our quirky neighborhood ghost whisperer. "And if that doesn't work?"

"Then we return to the séance idea and bring in a sexy physical medium to act as our arbitrator. Lucky for me, I happen to be spooning with one tonight."

The idea of being the go-between during this particular séance settled in my gut like a plate of extra-greasy fried liver nuggets. "Why me?"

Natalie snorted. "Because you have a big mouth, babe. Everyone knows that."

I gnashed my teeth at her. "The better to take a bite out of both of you."

"Where is Cornelius?" Doc asked Natalie.

"Follow me."

She led us into the kitchen where the overhead lights had been dimmed considerably. I stopped short at the sight of Cornelius flat on his back on the table with his long legs hanging over the edge, feet almost touching the floor. He was dressed in black silk pajamas with bare feet on one end and a pair of over-ear headphones on the other, which explained why he hadn't heard us arrive. A matching black silk sleep mask covered his eyes.

Doc and I shared wrinkled brows.

"What's going on here?" Doc beat me to the question.

Natalie leaned back against the counter, her arms crossed. "I'll give you one guess."

I ran my fingertip over the tablecloth spread out underneath Cornelius. It was rough and scratchy. "What kind of tablecloth is this?"

"It's not. It's a welding blanket."

"What's a welding blanket for?" Was this some kind of special spiritual blanket he'd ordered online for clearer reception when chatting with ghosts?

"It's for welding, you dork." Natalie thumbed toward Cornelius. "He needed something to lay on that wouldn't catch on fire, so I brought mine along."

"Why in the world would he be worried about catching on fire?" Sure, it was extra warm in his apartment thanks to Jerry cranking up the heat downstairs, but this was taking it a little far.

Doc shucked his coat and draped it over a chair. "Let me guess, he's clearing out his chakras."

"Close enough. He's trying to open his third eye."

"And that might cause a metaphysical fire?" I asked.

Doc joined Natalie at the counter. "One school of thought on clearing your third eye is to focus inward and burn everything in your mind, such as ignorance and any fears. This will create a vacuum, and whatever is blocking your third eye is sucked inside. Your third eye is then opened and the bad thoughts and feelings that you burned come out through your pores as black ash."

Natalie nodded. "When I got here, he mentioned something about the danger of trying this method. That spontaneous combustion was a risk."

I snort-scoffed. "Get the hell out of town."

"That was my first response, too, but he insisted it could happen. So, here I am playing firefighter with that close at hand, just in case." She indicated a fire extinguisher next to the pantry door.

I leaned closer to Cornelius, trying to see if he was actually asleep rather than meditating, or cleansing, or lighting fire to his mental trash.

"Be careful, Killer," Doc jested from behind me. "You don't need to get burned today, too."

Singed eyebrows would really top off my day. "Did he say why he's doing this? I mean, why right now?"

"No."

I looked back at Natalie. "You just came over without wanting to know any details, welding blanket in tow?"

"Pretty much. Yep."

"Were you desperate for entertainment or something?"

"Very. Coop is determined to keep me out of trouble, giving me a long list of what I can't do each morning. It's total bullshit."

"Have you told him that?"

She guffawed. "Have you met me?"

Of course she'd told him. She'd probably added a solid thump to his ears as an exclamation point. "But you're obeying the law dog anyway?"

She shrugged. "For now." She looked down at Cornelius. "When he called, I was happy to come over. It beat watching the paint dry, which was literally what I'd been doing in the upstairs hallway at the time."

"How long has Cornelius been like this?" Doc asked.

"If you mean zoned out in la-la land, about a half hour."

"You're kidding me." I turned to Doc. "How long does it normally take to open a third eye?"

He looked back at me as if I had a daisy growing out the top of my forehead right above where my third eye should be. "How would I know?"

"Because you know every-gobblygook-thing about metaphysical and supernatural and financial stuff."

He shook his head. "That's not true. You keep schooling me on all sorts of new tricks, *Scharfrichter*."

I sighed, glancing around before focusing on Natalie again. "You wouldn't happen to know where he put the Hellhound clock, would you?"

"Actually, I do." She pushed off the counter, leading the way out of the kitchen, through the living room, and into Cornelius's bedroom.

The clock was sitting in the middle of the floor. The bed had been shoved against the far wall, well clear of a circle of some grainy white powder surrounding the clock. Even from the doorway I could see that the hands were still spinning the same speed as before.

"That's salt around it," Natalie said. "I taste-tested it while Corny was busy unblocking."

"Salt for protection." I repeated what I'd heard Aunt Zoe say many times.

Doc frowned down at the clock. "He's not taking any chances."

I tugged on my earlobe. Hmm. Yesterday, when Harvey and I had visited, the clock had been sitting on the coffee table in the living room. There'd been no ring of salt around it. Why the new location and extra protection? Had the spinning made Cornelius uneasy? Was that why he was trying to unblock his third eye? Turning to metaphysical measures in order to figure out why the hands kept spinning? Or had something changed within the clock itself?

Easing a few steps closer, I studied the beast carving on the clock face. It looked the same as before. Pointy ears and a snout. The detailing was exquisite on the carved walnut timepiece, with each tooth in the beast's open jaws carved into the wood. The same was true of the sharp claws reaching up toward the cuckoo door, behind which I knew was a blond girl with red stains on her hands and neck.

The disturbing vision I'd had a month ago when I'd been storing this clock in our basement still gave me chills. Especially the part when Addy had come downstairs and touched the girl cuckoo carving, causing black smoke to come out from the clock and wrap around her finger.

Shuddering, I eased backward, closer to Doc. Yep, same creepy clock. I pulled the key out of my pocket, holding it toward him. "Want to do the honors?"

He shook his head. "You're the Timekeeper."

Puffing my cheeks, I blew out a breath. Doc was right. I had a job to do. I crossed over the salt barrier and knelt next to the clock, carefully flipping it over while searching for something to unlock.

There was no locked door on the back, only a small panel that was latched closed. I opened it, peeking inside. The workings of the clock appeared normal enough, same as some of those in Ms. Wolff's apartment had looked when Cooper and I had checked well over a month ago.

"Here, let me help." Doc knelt next to me, withdrew a penlight from his pocket, and shined it inside on the mechanical gears and whatnot.

"Do you see anything?" he asked.

"Not really. Only the autograph." I assumed it was the signature of the clock's maker. It looked similar to a name I'd seen written in another clock. Maybe the same clockmaker had created both.

"Let me see the key, Vi." Natalie joined us inside the salt circle, down on one knee.

I handed her the key, which had a heart shape on one end and jagged teeth cut into the other.

She looked at the jagged part and then the clock. "Tip the bottom up toward me."

Doc handed me the flashlight and then lifted and turned the clock for her.

"Vi, shine the light here," she said, pointing at the bottom edge. After I'd lit it up, she leaned closer, running her fingertips along the glossy wood. "Ah ha! Found it."

"Found what?"

She pointed at a tiny hole next to one of the weight chains. "There's a small door here. The craftsmanship of the clock is so good, though, that you wouldn't notice it if you weren't searching for it."

She handed the key back to me. "Stick it in and turn it."

The key slid in smoothly and rotated with ease. I heard a clunk.

I glanced at Doc. He nodded.

With a slight pull on the key, a small wooden door flapped open. I leaned closer, shining the light into the nook.

"There's something in there," I whispered.

Natalie put her head close to mine, peering inside, too. "There'd better be after all of this damned suspense."

"Hand me the light." Doc held out his hand. "I'll shine, you go fishing."

Hands free, I started to reach my fingers into the compartment but then pulled back.

"What's wrong?" Natalie whispered.

"Remember that weird sleepwalking dream or vision I had? The one where Addy reached toward this very clock and black smoke snaked out and wrapped around her finger?" I made a face at the clock. "Makes me nervous to stick my finger in there."

"How about if I reach for it?" Doc offered.

"I don't want anything to happen to you either." I glanced at Natalie. "Neither of you."

She smirked at me. "You want me to go find some stranger on the street?"

"Better yet, smartass, go get Detective Hawke."

"Hold on." Doc stood and walked over to the nightstand next to the bed. He returned with a pencil. "Use this to fish it out."

I took the pencil and bent down, with Doc back to holding the flashlight and Natalie back to holding her breath.

I hooked what looked like a thin cord of leather and carefully pulled. The leather cord slid out, unraveling. Another pull and a dark gray stone the size of a little cookie clattered onto the floor.

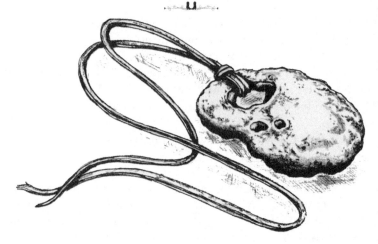

Still using the pencil, I lifted the leather cord. It had been threaded through a finger-size hole in the center of the stone, which now dangled in midair in front of us.

"Is there anything else in there?" Natalie whispered.

Doc shined the light around inside of the nook. "Not that I can see."

"What do you think this is?" I angled my head one way and then the other, checking to see if there were carvings or scratches on it, but finding nothing. "And why is it important enough to be locked away in a clock?"

"Some kind of stone pendant necklace." Natalie reached out and tapped it, making it swing back and forth in the air. "But whose?"

"It's a hag stone," Cornelius yelled, right behind us.

I squawked, taking a card from Elvis the chicken's deck, which made Natalie jump and bump into my shoulder. The leather cord slipped off the end of the pencil, but Doc caught the stone before it hit the floor.

"Damn it, Corny! Take off your headphones." Natalie hopped to her feet. "You nearly scared the ghost out of Vi."

"Oh, right." He tugged the headphones down so they ringed his neck. "Sorry about that."

"What's a hag stone?" I asked, my heart still beating the bongos in my chest. I'd heard that term before, but I couldn't remember the details.

Doc held up the pendant, peeking through the hole at me. "It's a stone that's believed to contain magic."

"Phenomenal magic," Cornelius added eagerly, joining us inside the salt circle in his bare feet. "Might I see that?" he asked Doc.

"Exactly what sort of magic are we talking?" I asked both of them. "Like a rabbit in a top hat show? Or casting spells with a wand stuff?"

"That depends." Doc rose to his feet, offering his hand to haul me up. "Some believe it can protect you from sickness, curses, and bad dreams."

"I like the sound of that," Natalie said, watching Cornelius inspect the pendant.

"And protection from the dead." Cornelius turned the piece this way and that in the light. "Some say hag stones were used by witches for spells and rituals. Others say they were used to neutralize the curses and hexes cast by witches." He held it up to one of his eyes, looking through it at me. "And then there's the theory that you can see invisible creatures from the land of the Fae simply by closing one eye and peering through the hole with the other."

"By Fae, you mean the plural of fairies?" I asked. "As in tiny mythical creatures from old folktales?" The story of Peter Pan came to mind, since I'd read it to my kids over and over years ago.

Natalie cleared her throat and held out her hands, palms up. "Faeries, come take me out of this dull world, for I would ride with you upon the wind, run on the top of the disheveled tide, and dance upon the mountains like a flame."

I gaped at her. "Did you just pull that out of your ass?"

"Oh, hell no." She grinned. "It's a quote from William Butler Yeats that I memorized for a drama class back in college. We had to recite a monologue, so I put together a combination that included that bit from 'The Land of Heart's Desire.'"

"Bravo, fair maiden." Cornelius bowed his head at her. "My grandmother often said there were naked fairies living in the swamp behind her house. As a testosterone-filled teenager, I would sit out back of her house at night, very eager to see one."

"Now you've gone and made this awkward," I said, wrinkling my nose at him.

Doc chuckled. "I once read you could use hag stones to open windows to other realms."

"With my luck lately and that stupid Tower card of Cornelius's, this particular stone would lead to a realm full of more imps."

"It could be worse, Vi. It could be a realm full of *Nachzehrer*." Natalie cringed. "It seems like I saw a movie once where a hag stone necklace was used as protection from an evil magician's spells and wards."

That made me think of the symbol Cooper and I had seen on that garage door in Lead. And the wards Masterson had on the walls of the Sugarloaf Building to keep his "pets" caged. *And* Aunt Zoe's protection wards. It would be interesting to hear what she had to say about the hag stone.

"I read an old myth once about a hag stone being used as protection against evil winds," Doc said.

Cornelius ran his thumb over the stone. "That almost echoes with the school of thought that hag stones can be used to control the weather."

"I am getting really tired of all this snow." Natalie held out her hand to Cornelius. "May I see it?"

He handed it over. "There are others who swear hag stones can recharge your body, mind, and spirit simply by hanging one over your bed."

"Really?" I watched Natalie dangle it in front of her face like she was trying to hypnotize herself. "All of this from a stone with a hole that was probably made simply by water erosion over time."

"Ahh, but the water is key," Cornelius said. "Since hag stones are usually created by water erosion, and magic and spells supposedly can't affect moving water, the stone protects the holder from evil."

Doc nodded. "The idea is that only good things can pass through the hole. Bad luck or other evils will get stuck."

Natalie looked through the stone. "So Vi could hang it up over her doorway like a horseshoe and keep nasty spirits away?"

"Or she could wear it around her neck," Cornelius suggested.

"To keep evil spirits out of my head?" I joked, but then thought about the evil terrors Prudence claimed were locked away behind a door in Cornelius's mind. Maybe he needed to wear the hag stone.

"And for good health and healing." Cornelius looked at Doc. "I believe it's flint, by the way."

"Interesting," Doc replied, his forehead lined.

My gaze bounced back and forth between the two of them. "I take it flint is special for some reason."

"Flint is beneficial to all chakras," Cornelius answered first. "It is believed to gather any negative energy as well as protect its owner."

Natalie handed me the hag stone. "Vi could use all of the protection she can get these days, that's for sure."

"Yeah, but will it repel a big bumbling bozo hiding behind a detective badge?" And how about ex-assholes who try to manipulate for their own career aspirations?

I palmed the stone. It felt cold and lifeless. How could one small stone possibly do any of those things, let alone several of them? It would make a weighty necklace. I could probably use it to clonk someone on the noggin with a good swing. Leave a nice goose egg behind.

"It is also said to make its owner courageous and strong," Doc said, playfully squeezing my triceps. "A true warrior."

"If you think of all of the tools made with flint since mankind was young," Natalie said, "that sort of makes sense."

What couldn't this holey stone supposedly do? "If only it could sweep and mop the floors, too," I joked.

"Dream on, Mickey," Natalie replied with a grin. "But this is Deadwood, not *Fantasia*."

I wasn't sure which place was more trouble filled lately. "Mr. Black had said that whatever was kept in the clock would be unique to each Timekeeper, so I guess I'm supposed to use this somehow at some time." I looked back down at the clock's spinning hands. "Let's just hope I can figure it out before I run out of time."

Doc wrapped his arm around me, pulling me closer. "We'll figure it out, Killer."

I smiled up at him. Or at least tried to. My worries wore heavy tonight, weighing in as frowns.

"So, Corny," Natalie said. "Were you able to unblock your third eye?"

He glanced toward the open bedroom door. "Partially. However, the resulting vision did not yield the answers for which I'd hoped going in."

I hesitated to ask but did anyway. "What do you mean?"

"You need to witness the conundrum as I did."

I really didn't like the sound of that. It bordered on ominous with a toe over the line into downright doomy.

"Come along," he said and walked out of the room.

With a shrug, Natalie followed. Doc waited for me to lead the way.

Cornelius waited for us at a bank of five dark computer monitors in the corner of the living room. His ghost monitoring command center, Harvey had called it yesterday. He rolled a leather office chair over in front of the monitor on the far left, dropping into it. One tap on the keyboard and all five of the screens lit up, showing different rooms from Calamity Jane Realty's office on the monitors.

"These are live, right?" Natalie asked.

He nodded. "Let me load the footage from earlier, a few minutes after everyone had left for the day."

He clacked away at the keyboard, reminding me of Mona. The screen in front of him froze and then went dark. When it lit up again, we were looking down at Jerry's office from up high. The camera was the one in the corner opposite the office door and closet door, both of which were closed currently in the video feed. We could see Jerry's heavy oak desk and executive style chair from this vantage point, but not the filing cabinet and bookshelf, which were along the wall directly below the camera.

"Here we are then." Cornelius stood, holding out the chair for me. "Have a seat. The show is about to start."

I hesitated, holding tightly to the flint hag stone. "What kind of show?"

After having gone down through the trap door in the closet floor before and almost not making it back out alive, I wasn't giddy to grab a bowl of popcorn and cozy up to the screen.

"You'll see," he countered.

"Maybe I don't want to see, though." I frowned down at the chair and then back at Cornelius. "Does this show have anything to do with why you were trying to unblock your third eye?"

"Not entirely. I've been wanting to clear it for a while now, but with Mercury retrograde until this week, I didn't have the motivation."

Natalie sat down in the chair. "If you don't want to watch, Vi, walk away. I'll give you the rundown later."

I wrung my hands together, glancing back and forth between Doc's steady gaze and the screen.

"Your call," he told me.

I cringed in anticipation, but nodded. "Let's do this."

"Look!" Natalie said, leaning closer to the screen. "Jerry's office door opened."

Doc and I huddled around her, while Cornelius stood off to the side, listening. How many times had he watched this already?

On the screen, the office door slammed closed. *Bang!*

I jumped thanks to the crisp clear sound coming through the speakers right in front of us. I remembered when Cornelius had installed his fancy microphone down in Jerry's office. That was before I'd realized there was a Hellhole down below Calamity Jane Realty. And before I'd seen what was down in it.

Nothing moved for a few seconds on screen. All was quiet.

"Is that it for the show?" Natalie asked, her gaze glued to the screen. "Because if so, I'm going to want my money back."

Cornelius crossed his arms. "Does a frog request a refund from the fly? I think not."

I tried to wrap my head around that but gave up when something moved on the monitor.

It was the desk calendar. A corner of the paper lifted and dropped. A slight fluttering sound came through the speaker. It lifted again, higher, only to fall once more. Then the whole calendar sheet lifted and flipped over the front of the desk, knocking off a pencil holder, which clattered onto the wooden floorboards.

A couple of pencils rolled a short distance before everything went still again. Silent.

"That was a little creepy," I whispered.

"You're going to enjoy this next part then," Cornelius said.

A pencil floated up from the floor.

Chills ran up my arms. Even though I knew we were watching Jane haunt her old business, I still couldn't quite get used to seeing things move on their own.

The pencil began to zigzag on the calendar. I leaned closer to the screen, trying to see if the drawing was legible. It looked like it was making stars or lightning bolts over and over in the same place, going back and forth and ...

The office door crashed open, banging into the wall behind it.

"Shit!" Natalie jerked back, almost head-butting my chin. She held her hand over her chest. "That scared the—"

"Keep watching," Cornelius interrupted, his tone ominous.

The calendar flew off the desk toward the open door, but it hit something in the middle of the room and fell to the floor. Something invisible to the camera. I leaned closer. For a second there I thought I could see some kind of aura or distortion.

The door to the closet flew open.

I gasped.

Then it slammed shut. *Bang!*

"Did something just go into the closet?" Natalie whispered.

"Or came out of it," Doc said, a frown etched deep into his forehead as he watched the screen.

The closet door opened again, hitting the wall behind it so hard the door shook.

Then it slammed shut again. *BANG!*

"What in the hell is Jane doing?" I said, worrying my lower lip.

The brass desk lamp hovered a few inches above the desk for a moment, and then sailed through the air, crashing into the closed closet door. Glass shattered, raining to the ground. The brass base bounced off the floor before rolling toward the opposite corner.

"This is some crazy-ass shit," Natalie said.

I shook my head in amazement. Had this really happened this afternoon? The time stamp on the video said so. Cripes, my desk wasn't thirty feet from this room.

Back on the screen, the closet door started to open again. Then it seemed to be caught in limbo, inching closed, then wider, then closed, then wider yet.

"Can any of you see anyone there?" I said, trying to make sense of what was on the screen.

"No," Doc said. "We need Coop here."

The closet door closed again, all the way. Then the desk began to slide toward the door, slowly at first before picking up speed and ramming into the closed door.

A book came out of nowhere and hit the wall next to the closet door. *Thud!* Then another. And another. *Thud! Thud!*

I pulled my hand down my face, utterly baffled. "Why throw books? Is Jane pissed off about something?"

The desk lurched a short distance away from the closet door, which then opened partway, ramming into the edge of the desk.

I waited, my breathing shallow, watching that darkness through the half-open door. "Just to warn you guys, if red, webbed monster hands come out from the closet, I just might pee my pants right here and now."

Natalie frowned up at me. "Don't stand so close to me then. Share those golden showers with your boyfriend."

I flicked her ear.

"Here it comes," Cornelius said, now standing over my shoulder, watching along with us.

I focused back on the scene as the closet door slammed shut again. In a blink, the desk flipped up on its end and smashed against the door, hitting so hard one of the drawers popped open. Pens and pencils, a tape dispenser, and a stapler clattered to the floor. The filing cabinet came sliding into view, crashing into the desk. Next came the bookcase, scraping across the floor, forced up against the filing cabinet.

"Damn," Doc said. "That old saying, 'Katy bar the door,' comes to mind."

"Make that 'Janey bar the door,' " Natalie said.

"Is Jane keeping something in or out?" I wondered aloud.

The scene on the screen stilled, except for one pencil that rolled a few feet before coming to a stop.

"Wait for it," Cornelius whispered.

"Wait for what?" I glanced his way.

A loud *BOOM!* echoed through the speakers.

I almost swallowed my tongue.

"Okay, that almost made *me* pee my pants," Natalie said, pressing back into the chair as if something might reach out from the screen and grab her at any moment.

BOOM!

It came again.

Cornelius leaned forward, pointing at the open desk drawer. "Watch closely."

BOOM!

The drawer jiggled, and a roll of tape fell out.

"Something is hitting the closet door from the other side," Doc said. "Hard."

BOOM! BOOM! BOOM!

Then it all stopped. I waited, half-cringing in anticipation.

"Is that it?" Natalie asked, still holding herself away from the screen.

The camera jerked, as if it had been bumped. The screen glitched once, twice. Then everything went black.

"That's it," Cornelius said, hitting a button on his keyboard. "Show's over, folks. Throw your trash in the waste receptacle on your way out."

I crossed my arms, unsettled clear to my toes about what I'd just witnessed. "I don't get what Jane was doing in there."

Natalie spun around in the chair to face us. "It's almost as if we were witnessing her having some sort of meltdown."

When Doc stayed silent, I looked up at him. His face was a patchwork of furrows and worry lines.

"Is this why you were trying to get your third eye to work?" Natalie asked Cornelius. "So you could see what was going on?"

"No. Even unblocked, that wouldn't work because seeing ghosts is not in my repertoire."

Doc was right, we needed to get Cooper here to see this recording. "Then why were you trying to clear your third eye?"

He took off his headphones and set them on the desk. "Third-eye vision is a powerful art that has been used by seers since the time of the ancient Egyptians and possibly before. This vision can be used to gather an overview of life, as if looking down from high up in the air and being able to see a snail move over the mud."

I glanced at Doc, who was still staring at the dark screen, his gaze narrowed.

"So," Natalie said, "you wanted to look down at all of this spooky shit and make better sense of it?"

"No. I needed to sharpen my senses to be able to see beyond the obvious."

Doc turned sharply toward Cornelius. "That wasn't Jane, was it? At least not Jane alone."

Cornelius touched his nose and then pointed at Doc. "The Oracle saw that which I needed to sharpen my senses to fully grasp."

Fingers of dread tickled down my spine. "If it wasn't only Jane, who was with her?"

"For that answer, we need someone who can see beyond the camera's visual limitations."

Natalie sighed. "Coop's not going to be happy about this."

"Since when has Cooper been happy about anything?" When she smirked at me, I added, "Well, anything besides playing naked patty cake with you."

"He's more partial to pin the tail." She winked at me.

"You mean pin the tail on the donkey."

"No, I don't."

I grimaced. "You know the rules. No talking about sex with that porcupine in front of me."

"Rules are for fools," she said with a grin.

I took Doc's hand, pulling his attention my way. "So now what? Call Cooper and wait for him to watch the video?"

He shrugged. "Or we go downstairs and take a firsthand look ourselves."

"You mean go in blind?" Doubly blind, even, since the camera had been taken offline, too. I shook my head. "What if whoever else was in there with Jane figures out how to open that closet door?"

"What if it's Jane who was shut away behind the door?" he shot back. "And she needs our help."

Eek. I hadn't thought of that.

"We could have a séance," Natalie suggested, excitement in her voice.

I scowled at her. "You really need to get out more this winter. Spend some time with your living friends."

"Tell me about it," she muttered.

"Or maybe get a dog. We have one named Rooster if you'd like to borrow him."

"Maybe. Addy did tell me she's teaching him how to dance. He'd at least be willing to dance at the bar with me."

Doc chuckled. "So, what do you say, Killer?" Doc thumbed toward the darkened monitor screen. "You feel like trying to talk to the dead before supper?"

CHAPTER TEN

Wednesday, January 30th

I was brushing my teeth the next morning when Aunt Zoe knocked on the bathroom door.

"Violet, Cooper called. He's on his way over."

I frowned in the mirror. Couldn't a girl brush her teeth in peace these days?

Doc had taken the kids to school and then headed up to Lead for an early morning appointment with a client, giving me the morning off to enjoy since I didn't have to go to work today. It appeared Cooper hadn't gotten the memo that I was supposed to be relaxing and unblocking my chakras after a few frustrating days.

The chakra clearing was Cornelius's idea this morning, not Doc's. My daily tarot guru had called while I was pouring my first cup of coffee, and I'd answered, thinking he might have some news about the Hellhound clock or Jane's ghostly overnight adventures. Silly me, I should have known better.

The good news was that for once the danged Tower card hadn't shown up in my metaphysical forecast. The bad news was that according to the cards, I was currently feeling overwhelmed with choices and needed to pick one course and go forth, said the Seven of Cups. And while I desired to overcome obstacles along with the Seven of Wands, and I had the Wheel of Fortune card in my corner to help me experience a change of fortune, the King of Swords was challenging me. When I asked Cornelius what that card meant, he said it sometimes represented a man in uniform who was connected to the law in some way, which inspired a growl from me, as law dogs often did. This led to my final card, representing the outcome for the day—the Two of Swords. And after giving me a verbal drumroll through the line, he'd declared my day would end in a stalemate.

When I told Cornelius where he and his cards could shove the stalemate, he'd reminded me that the results from tarot readings were not set in stone. That I could change my outcome if I desired. To do so, he suggested I try to flush my chakras through breathing in color energy.

At that point, I hung up on my unsolicited, self-appointed life coach and focused on the color brown, as in my coffee.

Aunt Zoe knocked again. "Violet, are you okay in there?"

Not really. The tarot gods were being mean to me, I had no idea how to catch that damned imp, and I sucked at my new Timekeeper job. To be fair, I hadn't really been trained on that last one. Obviously, though, I had no natural inclination for the role.

"Doc's not here," I mumbled back through a mouthful of minty toothpaste. "Tell Cooper to come back another time."

"He's not coming to talk to Doc."

I snarled at my reflection, doing my best rabid law dog impression before spitting out the toothpaste. "Why does he want to talk to me? Does this have anything to do with last night?"

"What happened last night?" she asked.

"Nothing." I rinsed out my mouth before adding, "At least nothing more than what we told you regarding the whole song and dance in Jerry's office."

And "nothing" pretty much summed up that ghost-filled matinee.

Cooper had joined the four of us at Cornelius's apartment about fifteen minutes after Natalie had texted him that we needed him and his ghost goggles. We'd all watched the video again together with Cooper in the front row seat. It was even spookier the second time through, especially the closet door battle scene.

However, Cooper hadn't been able to see anything more than we had, which was odd, but not entirely strange. Previously, Jane had been able to control when Cooper could see her, so she apparently hadn't wanted an audience during the brouhaha in Jerry's office. As to why that would be, we all had varying theories, but the answer wouldn't be clear until we somehow made contact with Jane.

Without being able to see who was doing what during filming,

we were also at a loss as to who might have been in there with Jane.
I suggested that it could've been the old crotchety ghost who used
to roam the office before Jane died. Doc wondered if maybe there
was a new ghost in the area, one that had been pulled in by Cornelius
with his pied piper skills. Natalie thought it was clear that Jane didn't
like this other ghost, so she shut it in the closet. Cornelius kept
kicking himself for not having an SLS camera already installed in the
room, which Doc explained would pick up ethereal forms not seen
with the naked eye and would work in darkness or light. That left
Cooper, who refused to voice his thoughts because he needed more
proof first and believed unverified speculation at crime scenes was
for amateurs.

After numerous "boos" and swearing (mostly on my part) aimed
at the arrogant detective, Doc had volunteered to go downstairs and
check out the scene in person while the rest of us watched via a hand-
held video camera. Cooper insisted on joining him, so we laid some
ground rules detailing when to turn tail and run, and downstairs they
went.

The office had looked the same as what we'd seen in black-and-
white night vision on the monitor screen before it glitched out, only
more colorful because Cooper turned on the lights when they
arrived. We were glued to the screen as Doc and Cooper tried to
reach out to Jane's ghost. After several breath-held minutes for
Natalie and me, Doc looked into the camera and told us she wasn't
there. Jane was either gone, lounging around wherever ghosts did
when they weren't toying with the living, or she was stubbornly
refusing to show herself.

They quickly moved the furniture back where it belonged, put
the various debris that had been tossed around back in place, and
swept up the broken glass mess from the lamp. When they checked
the closet, it was locked up tight. There would be no budging it until
Jane—or whoever—released the door, same as before.

Unfortunately, the camera in the corner was out of commission
no matter what Doc did to try to fix it. Cornelius told them to leave
it be for now. He'd replace it later.

After locking up the place, they'd met us in the parking lot. We'd
all headed to Aunt Zoe's to eat, including Cornelius, who'd gotten
over his camera woes when he heard that Harvey was making curried
chicken soup and rice for supper.

And yum, the soup had been bowl-licking good, even though Harvey had been in a hurry to make supper because he had another hot date with his latest "honey," Junie.

"What aren't you telling me, Violet Lynn?" Aunt Zoe asked from the other side of the door. "I can hear it in your voice, and I'm not leaving until you spill."

I put my toothbrush away and then opened the door, waving her in. "I'm feeling like a *piñata* this morning, twisting this way and that in between taking a beating. And now that I've said that out loud, I'm regretting it because I sound like a big whiny puss when I'm supposed to be this badass killer." I ended my pity party by blowing a raspberry at the woman with the scratched face in the mirror.

Aunt Zoe came up behind me, smiling as she wrapped me in her arms and squeezed. "You are a badass, baby girl. And you're smart, too. But that doesn't mean you can't stumble here and there along your journey."

I clutched her forearms, holding onto her. "I'm not stumbling, though. I'm falling flat on my face."

"Nah," she said, pressing her cheek to mine. "You're learning through trial and error. In the end, this process will make you stronger."

"In the end," I grumbled, "this process might be the death of me."

She pulled back and turned me around to face her, holding me by the shoulders. "Violet, you are a warrior woman. You will take hits and bleed now and then, but I have total faith in your ability to do what you need to do in the moment. You share the blood of generations of badass babes. Never forget that." She smiled and kissed me on the forehead. "Now, it's my job to help you get back on track. So let's figure out what you need to do next."

I turned back to the mirror. "First, I need to finish making myself presentable in public, and then I'll be ready to face Cooper. Did he say what he wanted to talk to me about?"

She half sat on the counter next to me, looking comfortable in a pair of faded jeans and a wine-colored hooded cardigan over her white shirt. "You know Coop. He doesn't like to let anyone else see his cards until he's ready to show them."

I said a few not-so-kind words about Cooper's stupid cards while twisting my hair into a French knot. "You look nice this morning and you smell good, too," I told her. She was wearing her favorite exotic fruity-scented perfume. "You have a breakfast date or something?"

Her dark blue eyes narrowed. "Violet, don't start."

"I'm not starting anything. I'm just saying that you aren't dressed to go out to your workshop, and you look pretty in that color, especially with your hair loose."

"It's not loose."

"Okay, mostly loose. That's a very pretty hair clip. Did you make those little glass flowers?"

"You know I did."

"So, are we receiving any visitors this morning besides Cooper?"

"Receiving visitors? We come from a long line of killers, not royalty."

"Being royalty wouldn't be as much fun. Always having to toe the line and keep emotions out of the spotlight. Blech. Speaking of spotlights and fire captains, have you heard from Reid lately?"

"That was a lousy segue."

"I know, but as you've told me before, sometimes we have to take a big leap."

I finished with my hair, all of the curls corraled for now. My face was a whole other matter, and no amount of makeup was hiding the scratches, as my kids had proven last night when they plopped down at the supper table across from me.

Addy had squealed in a mixture of surprise and horror. Layne, on the other hand, had gaped for a few seconds, and then he'd come around to my chair to inspect the wounds up close. Both had seemed to buy my lie about falling on the ice in the parking lot and landing on my face, neither seeing my crossed fingers under the table. I didn't like to tell fibs to my kids, but an imp was not a normal foe. The truth might have caused nightmares, or worse, more curiosity.

I lifted my chin, turning my head from one side to the other. Darn it, pulling my hair back only made the imp's handiwork more visible. With a sigh, I started plucking out the pins.

"What are you doing?" Aunt Zoe asked.

"It's no use."

"I agree. You're beautiful as is."

"And you're biased." I raised one eyebrow. "So, what about Reid?"

She opened her mouth, then closed it again, shaking her head. "We're not going to talk about him, Violet."

"That won't make anything go away. I should know, I've tried that when it comes to this *Scharfrichter* gig. Troubles continue to fester until you have to face them." I shook out my hair and gave her a lopsided smile. "At least with Reid, he's nice to look at when you're facing him."

She grinned. "That's true." Then her grin faded. "I'm too old to nurse a broken heart back together again."

I pshawed. "You're not too old. And what makes you think your heart will end up broken?"

"Please, it's Reid. Breaking hearts and fighting fires are what he does best."

"You're still mad because he didn't tell his son about you back when you were first dating years ago, aren't you?"

"Of course I am. My whole family knew about him."

I raised my hand. "I didn't."

"You were too busy raising kids to care about who I was seeing then."

"That's not true. You chose who you told about Reid for whatever personal reasons. He did the same."

"Fine. That's a legitimate point. But he refused to commit in the end."

"Not true. Neither of you died, so that wasn't the final ending. He's back, so the story continues. At the moment, however, you seem to be trying to wrap it all up in a way that I don't think will make either of you happy."

She scowled at me. "Reid comes with a lot of uncertainties, and I'm not sure I'm willing to ride that roller coaster with him anymore."

"Fine, fraidy cat. Then why don't you go scurrying over to Dominick's place with your tail between your legs. That slickster offered you the world on a silver platter. With his unnatural charm making your head ooze little popping hearts 24/7, you wouldn't even know if there were any steep hills or loop-the-loops to come."

"When you put it that way, Dominick doesn't seem so bad after all," she said with a smartass glint in her eyes.

I pointed at her face. "No. You cannot take the easy way out. I won't be able to stand visiting you, partly because of how starry-eyed you are when you're under Dominick's spell. But mostly due to the fact that being near him makes me want to upchuck. Christmases would require me to carry around a vomit bag."

She grimaced. "Dominick is a Stepford wife nightmare. I'd sooner spend the rest of my life alone with my broken heart."

"Good to hear. So, how about we invite Ox and Reid over for supper tonight?"

"I don't know. Let me think about it."

"Fine, but don't think too long. I've seen other women around town sparking on Reid. He's a hot catch." When she frowned at me in the mirror, I added, "Get it? The fire captain is a 'hot' catch because he's on fire with good looks, making the ladies spark?"

"You've been hanging around Willis too long." She crossed her arms. "Now, what are you going to do about Dominick pestering you regarding the whereabouts of his *lidérc*?"

I cringed slightly at that particular dilemma. "I don't know yet. Either I pretend to try to catch it and keep failing, or I come clean and tell him that I had to get rid of it before it killed me and my family. If I do the latter, I'll keep my fingers crossed and maybe throw in a bonus lollipop to help him get over the loss of his precious Hungarian devil."

"What kind of lollipop?"

"An imp-flavored one."

She rubbed her chin. "That's an idea. Now we just have to figure out how to catch it."

"Yeah, that's the key, isn't it?"

"Speaking of keys, I'd like to see that hag stone you found in the clock."

"Sure, it's in my top dresser drawer. Have at it." I fluffed out my curls so they'd hide my face a little better. "Have you seen anything in our family history tome about a hag stone?"

She shook her head. "Nothing about a *Duzarx*, either. Apparently, you're the first in our line who has come across one."

"Lucky us. Although Prudence knows about it, so maybe I should ask her for more details."

"Why are you making that face?"

"This face here?" I pointed at my wrinkled upper lip and bared teeth. "Because I'm still pissed at her for dragging Zelda to the old school yesterday. Even if she stopped short of taking Zelda inside, Doc and I didn't know and went in after her. We could have been walking into a trap."

"You're a fellow Executioner in Prudence's eyes. Maybe she figured you could handle yourself."

"Yeah, well, it would have been nice to have a little heads-up from her." I thought back to the mixed vibes I kept experiencing in that place. "There's definitely something in that school. An *other* of some sort."

"Maybe it really is the *Duzarx*." She looked down at her hands, rubbing her knuckles. "You need to find some way to make peace with Prudence."

I shook my head. "It'd be easier to eat sugar with a sewing needle. Prudence only likes herself. Well, her and Zelda. But there is no such thing as peace with that ghost. There's only listening to her demands and dodging her blows."

"Okay, let's give Prudence a rest. What are you going to do about the imp?"

"I wish I knew." I leaned against the counter next to her. "If I'm going to use it as a pawn in exchange for Dominick's *lidérc*, I'm going to have to catch it alive." I thought back to our first round in the front of Harvey's pickup. "There's no way it's going to crawl into a cage and let me lock it back up for good. Did I tell you how it kept saying 'No cage' over and over?"

She nodded. "Catching the imp by surprise might be nearly impossible now that it knows you're looking for it."

"If I can't get it out into the open, I'll risk losing a finger—or all five—trying to get a good hold on it."

"Maybe you can use the honey to make a trail that will lead it into a camouflage trap."

"That seems too easy."

"Yeah, probably. They are incredibly smart little bastards. That's partly why they're so hard to kill."

"What's the other reason?"

"They have very good hearing. According to one of the notes in our family history accounts, an imp can hear a human breathing before the person is even within sight."

"So, there's no sneaking up on this sucker." That explained why the imp in Harvey's truck heard me in my stealth mode, even though it had been asleep initially. "We'll have to take it by surprise some other way."

"Maybe if it doesn't think you're—"

Rooster barked two times quickly downstairs, doing his doggie door alert trick, which Addy had been working with him on the last couple of weeks.

"Coop must be here," Aunt Zoe said.

No sooner had she gotten the words out, we heard, "Parker? Zoe?" Cooper called up the stairwell. "Either of you up there?"

"Be right there, Coop," Zoe hollered back. "Make yourself some coffee if you want. Oh, and there's leftover bacon in the fridge."

I frowned at her. "How dare you share our bacon with that law dog!"

She laughed and tugged on my arm. "Come on. Let's go see what has earned us a visit from our favorite cop."

"He's your favorite," I muttered, taking one last look at my beat-up face in the mirror before following her out. "I'm just stuck with him. He's like a tick head lodged in my skin."

She turned back to me, her hands on her hips. "Really, Violet Lynn? Coop is always watching your back. He might snarl a bit now and then, but his tail is wagging at the same time."

"Fine, you're right. Cooper is more like a sliver under my skin. Detective Hawke is the dick head." I faked a gasp. "Oops, I meant tick head."

A grin hovered at her lips. "I think you were right the first time."

Cooper waited for us in the kitchen. Dressed in jeans and his Deadwood police coat, he was pouring himself a cup of coffee when we joined him. A couple of slices of bacon lay on a plate on the counter next to him.

"I let the dog out," he said without turning around.

"Thanks, Coop." Aunt Zoe patted him on the shoulder.

I took a seat at the table, figuring if he were making a house call, it wouldn't be to bring me a teddy bear and some hot chocolate. I might as well get comfortable while I waited for more bad news.

When he looked over at me, he winced. "Damn, Parker. Nat is right, you look like Edward Scissorhands, especially with your hair sticking out all over."

I hit him with a hard glare. "Yeah, well, you look like something the cat dragged in and the dog won't eat."

That wasn't really true, but he did look tired around the edges.

"You're stealing lines from Uncle Willis."

"True, but I'm limping along this morning after dragging axle for ten miles of bad road, so cut me some slack and get to the point of your visit."

He looked at Aunt Zoe, eyebrows raised. "Did she wake up like this?"

"Doc warned me that she was feeling feisty before he left with the kids." She pointed at a large envelope on the counter next to where he stood. "What's in there?"

He waved for her to join him at the table, pulling out a chair for her next to mine before sitting across from us, along with his bacon and coffee. "I combed back through the other scenes where Parker's imp made a mess."

"It's not *my* imp."

Cooper gave me a cross look, then opened the envelope. "Anyway, at each scene, I found the same marking." He pulled out several pictures and set them on the table.

"A ward?" I leaned forward, along with Aunt Zoe.

"Actually, it's more like a sigil," she said.

Sigil? I'd heard that word before, but I was curious about her take on it. "Explain the difference."

"Well, sigils are the actual symbols that are often used along with wards for protection. Like what we saw upstairs in the Sugarloaf Building. There was a ward keeping the *lidérc* caged. The sigils on each window and door had been charged by the ward to form a barrier. Some who practice this sort of magic use wards and sigils to keep things in, others use them to keep something out."

"And the jewelry you've given me to wear for protection?"

"Those pieces are a sigil of sort, but without the wards I created to awaken and strengthen them, they are just pretty jewelry."

"So this sigil the imp is creating at each site means what?" Cooper asked.

"Well, we don't know yet." Aunt Zoe picked up one of the pictures, holding it closer. "We have to figure out the purpose behind it."

"Were these photos all stored in police evidence?" I asked Cooper as I checked out one of the pictures, which was a close-up of the symbol—or sigil. "If so, Detective Hawke might be planning on using these to prove his theory about me being a witch."

"No, lucky for you and your evil broomstick." He was sporting a hint of a grin when I glanced over the top of the photo at him. "There was only one picture in the files that had any markings, and that one was blurry. I only recognized the sigil because I was looking for it." He pointed at one particular picture. He was right—it was too blurry to make out any details. The sigil looked more like a scuff mark.

"Then where did you get these?" I picked up another picture. This one looked like it was on that police car the imp had trashed.

"I got up early this morning and went to each of the locations where the imp had wreaked havoc."

He must have woken up really early, because he'd not only gone and taken the pictures, but printed them out, too. "And all of the crime scenes had one?"

"The scenes I could get to, yep. That first store the imp broke into was closed. And the bank next to Piggly Wiggly was also locked up, but the imp left its mark outside below one of the bank's windows."

Aunt Zoe stood and walked over to the junk drawer next to the phone on the wall. She pulled out a magnifying glass, returned to her seat, and held up one of the pictures, peering closely at the sigil. Then she did the same with the other photos, worry lines covering her face from forehead to lips.

"Typically, sigils are associated with magic. Or witches." She lowered the magnifying glass. "I don't remember reading anything about an imp using magic. From what I've learned about imps over the years, they don't typically need magic to deliver their type of destruction."

"So, you think this imp is different?" I asked her. "More intelligent, maybe? Wilier than others?"

Cooper smirked. "You're just trying to find excuses for your inability to apprehend it yesterday when it was already confined in a pickup."

I reached across the table and stole one of his pieces of bacon, pointing it at him. "If you hadn't let the damned thing loose up in the Sugarloaf Building in the first place, I wouldn't have to—"

"I know!" Aunt Zoe interrupted. "That's the next step we need to take. We have to go up to where Dominick had it caged in the Sugarloaf Building and see if there are any sigils there that match these." She turned to me. "The warded sigils that were being used to hold the *lidérc* were different from this, weren't they? I can go get my notes to double-check, but you had a picture of one on your phone, didn't you?"

I took another look at one of the photos while chewing on the bacon. It was cold, but still smoky and crunchy and slightly sweet. Harvey had a way of making bacon taste better than usual thanks to a dribble of maple syrup mid-fry. That was why I didn't like sharing it, especially with Cooper after he poked sticks at me.

"Yeah," I said to Aunt Zoe. "This is quite different."

"I think I can get Reid to let me in there tonight." Cooper picked up his other piece of bacon, squinting at me as he took a bite out of it.

"I'll go with you," I said.

"I don't think that's a good idea, Parker."

"If this is about stealing your bacon, there is more in the fridge."

"It's not about the bacon, but we both know that contrary to what Nyce and Nat think, you're mean enough to steal flowers off a fresh grave."

"I'm not mean." I turned to Aunt Zoe. "Am I?"

She sucked air through her teeth, shrugging slightly. "Depends on the morning." Then she laughed when I gasped. "You do tend to spit poison around the Deadwood cops."

"That's because they call me names." I wrinkled my nose at Cooper. "And make fun of my hair."

He held up his hands. "Guilty as charged. But I still don't think you should come with me to the Sugarloaf Building."

"Cooper, we don't know what else might still be in that building."

"You're right, but with Masterson still hot on your tail about that *lidérc*, we can't take chances with you being seen going into that building."

Crikey. I hadn't thought about Dominick seeing me. Cooper had a good point there.

"I'll take Nyce with me instead. He can sniff out any potential problems."

"No way." I crossed my arms.

"He's a big boy, Parker. He'll be fine."

"He is a big boy and he is hubba-hubba fine," I said, earning an eye roll from the detective. "However, he is an Oracle, and while I don't know what that might mean in this situation, I've learned enough to know that he is an extremely valuable commodity for those who have ill intent."

"It is a risk for Doc," Aunt Zoe agreed. "But I know someone who could go with the right protections to keep everyone safe enough for this quick trip."

"The right protections, huh?" I snorted. "You mean you along with your bag of tricks."

"Yes, and they aren't tricks." When she saw me shake my head, she added, "We could have you parked nearby in someone else's vehicle and right there on the walkie-talkie with us in case something new showed up to give us trouble."

"I still don't like it, but that seems more feasible."

Cooper pulled out his cell phone, hit some buttons, and then held it up to his ear. "Martin," he said into the phone. "I need to get into the Sugarloaf Building tonight." He paused. "No, the upstairs." His gaze moved to Aunt Zoe. "No, not that Parker. Zoe is coming with me." He frowned as he listened. "I don't think she's going to like that."

I didn't have to hear Reid's end of the conversation to know what he was saying. Neither did Aunt Zoe by the quick narrowing of her eyes.

"He doesn't need to come along," she told Cooper.

"You hear that?" Cooper said into the phone, and then listened. His frown burrowed deeper. He lowered the phone, speaking to Aunt Zoe. "He says either he comes along or nobody goes inside."

I chuckled. "Reid knows how to play hardball."

Aunt Zoe threw up her hands. "Fine, he can come, but I can't guarantee I won't knock him on his ass again."

Grinning, Cooper relayed her message into the phone. Then he settled with Reid on a meeting time at the building later tonight and hung up.

"Martin says he's going to bring his sparring headgear just in case you're feeling ornery."

She shook her head, a worried glint in her eyes. "You'll need to keep an eye on him in there, Cooper. Even though it appears the *lidérc* is no longer in residence there, that devil tried to get to Reid twice. I don't want it to miraculously show up and have the third time be the charm."

"Will do, Zoe."

"I'll bring protection for us, just in case," she said and then looked my way. "You can have your mace and be ready to come running."

"And swinging." I pointed at the pictures. "And if you do find some sigils similar to these, then what?"

She shrugged. "We might need to backtrack."

"What's that mean?" Cooper asked.

"Violet, didn't Dominick tell you that he took the imp from someone who disobeyed him and who was killed because of it?"

"Yeah, something like that."

To Cooper, she said, "We might need to figure out who was in charge of this imp before Dominick." She held up one of the pictures. "If it's using a sigil for some magical purpose, this could be something it learned from its previous owner."

"Meaning the owner might have been a witch?" I asked.

"Maybe, or just a sorcerer."

"Just a sorcerer," I said with a healthy dose of sarcasm.

She patted my arm. "Either way, I'll have to bone up on witchcraft history in this area. But if I'm right and the imp is using magic that it learned previously, we might be able to figure out the key to catching it."

"Hell, maybe Parker should borrow Reid's sparring headgear." He held his coffee out toward me. "You might have a fighting chance during round 2."

I flipped him off, not bothering to waste my breath on a rebuttal.

"In the meantime," Aunt Zoe said, focusing on me, "you and I are going up to Lead."

"We are? Why? It's my day off."

"Perfect. Then you won't have to watch the clock while we're paying Prudence a visit."

CHAPTER ELEVEN

An hour later, we were on our way up to Lead to visit a royal ectoplasmic pain in my ass. Yippity damn skippity.

I'd dragged my feet as long as I could at home until Aunt Zoe had threatened to call my mother and have her join us for the visit to Prudence's place. That got me hopping in a heartbeat. The idea of Prudence possessing my mom and chastising me with the whites of my mother's eyes showing would surely unhinge my brain and leave it flapping in the breeze, requiring a buttload of therapy to round up my marbles and put them back in my skull bag.

"I still think this is a bad idea," I told my aunt as we passed by the US Highway 385 cutoff that headed up Strawberry Hill toward Harvey's ranch. "Prudence doesn't like impromptu visits."

Aunt Zoe shifted in her seat to partly face me. "You cleared it with Zelda. I heard her loud and clear through the phone say that we are welcome. She even mentioned having hot cider along with something baked and ready for us to eat. Wouldn't Prudence have let Zelda know right away if our visit was going to be a problem?"

"Maybe Prudence was busy doing something else when I called."

"Like what? Going for a jog? She's a ghost."

"I don't know. Probably filing some of the teeth from her macabre collection."

Why couldn't my dead co-worker collect normal things, like antique teacups or hat pins? Or even weapons. Hell, in our vocation, a case full of swords or knives would have seemed reasonable. But eyeteeth? That was fruitcake nutty.

"I doubt it." She tilted her head to the side, eyes narrowing. "Are you afraid of a dead Executioner?"

"Yes!" I answered without hesitation. "And I'm not ashamed to admit that. Prudence is mean. Like angry hippo savage. Even dead she's still vicious. I can only imagine how tough she was when she was alive and kicking ass."

Aunt Zoe chuckled. "She'd cut your throat for a dime and give you a nickel back."

"Exactly. She's more brutal than a night in Antanimora Prison."

"A night in …" Aunt Zoe's forehead lined. "Where's that?"

"Madagascar."

She shook her head. "Have you been watching documentaries with Coop again?"

Nope. He and I typically stuck to old westerns, at least we had when he was staying at Aunt Zoe's last fall.

"It was Natalie, actually. Cooper really needs to loosen her shackles when it comes to helping me with Detective Hawke. I think the *bandida* side of her brain is planning a prison riot."

My cell phone rang. Rather than take the call myself, I handed it to Aunt Zoe. "Help me out. If it's my work, don't answer. It could be Jerry, and I'm not coming in today, not even for some new clients he *thinks* are interested in buying a place."

"Oh, I'm answering and hoping it's your boss." She took the phone. "I'm going to give that big meathead a piece of my mind for putting my niece on display like she's store window candy."

I held out my hand. "On second thought, give the phone back to me."

She held it away. "No. You're driving. Besides, it's not your office." She took the call. "Hey, Willis. Hold on, you're going on speaker." She punched the button, tuning in as Harvey asked, "Where's Sparky?"

"I'm driving."

"Where are you two headed?"

Aunt Zoe and I exchanged raised brows. I shrugged. She nodded, so I told him, "We're going up to see Prudence."

He harrumphed. "Of all the leather-brained … Tell you what, I got a better idea. How about you two go pee on an electric fence. That'll be less painful in the end." He snickered through the line. "Get it, I said 'in the end.' As in your hind end." He snickered some more. "That reminds me of this rather 'robusty' sidewalk hostess from a town a smidgeon east of Reno that I knew a few years back."

I frowned at Aunt Zoe. "Robusty?"

"You know," Harvey said. "Sturdy down below and heavy up top. Nice and robusty. Anyhoo, she was real partial to being zapped with electricity, so she'd take battery cables and clamp them on her—"

"Harvey!" I cut off a story that was sure to make me want to rinse my memory in bleach. "Why did you call?"

"I think I know where your imp might be purty soon."

"Really? How?"

"The 'how' part in that matter ain't important right now. The 'how' we need to be thinkin' about is *how* we'll be catchin' the critter this time without you takin' another beatin'." I heard the sound of his pickup starting. "Are you two up at ol' Prudy's yet?"

"Almost," I said, turning right off Lead's main drag.

"Well, slow down. I'm joinin' ya."

"Why? You usually whine and buck when I want you to come with me to visit Prudence. Aren't you worried about losing a tooth?"

"Well, I've been thinkin' about that ol' gal a bit lately. I don't think she's gonna take any of my choppers. She's had plenty of opportunities and left me and mine alone." There was a pause, and then, "Except for those two times she snuck inside my noggin' and took over the controls. But if Zelda is home, I'm mostly certain Prudy will probably leave me be."

"Fine, we'll wait in the driveway. Are you coming from Deadwood?"

"Nope. Just leavin' Junie's place."

Aunt Zoe shared a sly grin with me. "We'll see you shortly, Willis."

"Wait!" he hollered before I could end the call. "Did Zelda mention anything about bakin' some tasty tidbits for your visit?"

"Ah ha!" I smacked the steering wheel. "That's the real reason you're tagging along. You're in it for the food."

He cackled. "Nobody bakes like Zelda. See you in a hiccup."

We had been parked in Zelda's drive for about a minute when Harvey rolled in behind us.

Aunt Zoe rubbernecked out the windshield at the house. "The place is still in great shape."

I couldn't agree more. Prudence had chosen a beautiful abode in which to permanently retire. The Gothic revival–style house had held onto its elegance for well over a century. A leftover aristocrat from the gold rush years, the two-story home stood stately in the weak winter sunshine.

"I haven't been up here in a while. I do love that color."

I stared out at it, too. "With the ornate trim and arched windows, it reminds me of a fancy buttercream-colored wedding cake with chocolate piping." In the attic window, the sheer curtain moved slightly. "Prudence knows we're here."

Harvey pounded on my side window, making my heart rattle, dammit. He stood there in his faux fur–lined trapper hat, grinning so wide his two gold teeth were shining in the sun. It appeared that Junie Coppermoon was doing wonders for his disposition.

"What's wrong?" he asked, his voice muffled by the closed window. "You two hit a knot or somethin'? Let's get movin'. I'm freezin' my chicken tenders off out here, and I need 'em in good shape for another round with Junie tonight."

I motioned him to step aside and joined him out in the freezing wind. Huddling deeper into my scarf, I glowered at him. "You're seeing her again? That's going to be three nights in a row."

"Who put you in charge of keepin' score of my dance card?" He grinned wide, looking cock-a-doodle-doo proud. "That girl can't get enough of me and your honey."

Good Lord, I'd created a monster.

Aunt Zoe came around the front of my vehicle. She patted Harvey on the back. "You picked a good one there. Junie Coppermoon is a smart cookie and in tip-top shape."

"You should see her in her nothin'-alls. Boy howdy, that woman is hotter than a brandin' iron."

"Time out," I said, making a T with my hands. "I'm leaving the locker room before the towel-snapping commences."

"Ah, Sparky. I was just gettin' ready to drop the soap."

Aunt Zoe laughed, but that faded when she looked toward the house. "I see her in the front window."

I turned. Sure enough, Zelda stood there with the curtain pulled aside, waving out at us.

I waved back. "That's Zelda. She's a sweetheart." Unlike her roommate.

Aunt Zoe waved, too. "I'm talking about the blonde behind her in the high-necked dress with a blood-stained collar."

My breath hitched. "You can see Prudence?"

Harvey pushed his fur hat back off his forehead. "I didn't know you could see ghosts, Zoe."

"I don't often, but every now and then I come across a specter that seems to want to be seen."

"Well, I did text Zelda after we hung up and let her know my *magistra* was coming along, and that I'd appreciate it if Prudence behaved herself around you."

"Apparently, Prudence has something to show me." Aunt Zoe grabbed me by the elbow and urged me forward. "Let's go see what the dead Executioner has planned for us this morning."

"She's going to give me shit about my face," I said, marching up the gravel drive toward what was sure to end with me being the belle of the brawl yet again.

I climbed the steps onto the wide front porch, leaning into the frigid wind gusts whooshing over the Open Cut mine on our left.

"Woo wee!" Harvey hurried up next to me. "Ol' man winter is tryin' his damnedest to turn me into a flesh kite."

I turned back toward the drive, wishing I were already on my way out of this place. I noticed the driver's side window on Harvey's truck looked closed. The imp had just shattered that yesterday morning.

"Hey, did you get your window fixed already?" If not, driving around in this weather must be hard on his joints. It would be for me even at my age.

"Yep. But the inside is still a mess."

"That was fast."

"I know a guy at the body shop in Lead. He had a couple in stock and owed me a favor."

I shivered for reasons other than the cold wind. I shoulder bumped Harvey. "You ready to catch me if I fall in there?"

This house was the site of my near death last summer, thanks to a crackpot bitch who thought I'd be the perfect candidate to not only help raise a demon to this plane of existence with my blood, but also copulate with the nightmare and bring its hellish baby into the world. I shook the tension out of my hands. I still had some sweaty qualms when I was under this roof about the demon coming back to finish what had been started.

Harvey gave me two thumbs up. "I'll be there with bells on. Just do me a favor, Sparky, and try to time it so I'm not in the middle of eatin' whatever goodies Zelda has for us."

"Nice. I see where I rate in your book."

"Well, there's pie, then honeybuns, and then you." He scrunched half of his face. "Unless she's made some sort of fruit cobbler, then you're after that."

After holding my fist up to the buzzard, which only earned me a wheezy laugh, I turned to knock on the screen door. But before my knuckles found purchase, Zelda was there to greet us. She looked cute as a button in an apron covered with green and red apples. Her curly auburn hair was tied back and a dusting of what appeared to be flour covered part of her left cheek.

"Violet! It's so good to see you. And you must be Zoe. It's nice to meet you. Please, come in out of the cold. All of you." She stood back, allowing room for me to step inside the foyer with Aunt Zoe on my tail. "I whipped up some chocolate cherry cobbler, and it just came out of the oven." She smiled wide, her green eyes sparkling when she turned to our third musketeer. "I think you're really going to like it, Mr. Harvey."

"Winner, winner, chicken dinner!" Harvey pumped his fist, hustling in and closing the door behind him. "I'm sure glad you invited me along, Sparky."

Truthfully, I was too, even though he'd come mostly for the food.

The house smelled like the inside of a chocolate cake. I might have drooled a little as I was taking off my coat, which I handed to Zelda, who collected our winter gear and hung it in the hall closet before leading us along the narrow hallway.

"These stained glass sconces are absolutely gorgeous," Aunt Zoe said, reaching up to touch the Tiffany-style stained glass.

"I agree," Zelda said, waving us toward the living room. "Wanda Carhart had immaculate taste."

Upon entering the living room, Aunt Zoe came to a standstill. Her gaze widened as she took in the birch flooring, plush cream rugs, flower-covered silk wallpaper, high ceiling with pearlescent-painted tin squares, velvet curtains decorated with lace patterns, maple hand-crafted molding, and burgundy leather furniture.

"Wow!" Her voice sounded slightly breathless. "This house is even more lovely on the inside than the out." She turned to me. "You should have brought me along to meet Zelda and Prudence sooner."

Zelda hugged herself. "I fell in love with this house right out of the gate. And while Violet's news about some of the unpleasant events that had taken place within its walls made Zeke and me hesitate, I couldn't stop daydreaming of what our life could be here."

I had to wonder if Prudence had played a part in planting that happy-go-lucky seed in Zelda's brain. She'd put a trigger word in Detective Hawke's head with ease, so it probably hadn't taken much work to push Zelda into signing the contract. Especially since the middle-aged librarian was an open mental channel for Prudence, even more so than Wanda Carhart had been before her untimely death.

"I can see why," Aunt Zoe said, looking at me with a slight furrow in her brow.

Actually, she was staring past me, over my right shoulder, toward the wide, carpet-lined stairwell. I had a feeling she wasn't admiring the ornately carved banisters with their pineapple-shaped newel posts.

"Prudence is standing behind me, isn't she," I said, bracing myself for what was to come.

Harvey grunted and hustled over to the front window, putting a healthy amount of space between us. Some bodyguard he was.

"Yes," Zelda said, sounding surprised. "How did you know?"

I pointed at my aunt. "She can see her."

"Oh, how interesting." Zelda leaned against the back of the sofa, her hands clasped together. "Can you hear her as well?"

We all focused on Aunt Zoe, who continued to stare in the direction of the stairwell.

"I don't know. How does she usually communicate with you?"

I snorted. "Via blunt objects and barbaric strength."

Harvey snickered. "Prudence ain't one for small talk."

Aunt Zoe glanced my way, her grin barely suppressed. "I was talking to Zelda."

"Since the beginning," Zelda explained, "Prudence just started speaking in my mind. At first I thought my porch light might be flickering, you know." She giggled, tapping her temple. "But then Prudence showed up behind me in the bathroom mirror one morning after Zeke had left for a week-long contracting job." Zelda giggled some more. "After I picked myself up off the floor and found her still standing in the mirror kind of shimmering, I realized she was a ghost and I couldn't have been happier." She turned to me. "Violet, you remember how I'd told you we were looking for a house that was haunted?"

I nodded. I used to think that was an odd request, but these days, thanks to the *Paranormal Realty* TV show, it had become as normal in my world as peanut butter sandwiches and stray pets.

Zelda clapped her hands together. "Ever since then, Prudence has been here to keep me company, which I really appreciate since Zeke tends to have longer stints away for his job than I like."

"You mentioned before that Zeke knows about Prudence, right?" I asked, wondering how the retired pro wrestler felt about his wife hanging out with a wispy pal.

"Yes." She tittered, leaning in. "At first he was a little concerned for me and my mental health, but then he saw how happy I was to have Prudence's company. I used to get so lonely during his absences. But not anymore. It's like I have a best friend rooming with me."

All of that sounded cute and bubbly and lovely, but did Zelda realize she was living with a cold-blooded killer whose tooth collection rivaled head-hunter scalps? Maybe so, maybe not. I guess if Prudence were protecting Zelda, then it was all water under the bridge. However, there was the matter of what happened yesterday at the old school.

Oh, that reminded me. "Zelda, I have your daisy scarf that you must have dropped at the middle school."

She smiled. "I'm so glad you found that. It was a gift from Zeke's mother. It must have fallen out of my car when I got out. I didn't realize it was gone until we returned home."

Probably because Prudence had been at the helm and super eager to get to the *Duzarx*.

I scowled toward the stairwell. "What were you thinking, Prudence, taking Zelda to that crumbling school? That place is dangerous for more reasons than it being on the verge of falling down on her head."

That might have been a bit of an exaggeration, but I was trying to make a point.

Zelda hurried over and grabbed my arm. "Please, Violet. Don't start squabbling with Prudence already. She did promise to keep her temper in check since your aunt was coming."

"Hear, hear," Harvey said. "No pecos promenadin' between you two, at least not until we've filled our bellies."

"Fine." I walked around Aunt Zoe and sank into the leather sofa cushions. "But Prudence had better let me eat this time. Chocolate will stain your white carpet if she does her utensil-flying parlor trick again."

Zelda paused, listening for a few beats. "She said—"

"That out of respect for me," Aunt Zoe interrupted, "she will refrain from teaching you manners this visit."

There was our answer—Aunt Zoe could hear Prudence as well.

"How do you like those apples?" Harvey linked his thumbs in his blue-pinstriped suspenders. "You think Prudy will want to hop inside your aunt's melon and take her skin suit for a spin, too?"

"No." I turned toward the stairs. "Prudence, no possessing my aunt."

Zelda smiled. "She's standing right next to you now, Violet." When I cringed, she patted my shoulder. "But don't worry, she says to tell you that she has agreed to your terms."

Splendid, but which terms in particular? I didn't trust Prudence not to bend the rules to her advantage.

Zelda glanced toward the kitchen. "How about I go get us some cider and cobbler, and then we'll get the show on the road."

"I'll come help you," Harvey said, rubbing his hands together as he hustled after Zelda.

Silence settled in the room, interrupted by a burst of laughter from Zelda coming from the kitchen. The cobbler gods only knew what Harvey was up to now. Probably spinning another X-rated yarn about some courtesan he knew down in Nevada.

"And then there were three." I looked over at Aunt Zoe. "At least I'm assuming Prudence is standing here yet."

"She is." Aunt Zoe went over to the front window, glancing back at me. "But she's actually sitting right next to you."

I jumped to my feet, my gaze darting all around, only to realize Aunt Zoe was quietly laughing.

I aimed a mock glare at her. "Not funny."

"It was a little. Prudence agrees."

I didn't know what had me more on edge—this whole chummy

relationship the two of them had right out of the gate, or my aunt being able to not only see, but also talk to the snooty ghost. This must be Prudence's doing somehow. If that were the case, why wouldn't she let me see her, too?

I lowered my hiney back down onto the sofa, warily glancing around as if I'd be able to see the arrogant haint. "Ask Prudence how she knows the *Duzarx* went into that school building."

Aunt Zoe stepped closer, standing across the coffee table from me. "She says that she can hear you, so you need not have me repeat questions."

"Fine." I looked up at the ceiling since I didn't know where Prudence was hovering. "Then answer the question."

There was a moment of silence, then from Aunt Zoe, "Prudence doesn't approve of your incivility."

"Here we go again." I sighed, squeezing my temples. "Prudence, will you *please* tell me what makes you think the *Duzarx* went into the old school?"

"A little less tone, Violet," Aunt Zoe said, barely holding in a smile.

My chin jutted. "Did Prudence say that?"

"No, I did."

I flipped off my aunt, which made her laugh. "That seems to be your go-to this morning. First Coop, now me."

"Yeah, but with Cooper I meant it times two. With you, this one finger is full of love."

Aunt Zoe glanced toward the sideboard to my right, her brow tightening. "Prudence wants to know what happened to your face."

"If she answers my question, I'll answer hers." I was sticking to my guns until the chocolate cherry cobbler showed up, and I was rewarded for my efforts here.

Aunt Zoe moved to the chair, settling in, appearing quite at ease jawing with a ghost. "Prudence says that a *Duzarx* emits a telltale reverberation. That's how she was able to track it to the building."

Before I could get a word in, Aunt Zoe asked Prudence, "What sort of reverberation?"

I sat forward, curious about that, too.

She waited a moment and then spoke again. "No, I have not read anything about the *Duzarx* in our family history volumes."

Again, she paused, her gaze now centered near the front

window. "Yes, volumes. Plural. There are several of them full of ancestral anecdotes written down by past *magistras*."

Aunt Zoe had transcribed many of these writings during her lifetime, but there were more still in older languages. Apparently, our family had been killing for a long, long time.

Her head lowered. "Really? Your line never kept any notes or records?"

Then how had Prudence's ancestors passed on any information to help the current slayer succeed? I guess that didn't matter now, since Prudence was the last of her line.

Aunt Zoe's eyebrows raised. "That's quite impressive, Prudence. We've had to rely on written histories." After a moment, she shook her head. "It's not a matter of memory issues. Although as I age, I do tend to forget the finer details if I don't write them down. It's more that twin babies are common in our line, so we've had many a *Scharfrichter* called into action over the centuries, often even two at once." She sent a smile in my direction. "Violet and her daughter are an example. Adelynn is not yet ten, and already her innate abilities are emerging."

Normally, Prudence made a practice of insulting my family line, but from the sounds of this side of the conversation, she was being respectful for once. Then again, Aunt Zoe did have a lot more knowledge when it came to our past. Her position as a *magistra* might also have been one requiring respect in Prudence's time.

I wondered how the knowledge that my daughter was already on her way to becoming a fellow killer settled with Prudence. Hell, she would undoubtedly reprimand me if she learned that I kept dragging my feet on training Addy. Then again, Doc had been working with both kids on how to defend themselves, so we weren't keeping Addy in the dark entirely.

And what would Prudence think if she found out my son was a … crap, what was that name again? *Besh*-something. Screw it—he was a Summoner. Or at least Layne's powers as one were developing, same as his sister. It was only thanks to Layne's youth and Aunt Zoe's protective charms that the monsters had been kept at bay so far.

I blinked back to the present conversation, realizing that Aunt Zoe wasn't speaking English anymore. I leaned forward, trying to figure out what language I was hearing. It sort of sounded like

German, with a lot of friction in the mouth, but what did I really know of that language outside of what I'd heard in *Indiana Jones* movies?

I waited until there was a break in Aunt Zoe's side of the conversation. "What is going on?"

"I believe Prudence is testing my knowledge of Old German." She looked toward the window. "Am I correct?"

After a moment, she nodded and turned back to me, her eyes filled with mirth. "She says I have passed her test, but she wonders why you are such a fumbling fledgling."

Before I could come up with a smartass reply, Zelda and Harvey returned with two serving trays. Harvey set his tray on the coffee table. It held bowls of steaming cobbler topped with a dollop of whipped cream, shavings of dark chocolate, and a maraschino cherry. My stomach rang the dinner bell even though breakfast hadn't been that long ago, kicking my salivary glands into high gear.

Zelda's tray held cups of steaming apple cider with sticks of cinnamon dipped in them. God, I loved this woman. If only she didn't come with such a persnickety sidekick.

"Giddy up!" Harvey said, sitting at the opposite end of the couch from me.

Zelda settled in between us, playing hostess, handing off the bowls of goodness.

I took the spoon and napkin she handed me, licking my chops as I dug into the warm bowl of chocolate heaven. I groaned and closed my eyes. Harvey was right, this was worth risking a tooth. The cider was both sweet and tart somehow, finishing with a zingy bite— just how I liked my man.

Aunt Zoe took one mouthful and sighed. "Zelda, this is absolute nirvana for the taste buds."

"Thank you." Zelda dabbed the side of her mouth with a napkin. "My grandmother used to make it every Christmas." Her smile took on a melancholy air. "She was the one who taught me how to bake. I miss her every time I'm in the kitchen."

Harvey scooped up a second steaming bowl of cobbler before I was even halfway through my first. When I looked at him with raised brows, he said through a mouthful of chocolate and cherries, "I need some calories to make up for last night's lesson on the birds and the bees."

Zelda chortled. "Mr. Harvey, you are incorrigible."

"That's why the ladies love me," he returned with a wiggle of his bushy eyebrows. "Goody two shoes aren't sexy at my age."

Prudence let me finish my dessert without disruption. Whether she stuck around for our mini-feast was beyond my ability to see. Neither Zelda nor Aunt Zoe spoke to her, so I assumed she'd gone wherever ghosts go when they wanted to be left alone.

After I set my bowl down, I wiped my mouth, thanked Zelda, and then leaned toward Aunt Zoe. "Did Prudence ever say what kind of reverberation the *Duzarx* emits?" Was it loud and banging, or a low drone that Cornelius could pick up with one of his fancy gadgets?

Aunt Zoe was working on her last few bites. I hated to interrupt her enjoyment of Zelda's *pièce de résistance*, but it was time to get back to the business of why we were here. This was my day off, and I wanted to spend it cleaning out my closet and paying bills.

Who was I kidding? I wanted to lollygag on the couch watching old movies and pretending I lived a normal life. Visiting with ghosts did not fit into that "normal" daydream.

"No." Aunt Zoe focused on Zelda. "Is Prudence still here and I'm not seeing her?"

"She's here." Zelda finished the last bite of her cobbler and then took a sip of cider. "Hold on and let me reach out to her. I know she had something she wanted you to see."

See what? What did Zelda mean by reach out to her? And why couldn't Aunt Zoe see Prudence now? I held my tongue, trying to remain patient while waiting to see what Prudence's newest parlor trick was going to be.

Zelda leaned back on the sofa and closed her eyes. Harvey and I exchanged frowns. We'd seen this part before. Zelda's eyelids would open, revealing eyes rolled back to show the whites. Then Prudence would start talking in her Katharine Hepburn–like accent, spouting orders and insults.

I scooted a few inches away from Zelda, debating on standing to put more distance between us so she couldn't lay a hand on me and inflict pain in one way or another.

Harvey actually did stand, moving over to half sit on the arm of Aunt Zoe's chair.

Chicken, I mouthed.

He shrugged and nodded, and then scooped up another bite of cobbler. Food before pride in his book, in other words. I could accept that.

"Violet," Zelda said, her eyes still closed. Only it wasn't Zelda's tone.

"Hello, Prudence."

CHAPTER TWELVE

Somewhat recently, I'd read an article about how to deal with toxic co-workers. This was after Ray, the horse's ass, had been fired, so my interest in the topic had nothing to do with him. My reason for digging into this subject had to do with Prudence.

Aunt Zoe and Doc had both said to me at different times that I needed to reach some middle ground with the dead Executioner. The problem with that notion? I doubted Prudence cared about compromising with me. I had a gut feeling that she liked to be the alpha, controlling the who, what, when, where, and how of the world around her. In her mind, there was no "middle." There was her way, and then there was the way to which I should agree based on her opinion—and both were one and the same. For instance, if I were to say the sun was shining, she'd insist it was raining and proceed to order me to use an umbrella and for how long.

But back to the article on toxic co-workers.

According to the author, some Dr. So-and-so, I first needed to create a physical distance between us, which I was trying like hell to do. Unfortunately, Prudence kept intruding on *my* space with Zelda's help. Calling me out of the blue to come to the school yesterday was a great example.

That led to the next tip—refusing to participate, as in with gossip or rumors, or with a narcissistic Executioner who insisted that she was always right. Following this was a sticky wicket for me. I had a history of charging into battle with my big mouth, and that tended to land me in shootout-at-high-noon situations.

Another idea was to set solid boundaries, both conversational and physical. In my defense when it came to past confrontations with Prudence, I had tried to draw a line in the sand and keep my distance from whomever she was possessing at the time. Especially that day with Cooper and his superhero grip. And the experience with Ray. Oh, and Detective Hawke, too. And *all* of the times with Zelda, because exchanging any blows with her could hurt my daisy-loving pal, and that was the last thing I wanted to do.

If I were honest, though, I would've liked to have socked Ray in the nose while Prudence was in his noggin. And Detective Hawke, as well. Maybe even Cooper. No, maybe not Cooper. Well, at least not his nose again. I'd done that plenty already. Just a solid flick on his forehead would have been rewarding. Or maybe a good hard pinch on his … Stop. I was heading down a rabbit hole and now was not the time for wishful daydreaming.

The final resonating bit of advice was to take care of myself, first and foremost. Dr. So-and-so had mentioned something about a self-care routine, which jibed with Cornelius's various bits of advice about plunging out my chakras, scrubbing my aura, sharpening my medium skills, taking a fire hose to my negative thoughts, and dancing the horizontal polka with Doc.

Actually, that last suggestion was Natalie's when I told her during a coffee break about how I was working on getting along better with Prudence. She'd gone into detail on several more mattress dances she and Cooper had performed of late, which made me first wince, then cringe, then plug my ears, and finally pretend to fall off my chair and die. I should have won an Oscar for my performance, but Natalie gave me a noogie instead after yanking me back upright.

Anyway, contrary to what everyone might think, I was truly trying to improve my relationship with my co-worker in killing. Doc's smartass idea of Prudence and me going on a spa retreat together and doing some trust-building exercises would happen when the Rocky Mountains went flat. For now, I'd have to continue to work on controlling what was within my means when I was around Prudence and not spiraling into any more chest-beating matches.

"How have you been since we last talked?" I asked Zelda—well, Prudence, who was keeping her host's body in a relaxed state and her hands to herself for once. Nonetheless, I shifted as far away from her as the sofa would allow, putting the article's advice about physical distance into practice. "I hear you enjoyed some fresh air yesterday afternoon."

Prudence sighed, rather overdramatically in my opinion, but I kept that to myself. "Why is there always an abundance of buffoonery when it comes to you completing your tasks?"

I expected to be on the receiving end of a whites-of-her-eyes glare at this point, but she kept Zelda's eyelids closed.

I opened my mouth to comment on what I thought of her stupidity in dragging Zelda to the school yesterday, but then I remembered I supposed to refuse to participate when it came to my hare-brained, toxic co-worker's negativity and not engage in her mud-slinging attempts.

So, instead, I asked, "And how are things in your attic lately? Do the spiders appreciate your sparkling personality as much as the rest of us?"

Aunt Zoe cleared her throat, shaking her head at me, but a smile hovered at the corners of her mouth.

"A simpleton would fare better against her adversaries than you," Prudence declared, as if I'd asked for her haughty opinion.

Simpleton? I crossed my arms. And here I thought Zelda and I had set some boundaries with Prudence prior to my arrival. "You said you were going to play nice today."

"With the *magistra*, yes, out of the respect she has earned. You, on the contrary, have yet to do as I have told." She sniffed. "The great irony is that I stayed in this uncivilized locale, as was planned, and for what? To brandish weapons side by side with a fool."

"I'm not a fool, Prudence," I said, taking a deep calming breath. Self-care often started with breathing right, according to Cornelius. Or was it breathing in the right colors? I should really carry a color chart on me, like a tip card, so I could make sure not to breathe in the wrong hue. "Nor am I your trained monkey."

"Oh, I know. A simian would run circles around you."

Harvey chuckled, earning a quick glare from me.

My glare for Prudence was twice as long. "Why would a monkey run in a circle? That's just silly. It's not a goldfish, for crissake. It's an intelligent—"

"Digressing," Aunt Zoe said in a sing-song voice.

I closed my lips and breathed in the color pink. Pink had to be good, didn't it? Cotton candy was usually pink. And sweet.

"Listen, Prudence, I didn't drive up here to—"

"*You* will be the one to listen, *Scharfrichter*."

I bristled from head to toe at her tone, but I buttoned my lips and waited, along with Aunt Zoe, who was leaning forward in her chair in anticipation. Harvey, on the other hand, was gulping down his cider. Jeez, Rooster the dog was quieter when he drank from his water bowl, although Harvey splashed a lot less.

"Traditional methods of trapping an animal will not achieve the desired results when hunting an imp," she said.

Had I mentioned trying to trap the imp? I did remember telling her during one of our visits that I had to catch it. "Duly noted, Prudence."

"Imps have incredibly strong fingers and jaws, which it is obvious you witnessed personally."

I touched one of the scratches on my face. It was still tender, but I was healing quickly, as I tended to do when injured by an *other*. That was one of the few blessings that came with my Executioner DNA.

"You figured out what happened to my face." I clapped three times. "Nice job, but that was an easy mystery to solve."

I waited for a condescending comment about how I was lousy at my job, but nothing followed. There was only the sound of Zelda's slow, deep breaths.

And Harvey's rattling of a plastic wrapper as he opened a piece of candy and popped it into his mouth. Goody gumdrops! How much sugar did he need in one sitting? Was he preparing for the starring role in the next version of *The Fly*?

"The creature will either bend the wires of the cage," Prudence continued. "Or rip a hole through the steel with its teeth. It is no fool, nor is it feeble. This is why imps are long-lived and require cleverness to not only catch but hold as well."

I looked at Aunt Zoe, who had snared an imp once and even killed it. She certainly fit the "clever" bill, considering that she'd been able to see it only in the reflection of a special mirror.

"It is true the creature is drawn to honey." Prudence wasn't done, apparently. "However, you must reconsider your rather simple method for using the viscous substance as bait. Simply coating the bottom of the cage will not suffice. The results of so much arduous exertion from honeybees is squandered there. The same could be said pertaining to such puerile carnal diversions."

Huh? Carnal diversions? "What are you talking about?"

It seemed like I was being schooled and scolded for an offense I hadn't made. While this type of interaction with Prudence wasn't really something out of the ordinary, she was certainly being oddly specific about a crime I hadn't committed. Not yet, anyway.

Sure, I had considered getting the cat carrier to transport the imp, but it was plastic, not a steel cage (which I now knew would be a really bad plan). As for the idea of coating the bottom of the carrier with honey, that hadn't even occurred to me because I was going to knock the little sucker out before caging it.

"Buggeration!" Harvey hopped off the arm of the chair, his expression aghast. "Prudy's readin' my goldurn mind!"

"Really?" Aunt Zoe gawked from him to Prudence and back. "So, you're the one thinking of using a steel cage to trap the imp?"

Before he could answer that, I had a question, too. "Is that why you told us you knew where the imp might be?"

"Yessirree to both of you." He backed toward the front window, clearly putting space between Prudence and him, as if distance would stop her from radioing in on his thoughts. "I picked up a couple of traps yesterday that the local wildlife folks use to catch stray critters." He held out his hands. "The nice kind, don't worry. Coop has made me swear to stop usin' the other kind unless I'm huntin' one of those monster critters out of Slagton. If I don't, he'll take away my cannon."

"Addy will be glad to hear that," Aunt Zoe said. "I take it you set these honey traps already."

He nodded. "Early this mornin'. I figured we'd have us an imp in a cage in no time. Then it'd be up to Sparky on what to do with the li'l bastard." He combed his beard with his fingers, frowning toward Zelda. Or Prudence. "The odd thing is, I haven't been thinkin' about that cage at all since we got here, so how does she know about it?"

"What were you thinking about?" I asked.

"Besides Zelda's baked goodies, I was making some plans for fun and games later with Junie." He grinned and shrugged. "That lady has my number and keeps calling me up to the counter."

I looked back at where Zelda sat in her Zen pose. "Is this what it was you wanted me to see, Prudence? That you can read minds? If so, you've shown me that before, remember?"

Doc and Cornelius and Cooper had been here with me that time. And before, she'd read Detective Hawke's mind and filled me in on what crimes he thought I'd committed.

"Of course I remember." Prudence's sigh had a solid dose of annoyance. "I am not simply reading the lothario's mind. I am recounting what I have observed."

I chewed on that for a moment, trying to nail down the exact difference she was aiming to clarify.

Aunt Zoe rested her elbows on her knees, one eyebrow lifting. "Are you telling us that you're able to not only briefly possess Willis when he is within your sight and read his mind, but you can also go where he goes and view what he sees?"

"Essentially, although I would not use the word 'possess' in the latter case."

"Is this the same thing you can do with Zelda?" I asked. "Slip into her skin and walk her around?"

"Not the same."

Actually, I had witnessed Prudence do something along these lines when Harvey and I were in the basement of the courthouse with the *lidérc*, but I'd assumed it was enabled somehow by our connection as Executioners. And maybe along with the mystic mirror that was there with us, too.

"Not possession, then, but you did watch Harvey set up the trap this morning?" I asked. It seemed that Doc had talked about this ability, calling it something like distance viewing. Or was it remote viewing? Wait, was this a telepathic thing? I'd have to ask him later.

"Correct."

"Errr," Harvey started, and then cleared his throat. He squirmed, as if she were under his skin at this very moment, and tugged at the neckline of his shirt. "Uh, Prudy, were you also watchin' while I was … uh … visitin' with Junie before that?"

"Visiting?" She scoffed. "Is that what you call your vulgar display of amorous congress?"

I grimaced at Harvey, whose cheeks flared bright red. "Prudence, were you in Harvey's head watching while he and Junie were … " I stopped, because the man in question was visibly cringing, which made me wonder what in the hell he and Junie had been doing this morning.

Then again, I didn't really want to know.

"*Forniquer,*" Prudence snapped with a good dollop of pompousness.

"That's French for fornicating," Aunt Zoe translated.

"Although I believe I would classify what *Monsieur* Lothario was doing as bawdy coupling, commonly performed in uncultured brothels."

Harvey's face was frozen in one big wince. "You're tellin' me I was in bed with *two* women this mornin'," he said, his voice higher than normal. "Well, don't that take the whole biscuit?"

"You speak untruths," Prudence said. "There was no bed involved. And unlike your partner, I was not enjoying your ridiculous burlesque performance. Frankly, the tassels were absurd enough. The feather scarf was too much."

Oh, brother. That painted a picture I sure didn't want to visualize.

Damn. Too late.

"Really, Willis!" Aunt Zoe snorted in laughter. "A feathered boa? I never would've thought Junie to be so adventurous. Although she does love the theater."

Harvey's face was now the color of cooked beets.

Trying to move past the jazzy blend of trombones and clarinets and pianos playing striptease music in my head, I focused on Zelda. "Prudence, how long have you been able to do this little 'seeing' trick with Harvey?"

"Since the first time I met him."

An "erp" came from my feather-dancing bodyguard.

That was way back when I first brought Harvey along to keep me company while I talked to Wanda and Millie Carhart about selling their house. All of that time she'd been able to see through his eyes at whim. A look at Harvey's wide peepers made it clear he was adding up the months, too, and all that had happened between then and now.

"Why?" I asked her. "What made you choose Harvey? Or are there others I've brought here that you are also using the same way?"

Such as Doc? Was I having sex with two people, too?

"Do not fret, *Scharfrichter*. The Oracle is impossible for me to observe for any length of time. His mind is too slippery due to his own abilities."

Oh, thank God! Doc and I could skip the blindfolds during naked playtime. Then again …

"What about Detective Cooper?" Aunt Zoe asked, pulling me back on track.

"I considered the constable, but Violet was very tense in his company, so that didn't benefit my purpose."

"I was tense because you had Cooper trying to squeeze my leg in half for most of the time he was here." It took weeks for those finger bruises to fade.

"As for the Spirit Miser," Prudence started, but then paused. Zelda's body actually shuddered. "What I saw in his mind would have turned a weaker soul to stone. I would not be at ease enough to explore the view from his eyes for any length of time."

That was what Prudence got for dabbling in people's heads. Although Doc had also caught a glimpse behind the locked door in Cornelius's head and talked of terrors he hoped to never see again. As curious as I was about what they'd seen, I'd rather keep that door closed and barricaded. I had enough monsters to deal with outside of Cornelius's brain.

"You should take great care around the Spirit Miser," Prudence warned. "In fact, executing him as soon as possible would be the wisest course of action."

I scoffed. "I'm not killing Cornelius."

"Then bring him here, and I will have Zelda do it."

"No, you are not killing him either. Especially not by Zelda's hand. Besides, he's helping me."

"He will go rogue," she growled in a deep, loud timber, her tenor a goosebump-inspiring mix of doom and destruction.

"We'll cross that bridge if we ever come to it. And that's a big *IF*. For the time being, Cornelius lives. End of discussion." I went back to what she had said about Cooper. "What did you mean about the constable not benefitting your purpose? To what purpose are you referring?"

"When I realized that you were an Executioner, albeit a sad excuse for one, I knew you had come to finish what had begun long ago. Or, if not to follow through to completion, to die poorly while trying."

"Gee, thanks for your vote of confidence."

"You are a clodpoll when it comes to your purpose. Do you

deny it?"

I would probably deny it, yes, if I knew for certain what a clodpoll was. Since this was Prudence talking, I assumed it was not a flattering noun, and she meant it to be a sucker punch about my abilities as an Executioner.

"Prudence, you have to understand something." Aunt Zoe stepped in before I could formulate any sort of rebuttal beyond *I-know-you-are-but-what-am-I?*, which would have sunk my battleship in the who's-a-better-Executioner contest.

"You have to understand that in our ancestral dynasty," Aunt Zoe said, "we wait until the *Scharfrichter* shows signs of developing before training begins."

"Why would you not train from birth, *magistra?*"

"Because there have been whole generations skipped when it comes to being called into action. The *magistra* is meticulously trained so that the necessary knowledge is shared from one generation to the next, but each *Scharfrichter* is born with an innate ability to fight and kill. It only takes a short time to bring them up to speed once the need arises, and then the pair work as partners. Otherwise, the non-active Slayer is given the opportunity to live in peace and hopefully bear a future *Scharfrichter*, since those who end up having to fight often do so to the death."

I frowned down at my hands, not liking what that likely meant for my future now that I'd been called into action. Fighting until I keeled over was for Vikings and their Valhalla hopes. I was more into taking bubble baths and watching cloud formations. But I would fight, especially if it meant Addy didn't have to do the same and might yet be able to live in peace and make more *Scharfrichter* babies—only after she finished college, of course, and found a nice partner who treated her well.

"An imprudent waste," the haughty haint snapped. "Time would be better spent training a much superior Slayer, whether needed or not."

"You don't understand." Aunt Zoe reached over and patted my knee. "This *Scharfrichter* came out of the box already a superior Slayer. Once activated, she simply needed to be given a weapon to start killing."

Wow, that made me sound a lot more razor-sharp than this blunt butter knife felt.

Harvey gave Aunt Zoe a doubtful stare that probably matched mine. "We are talkin' about Sparky, right?"

"Yes, Willis. You've seen her in action, have you not?"

I didn't wait for Harvey to answer that, considering his most recent viewing of my "action" against one small imp. "Prudence, to be clear, you hooked up with Harvey to monitor my actions?"

" 'Hooked up' is a simplistic way of describing a skill that is clearly beyond your mental capabilities."

"Yeah, yeah, sticks and stones." I brushed off her insult. "Why did you choose him?"

"Is it not obvious? He is your shadow. I was able to read his intentions to join your crusade, if you will, almost immediately."

All of this time she'd been able to watch me at will whenever Harvey was around, like some ghostly voyeur. How weird. Unnerving, too.

"That's how you knew about Sparky's actions back in Slagton with the chimera before she'd told you," Harvey said. "It's because you were there watchin' with me."

"I saw her lack of finesse in killing, yes."

"You hear that?" I asked Aunt Zoe. "She's impossible."

"Stay focused, Violet Lynn," she replied and gave me an encouraging smile.

Focused, right. We were in some serious need of boundary lines in the sand here, dang it.

"Can I shut you off when I want?" Harvey asked, apparently riding the same train of thought as me.

"The choice is mine, not yours." Zelda's arms began to tremble. Quickly, the tremors spread to her shoulders, lips, and then down her legs.

"Is Zelda okay in there?" I asked.

"Of course." The trembling was becoming more visible.

"Then why is she shaking?"

"You mind your business, *Scharfrichter*, and I'll mind mine."

"Please! You're the one nosing into my business through Harvey's eyes."

"Your business is mine, too. If you continue to fail, all I have sacrificed will be for naught."

"What did you sacrifice?" Was she talking about her family at the time of her death?

"Again, mind your business."

I looked at Aunt Zoe. "She sounds like Cooper."

"And if you must hunt the imp, do so with great care." Her voice was beginning to quiver, too. "Trust me, the last thing you want is an imp hunting you." Zelda's body jerked enough for her feet to come off the floor. "I will take my leave now. Zelda must wake."

"Prudence, wait!" I called, leaning toward her. "I need to know how to find the *Duzarx*."

Zelda reached out and boxed me upside my right ear with lightning speed.

"Son of a—ouch!" I fell back against the arm of the sofa, cupping my stinging, ringing ear. "What the hell, Prudence?"

Zelda's eyelids opened. I cringed at the whites of her eyes aimed straight at me. "Do you hear the ringing?"

"Yes, dammit." I felt the burning, too.

"The closer you are to a *Duzarx*, the louder the ring. They emit this perceptible sound at a level an Executioner can hear, but not a human."

"Jeez, you could have just told me that." That meant I hadn't come across the *Duzarx* when Doc and I were in the old school. So what had been in that classroom?

The corners of Zelda's mouth crept upward, looking like they'd been pinned to her cheeks while the center of her lips drooped. "There is no pleasure in words. The use of force is a far more gratifying courier."

Zelda's head fell forward.

"Is she okay?" Aunt Zoe whispered.

I figured she was, but I wasn't going to move closer to her until I was sure Prudence the Pugilist was long gone.

Harvey harrumphed, crossing his arms. "This is gonna mess up my game."

"What do you mean?" I asked, gently rubbing my burning ear. The ringing was still going strong.

"I was gonna go for a hat trick tonight with Junie, but I'm not sure Big Willy's gonna work if I know ol' Prudy might be watchin'."

Aunt Zoe let out a bark of laughter.

I groaned and shook my head.

"This ain't funny, you two," Harvey said, scratching his beard. "Poor Junie. She might not like havin' a threesome with a ghost."

Zelda's head raised, her green eyes smiling and friendly, although lined at the edges. I thought Zelda had said before that Prudence's possession usually left her energized. What was different today?

"What did I miss?" she asked.

"Trust me, you really don't want to know," I said, still shaking my head.

"Dang it," Aunt Zoe muttered. "I meant to show Prudence the sigil the imp keeps leaving around town and see if she recognized it or had any thoughts on why an imp would leave a sigil."

Zelda looked toward the stairwell, her brow lined slightly when she turned back to us. "Prudence says that if there's a sigil, then the imp was likely taught some form of sorcery. This would make for an even greater foe if it decides to hunt Violet in return."

I scoffed. "Great, a magical imp. What's next?"

Zelda was focused on the stairwell again. "She also says that you must kill the *Duzarx* before the next blood moon."

"I know." I looked toward the stairs as well. "Prudence, you told me that already."

"Yes, but she doesn't believe you're capable of doing it." Zelda patted my arm. "I think you can do it, though, Violet. Don't let Prudence be a buzz kill. She's just been pushing herself harder lately, and it's making her more gloomy than usual."

"That's it. I'm putting some physical distance between Prudence and me." I stood, motioning for Harvey and Aunt Zoe to join me. "Zelda, thank you for the cobbler. It was delicious, and I always appreciate your kindness." I glared toward the stairs. "Prudence, mind your own damned business and stay out of Harvey's head."

"Violet, wait." Zelda rose from the sofa as I started to walk away. "Prudence says not to forget about executing the *caper-sus* and the *Draug*, the other white grizzly, and something called a *Fhain-Hai*, which will skin you alive." She cocked her head for a second, and then added, "Oh, and the Guardian Knave. She says he is especially treacherous for you and your *Scharfrichter* offspring."

I frowned at the stairs while chills ran sprints up and down my spine. "I think I'm gonna need some tequila therapy to help process this."

"Violet Lynn," Aunt Zoe said, taking me by the wrist, same as she had when I was a child. "Let's go home."

"Yeah, let's." I shrugged off my worries for the moment. "I'm leaving, Prudence," I said loud and clear. "As for your gloomy predictions, I'm going to find a loophole, so that I don't end up rattling chains alongside your crabby ass for all eternity."

CHAPTER THIRTEEN

A red dually pickup sat next to the curb in front of Aunt Zoe's house when we got home.

"Ah, hell," Aunt Zoe said as I killed the engine. "What's he want now?"

On the front porch, Reid Martin leaned against one of the posts. Wearing jeans, a sheepskin-lined coat, and a blue beanie hat, he looked lumberjack tough and cowboy rugged. To my eyes, he was a bright ray of sunshine on a shit-stormy day.

I smiled at the sight of him. "He wants the same as always, I'd guess—you."

"Yeah, well, he can keep on wanting."

I glanced over at her scowl. "I thought we'd talked about this earlier."

"*We* didn't. *You* did."

"Then why is he here?" I certainly hadn't rubbed a genie bottle today and made a wish.

"We're going to the Sugarloaf Building, remember?"

"Not until tonight."

She reached for the door handle. "Well, I might have texted him about bringing his son for supper, but he should have just texted me back with his reply."

My smile widened.

Before I could get a happy word in edgewise, she cut me off with, "Don't go making something out of nothing, Violet Lynn. Since he's helping us with the imp, I thought we should feed him first."

"Sure you did," I said, not believing for a moment that was the only reason he'd been invited to supper.

She aimed a hard squint at me.

I held up my hands in surrender. "Okay, okay. Let's go see why he's here so early."

She was out of my rig in a heartbeat, slamming the door hard enough to rock the SUV in her wake. For someone who was trying her damnedest to act like she didn't want Reid gracing her porch, she was certainly in a big hurry to talk to the hunky fire captain.

"What do you want, Martin?" she asked, loud enough for me to hear not only through my closed window, but the neighbors' windows, too.

Reid pushed away from the post, standing front and center at the top of the porch steps as she strode up the sidewalk. His smile was wide but visibly wary—the look of a wise man who'd ended up on the wrong side of her double-barreled shotgun before.

"Hey, Zo," I heard, but everything after that was too quiet. Unlike my aunt, Reid wasn't broadcasting his side of the conversation to the neighborhood.

I stayed put behind the wheel with my gaze averted, wondering if I should get out and join them or slink down in my seat and give them some privacy. Too many times I'd been stuck in the middle of their arguments, squirming in my boots while not sure where to look, wishing I could dig a hole in the dirt and bury my head in it until they'd finished.

Maybe I should pay Doc a visit. And if he was too busy prepping for his afternoon appointment, I could check in on Cornelius to see if Jane had been up to any more funny business this morning, or if the Hellhound clock had stopped spinning.

"Violet Lynn!"

At the sound of my name I looked over to see Aunt Zoe standing on the porch next to Reid, gesturing for me to join the two of them.

I grimaced and shook my head.

She nodded and waved me in with attitude this time.

On second thought, maybe I'd say "Hello" to Reid and then go inside and hide upstairs until he left.

I hopped out of my SUV and crunched my way along the salt-sprinkled sidewalk to the porch.

"Hi, Reid." My smile matched his in cheerfulness in spite of my urge to get the hell out of Dodge.

"Hey, Sparky," he said, and then shivered when a freezing gust blasted us. "You think I could come in for some warm coffee?" His gaze shifted back to Aunt Zoe. "Or something?"

It didn't take a monkey who could run in circles to read what that "or something" might be. I definitely should've stayed behind the wheel.

Aunt Zoe's eyes narrowed. "Or you could tell me why you're here now when my invite clearly included the word 'supper' in it."

I tentatively raised my hand, drawing their attention. "May I please be excused to go inside?"

Reid chuckled, nodding.

Aunt Zoe shook her head. "Not yet, Violet." She returned to Reid. "Spit it out, Martin. I need to get busy on an order."

An order, huh? She sure didn't seem to be in a hurry to get to work this morning when I was dragging my feet about going up to Prudence's lair.

His expression sobered.

Oh no, here it came. I cringed and stared at the top of my snow boots.

"It's about this evening," he said.

"Listen, Martin, I understand if you don't want to go inside that building with Coop and me after what you experienced with the *lidérc*. Seeing your father like that, rest his soul, had to be difficult."

"Oh, I'll be joining you in the Sugarloaf Building. And just so you know, seeing Dad was tough, but what you did was worse."

She jammed her hands on her hips. Two bright pink spots warmed her cheeks. "What *I* did? Violet is the one who used you as bait."

"Hey!" I nudged her with my elbow for throwing me under the bus. "I apologized for that."

"Yes, you did," Reid said to me. "And I accepted it because you were acting on instinct in the face of danger, and as a firefighter, I completely understand that." He focused on Aunt Zoe again. "But you knowingly knocked me out."

Her brow lined. "I was acting on instinct, too, and protecting your ass."

He pointed at her. "No, you were being hard-headed about accepting my help and rather than work with me, you removed me from the equation."

"He kind of has you there," I said to her.

She turned on me with her gunslinger squint.

I wrinkled my nose in return.

Reid hunched into his coat when another cold gust tried to knock us over. "That's not why I'm here, though, Zo."

"Why then?"

"It's about your invitation for me and Ox to come to supper."

"You don't have to come," she said quickly, looking away. "It was just an idea Violet had."

I gaped at her. What the ever-lovin' hell? Was I some kind of human shield this afternoon? It was not like Aunt Zoe to hide behind anyone, especially me. It had to be because of Reid. She could deny her feelings for him until she was blue in the face, but two things were crystal clear to me at this moment: the moon orbited the Earth and Aunt Zoe was still gaga for Reid.

"Violet, huh?" Reid grinned, giving me a wink. He wasn't buying her bag of baloney either. "That was some good thinking on Sparky's part."

"Yeah," I said with a shrug, taking the blame in stride. "I thought it would be nice to get to know your son a little more. You know, welcome him to the family."

Aunt Zoe growled at me.

"I mean, we would be welcoming Ox to the community family, you know," I said, gesturing wildly while wincing as I spoke. "Like all of Deadwood. And ... and Lead, too." Reid's grin widened at my fumbling, but I kept bumbling along anyway. "And our family would be enjoying his ... um... here-ness, bodily, of course, as well."

Dear Lord on a surfboard! Someone please cram a large potato in my mouth.

Aunt Zoe took mercy on me, giving me a side hug. "That's our Violet. Always so thoughtful of others. How is Ox doing?"

Reid's son was moving to Deadwood to be closer to his dad, which was making Reid much more chipper these days. Both men had made a career out of fighting fires, so they had more in common than just their DNA. After working on wildfires all around the country for several years, Ox was hoping to settle down now. At least that was what my little spies, aka nosy kids, had told me after they'd grilled Reid's son the last time he was in town and had been over for supper with Aunt Zoe. Doc and I had been in Spearfish the night of Ox's visit, hanging out with a banshee in a haunted jail that had been repurposed as an escape room. Cooper, Natalie, Cornelius, and Harvey had been locked up in the jail with us, so we'd all missed out on the meet and greet.

"Ox is good." Reid focused on me. "I'm sure he would have enjoyed being welcomed to the 'community' family if he weren't delayed back home."

"Oh, I'm sorry we won't get to see him." I really was. Aunt Zoe had seemed to like Reid's son out of the gate. I had a feeling he might be somehow beneficial to my matchmaking efforts. "He is still moving here, right?"

"Yeah, definitely. It's just there were some complications that needed to be dealt with first, so he's not going to be here for a bit longer." He turned to Aunt Zoe. "That's why I wanted to talk to you. I wasn't sure if the invitation stood for me alone."

She stood frozen, her forehead lined.

Apparently, she was hoping for Ox to be here tonight as a buffer. But maybe with only Reid present, the two of them might have an opportunity to work out their past issues a little more if given some time to talk alone.

"Of course the invitation stands," I said, breaking the silence. I didn't give Aunt Zoe the chance to get a word in, adding, "Natalie is cooking tonight, so I don't know what we're having, but beer is always a welcome addition at our table, right, Aunt Zoe?"

I nudged her.

"Uh, yes. You know we like beer."

His relief was plastered all over his face. "I'll bring something local. I've been holding onto it until the next poker night, anyway."

"Oh yeah, poker night. Crud." I dug in my purse for the house key, eager to make an escape while the going here was good. "I'm sorry we're screwing up your guys' fun with this trip up to Lead."

Wednesday nights were when Doc, Cooper, Reid, and Harvey (or whoever could make it if Harvey was too busy dancing the cabaret with one of his old flames) got together to play cards and talk about whatever guy stuff was on their minds, like tire sizes, demolition derbies, and the best-tasting whiskey. Oh, and anything having to do with firearms, thanks to Cooper's obsession with all things "gun."

"No worries, Sparky. According to Coop, the sooner you can get rid of this critter, the better. Besides, he's been playing even shittier than usual lately. I have a feeling catching this imp might be the cure to his inability to focus on his cards."

I had to wonder if Natalie and her complaining about being on a leash had anything to do with Cooper's focusing issues. But I kept that to myself.

"I'll see you at suppertime then, Reid." I slid the key in the lock. I was almost free!

"Violet," Aunt Zoe said as I opened the door.

"Sorry, I can't talk anymore." I turned back in the midst of a cringe. "I'm gonna go up to my room and meditate. I need to unblock my chakras and figure out what to do next about this whole mess with the imp." Not to mention the laundry list of other shudder-inspiring creatures Zelda had rattled off.

"Unblock your what?" Reid asked.

Aunt Zoe crossed her arms, her lips itching to grin. "What are you really planning to do?"

I might as well come clean. "I'm going to lock myself in my bedroom and read a hot and steamy romance novel."

Reid chuckled. "Enjoy some steam for me."

I gave him a thumbs-up. "You got it, hose jockey! Have fun, you two. Reid, have her home by midnight, or she'll turn back into a wolverine."

I closed the door on his laughter and blew out a breath of relief. Before Aunt Zoe opted to drag me back into the middle of their *tête-à-tête*, I kicked off my boots, raced up the stairs two at a time, and slid into my bedroom, closing the door behind me.

"Now, where did I leave that book?" I'd been reading it in bed the other night while waiting for Doc to get out of the shower, but it wasn't on my nightstand.

Bogart the cat looked up at me from the middle of the bed and meowed.

I glared back. "Bogart, you didn't bring any squeaky pals in here with you this time, did you?"

The cat looked away, bored with our conversation before I'd even started. Or maybe that was the feline version of pleading the Fifth.

"Fine, but if you're going to be in here, you have to act as my therapist. You owe me that for all the food and litter I buy each month."

She sighed and gave me two tail flicks.

I flopped down next to Bogart, who suffered my touch while I tried to use petting therapy to work through my Prudence-inspired anxieties. Cats were supposed to be like fluffy stress balls according to Addy, who continued to try to sell me on how great it was to have Bogart in our lives, even though I'd already consented to the fur ball sharing the house with us long ago.

It turned out Bogart didn't want to hear about my blocked chakras, though. She turned her back to me when my tone grew whiny, and then thumped her tail several times in annoyance when I socked my pillow in frustration. And when I started venting about that dang tarot deck, the big puss up and left the bed, meowing by the door until I opened it.

After the cat had gone, I covered my head with a pillow in an attempt to muffle the outside world and the mushroom cloud of troubles building on the horizon. That didn't work, so I moved to my closet.

My intention was to clear out some of my summer clothes and make more room for Doc's shirts, dress pants, and shoes, but then I realized that Elvis had escaped her cage and was currently sleeping on the monster-feet slippers the kids had bought me for Christmas a few years back. Not wanting to disturb her chicken dreams, I sat next to her, huddling under my shirts and dresses, contemplating what my life had become. But contemplation got me nowhere, so I opted to talk to the bird instead.

Elvis, bless her chicken heart, listened to my bemoaning without giving a single cluck. Of course, that was mostly because she was still sleeping. At some point, I must have fallen asleep, too, because I jerked awake later to find myself alone in the closet with nothing but a few stray feathers for company.

Deciding to skip out on the closet cleaning, I switched gears and moved to first Layne's room and then Addy's, where I picked up dirty clothes and books and various weapons strewn across their carpets. At least there was no fake blood this time.

While the gerbil's cage in Addy's room had been recently refreshed with clean wood shavings, The Duke was low on pellets and water. I refilled his bowl and bottle, bellying up to Addy's dresser to complain to him about the Hellhound clock. He wiggled his whiskers at me when I moved on to my woes with Timekeeping in general. But when I started in on my real estate job and all of the ghost-groupies I had to keep touring around town with no financial gain for my troubles, he hopped on his wheel and started running. I took the hint, wishing I could run from my calamities, too. Actually, I wasn't much into running unless there was an ice cream reward at the end.

I took The Duke's not-so-subtle hint and headed for the bathroom, which was in need of a serious scrubbing, thanks to the kids' inability to keep toothpaste in the sink. A glance at the shower in the bright light of day confirmed that before any further imp-hunting was going to be done, a total bathroom scouring would be necessary. As a bonus, I figured some solid strenuous work would make for good meditation and leave both my brain and the tub sparkling. I grabbed some rubber gloves from under the sink and got to work, wondering how Doc liked sharing a bathroom with two kids who didn't seem to mind if dental floss actually made it into the wastebasket. He hadn't returned to his own house yet, so I took that as a good sign and decided to keep bribing him to stay with sex.

Rooster showed up halfway through the Great Clean and plopped down on the bathmat to watch me de-stress. Like a good buddy, he whined along with me every now and then in support as I moaned and groaned about the cards I'd been dealt—both in life and from Cornelius's tarot deck.

I wasn't sure that I really meditated while I swabbed down the tile and porcelain, but I did do plenty of cussing under my breath about the imp and the *Duzarx* and Prudence and Dominick. While I was at it, I also cursed Detective Hawke for being a constant thorn in my side since the get-go, and Ms. Wolff for forcing me into a new role I didn't know squat about without asking me first.

All of that swearing and scouring made me hot and sweaty, and not in the good way the romance book therapy was supposed to have worked, so a nice long bath in the clean tub came up for debate. When asked for his opinion on the matter, Rooster barked in agreement with my decision to enjoy a nice long soak. Since he was so positive about my decision, I asked him which he thought would be more likely to clear my chakras, the strawberry- or coconut-scented bath bubbles. His attempt to eat the bottle of coconut-smelling bubbles made his answer crystal clear.

Aunt Zoe had left in the midst of my bathroom cleaning frenzy, hollering up the stairs that she needed to run to town. I didn't ask her how things went with Reid because I wasn't sure I wanted to hear anything negative. I was still in the midst of trying to find my happy place, which was why I called Doc on my cell phone as soon as I'd settled into the warm, bubble-covered water, putting him on speaker, and proceeded to fill his ear with all that had happened with Zelda and Prudence.

He agreed that it sounded like Prudence was able to use some form of remote viewing or clairvoyance whenever she wanted to see what Harvey did. He also laughed quite hard when I told him about Prudence witnessing the feather-boa dancing and bawdy "amorous congress" between Harvey and Junie.

I finished my long-winded tale with a sad ending: "I didn't get to enjoy my romance book because I needed to clean more than read." I blew a valley through the mountain of bubbles bobbing in front of my face. "But now that I have you on the phone, maybe we can act out one of the hot and steamy parts." I looked over at the dog, who was sprawled out on the bathmat, snoozing. "Rooster, cover your ears."

Doc chuckled. "I'd rather come home and practice the scene in person."

"But you can't."

"But I can't. At least not for a couple of hours. By then, your bath will be cold."

"I'll still need some warming up." I leaned closer to the phone and purred.

There was a pause on his end. "Are you gargling?"

"No. That was supposed to be a sex-kitten purr." I did it again.

Rooster looked up at me with wrinkled doggie eyebrows and barked.

"Was that a sex-puppy bark?" Doc asked, clearly laughing now.

I shushed him and the mutt.

"Do you want me to pick up the kids after school so you can read your book?"

"Aunt Zoe said she'd get them today." I scooped up a handful of bubbles and blew some toward Rooster, who looked unimpressed with them now that he'd tasted a few and found them gag worthy.

"How long until your afternoon appointment arrives?"

"About thirty minutes."

"Good. That's just enough time for me to tell you about what I'm wearing."

"I thought you were taking a bath."

"I'm talking about the bubbles and what they're covering."

"Hmm. I'm more interested in what they're not. Let me close my eyes first, Boots." I heard his chair squeak through the phone and pictured him leaning back. "Okay, ready. Start up top and don't leave out any details."

The phone down in the kitchen started ringing.

"The phone," I announced. Crap, I hadn't thought to bring it into the bathroom with me.

"The bubbles aren't covering your phone?" Doc asked. "That's not very sexy, Boots."

"No, I mean the phone downstairs is ringing."

Three rings in, it stopped.

"Never mind, whoever it was must have hung up." I double-checked my cell phone to make sure nobody had tried calling me while I'd been talking to Doc. Nope, nothing.

"Good," he said. "Now where were we? Oh yeah, you were going to tell me about the bubble-free landscape."

"Hills and dales as far as the eye can see." I smiled, imagining his hands exploring the countryside from my head to my toes. "Lucky for you, we are experiencing some bubble shrinkage and two peaks are now sticking up through the clouds."

"Trust me, Boots, I'm thinking about those two peaks and we definitely don't have shrinkage."

I giggled and slipped deeper into what was left of the bubbles, closing my eyes, sighing in contentment.

"Damn," he said, his voice husky. "Sigh like that again and tell me what you're doing with your hands."

I sighed, making sure not to purr this time, imagining he was doing the touching instead of me. "I'll start with caressing my—"

Creak.

My hand froze. I opened my eyes, peering out over the bubbles. That sounded like someone walking up the stairs.

Was Aunt Zoe home? If so, why hadn't she called my name like she usually did? I hadn't heard her truck pull in the drive or the front door opening, but then again I'd been giving Doc an earful about my adventures with Prudence for the last fifteen minutes.

"Caressing your what?" Doc asked again, his voice still deep and husky.

Rooster's ears perked up. He looked toward the closed door, letting out a slight whimper.

Creeeaak.

I heard it again. This time, I knew exactly what made that sound—a step midway up the stairs. Almost ten months of living in this house had taught me what creaked and where, both upstairs and down.

I sat upright and grabbed the phone, taking it off speaker. Rooster sat up, too. We both stared at the door, listening. Waiting. Was the dog's heart thwapping against his ribcage as hard as mine? Probably not. He was braver than me, especially in the dark.

"Boots, you're killing me here." Doc's voice came through the line, only tinnier and much lower in volume. "What are you caressing?"

I held the phone to my ear. "Doc," I whispered as quietly as I could. "Someone is here."

"Who?" he asked, seeming to miss the point. "And why are you whisper …" He paused. His chair squeaked. He cursed and then whispered in return, "Violet, who's there?"

"I don't know," I said under my breath. "But they're coming up the stairs."

CHAPTER FOURTEEN

J eepers creepers," I whispered to Doc. "Is it too much to ask for a little steamy bubble therapy and some hot phone sex?"

"Killer," Doc whispered back. "Get out of the tub now."

"Already in process." I sat up as silently as possible, trying not to make sloshing sounds in the water.

"Are you sensing anything not human?" he asked.

I took that to mean an *other* who might be hunting me for the bounty supposedly on my head.

"No. Not yet."

I had a few goosebumps, but not the spine-chilling kind. They were from sitting upright in a bath on a cold winter day in the upstairs bathroom of a house more than a century old. Besides, Aunt Zoe's protection wards were supposed to keep *others* out of the house, weren't they?

Another creak followed.

"That was the top step," I whispered to myself as much as Doc and slowly stood up in the tub.

Rooster began to growl quietly. He stood on all fours, his focus glued to the door.

"Jesus!" Doc's voice was thick with tension. "You need to get out of there."

"And go where? The only exit route is blocked."

Who was sneaking up the stairs?

Hadn't I locked the front door? I thought so, but maybe I'd left the back door unlocked when Rooster had come inside after going out to pee.

Maybe it was someone looking to grab a few valuables and run.

I looked around for something to swing at the intruder.

"You need to find a weapon." Doc was reading my mind.

"I know." Anything that I could hit hard with would do.

"And quick."

"I'm trying."

"Try faster."

A hairbrush lay on the counter. That would sting, but it was too small. The toilet cleaning brush would be gross, but too flimsy to do any damage. Maybe the towel bar? Although I'd have to pull it free of the wall first and probably make a lot of noise in the process. Damn it, I really wanted something heavier than that. I looked at the toilet, and then the lid on the back of the tank.

"That will do," I said. As quietly as possible, I stepped out of the bath onto the mat behind Rooster.

"What will do?" Doc sounded slightly winded. "Never mind. Violet, keep the door locked and hold on. I'm coming home."

I heard the hard scuff of a shoe heel across wood out in the hall, and then a slight groan from the floorboards. Those two loose boards were a few steps after my bedroom.

"There's no time, Doc. They're right outside the bathroom now."

I grabbed my robe from the hook. Rooster's left ear turned in my direction, but his attention remained on the target, his growl low and steady.

"I'm going to set you down, Doc. Try to be quiet."

"Christ!" I heard him say as I set the phone on the bathroom counter.

I slipped on the robe and belted it tight. Next came the porcelain tank cover off the back of the toilet. It *thunked* slightly as I lifted it. I winced. Water trailed down my legs and dripped onto the floor, making things slippery.

Meanwhile, no sound came from the other side of the door. I frowned at the wooden barrier between me and the creeper. Not a creak or a scuff or a …

Shit! The door was unlocked.

I tiptoed forward, avoiding the squeaky floorboards in front of the sink. Rooster moved along with me, his toenails clacking lightly on the floor.

When I was close enough to reach the light switch, I killed the lights and then took a step back.

Through the crack under the door, a shadow moved.

It was now or never. I raised the tank lid and took a steadying breath.

A white envelope slid under the door, coming to a stop in front of my bare toes.

Rooster and I both looked down at it.

Thanks to the dim afternoon light coming through the bathroom window, I could read my name scrawled on the front in cursive writing.

What the hell?

I lowered the tank lid to reach for the envelope, but then realized the intruder was still on the other side of the unlocked bathroom door. Maybe that envelope was just bait, sent through to distract me so I'd lower my guard and bend to pick it up. Then the intruder would have the jump on me.

That was a good try, but I was coming out swinging. I was going to belt whoever had interrupted my bath clear up to Mount Moriah cemetery.

I counted to three. Then I raised the toilet tank lid, yanked open the door, and roared my head off.

Cornelius stood in the hallway with his hand raised to knock. Below his furry Russian Cossack hat, his cornflower blue eyes widened at the sight—and sound—of me. He bawled back like a startled cow, ducking slightly.

Rooster barked twice and flew past me.

"Rooster, no!" I shouted … too late.

The dog hit Cornelius at chest level, doing the work of the tank lid for me.

Cornelius stumbled backward with the dog clinging to his wool coat and crashed into the small library table across the hall. His hat went flying, along with two of the picture frames sitting on the table. Both frames hit the floor with the telltale *crash* of broken glass. Cornelius slid to the floor after them, taking the dog, who was too busy licking our visitor to death to notice the mess he'd caused, down with him.

"Holy hell," I said when the dust settled and all was silent except for Rooster's thumping tail.

I leaned the tank lid against the bathroom door jamb, grabbed my slip-ons, and tiptoed over to pick up the photo frames. Luckily, the glass hadn't shattered, only cracked inside the frames. I set both facedown on the table and frowned at my intruder.

It appeared that Rooster remembered the liver-flavored treats Cornelius had brought him last night and was checking his benefactor's face and neck for more. Or maybe Cornelius was wearing liver-flavored aftershave. Either was a perfectly viable possibility.

"You scared the shit out of me." I shooed Rooster away and held out my hand to help Cornelius stand. "What are you doing here?"

For a tall, stick-like insect, he was as heavy as a ship's anchor. "I need to borrow your hag stone."

"You could have called. I'd have brought it to you after I finished my bath and saved you the trip."

Was he the one who'd called the land line and hung up after three rings? No, he would have been inside the house by that point.

"Calling is passé." Cornelius tried to brush the dog hair and drool off his coat, but soon gave up. "I tried to reach you via telepathy, but you didn't reply."

His faith in my supernatural abilities was irrational at best. "My telepathic lines are down." I thumbed back toward the bathroom. "What was with sliding your envelope under the bathroom door?"

"That's not my envelope. I found it inside your front door below the mail slot." He looked over my shoulder toward the bathroom doorway, his brow furrowed. "Violet, don't you think it would be wise to secure your doors when you're home alone taking a bath?"

I thought I had. "Because of the bounty hunters?"

"Because of sprites."

"You mean the reddish flashes of light that shoot upward way up in the clouds during lightning storms?" Layne had watched an interesting documentary on sprites last year during his weather-bug phase.

"Of course not," he said, as if I were nuts to think that. "I'm talking about the fairy-like, mythical creatures who hang out near water and love to play tricks on humans."

"Oh, those sprites. Right. What was I thinking, taking a hot bath in the middle of an icy winter's day?"

He gasped. "Were you steam cleaning your chakras?"

"Yeah, something like that."

"Brilliant!" He leaned closer, sniffing around me until I swatted him away. "I certainly hope you weren't using coconut for the cleansing."

"What's wrong with coconut?"

"Of all the silly questions." He laughed loudly.

I contemplated batting him with the tank lid after all.

"Violet!" came a faint voice from the bathroom.

"Do you hear that?" Cornelius leaned to the side, looking up and down the hall. "It appears there is a sprite already here calling for you." He focused on the bathroom doorway again. "You weren't steam cleaning your chakras in front of a mirror, were you?"

"Why? Would that be a problem, too?"

He snorted. "Only if you're looking to provoke your inner evil eye."

Oh, boy.

"Violet!"

We heard the tinny voice again.

"That's Doc," I told Cornelius. I held up my index finger. "You wait here. I need to go handle that and get dressed."

A string of curses rattled through my phone as I lifted it to my ear. "It's Cornelius," I said, interrupting Doc's tirade. I closed the door and locked it this time.

Doc groaned. "Woman, you're going to give me a heart attack one of these days."

"In or out of the sack?" I joked as I shucked the robe and stepped into my underwear.

"Both." He blew out a breath.

"Look on the bright side." I put him on speaker so I could pull my camisole over my head. "I keep our love life exciting."

"You certainly do." He sniffed. "Are you okay?"

"I think so." I looked in the mirror at my cheeks. They were still flushed from the warm bath, which made the scratches and bruises a little less noticeable. "Yeah, I'm good. Although my evil eye might be pissed at me."

"What?"

"Never mind."

"Is Cornelius okay?"

"Well, he almost got creamed upside the head by a toilet tank lid, but instead got tackled by a dog."

"Was that the crash I heard?"

"Yep. The two of them hit the table out in the hall and knocked off a couple of picture frames." I yanked up my yoga pants. "But he's back topside again in spite of Rooster's attempts to slobber him to death."

"Good. Violet, please promise me you won't take any more baths without locking the doors first."

I tugged my shirt over my head. "But then how will you sneak in and splash around in the water with me?"

"I'll figure out a way." He was quiet for a moment. "I love you, Killer."

"That's music to my ears." The swooning kind.

"I need to go. It's going to take me a minute to level out my pulse and get my head back into numbers-land."

"Okay." I smiled at my reflection as I pulled out the hairclip I'd used to keep my curls out of the water. "Hey, Doc?"

"Yeah?"

"Smell you later, sexy boy."

He groaned and hung up.

Back out in the hall, Cornelius was sitting on the top stair step next to Rooster. They both looked over their shoulders as I came up behind them.

"I'll get you the hag stone."

I detoured into my room and fished in my underwear drawer where I'd stuck the hag stone yesterday so my kids wouldn't find it and think it was a cool toy necklace. But the stone wasn't there. Then I remembered that Aunt Zoe had been looking at the stone pendant earlier. She'd probably left it in her bedroom.

"Stay," I told the two of them as I paused behind them on the way to her room. "I'll be right back."

Cornelius looked at Rooster. "I believe she has mistaken me for a fellow canine."

Rooster barked and tried to lick Cornelius's ear.

I left the licker and the licked, heading down the hall. On the way to Aunt Zoe's room, I made a side trip to the bathroom and grabbed the envelope off the counter where I'd left it after hanging up from Doc's call.

I flipped it to the front. There was no stamp, so it hadn't come via the mailman. Someone must have dropped it off after Aunt Zoe left. Or maybe she'd seen it on the porch on her way out and stuck it through the mail slot rather than bother with unlocking the door.

Her bedroom smelled like a blend of honeysuckle and her exotic fruity perfume. I shooed Bogart off her goosedown comforter, earning an annoyed meow in return.

"Yeah, well that's what you get for not wanting to listen to my problems," I said as the cat strolled out into the hall.

The hag stone pendant was sitting next to her journal on the dresser. She must have been making some notes in it. I didn't bother taking a peek at her journal because I was living the real deal about which she was writing, and I knew she'd tell me if there was something important she'd discovered.

After closing the bedroom door behind me to keep Bogart out, I returned to Cornelius, handing him the stone.

"Why do you need that?" I asked, nodding at the hag stone as I tore open a corner of the envelope.

"I've been thinking about the Hellhole," he started to explain, but then paused, his head crooked to the side. "Which reminds me of something else."

"What's that?"

"You had a phone call."

I ripped open the envelope the rest of the way. "Did my cell phone ring?" I hadn't heard it.

"No." He took the envelope from me and lifted the hag stone, staring at the letters of my name through the stone's hole. "The phone on the wall in the kitchen did."

That was right. I'd heard it before the stairs had creaked. "You answered that call?"

I watched him inspect the envelope, wondering what he thought he could see through that hole. It wasn't a magic magnifying glass, for crissake. Then again, maybe it was. What did I know?

"Of course I did. A ringing phone requires answering. It's common protocol. Surely you know that by your advanced age." He flipped the envelope over, examining the backside.

I let the age crack slide by for now. "Yeah, but I don't answer strange phones."

He looked up at me with one raised eyebrow. "That explains so much."

"Oh, here we go." I snatched the envelope back. "Explains what?"

"Karmic will."

"What about it?"

I started down the stairs with him following, pausing to gingerly pick up one of Rooster's tennis balls, which was resting in the corner of a step. What had I told the kids about leaving dog toys out?

"Past actions affect the present. You will reap what you have sown."

I glanced back at him as I reached the bottom of the stairs. "All because I don't answer strange phones?"

He shrugged, pausing on the final step. "It all starts with the pea, princess. The shapes of the mattresses above are then altered."

I decided to skip veering off onto that sidetrack and returned to the phone call. "Who was on the phone?"

"I didn't ask."

Rooster bounded down the stairs, snatched the ball from my fingers, and raced into the kitchen.

I trailed after the dog, asking over my shoulder, "So, you answered the phone and heard my name and then put the phone down to come get me?"

Had someone besides Doc been listening to the commotion upstairs all of this time? Although the yells and crashes would have sounded much fainter from down here.

"No." Cornelius followed Rooster and me. "I answered the phone, listened to the request to talk to you, and then hung up."

I stopped and turned. "You hung up?"

"Of course."

"Why? I thought it was protocol to answer."

"I had obeyed protocol. But the call was not for me."

"Well, of course it wasn't." He'd answered but then hung up? Not for the first time I had to wonder what corner of our solar system Cornelius hailed from. "So, you didn't find out who was calling?"

He looked at me as if I were the one filled with nuts and nougat. "It was not my business."

I shook my head. "You could have at least gotten the name of the caller, and maybe even why they were calling."

"I didn't need to ask the name."

"Don't tell me you have the psychic ability to know who is calling on a phone."

"Of course not. My telepathic range is more limited than that, as you proved earlier when I tried to reach out to you via my mind and received dead air in return."

I started to cross my arms, but then remembered the envelope in my hand. I pulled out the paper inside while asking, "Then how do you know who called?"

"Because the caller announced his name."

"What do you mean?" I started to unfold the paper. "Announced how?"

Cornelius took the folded note from me before I could read it, wadded it up, and threw it across the kitchen. Before I could do more than sputter, Rooster raced over and scooped it up, speeding off with it toward the dining room.

I gaped after the dog. "What did you do that for?"

"Focus, Violet." Cornelius turned my chin back toward him. "The caller said, 'This is Detective Hawke of the Deadwood Police Department. I need to speak with Violet Parker.' At that point, I realized the call was not meant for me, so I hung up."

A laugh escaped before I could stop it. Then a couple more, which I let fly because Hawke was apparently after me again for some crime he hoped to pin on me in order to win a Detective of the Year award.

"You hung up on Detective Hawke?" I asked when I corralled my laughter.

"It would seem so." He lifted the hag stone and peered at me through it, a grin tilting the corners of his mouth. "Next time he should be less definitive in his request for an answerer."

Cornelius knew of my past battles with Detective Hawke. I had no doubt he'd hung up on Hawke with that same grin before coming upstairs to scare the dickens out of me.

"Thanks." I pretended to poke him in the eye through the hag stone's center hole. "You never did say why you need this stone."

"I think we might be able to see what is bothering your previous boss's ghost."

"You mean by watching that video recording of Jane through the stone's hole?"

He lowered the pendant. His bright blue eyes were suddenly

dead serious. "I mean by looking through it while down in the basement of the courthouse where you previously accessed the Hellhole tunnel."

"No." I wasn't going near that damned hole again.

"I believe this hag stone might help us channel from there, since the other way to the Hellhole is blocked. This might allow us to speak with whatever it was that Jane battled in her office."

"Oh, hell no."

He pocketed the hag stone, his mouth a straight line. "I need you to come with me, Violet, because I'm going to figure out what was happening in that office yesterday, and I might run into something that needs killing while I'm down there."

* * *

Later that evening, I was freezing my ass off on a dark side street in Lead.

Doc and I were on watch duty, sitting together in the cab of the Picklemobile, Harvey's old Ford that Doc was driving while his muscled-up 1969 Camaro hibernated in his garage. We were parked a hop, skip, and a vroom away from the Sugarloaf Building with the engine off, blending in with the scenery while we waited to hear from Cooper on the two-way radio sitting on the dashboard.

Scooting to the middle of the bench seat, I snuggled into Doc's side to share body heat and stared through the windshield at the Milky Way. This was the closest thing we'd had to a date night in weeks.

I tried to pretend we were out soaking up some star gazing instead of doing reconnaissance on a sharp-toothed little bastard that might be able to zap me with dark magic. Seriously, though, the sorcery notion seemed too farfetched, but maybe the imp could tell my possible future with better results than Cornelius's dang tarot cards.

Natalie was back at my aunt's place listening in on another walkie-talkie while keeping an eye on my kids. She was waiting along with us to hear if Aunt Zoe, Reid, and Cooper found any sigils located near the antiquated stove where the imp had been caged for years.

Harvey had pocketed his walkie-talkie and headed off to Junie's place after the supper dishes were cleaned up. But he'd been uneasy about tonight's date. Before leaving, he'd asked Doc and Cooper to look into his eyes and check for any sign of Prudence. It would have been funny if it weren't a distinct possibility. I'd be sweating bullets, too, if Prudence could hop into my head at will.

Doc turned the key enough for the dash lights to come on. They added a soft radiance to his profile. He smelled tasty good, like a blend of cinnamon and citrus. Call me kooky, but I found the whole stakeout downright romantic. I thought about licking his neck, taking a card from Rooster's deck, but I checked out the dials and gauges on the dash instead.

"I can't believe this is the same truck that I drove last fall," I said.

The pickup was like a whole new rig now, thanks to Doc tuning up the engine so it didn't burp, stutter, or fart when it started up, idled, or shut down. He'd also cleaned the old girl inside and out, put on some faux fur seat covers that were nice and warm beneath my yoga pants, and installed a new stereo that was surrounded by a blue glow.

"The old truck has good bones," Doc said, his breath steaming in the cold air.

I nestled deeper into his side, pulling his arm around me so we could lace our cold fingers. I looked up at him and wiggled my eyebrows. "You want to finish what we started earlier on the phone?"

I could feel his chuckle as well as hear it. "No way, Boots. It's too damned cold."

"Party pooper."

He kissed my temple. "You never did tell me what was in the envelope that Cornelius slid under the bathroom door."

"A note," I said, cupping my hands over my nose and mouth and blowing out to warm up my face.

"What did it say?"

"I don't know."

"You didn't read it?"

"Rooster ate it before I could get it out of his mouth."

"Shit."

I didn't bother placing the blame on Cornelius for wadding it up and throwing it in the first place. He didn't know Addy had been training Rooster to play fetch with tennis balls. Hell, I think Rooster had been as surprised as we were that he ate the note, judging by the way he kept walking around sniffing the carpet after he'd swallowed it.

"Did you see who it was from?"

"Nope. But I did find out that Aunt Zoe wasn't the one who'd slipped it through the mail slot, so she knows nothing about it."

"In other words, short of going around to all of the neighbors to see if anyone saw who'd dropped it off, you won't know what the note said until someone comes to you about it."

"*Exactamente.*"

"Maybe we need to invest in a door camera."

"That's what Cooper said."

"You sound like you're not onboard."

"I don't know. I guess I'm old-fashioned. Seems like there are too many cameras in the world already. And what happens if it captures something that we don't want on record and Detective Hawke gets his hands on it?"

"That's a valid point," he said. "I wonder what Hawke wanted on the phone."

I'd told Doc about the phone call earlier that Cornelius had answered. He'd laughed, same as I had.

"I'm sure we'll find out soon enough." I shivered, pulling my coat tighter around my neck. "I wish we were home in bed."

Doc cuddled me closer. "Cornelius said you're letting him hold onto the hag stone but made him pinky swear he wouldn't go into that hole in the wall under the courthouse."

"If he'd witnessed what I had down there, he'd run all the way back to Vegas."

"Maybe not," Doc said. "Judging from what I saw with Prudence's help behind that locked door in his mind, Cornelius has experienced some hair-raising nightmares."

"Did I tell you Prudence wants me to execute him?"

"No way."

"Yeah. And if I won't do it, she said she'd have Zelda commit the deed. She doesn't trust him now that she knows he's a spirit miser."

"Jesus."

"I refused and told her I needed him. She thinks I'm making a mistake letting him live."

"She must have been a real terror when she was alive."

I shifted slightly to ease a growing ache in my hip. "You think they're okay up there?" I looked out toward the dark Sugarloaf Building. "I can't even see flashlights. We should have had them take Cornelius's video camera along."

"Coop said he'd be on the horn if anything went sideways, so you could race up there and start walloping things."

"I'd start with him," I joked, and then remembered something else I meant to tell Doc and had forgotten about because the kids had come home excited about an assembly they'd had at school starring a dog trainer and his acrobatic dogs. Poor Rooster was in for it now.

"Speaking of cameras," I said, staring up at the Big Dipper in the sky. "Cornelius called later this afternoon with the idea of installing a camera in the courthouse basement that monitored the hole in the wall. Then he could try looking through the hag stone at his monitor and would be upholding his end of the pinky promise without losing a finger."

"How would he get it down there and set up without anyone seeing him or noticing his video camera? Courthouses tend to have guards roaming, watching for trouble, as well as their own cameras everywhere."

"I asked him something similar during the call. He answered that he'd wear an invisibility coat." When Doc chuckled, I added, "Yeah, that was my response, too, only I started with a snort of disbelief."

"What about his camera?"

"He'll hide it between some boxes. Nobody will even know it's there, according to him."

"Really?"

"He assured me he's done undercover work before."

"Okay then."

Doc reached under the seat and pulled out a small zippered duffle bag. Inside was a fleece blanket. He unfolded it and wrapped it around me, using it to tug me nearer and warm both of us. I pulled up my legs, turning myself into an egg, and squeezed even tighter against him.

"How's this for undercover work?" he asked, sliding his hand between my knees under the blanket. "Now all we're missing is a cozy fire and s'more makings."

"Here's s'more good stuff." I slid his hand a little farther north up my thigh where he was making things even warmer.

"Boots, are you getting fresh with me?"

"I'm trying to, but you keep whining about the cold."

He laughed. "A man has his limitations."

"For a guy who grew up in Colorado, I'm surprised you don't run around half-naked in the winter."

"For a girl who grew up in South Dakota, I'm surprised your fingers and toes get so damned cold. It's almost like you're part reptile."

"Did my wild Medusa hair give me away?" I hissed up at him like one of her snakes.

He leaned down and kissed me, cutting my hiss short. "No insulting one of my favorite things about you."

I smiled after he pulled away. "What else is a favorite?"

"Your lips. Always."

"You mean these?" I sucked in my cheeks and made fish lips at him.

"Yeah, those, my sexy guppy." He swooped back in for a second kiss.

What started as flirty fun flared into a heated exchange that had me reaching around his neck and pulling him even closer, taking my time kissing him back. His lips were warm and willing, and he tasted like a good time in the making.

He groaned deep in his chest. His hand inched further north, starting something that I really wanted him to finish. "I also love your fondness for yoga pants," he said as his mouth left mine and trailed down my neck.

"You sure you don't want to fool around?" I stared up at the stars through the windshield. His lips melted away my inhibitions.

"We're supposed to be on alert."

"We could make it quick. I'll crawl on your lap. A little wham-bam-thank-you-ma'am and we're back to waiting for Cooper's all-clear."

"You're such an old romantic, Boots."

I shrugged. "Hey, a girl's gotta do when a girl's gotta screw."

He chuckled. "So poetic, too. What's next, a sonnet?"

"Natalie saw that line written in lipstick on a mirror years ago."

"Let me guess—a truck stop bathroom?"

I shook my head "A club down in Rapid. What do you say, Romeo? You up for a little hanky-spanky?"

"Hmm." His warm hand slid inside my coat, reaching under my sweatshirt and camisole, finding bare skin. His fingers trailed up my ribs, his thumb circling in on the target. "Camisoles are another favorite of mine."

"Really? I'll have to buy you one. Do you prefer cotton or silk?" I reached for him under the blanket, happy to feel that he was as ready to play around as I was. "How about if I show you one of my fav …"

A *thump* came from the passenger side door.

Doc and I both froze.

"Did you hear that?" I whispered.

"Yeah. Why are you whispering?"

"I don't know. It just seemed …"

Thump!

This time it was louder.

He pulled his hands free as I sat upright.

"What the hell is that?" I asked, readjusting my clothes.

"It sounds like something keeps hitting the door."

I scooted over toward the passenger window, peering out at the dark hillside next to us.

A snowball slammed into the glass. I yipped and pushed back into Doc, who had slid over behind me. He caught me by the shoulders, holding me steady.

"Who threw that?" he asked, looking over my shoulder into the darkness.

"Hand me the flashlight." I leaned forward again, trying to see who was using us for target practice. I shined the beam of light out across the bank of plowed snow and the pine trees beyond it. "I can't see any—"

The imp popped out from behind a tree to my right, its red eyes glowing in the spotlight.

"Holy crap!"

As I gaped at it, the little sucker threw a snowball. This one slammed into the glass with a definite *clink* along with the *thump*. That one must have had a rock in it.

I winced. "That son of a bitch is gonna break the glass!"

"Violet, who is it?"

Before I could answer, another snowball with rocks in it hit the side mirror hard, leaving a big crack behind.

"That's it!" I opened the door and scrambled out.

My boots hit the icy road and slid out from under me. Before I could catch myself, I fell flat on my back. Talk about wham-bam. That was going to leave a mark.

I groaned. "Stupid Tower card and its peril prediction!"

A snowball whizzed over me, hitting the side of the Picklemobile where my head had been a moment before. Snow rained down on me along with some grit. A piece of gravel bounced off my chin.

I struggled upright in time to see the imp take off running down the street. "I see you!" I called after it in the dark, almost falling on my ass again as my boots slipped on the same patch of ice. I grabbed the pickup door, holding myself up. "You're not going to get away this time!"

"Are you okay?" Doc hurried up behind me, brushing off my backside. "Did you hit your head when you fell?"

"I'm fine." I pointed at the pickup. "Get in the passenger seat." I slid my way around to the driver's side and hopped in behind the steering wheel, slamming the door shut. "It's the imp," I told him while scooting the seat forward with his help.

"What?! The imp was throwing snowballs at us?"

"Yeah. Crazy, right? Welcome to my world."

"What are the chances of it being here right now?"

"Apparently very good." I pointed out the windshield. "I see it up there under the streetlight." In fact, the asshole was dancing in a circle with a couple of short ropes in its hands. What the planets? Was it drunk on mead?

Doc squinted through the windshield. "Where?"

"Trust me, he's right there." I turned the key, cranking up the Picklemobile. "Let's go catch that little fucker."

CHAPTER FIFTEEN

T
here he is!" I yelled, slamming on the brakes and taking a hard left.

"I'll take your word for it." Doc gripped the dash as the back tires skidded around the corner on loose gravel and slick slush. He caught the two-way radio as it tumbled along the dash toward his side. "Watch out for that trailer!"

I was so busy keeping my eye on the imp, I almost sideswiped a small utility trailer piled high with firewood. "That thing needs reflectors," I muttered as I corrected and hit the gas.

"It has them."

"Oh. My bad then. They shouldn't park so close to the damned street."

"Maybe I should be driving," Doc said.

I squinted into the darkness, looking for signs of the imp. "Damn it, where'd he go?"

The walkie-talkie made a crackling sound. "Nyce, come in," Cooper's voice rang out. "Over."

I caught sight of movement ahead on my right and pointed it out. "He just went around that two-story house."

Actually, it looked more like an early twentieth-century duplex as we drew closer. A bit long in the tooth with a sagging porch roof and boarded-up windows, but with plenty of potential given some cash, a lot of elbow grease, and … What was I doing? Now was not the time to be thinking about real estate. Where'd that damned imp go?

Doc lifted the radio. "Nyce here. Over."

I eased past the duplex, looking for any sign of the pipsqueak.

"We need some help here," Cooper said. "Over."

Doc gripped the dash to keep from tipping into me as I took a sharp right down a street that ran along the other side of the duplex. "Is everyone okay there?" he asked into the radio. "Over."

"We're fine, but we have a vehicle issue. Over."

"There!" I spotted the imp. It was climbing up a partially broken trellis toward the second story. The window above was boarded over, so I didn't know where it thought it was going. "It's heading up the side of the house."

"What kind of issue?" Doc asked into the radio while peering out the windshield at the duplex's second story, forgetting to say "over." He glanced at me. "Is it still up there?"

"No. It pulled itself up onto the roof. That thing could definitely be in the circus." I slowed to a stop in front of what looked like red and black snakes in the road.

"Reid's rig won't start," Cooper explained. "You have tow straps with you? Over."

Of course they weren't snakes. Not in the dead of winter. Nor were they the ropes I'd thought the imp was holding after the snowball attack. Whatever they were, the little shit must have dropped them before scaling the side of the duplex.

"Yeah," Doc said into the walkie-talkie. "Is it a battery issue? Over."

"Not in the usual sense," Cooper said. "Let's just chalk it up to vandalism and theft. Over."

I frowned at Doc. Who would be out messing with vehicles on a night like this? It was too damned cold.

He held the walkie-talkie to his mouth. "What in the hell was stolen?"

"Cables and hoses for starters. Trust me, Nyce, you're going to want to see this for yourself. Over."

"We'll be there shortly." He started to lower the walkie-talkie, but then added a final "Over."

"Cables, huh?" I said, pointing out the windshield.

"Yep." He reached for the door handle. "I'll be right back." He climbed out into the wind, grabbed the cables, and was back inside in a flash, bringing the smell of cold fresh air with him.

"Battery cables," he confirmed, dropping them between us. "Do you see the imp?"

I shook my head. "I could hop out and go search for it while you head over and help with Reid's rig."

"Not an option, Killer. We'll have to hunt the imp together another day. Those guys don't need to be stuck out in this cold for too long."

He was right. The imp could wait. The humans, not so much.

I started the truck rolling and made a right at the end of the block, heading back toward the Sugarloaf Building.

When we got there, Aunt Zoe and Reid were sitting inside the truck while Cooper leaned against the front quarter panel, staring toward the century-old rundown building. He shielded his eyes as I pulled up in front of Reid's rig.

Doc let out a low whistle at the sight of the hood. "Holy shit," he said, shaking his head. "That imp peeled up the hood like it was opening a can of sardines. How in the hell can it have that kind of strength?"

I couldn't believe my eyes. Prudence had talked about the thing ripping and chewing through a wire cage, but bending back a metal pickup hood? Criminy!

"How is Reid going to explain this to his insurance agent?" When Doc gave me a smirk, I added, "What? I don't think they're going to accept an invisible imp as the cause."

"Probably not. We'll need to rip the whole thing off and hope that fits under the vandalism category."

"If Detective Hawke catches wind of this and where it happened, he's going to come for me again, only with handcuffs this time."

"Don't worry about Hawke. Coop will keep this off the record. Your focus needs to be on the imp first and foremost." He opened his door and joined Cooper, forgetting to grab the battery cables in his haste to see the damage. "Let me see your flashlight," I heard him say before he reached back and shut the passenger door.

I set the parking brake, leaving the engine running, and gingerly stepped out of the Picklemobile. I wasn't going to fall on my ass again. One butt bruise a night was plenty for me.

By the time I made it safely to Reid's truck, Doc was leaning over the part of the engine exposed to the elements, shining a flashlight around inside.

I handed off the cables to Cooper. "Here's some evidence the imp left a few blocks away."

"Fuck," he muttered, pulling out his cell phone. "I need to call Nat and give her the lowdown on the situation before she drags your kids up here with her to rescue us."

"Awww, she loves us," I said in baby talk. "She really, really loves us."

He grimaced. "Hey, Nyce. I don't think your girlfriend's brain cells are holding hands right now."

Doc wisely remained silent.

I wrinkled my nose at Cooper, returning to my normal voice. "I don't know if she loves *you*, though. You're very prickly to the touch and leave aggravating barbs under the skin after you leave."

"Are you done, Parker? Where's your off button?"

"I won't be done until you give me a big bear hug and tell me how much you miss watching old westerns with me in the middle of the night."

"Are you drunk?"

"On adrenaline. Now call my best buddy and stop bugging me." I turned away from him and shouldered up next to Doc. "How bad is it?" I asked, peeking into the engine compartment. I wasn't sure what I was looking for, but from what I could see, there looked to be a definite lack of the hoses and wires and belts I was used to seeing.

"It's fixable," Doc said, moving the flashlight around. "But not right now. We'll have to tow it to Deadwood." He leaned back and touched the peeled-up metal. "This, however, is not reparable." Doc aimed the light at the left corner of the grill. "It tore a hole clear into the radiator."

I looked closer. "Wow. That bastard has to go."

He moved the beam of light around some more, looking in the nooks and crannies. "What a mess."

Cooper was back a minute later. "Shine the light over there, Nyce." Cooper pointed toward the snow along the side of the pickup.

Doc did as told, lighting up tracks in the snow.

"This asshole might be invisible to all but Parker, but we could be able to track it in the daylight if the wind doesn't cover its prints overnight."

"We'll come back in the morning then."

Cooper turned to me. "You have an eight o'clock appointment tomorrow."

"No, I don't." And how would he know my schedule?

"Yes, you do. Tell your boss your client wants you to show him some houses in Lead."

Ohhh, now I got it. "By the way, Cooper, are you interested in buying an old building to live in?" I'd forgotten to ask that on Ben's behalf until now thanks to the whirlwind that was my personal life.

"Depends on the building and what shape it's in."

"What did you think of that listing in Central City that I sent you the other day?"

"No."

That was it? No questions or explanations? "Hey, thanks for thinking about it, though." It was a nice place at a good price with plenty of garage space for his Harley. I frowned at him. "Why not?"

He spared me a glance. "It's too close to the creek."

"You could fish from your backyard."

"Or from inside my living room when the water is running high. No thanks. Keep looking, Parker."

Dang persnickety … "Will do, Goldilocks," I muttered.

Doc chuckled.

The driver's side door opened and closed. Reid stepped up next to me.

"How do you like my rig's new look?" he asked.

Doc shined the flashlight over the hood again and shook his head. "Unbelievable." He turned to me. "Think of what it could've done to your face if it'd wanted to, Killer."

I cringed. Maybe I was luckier than I figured in spite of what Cornelius's tarot cards kept telling me. "I'm going to wear a welding mask when I try to catch it next time."

Doc put his arm around my shoulders. "When *we* try to catch it." He kissed my temple with cold lips.

Aunt Zoe got out and came around to the front of the battered truck.

"I'm sorry about this," I said to Reid.

"It's not your fault, Sparky. Cooper is the one who let it out of that old stove in the first place."

"Hey!" Cooper growled. "I told you that in confidence." He pointed at me. "I let it out of the cage, but Parker batted it out the window."

Reid shook his head as he looked at the imp's handiwork. "I've seen some things in my life, but nothing like this. Hey, Zo, how big did you say this imp is?"

"About the size of a beagle. Maybe a little bigger." She shivered and looked my way. "Is that about right, baby girl?"

I nodded. "Give or take an inch." I thumbed toward the Picklemobile. "You want to go warm up in there?"

"Good idea."

As she passed me, I grabbed her arm. "Did you find any sigils?"

She nodded. "There was one inside the stove that matched those the imp has been leaving around town. Then there was a different symbol carved into the metal on the outside of the stove. I suspect that was used to keep it trapped in its prison. Another smaller sigil, different from the others, was carved into the wall down near the floor. I'm wondering if that was a final checkpoint in case the imp made it that far from its cage."

Yet somehow the imp was able to pass all of those sigils while riding on Cooper's shoulder. How did that work?

Another thought came to mind. "Or maybe that sigil near the floor was used to contain something else that Dominick is keeping caged in the building."

"There's a thought. Or it was a deterrent for the *lidérc* so that it couldn't enter the kitchen for some reason."

A gust blasted us, trying to flash freeze my nose.

"Good gravy!" Aunt Zoe said from behind her cashmere scarf. "It's colder out here than a cast iron toilet on the north side of an iceberg. I'm going to go thaw out."

Doc was pulling out the tow rope from behind the front seat when she approached. He held the door wide and then closed it behind her before returning to my side. "You want to take your icy toes and wait in there with Zoe while we tie off the tow strap?"

I shook my head, pointing toward the building. "Mind if I borrow the flashlight to go look around the backside of the place?"

He handed it off. "Don't wander too far alone. I know you're a big bad *Scharfrichter*, but you're my favorite killer, and I don't want you to get hurt any more than you already have been by that imp."

I tried not to look too much like a lovesick puppy when I smiled up at him. "You think it will come back here tonight?"

"I have no idea, but the way it showed up while we were here and whipped those snowballs at the side of the truck makes me wonder if Prudence was predicting the future—it's hunting you now."

I nodded, staring in the direction I'd last seen it. "I'll stay close."

"Okay. We won't be long."

Reid helped Doc and Cooper hook up the tow strap while I scouted around the Sugarloaf Building, wondering if there were any other so-called pets Dominick kept stowed away in the place. I had explored both floors in the past, but there might be a basement or crawlspace down below. Maybe even some sort of attic, too.

Around the back of the building I found a grated window at ground level that was mostly covered by a snowdrift. I kicked some of the snow away from the grate, but the flashlight wouldn't pierce the darkness. Either there was something blocking it, or the window had been painted over to keep a nosy nellie like me from seeing inside.

I stood back and stared up at the big old building. How could we access this lower level? I hadn't seen any stairs going down when we were in there last. Maybe Reid would know since he had done fire safety inspections here for years.

"Violet," Reid called.

Huh, speaking of fire captains. I returned to the front of the building. Aunt Zoe was sitting back in Reid's truck now.

"Doc's going to tow us while I drive. Zo is riding with me. Coop is joining you two."

I raised my brows. "Aunt Zoe is willingly riding alone with you?"

"I think she feels guilty about what happened to my rig," he explained in a lower voice.

"Gotcha. I assume you're playing that for all it's worth."

"Every damned penny."

I regarded the front of his pickup. "I really am sorry about your rig, Reid."

He shrugged. "It's not your doing. I'm the one who insisted on joining Zo and Coop tonight. Besides, when it's all said and done, maybe Zo will give me a kiss to make me feel better."

That made me laugh out loud.

"Parker!" Cooper barked. He was holding the Picklemobile's passenger door open for me. "Let's hit the road."

Doc was already settled behind the steering wheel when I slid inside and snapped on the middle seatbelt. "Long time no see, Gomez."

"Too long, *querida*," he replied in his Gomez Addams accent. "How long has it been since we last waltzed through the graveyard?"

Cooper slammed the door. "None of that French-smoochie shit, you two." He looked out the passenger side window and did a double take. "How long has this mirror been cracked?"

"Since tonight," Doc said.

"What happened?"

"The imp happened with rock-filled snowballs. It was aiming for my head, but the mirror got in the way."

"That fucking imp," he growled.

"Did anyone hear from Harvey?" I asked as Doc started rolling forward.

"Uncle Willis has gone dark. He didn't reply when I radioed him earlier."

I wondered what game he and Junie were playing tonight and if Prudence might be tagging along.

There was a slight tug on the Picklemobile, and then we were on our way back to Deadwood. As we towed merrily along, Doc and I filled Cooper in on the imp's snowball attack and how I'd tried to chase the bastard down but lost him at the boarded-up duplex.

"You need to show me what duplex you're talking about when we come back in the morning," Cooper said as we slowed to a stop in front of Aunt Zoe's house.

"I can drive," Doc offered.

"You don't have any appointments tomorrow morning?" Cooper asked.

"My calendar is clear all day."

I bumped his leg with mine. "Maybe I can stop over for lunch or something."

"Or something," he said with a wink.

Cooper snorted.

"Don't tell Cornelius you're free," I said to Doc. "He'll want you to check out the Hellhole with him."

"You're not going down there again, Parker."

Apparently, Natalie wasn't the only one on Cooper's boss-around list. I smiled and leaned my head on Doc's shoulder. "I think

Coop is finally starting to like me."

"It's 'Cooper' to you, Parker. And don't get your tail wagging. That Hellhole is off limits to everyone."

"But I like it when Violet wags her tail," Doc said, shifting into park. "Be right back. I'm going to unhook the tow strap."

After Doc shut the door, Cooper frowned my way. "I don't want Nat thinking she needs to go in that Hellhole with you so she can watch your back."

I crossed my arms, not sure Natalie would appreciate him determining where she does or does not go. "You're locking her down too much, if you ask me."

"I didn't ask you," he said, his tone loud and clear that this discussion was over.

Lucky for me, I was tone-deaf when it came to my best friend's welfare. "Maybe you should, though. I've known her for a long, long time. She's gnawing at that leash you have tied onto her these days."

His scowl deepened. "Did she tell you that?"

"In so many words, yes. Why do you think she was willing to go watch Cornelius unblock his third eye?"

He shrugged. "Because they're friends."

That was true, but that was only surface level. "She's bored stiff being sidelined. If I know Natalie, she'll put herself in the game with or without your consent soon enough, and tell you where you can shove your whistle if you try to call a timeout."

Holy basketball! I was starting to sound like my boss, the ex-hoopster, during one of his office pep rallies.

Cooper stared out the window toward the house, where Natalie now stood under the porch light waving at us to come inside.

"I don't want anything to happen to her," he said quietly. "You play with monsters who rip out guts for fun."

"Yeah, don't remind me." I gave Natalie the one-minute signal with my finger. "But you can't lock her in a cage to keep her safely tucked away. Look at what's happened with the imp now that it's finally free. Total chaos."

Doc walked by the driver's side and tossed the tow strap into the back of the Picklemobile.

"Total chaos," Cooper repeated. "Isn't that your middle name?"

I chuckled as Doc opened the door. "Zoe is going to drive Reid home," he said.

"Seriously?" I clapped. Maybe Reid would get that kiss yet before this was all over.

Doc nodded. "He's going to come back tomorrow afternoon when his shift is over and deal with his rig. For now, he covered the torn-up hood with a tarp he had in the bed of his truck."

"Good thinking," Cooper said. "We don't need nosy neighbors asking about the damage."

"Natalie is getting ready to head out," Doc continued. "Do you want me to give you a ride home, Coop, or are you going over to Natalie's place?"

"She's coming to mine—well, your house."

"Same thing," Doc said.

"She'll take me home." Cooper got out and closed the door without another word to me.

"You're welcome, *Coop!*" I yelled as he walked away.

He stopped and glared back, pointing at me as he said something I couldn't hear.

Figuring it was his usual mantra about using his full name, I waved at him, giving my best impression of a killer-clown smile.

He winced and shook his head, turning away.

Doc reached in, shut off the engine, and collected the keys. "Slide this way, Killer, and I'll make sure you land right side up this time." He held out his hand, offering to help me.

I took his hand, letting him tug me his way.

He smiled as I scooted closer. "Or do you want me to lift you out of here and carry you over the threshold?"

I paused for a split second at the words "carry" and "threshold." They reminded me of wedding dresses and marriage vows, subjects that I preferred to skirt whenever possible so that I didn't end up falling ass-over-teakettle into Rejectionville, which was located in the tenth circle of Hell—the one Dante forgot to mention in *The Inferno*.

"You should be careful talking like that, Candy Cane," I joked, swinging my legs out from the cab.

"Why's that?" He helped me step down and gain a solid footing.

"If certain young ears hear you, they might get the wrong idea." I eased back, making room for him to close the door.

"What idea is that?" he asked after the door was shut.

I looked down the dark street, wishing I'd kept my cakehole shut about his word choice. "Golly, you're just full of questions tonight, aren't you?"

"I'm full of questions many nights, wondering things like what you're wearing under your bathrobe, how soon until I get to feel you up again, and if your feet will be just slightly cold or two ice bricks I could use to build an igloo."

I laughed, taking the crooked arm he offered for me to hold onto as we crunched through the snow toward the porch. The smell of wood smoke lingered in the air in spite of the gusts of wind moving through the gulch.

"You really have an obsession with my feet."

"I'm obsessed with all of you, Boots, including your unnaturally cold feet."

"You'll appreciate them come summer. Then you'll be begging me to touch you with them."

He paused at the bottom step, pulling me to a halt. "Violet?" he said quietly.

"Yes?"

"What wrong idea are you talking about?"

I stared up at him in the dim glow coming from the porch light. His expression was unreadable. A game face if I'd ever seen one.

I decided to play it straight in return. "Well, a phrase like 'carry you over the threshold' might make Addy get certain ideas about us." And maybe not just Addy.

He nodded, his mouth a thin line. "And these ideas would be 'wrong,' in your opinion?"

Hold on a second here. What was going on? Was he talking about marriage? As in marriage to him? As in *my* willingness to get married to him?

"Not wrong in the negative sense of being immoral or undesirable," I explained, licking my suddenly very dry and very cold lips. "More like being just incorrect."

"Incorrect," he repeated, his gaze still holding mine.

"Yeah. I guess."

He frowned and looked to the side. "What if it wasn't incorrect?"

I stiffened.

The wind rattled the branches of the cottonwood tree over our heads, biting at my cheeks and nose as it whipped past. But I didn't care one iota about Old Man Winter's attempt to freeze me solid at the moment.

I stared at Doc's profile in silence until his focus returned to mine. Were we really talking about the idea of marriage or was this something else and I was being a buffoon, my usual *modus operandi* according to Prudence?

I considered inquiring outright if he was sort of asking me to consider entering a marriage with him, because this certainly didn't feel like an absolute proposal. However, after the physical beatings I'd taken lately, I was hesitant to open myself up for a mental bruising. Or worse, a heart flogging.

"If it wasn't incorrect," I said, tiptoeing through my answer, "then it wouldn't be a wrong idea, I guess."

His gaze held mine. "It's a good thing your fake marriage to old Hooch turned out to be a sham."

"Yeah, it is." I tipped my head. "Why do you say that?"

"Because I don't like to share when it comes to you."

He'd told me that before.

"Same here." So, maybe it hadn't been a sort-of proposal. Man oh man, was I glad I'd played it safe.

He pulled me into his arms, acting like he was going to kiss me, but holding back. His gaze traveled around my face, moving from my mouth to my cheeks to my eyes and then back to my lips.

"Doc?"

"Hmm?" His focus moved north, meeting my eyes.

"Are you going to kiss me or something?"

"Or something," he said, cupping my cheeks and tilting my chin up.

"Okay." I closed my eyes and then opened them, not sure how I should go into whatever came next.

"Violet." He frowned slightly. "I can carry you over the threshold." He paused long enough that I wondered if he wanted me to hop onto his back. "If you'll let me," he added in a low voice, sounding almost uncertain.

"If I'll ..." Was this simply a matter of him assuring me he could lift me up and physically move me? No. He was asking ... Jesus, leave it to Doc to be Professor Cryptic about spending the rest of our lives as husband and wife.

Fuck it. I was going to take a chance with my heart. "Doc," I gulped, my pulse running sprints. "Are you asking if I—"

I heard the front door open.

Dammit!

"Come on, you two," Layne said from the porch. "Enough with this mushy stuff. There's a show on about Hessian soldiers that you should watch with me, Doc. They have some really cool weapons. Some are like those ones in Aunt Zoe's old book."

I continued to stare up at Doc, not wanting to move or say anything to break the spell.

"Layne, you're letting all of the cold air in," Addy chastised her brother. The screen door creaked. "Hey, what are you two doing out here?" she asked. In my peripheral vision, I could see her in the doorway with her brother now.

"I think they're pretending they are frozen to death."

Doc started to laugh.

"Ah, isn't that sweet," Addy said. "Just like at the end of a romantic movie, only usually they're kissing."

"Eww." Layne made a retching sound. "Don't make it gross, Addy."

I heard the telltale *click-click-click-click* of Rooster's toenails on the porch boards, followed by two barks.

"What's going on out here?" Natalie asked next.

"I think they're stuck together," Addy said, giggling.

"Oh, man." Cooper groaned. "They're not doing that Gomez and Morticia crap again, are they?"

I started to giggle. After the emotional roller coaster of a day I'd had, it was a wonder I wasn't howling with mad laughter.

Doc's grin widened. "I enjoyed our date night, Tish."

"Same here, *mon cher*."

"Oh, that's French." His hand slid up my arms.

Cooper growled and pushed past us. "Make room, lovebirds. Nat, we need to get out of here before they start waltzing."

Addy clapped. "I love dancing."

My daughter, a romantic at heart like her mother.

"Okay," I said, putting on my mom face. "Addy and Layne, go back inside and shut the door. And take the dog with you."

Rooster barked again and raced inside.

"Sometimes I swear that dog speaks English," I said.

Doc put his arm around me. "Give him a month and Addy will teach him Spanish, too."

Natalie gave me a quick hug good-bye, and then followed Cooper to her truck, tossing him the keys. "Take me to your kennel, law dog."

Doc and I watched them back out of the drive in silence.

"Well?" I asked, turning back to him.

He dropped a quick cold kiss on my lips, and then bent and picked me up before I knew what was happening.

I laughed, putting my arms around his neck. "Put me down before you hurt your back."

"I have you, Tish." As he climbed the porch steps, the door opened again.

Both kids were standing in the way. Addy was dancing in circles with Rooster while Layne was watching us with a curious expression.

A chicken passed by on the way to the kitchen, which somehow seemed normal in my crazy life.

"What are you doing, Doc?" Layne asked.

"I'm carrying your mom over the threshold."

So, had I made a big deal out of nothing back there? No, there had been more to it. I'd bet Harvey's favorite nut on it. But I wasn't going to obsess about it. At least not too much. I had a pissed-off imp to catch and a spinning clock to figure out.

I looked up at Doc as he backed up and closed the door with me still in his arms. Before my self-doubt demon could gag me, I blurted, "There's a lot to carry here."

Kids. Pets. A *Scharfrichter* life full of monsters.

"I know." He winked. "Like I said, I have you."

He set me down, swatted me playfully on the backside, and then let Layne drag him off to the living room with Addy and Rooster skipping along behind.

I locked the door and leaned back against it.

"What in the hell was that?" I whispered.

"Mom," Addy called out. "Will you make us some popcorn, please?"

"Yes," I hollered back, and then blew out a breath while unbuttoning my coat. "And life goes on. Now where did that dang chicken go?"

CHAPTER SIXTEEN

Thursday, January 31st

A new day, a new set of tarot cards.

I leaned against the kitchen counter and pulled up Cornelius's name in my cell phone.

For a moment, I hesitated, staring out the window at the crooked snowman the kids had made next to the swing set, along with a snowdog, snowcat, and snowchicken. There might even be a snowgerbil at the end of the line, but from my vantage point, it looked more like a two-humped mound of snow. All four snow animals were wearing different colored stocking hats that my mother had knitted for our pets.

I took a sip of fresh coffee, debating on how much I really wanted to hear what Cornelius and his tarot deck thought my future may or may not hold. Seriously, how much stock did I put in those cards? It was all a matter of odd coincidences and chance happenings, wasn't it? For all I knew, I was subconsciously making things go the way of the cards.

Then again, seeing that the cards seemed to be hitting more than missing when it came to my daily trials and tribulations, would having a little heads-up hurt anything? Even if it weren't totally accurate and I might be making things swing one way or the other.

"Screw it." I tapped the call button, ready to belly up to the foretelling poker table.

Cornelius didn't answer.

Hmm. It was pretty early in the morning. He might still be sleeping. Or he could be scouring out his chakras again. How often did chakras need to be cleaned anyway?

I hung up without leaving a message because I wasn't going to even try to make beeping sounds in Morse code per his absurd voicemail instructions. Instead, I'd call him again after Doc and Cooper and I returned from looking for the imp's tracks up in Lead.

I heard the front door open. Doc must be back from taking the kids to school.

"Parker?" a voice called out.

I cringed. Not Doc.

"I'm in the kitchen." I rolled my shoulders, trying to work out my usual Cooper-inspired tension ahead of time. I really wasn't in the mood to bob and weave this morning in between snarky jabs and below-the-belt insults.

Cooper cruised into the room wearing a plain black winter coat. Apparently, he was playing undercover detective this morning. My gaze shifted northward, taking in his bloodshot eyes and scruffy jaw.

"Where is Zoe?" he asked, raking his fingers through his hair, which wasn't for the first time this morning, judging from the tufts sticking up here and there.

"She didn't come home from Reid's."

One blond eyebrow climbed toward his hairline. "Are you joking?"

"Yeah, unfortunately. She's in her workshop with Rooster and Elvis, taking out her frustrations with our favorite fire captain on some molten glass."

"Did something happen last night?"

"No, and I think that might be at the core of her vexations."

"Gotcha." He glanced around. "Your kids doing okay after being up later than normal last night?"

"They're a little sleepy, but they have tomorrow off."

"Why? It's not a holiday."

"It's a teacher workday."

"Lucky kids. They didn't have those when I was younger. I certainly could've used more days off from prison. I mean school."

"You sound like your uncle. Did you attend that old school in Lead, too?" I'd asked Natalie the same question the other day and she'd said they'd closed it down long before her time.

"I'm old, Parker, but not that old, although this morning I'm feeling damn near ancient. They shut that school down shortly after Uncle Willis was there, if I remember right. It's gone through several private owners since the state sold it off, all of them coming in with big plans, but none having the cash or gumption to follow through. Masterson owns it now, right?"

I nodded. "He hasn't mentioned any plans for it, but I suspect he's keeping troublemakers locked away in there."

"Nyce mentioned that theory. You're not thinking of going back in there any time soon, are you? At least not without me."

"Bullets don't always kill, Cooper."

"True, but they usually slow trouble down enough to make it manageable." He pointed at the coffee maker. "Mind if I have a cup?"

I frowned, feeling like I'd stepped into a parallel universe where Cooper was my pal. Or maybe this wasn't really him. If I hadn't already killed the *lidérc*, I'd suspect it was hiding behind Cooper's face this morning.

"What's going on?" I asked him.

"I want some caffeine."

"No, I mean between you and me." I stepped to the left to make room for him at the counter. "Right now."

He grabbed a mug from the cupboard. "You're going to have to be more clear if you want me to give you an answer."

"You're not barking at me right out of the gate for once."

"I'm tired. Give me time to pour some coffee down my throat

and maybe I can scrounge up a growl or two."

"What happened last night?" I remembered our conversation in the Picklemobile about Natalie. "Did you have a fight with your girlfriend?"

He yawned while pouring his coffee. "We didn't have a chance to get that far. A call came in that I had to go deal with, so she went home and I went to work. And that's why law enforcement personnel have a high divorce rate."

"You want milk for that?" I asked, pointing at his cup of coffee.

He shook his head. "The stronger the better this morning."

"Did the work call have anything to do with the imp?"

"Not this time." He took a sip. And then another.

"Did it have anything to do with why Hawke called here yesterday?"

"How would I know that? I don't read minds, I just see dead people." When I glared at him, he shrugged. "Hawke doesn't talk to me about you. He thinks I'm too soft on you. That you're casting spells to make me like you."

"The joke's on him. You like me without any spells."

He pursed his lips. "I don't know. 'Like' is a strong word."

"Shut up and drink your coffee."

He did just that. I did, too, leaning against the counter next to him with only the tick-tock of Aunt Zoe's Betty Boop clock breaking the silence.

"You heard from your uncle today?" I asked after a couple of sips.

"No. And I hope not to, at least not for a bit." He grimaced. "I don't think I can handle hearing about his latest escapades with Ms. Coppermoon, especially after all of his worrying about Prudence joining in on their R-rated fun."

"Me either."

"Ms. Coppermoon was my English teacher, you know. A really nice lady, although a bit strict with her grading scale." His grimace deepened. "I don't like to think of her as anything but a teacher. Uncle Willis doesn't seem to respect that notion."

"Maybe that will change with Prudence popping into his noggin every now and then."

"We can hope. Although I wouldn't wish Prudence on most anyone."

"Not even your partner at work?" I hid my grin behind my coffee mug before whispering, "Snollyguster," which was the magic trigger word Prudence had planted in Detective Hawke's mind the last time he'd been in her house.

Cooper pointed his mug at me. "Maybe him. But only on the days when he's being a jackass."

"Ha! That's every day I've been around him."

He shook his head. "Hawke wasn't always like he is now. When we were first starting out, before greed made him power hungry, he was a decent cop. A little full of himself around women even back then, but time on the force has tarnished his badge. You didn't hear me say that, though."

"Hear what?" I joked, then I glanced at the clock. Where was Doc? Had he stopped for coffee on the way home? "I'm going to have to drive separately up to Lead. Jerry called earlier. I have an appointment with a potential buyer at nine."

Cooper waved me off while yawning. "I forgot to tell you. The trip to Lead is off. There are no imp tracks. I checked about an hour ago. The snowstorm that blew through last night wiped out everything."

"Damn it. How am I going to catch that little shit?"

"You're going to need to patrol the area for twenty-four hours or more, for starters." He took another sip from his mug. "I called Nyce on the way over here and told him our imp hunt was off. He said to tell you he was going to the Rec Center and would like to catch up with you at lunch in his office. He's buying."

"Okay." I picked up the toaster to check my reflection and make sure my makeup was still holding up. The scratches from my imp fight were mostly healed, and the bruises were fading quickly, but it had taken an extra ten minutes of makeup work to fix my face this morning.

"What was your late-night call about?" I asked, setting the toaster down. "And if you tell me it's police business, I'll slap you with a piece of toast."

His brow wrinkled. "There is no toast."

"Nice sleuthing, Detective," I teased. "I'll put a piece in simply for the joy of beating you with it."

He smirked at me. "An accident."

"That's the reason you had to leave Natalie last night?"

"Yeah. It involved a pickup truck, an icy bridge, and a snowplow. No fatalities, thankfully, but the pickup spun around several times before nose-diving deep into the ditch. Took the tow truck a couple of hours to get it back on the road. Only minor damage to the plow, though."

"Why did you have to go to the accident? I mean, you're a detective, not a patrol cop."

"We're short staffed at the moment and I was on call." He took a sip of coffee. "The plow driver had pulled off to the side of the road prior to the accident. Claims he saw a light-colored bear in the ditch munching on a deer carcass right before the plow sent a blast of snow flying toward it. So, he pulled over and thought about going back to take a second look, but then the oncoming pickup hit black ice and bounced off his plow."

"A bear? It should be hibernating now."

He finished his coffee and walked over to the sink, grabbing the dishrag draped over the faucet. "That's why the plow driver stopped. He thought it might have been roused by some poachers. Maybe injured." Cooper quickly washed and rinsed his mug. "He was considering calling a friend who works for the South Dakota Game, Fish, and Parks Department when the accident happened."

"Did you look for the bear while you were out there?"

"Yeah, but it was snowing and blowing pretty hard." He looked around the counter. "We couldn't find a bear or tracks. But we did find the frozen deer carcass. It had clearly been torn open recently, bones gnawed on and innards scattered."

"That seems weird, doesn't it?" I grabbed a clean dish towel from the drawer and handed it to him.

"Everything is weird these days, Parker." He dried his mug and handed it to me to put away in the cupboard closest to me. "And it all started when you came to town."

"It's not my fault. It's genetics. And a calling." I closed the cupboard door, leaning back against the counter again. "Some days I wonder how my life would be if I were normal."

"I doubt you would ever be considered 'normal,' not with that hair." He grinned at my middle-finger salute, adding, "You'd be annoying, about that I have no doubt. Nyce probably would've taken pity on you still. He's got a soft spot for you that makes absolutely no sense on paper. Makes me think he's taken too many ghost hits to his head over time."

"That's it," I said, reaching for the bread box on the counter. "Get ready for a solid toast slapping."

Chuckling, he held up his hands in surrender. "I'm going home and catching up on some sleep." Hands still in the air, he headed for the front door.

I followed, seeing him out onto the porch. "Get plenty of beauty rest. You look like something Bogart dragged in that not even Rooster will eat."

"At least I have the excuse of no sleep, Frankenstein."

"It's Frankenstein's monster, law dog."

"You would know after looking at it in the mirror this morning." When he made it to his police Durango, he turned and gave me a mock glare. "Stay out of trouble, Parker."

I smiled. "See, I knew you liked me."

Shaking his head, he crawled inside and drove off.

I shut the door and took advantage of the extra time before I had to leave for work to enjoy another cup of coffee—my third. This time, I kept it to mostly milk with a solid hit of sugar and enough of the black go-go juice to give it nice color. I needed to woo my potential clients, not talk their heads off.

I tried Cornelius's number again and once more ended up listening to his voicemail. Shrugging, I switched to Natalie's number. She didn't answer either. I doubted she was doing any chakra cleansing, not with all of the painting she needed to do yet at Galena House.

I thought about calling Detective Hawke back and finding out why he'd called me here at home yesterday, but then I laughed at my silly notion and returned to enjoying milky coffee in a quiet kitchen with no cops, kids, dog, chicken, cat, or gerbil in sight.

A half hour later, as I headed into work early to prepare to meet my potential new buyers, my fingers and toes were crossed that this time they would actually want to hear about a house, and not only the ghosts that might live there.

* * *

"On a high note, my newest clients didn't want *only* a ghost story or two," I told Doc a few hours later as we sat in his office after enjoying some sweet and savory turkey cranberry sandwiches that he'd picked up for our lunch date.

Doc's laptop and paperwork were pushed aside, making room for my rump and our desk picnic goodies, including a shared bag of pretzels, an iced tea for him, and a diet ginger ale for me. After a total of four coffees this morning, I had to lay off the caffeine. My twitching eyelid had been a good distraction from my beat-up face as I'd led my potential buyers through a couple of Deadwood homes, but enough was enough. Much more and my twitch would move south to my shoulders, and then it was only a matter of time until I morphed from Dr. Jekyll into Mr. Hyde.

"So, they're legit buyers this time?" he asked, leaning back in his chair, his hands behind his head while his feet rested on a drawer he'd pulled out.

"Seems like it." I crunched on a salty pretzel. "Although they did want to know if I could sense any ghosts in the houses we visited. When I explained after the third house that I suffer from ghost blindness, they were content with learning whatever human-related history that I knew."

"Are they coming back to see more houses?"

I nodded, leaning back on my hands. "They scheduled another appointment with me for next week."

"That should make your boss happy."

"I'll know tomorrow. Jerry had to go back down to Rapid City this afternoon." I chewed on my lower lip. "You know, he's been going down to Rapid an awful lot lately. I sure hope he's not putting together some new marketing gig for us. His tendency to 'think bigger' when it comes to finding new buyers makes my palms sweaty. Hell, we still have one more *Paranormal Realty* show to go."

Doc lowered his boots to the floor, sitting forward, resting his elbows on his knees. "Did Coop tell you about that accident he was at last night?"

"Yeah. He was really tired this morning." I grabbed another pretzel. "I could tell because he didn't snarl at me. In fact, he was sort of nice to me. It was weird. Like *Twilight Zone* kooky."

"No way."

"Yes way." I crunched on the pretzel, washing it down with a sip of ginger ale. "He even talked to me a little about police business."

"Damn. You two are going to be shopping for curtains together before you know it."

I lowered my drink, frowning at him. "Is that what you think women do together? Shop for curtains?"

He struggled to hold back a grin. "Some days. Other times, they drink beer and talk about how to catch imps."

"That's more accurate." I hopped off the desk and turned around, forcing him to make room for me on his lap.

He obliged without complaint, wrapping one arm around my back while the other reached under the hem of my gauzy, mid-length skirt to play with my knee through my warm cashmere leggings.

"Coop told you about the bear?" Doc asked.

"And the gnawed-on deer carcass." I looped my arms around his neck, nuzzling his throat at the base of his short beard for a few seconds before leaning back to admire his handsome mug. "What's with the frown lines?"

"I'm worried about that bear, Killer."

I placed my hand over his heart, feeling it thump under my palm. "You think it might be rabid or something?"

"No. I'm afraid it might be the other Bone Cruncher."

Shit. A Bone Cruncher, or as the Lakota legend had it, a white grizzly.

I lowered my hand. "They hunt in pairs." I repeated the line from a note Mr. Black had sent me months ago after I'd killed a Bone Cruncher behind Harvey's barn.

"I could be wrong." Doc shrugged. "Maybe it really was just a snow-covered bear that came out of hibernation early to get a snack."

"Or a rare albino bear that nobody around here had happened to ever see before." I blew out a breath. "Either would be preferable to that bloodcurdling, milky-eyed son of a bitch."

Doc traced a circle around my kneecap. "If another Bone Cruncher is here, I have a feeling the local *Scharfrichter* is at the top of its hit list."

I leaned my head on his shoulder, staring out the front plate-glass window at the courthouse across the street. The sky had started spitting snow as soon as I'd joined Doc for lunch, and dark heavy clouds now ruined the chance of a sunny afternoon.

I shuddered at the memory of running into the first Bone Cruncher. All of those scythe-like claws and dagger teeth. And the fetid stench that had come from it, both before and after death, and stuck to the back of my throat. Blech! It made me want to gargle with Harvey's homemade, esophagus-burning hooch just thinking about it.

"It appears I'm going to have to work on Prudence's list sooner rather than later."

"Yes, *we* will." Doc's hand inched higher up my thigh. "Now, what have I told you about wearing these tights?"

I fluttered my eyelashes at him. "That they're soft and fun to touch."

"No, *you* are soft and fun to touch. These tights get in my way."

If this Executioner gig had taught me anything over the last few months, it was to appreciate each moment while I was still breathing, because I never knew which breath would be my last. Moments such as this one were a great example—alone with Doc, watching snow fall while safely wrapped in his arms. Make that wrapped in one arm—his other hand was busy scorching a path further north in spite of my thick leggings.

I smiled, returning to his neck for another nuzzle. "You smell deliciously spicy, Gomez. I think I'm going to lick you for dessert."

He chuckled low in his chest. "I'm all yours, Tish." He shifted me on his lap, fitting us together even better. "But we should probably move to the back room. The door is unlocked."

"Where's your sense of adventure?" I whispered as I nibbled my way toward his earlobe.

My cell phone rang before I could get a single lick in, dammit, playing the eerie tone I'd programmed into it while enjoying my third coffee this morning.

"That's Cornelius," I said, running my nails down the front of his shirt.

"You want to answer it?"

My hand kept traveling lower, heading toward his belt buckle. "I'd rather give you a good tongue lashing."

He groaned and caught my hand, stopping any additional exploration. "Me too. However, we have a problem."

I shifted in his lap. "I can feel that. It's one of my favorite kind of problems when I'm alone with you."

"Same here, but the problem to which I'm referring is staring through the front window at us."

I sat up and looked toward the glass.

Cornelius stood on the other side in his Cossack hat, long black coat, and a pair of galoshes. He had his phone held up to the window for us to see, and a box tucked under his other arm. "Answer your phone," he called through the window.

"Now what forewarning do the tarot gods have for me?" I reached for my purse to fish out my phone.

"That wooden box looks like the one for the Hellhound clock," Doc said, nudging me off his lap and onto my feet.

I gave up on finding my phone and walked over to the door, opening it a crack. A cold breeze pushed its way inside, fresh and shiver-inspiring. "You rang, Spirit Miser?" I called out.

Cornelius hurried to the door while pocketing his phone. "I'm looking for the Timekeeper."

I held the door wide. "Well, then you've come to the right place. What foretelling do you offer from your mystical tarot deck, oh great seer of futures yet unknown and undetermined?"

"That's kind of redundant, Killer," Doc said from behind me.

I pointed a stern finger at him. "No heckling allowed from the upper balcony."

"The news is troubling." Cornelius passed by me and went straight to Doc's desk, setting the box down on it. "I need no tarot cards at this time to see the looming storm on your horizon."

Doc stood, his brow lined yet again. "Why is the news troubling?"

Cornelius took off his hat and tossed it on the chair next to him. "I have been experimenting this morning." Static electricity made his hair stand on end over the top of his ears, giving him an eccentric, mad scientist look.

I locked the door and joined them at the desk as Cornelius took the lid off the wooden box. "Experimenting with what?"

He pointed at the clock. "See for yourself."

I did. It was ticking, but … "The hands aren't spinning." Relief should have been flowing through me, but Cornelius's lack of levity held me in check.

"That's a sound observation," he said. "I'm pleased to find your vision is still operational. I have a feeling you'll be needing it soon. If only you could develop the ability to see in the dark."

"That's my job," Doc said, looking down at the clock.

"Why is the lack of spinning hands bad?" I exchanged a frown with Doc. "There's no chiming or cuckooing or anything odd going on. This seems like a perfectly good thing to me."

"I didn't say it was bad, only troubling. Also, it is common knowledge that perfection is a fallacy." Cornelius sat on the corner of Doc's desk. "And at your advanced age, Violet, you know that 'good' is simply another four-letter word."

"Keep it up, wisenheimer," I said, my voice rising along with my confusion, "and I'm going to give you a perfectly good bump on your nose."

"What's going on here, Cornelius?" Doc intervened in a much calmer voice.

"This morning, I was pondering Violet's clock situation while I drank my protein shake." He focused on me. "You've probably heard about how the needle on a compass will spin when it sits over magnetic rocks, yes?"

I shrugged. "Sure." I'd seen that in a movie at some point in my life, but I couldn't remember which and when.

"Well, that's an incorrect notion. The needle does not spin when the compass is placed on top of a magnetic rock. In fact, you would have to move the magnetic rock around the compass to make the needle follow it in a circle."

I crossed my arms. "What's your point?"

"The clock hands are spinning due to a specific location."

"But you just said that the magnetic rock would have to be moved around the compass to make it spin, not the other way around."

"I know what I said. I also stated that the spinning needle idea is incorrect."

"So why are you bringing that false notion up now?"

"Violet, you cannot see the forest for the trees."

My gaze narrowed. He wasn't going to be seeing the forest either after I gave him a Three Stooges eye-poke.

"I brought up the spinning compass needle because I was thinking about the idea of it this morning."

"And it being wrong," I said, doing my damnedest to follow his meandering train of thought.

He touched his finger to his nose. "Now you've caught up with me."

I leaned closer, growling at him. "Your explanation is about as linear as a spinning compass, Cornelius!"

He stepped back, hands raised. "Have you considered placing a jade crystal at the center of your chest to alleviate your violent emotional reactions?"

Before I could climb over the desk and bite his head off, Doc pulled me into a sideways hug, only he didn't let go when it was over.

"What do you mean, the clock hands are spinning due to location?" Doc asked, holding me tightly against his side.

"The clock itself is not magnetic. I tested it. However, the whole idea of a magnetic-like vortex that could be revolving around the clock inspired the conclusion that I should experiment with transferring the clock to different locations."

"Like where?" I asked more calmly, now without baring my teeth after having taken a few deep breaths during Cornelius's explanation. "Besides here in Doc's office, I mean, where the hands are clearly not spinning."

"I started with my hotel, testing the clock on each floor."

I wondered if anyone noticed an eccentric man in a Cossack hat carrying a clock in a box around the hotel and considered calling the authorities. "What happened?"

"The hands remained stationary. Then I walked to Natalie's apartment, which was rather unpleasant in the cold."

"Did you see Freesia?" I asked.

"Are you speaking of the flower-named maiden who is the proprietor of Galena House?"

"How many other women named Freesia do you know?"

"You might be surprised. Many of my grandmother's friends were named after flowers, especially those that enjoyed flirting with younger males."

I was now sorry I'd asked. "Yes, I meant Freesia the owner."

"No." He tilted his head, which seemed to make one eyebrow raise. "But should I have?"

Freesia had a major crush on Cornelius, and I had yet to figure out why because he didn't appear to pay attention to her at all. That often made me scratch my head, because Freesia was gorgeous with killer curves that I'd think would inspire drooling from most mortal men. Then again, I continued to wonder if Cornelius might be from a planet located in the next solar system over from ours.

"I guess not, if Freesia wasn't there." I let that whole subject drop and returned to his story for him. "Was Natalie home when you went to her apartment?"

"Yes. However, she isn't anymore."

"Why not?"

"We'll get to that later." He pointed at the clock. "Stay focused, Timekeeper."

I glanced up at Doc and sighed loudly.

He winked back at me before returning to our lunch guest. "Did the hands spin while you were at Natalie's place, Cornelius?"

"No. The clock's hands remained motionless, same as they had at my hotel."

"Where else did you go?" Doc asked.

"Natalie drove me to several more locations in Deadwood, including the spot where the Hessler house was prior to Violet burning it down."

"That was an accident," I muttered.

"Then we went up to Lead, testing at a couple of cemeteries, then outside of the Sugarloaf Building, and finally, to the Opera House. Not once did the hands move on this clock. In fact, they remained at this same location no matter where we went." He indicated toward the clock face.

"Eight twenty-three," Doc read the time aloud. "That must be significant." He rubbed his jaw. "We know that the hour hand shows longitude and the minute hand shows latitude, but that doesn't mean anything if we don't have a key or map relating the clock times to locations."

It sure would've been nice to have received a user guide when this Timekeeping job landed in my lap. "You don't think it's just where the hands stopped spinning when Cornelius moved the clock?"

He shook his head. "Not with these Black Forest clocks. I think we have to figure that any hand movement has meaning."

"Right." I turned back to Cornelius. "And Natalie was with you the whole time?"

"Yes."

"That must be why she didn't answer my call earlier."

"No. When your call came in, I wouldn't let her take it."

"Why not?"

"I didn't want your energy to skew our test results, what with you being the keeper of time."

That actually made sense. Sort of. Could energy transfer through a cell phone, though? Like a black cloud coming out of the speaker? I didn't bother asking him. We didn't need to go down yet another rabbit hole.

"Okay," Doc said. "So, none of the locations you visited made the clock's hands spin?"

"Correct, except for one place other than my apartment."

"Where?" I asked.

He thumbed toward the wall abutting Calamity Jane Realty. "Next door in your boss's office."

My shoulders slumped. "It's the Hellhole causing it to spin, isn't it?"

"That's my theory."

Doc cursed, dropping into his chair.

"But why?" I asked, looking from Cornelius to Doc. "What does the Hellhole have to do with this clock? Are they somehow tied metaphysically?"

"That is what Natalie went to find out," Cornelius said.

"What?" My spine stiffened in a snap. "You sent her down into that hole in the floor in the office closet?"

"Of course not. The door still won't budge." He nudged his head toward the plate glass window. "She's in the basement of the courthouse."

I gasped. "You let her go there alone?"

"I'm not sure if you have noticed, but Natalie is a free spirit who goes where she wants." He rubbed his shoulder, grimacing. "She also knows exactly where to land a rather painful knuckle-punch if you try to block her path. Besides, the idea to install my newest camera in the tunnel was hers."

"Oh, no!" I looked around for my coat, forgetting where I'd left it in my panic to get to Natalie before something else did. "We have to go get her out of there."

"Remain calm, Violet. Focus on the color green to avoid overstimulating your heart."

I paused and looked at Doc, whose worried expression probably matched mine. "I'm about to start roaring like a lion here."

"Besides," Cornelius continued, patting his coat, "I have her right here."

"Oh, really? Next to your talking cricket?"

He pulled out a gadget the size of a large cell phone from his breast pocket that had a display screen on it. After pressing a couple of buttons on what looked to be a video screen, he held it out toward me.

I stared at the screen. "I can't see anything but a hole that looks like …" I trailed off, realizing that I was looking out at the courthouse basement wall from inside the underground tunnel that led to the Hellhole below Calamity Jane Realty.

Oh, fuck.

"Hi, Vi!" Natalie's whispered greeting came through the remote viewing gadget's speaker. Then her face filled the screen, blocking the view out through the hole. "Guess where I am?"

CHAPTER SEVENTEEN

Damn it, Natalie!" I snatched Cornelius's fancy remote viewing gadget from his hand, staring down at the display screen now filled by her dirt-smudged face.

"Damn it back at you." She turned the camera and moved her head to the side, giving me a view of the dark tunnel behind her. "Look what Corny and I figured out how to do." She held her arm out toward the tunnel. "For your viewing pleasure, we now have 24/7 monitoring of the tunnel leading to the Hellhole. He's going to order a few more cameras that we'll link together and then we can capture video even deeper."

She needed to get out of that tunnel before something captured her and dragged her even deeper!

I scowled at the screen. "It's good to see that your college education and common sense didn't get in the way of your ignorance today!" I huffed. "Cooper is going to blame me when he finds out you went in that tunnel and he's gonna blow up like a toad. Geez Louise, you had to go and do this just when he and I were starting to make headway on a wonderful bromance."

Natalie moved back in front of the camera, her wide grin centered on the screen. "Vi, you have to pee standing up on a regular basis to be part of the bromance club."

"You know what I mean." I lifted the screen closer. "And why is your forehead bleeding?"

"I played chicken with a rock on the way in here." She swiped at the blood with her shirt sleeve. "The rock won."

"Can she see us?" I asked Cornelius.

"No. She can only hear us via a speaker on the remote viewer attachment."

Doc stood, coming around his desk for a better look. "How are you getting this feed?" he asked Cornelius. "I wouldn't think a Wi-Fi signal is strong enough to make it through all that concrete."

"We tapped into the hardwire feed and then used some extenders to boost the signal."

I looked up at the tech-savvy whiz. "Did you two illegally break into the courthouse this morning?" Cooper was going to beat his chest and thump on the ground if Natalie was visible on any security cameras.

"Not officially," said the voice on the other end of the remote viewer.

"Natalie knows a female who is interested in paranormal investigation." Cornelius took the remote viewer back from me and started tapping some buttons on its side.

"And ... what?" I held up my hands, palms up, when he gave no further explanation. "This female works at the courthouse and let you two inside?"

"Actually, the female knows a male who works in the building and swears the basement is frequented by a phantom. He owed her a favor."

"A big favor," Natalie added. "A couple of phone calls later, we were inside. And after a solemnly sworn promise not to access anything but our live feed, we had what we needed to set up this system."

Cornelius turned the viewer toward me. "Natalie mounted the camera on a piece of wood, which she secured upright inside the hole in the wall, and *voilà*. We are live."

"Go team *Scharfrichter*!" Natalie cheered.

Doc shook his head. "Natalie, when you put your mind to a task, shit happens."

"Indeed," Cornelius said. "My dead grandfather would have said that between her stubbornness and hard work ethic, she'd wear out even a young mule."

I snorted. "That's something that a certain detective—or two—might want to keep in mind."

"I think I would've liked to have a beer with your granddad, Corny," Natalie said.

"Grandfather loathed beer. A Smoker's Cough was his drink of choice."

"What the hell is a Smoker's Cough?" I asked.

"You need to see it for the full effect. It's a shot of Jägermeister with a healthy dollop of mayonnaise on top."

"Eww!" I recoiled. "That's downright vomitrocious."

"You stole that word from Addy," Doc said with a grin.

"You should try a Smoker's Cough, Tall Medium," Cornelius said. "It tastes better than it sounds."

Doc shuddered. "Not even on a bet while I'm drunk."

"I'd try it for twenty bucks," Natalie said.

I guffawed. "Yeah, well, you ate a tube of lip balm for a dollar once, so that's not saying much."

"Make that five dollars," she shot back. "And it was cherry flavored."

"Mmm." Doc's eyes focused on my mouth. "I sure like your cherry-flavored lip gloss, Tish."

"Speaking of lip dehydration," Cornelius said. "Did you know there was a must-have book for new brides in the 1800s called *The American Frugal Housewife* that suggested earwax as a solution for cracked lips?"

"What flavor of earwax are we talking?" Natalie asked, her voice tinged with laughter. "Potato or carrot?"

"Good gravy! We've really run off the rails." I pointed down at the remote viewer screen. "Seriously, do we want to see what's going on down in that tunnel day and night?" I looked to Doc for an answer.

"Not knowing might be more dangerous than the alternative," he said.

Speaking of danger, I focused back on the viewer. "Natalie, I think you need to get out of there now. As in immediately, ASAP, and all that jazz. As clever as this setup is, you are vulnerable down there, and I'm too far away to get to you quickly if something comes out of the dark and grabs you or strangles you or tries to eat you for lunch." My words were flying faster and faster as I spoke. "So, pat yourself on the back, toot your horn silently, spike an imaginary football, and get your buns over here before all hell hits the fan and either your ass is grass, or mine is with your boyfriend by association."

"Whoa there, my little radioactive crack monkey," she said,

smirking into the camera. "Out of curiosity, how many coffees have you had so far today?"

"That's not important!" I shouted and then cringed. So did Natalie, Doc, and Cornelius. "Sorry," I said to one and all. "That was probably the extra caffeine doing the yelling."

Natalie pointed at me through the camera lens. "You should come with a warning label today, babe."

"Not just today," Doc said, chuckling, which earned him an elbow jab in the ribs.

Cornelius squinted at me, turning his head to one side and then the other. "Her aura is definitely red with intense physical energy. Crimson even almost, which could also represent a high sex drive."

"You don't say." Doc squinted at me, too, mimicking Cornelius. "Crimson looks good on you, Boots."

I scowled at all three of them, although Natalie couldn't see it. "It's all fun and jokes until something slithers out of the dark and—"

"Shhh." Natalie held her finger to her lips, looking behind her. She stared into the darkness beyond for a few beats, then turned back to us long enough to whisper, "Did you hear that?"

"Hear what?" Cornelius asked, holding the remote viewer's speaker closer to his ear, then lowered it, shaking his head.

"It sounded like a bunch of rocks falling. Not big ones, more like large pieces of gravel." She looked behind her again.

"Are you fucking with us, Nat?" I wouldn't put it past her to pull a practical joke in the middle of the Hellhole tunnel.

"No." She turned toward the camera, her eyes wide and overly bright. "I think there might be somebody in here with me," she whispered.

"Shit!" My heart was racing so fast it ran away with my breath. "I'm coming over."

"Vi, wait. Calm down. I can be through that hole and safely on the other side and down the hall in a flash." She leaned closer to the camera. "Hey, Corny, turn on the night vision. Let's see if we can pick something up on infrared."

"That thing has night vision?" Doc asked Cornelius.

"Thermal imaging, too."

"Damn. That's an expensive camera."

Cornelius tapped several buttons, moving through a menu

screen quickly. "You'd be surprised what a little money can buy these days." He glanced up at Doc mid-tap. "Or a lot, in this case." Two more taps and he held out the viewer so we could watch along with him. "Night vision is activated."

I crowded up next to Cornelius, while Doc looked on over my shoulder.

"What do you hear, Nat?" I whispered, chewing on my thumb knuckle.

"Something is moving around farther down the tunnel," she said in a whisper. "Maybe down under Calamity Jane's. It almost sounds like something is being dragged."

I couldn't see anything on the viewer, not even with the night vision, but my hackles were up and raring to go anyway, grabbing pitchforks and shovels. "Natalie, get out of that tunnel."

"Hold on, I forgot about this." She held up something in front of the camera, cutting off the top half of the screen. The edges formed a blurry circle. "Can you guys see through it?"

The camera tried to automatically adjust with no luck.

"Give me 4.5 seconds, Natalie." Cornelius tapped on a couple more buttons, scrolling through a menu. Then the focus adjusted, giving us a clear view of nothing but rock walls receding into the darkness.

"What is that?" Doc asked.

"It's the hag stone." Cornelius leaned closer to the screen. "Natalie, elevate the pendant two centimeters."

She raised it slightly. Now the image on the viewer was framed by the stone's inner circle. Still, though, there wasn't anything to see besides the rock walls and ceiling.

"Turn up the volume as loud as you can," she whispered.

Cornelius thumbed a button on the side, holding the viewer closer so we could hear it better.

I listened, breath held, hearing nothing. I glanced at Doc with raised brows. He shook his head.

I leaned closer yet, closing my eyes. If I shut off one sense, maybe another would crank up.

Still nothing. Eyes back open, I looked toward the door, wondering if we should high-tail it over there.

"We need to go get her," Doc said, apparently reading my thoughts.

"I'll get my coat."

"Just wait a second," I heard Natalie say.

We'd already waited too damned long, but I returned to Cornelius anyway, who'd handed the viewer to Doc while he messed with another gadget that he'd extracted from a different coat pocket. This one had a target on a digital screen at the end of a four-inch handle. It reminded me of a radar gun.

"Dammit, Nat," I said. "This is too risky."

"It might be a trap for you," she said so quietly that I almost didn't hear her. "Like before."

"No shit, Sherlock. That's why I didn't want to go down there again."

"I have an idea," she said, lowering the hag stone from the camera eye and replacing it with her face.

The night vision mode made her skin appear light green and turned her eyes into silver marbles. Slap a healthy coat of lipstick on her and she could be a variation of The Creature from the Black Lagoon, minus the gills.

"Forget it, Natalie," I said. "We're coming over there now."

"No. Hear me out."

I turned to Doc, torn. He nodded. Cornelius was staring down at the other hand-held gadget, his frown growing over his brow like a storm cloud.

She moved closer to the screen. "What if I—"

"Natalie," Cornelius said, cutting her off. Something in his tone chilled me to the bone. "The camera is set up and working. You need to come back now."

"In a minute. I just want to—"

"Leave now," Cornelius said, his voice gruff. "There is something coming toward you."

"What?!" I cried. "How can you see that?"

On the viewer Doc was holding, everything looked dark green on the screen behind her, but there was no movement from what I could tell.

Cornelius leaned over, showing me the screen on the other gadget while pointing at a green dot in the center of the target. "That is Natalie." His finger shifted to another dot at the edge of the display screen. "That is not."

I watched as the other dot moved toward Natalie's dot.

"Is that using the thermal sensor on the camera?" Doc asked.

"Yes. I programmed an estimated distance between the courthouse basement and the Hellhole entrance below Calamity Jane Realty. From what I can tell, whatever is down there with Natalie is about fifty feet away and closing in." Cornelius leaned toward Doc and tapped on the remote viewer. The display changed to show bright colors in place of Natalie's face. "The camera is now showing thermal imaging. Natalie, step aside."

I stared at the dark screen. A small spot of yellow appeared in the distance, the image slowly spreading on the screen like an ink stain.

"Forty feet," Cornelius said, taking the viewer from Doc, his attention ping-ponging back and forth between both gadgets in his hands.

"Damn it," Doc said. "Killer, we need to go."

"Natalie," I whispered. "Get out of there now. There's a sigil that's being used as a ward on the basement side of the wall." I remembered that clearly from my brush with monsters in that dark tunnel. "That will likely keep whatever is coming from escaping the tunnel." At least I hoped so. "Doc and I are on our way."

We'd made it to the door with Cornelius following on our heels when I heard Natalie's voice at full volume coming from the viewer. "Holy Hell! What are *you* doing here?"

I turned back to Cornelius. "Can you see anyone?"

He shook his head, shielding the viewer screen from the daylight coming through the open door. "But the other dot is now less than fifteen feet in front of her."

"Who is it, Nat?" I asked, hurrying back to him.

She didn't reply.

"Natalie?" I took the viewer from him, the screen turning from black to bright yellow and white. "What's wrong with this thing?" I asked, shaking it.

"Let me check." He took it back while I stared down at the screen along with him.

"The thermal reading is off the chart," he said.

"Violet." Doc grabbed me by the wrist. "Let's go!"

Then the screen went dark. Completely black.

"Natalie?" I called.

Silence.

I looked up and met Cornelius's worried gaze. "Please tell me the camera just died and not my best friend."

He stared at me with wide eyes for a split second and then shot out the door, racing across the street.

I ran after him, slipping on the slush and ice in front of the courthouse and almost landing on my ass next to a silver maple tree. Doc caught me, steadied me, and then we were off again.

Cornelius was already through the doors, moving fast.

My heart pounded in my ears as I struggled to keep up. Damned Natalie and her tendency to run into danger instead of away from it.

"Bravery badges are frickin' overrated," I grumbled.

Doc beat me to the courthouse doors, leading the way inside and across the fancy marble floor toward the elevator. I followed him, thankfully running into nobody else in the process, and hurried through a door off to the side of the elevator that he held open for me.

Inside was a stairwell leading up and down. I saw Cornelius one flight below, opening a steel door.

Doc raced after him, taking the stairs two at a time. He held the door open at the bottom for me. We careened into the basement as Cornelius ran away from us down the long, stone-walled hall over a wooden walkway covering the cement floor. We finally caught the long-legged ostrich a turn later. He stood in the deep alcove full of shadows that the fluorescent lights couldn't fully reach, where the stone-lined opening in the wall about the size of a manhole cover was normally hidden from view.

Earlier this month, after the mess with the *lidérc*, we'd blocked the entrance to the tunnel with boxes, crates, and wood-paneled doors, crossing our fingers that the sigil on the wall next to the hole would continue to do its job as a gatekeeper, as it had for who knew how long. Today, the area around the tunnel entrance was partially cleared, everything stacked to one side. Several black cords ran up the wall and into the tunnel opening.

It appeared that Natalie had made enough room amongst the doors and boxes to climb through the hole into the tunnel. She'd left several stacked wooden crates below as steps. Cornelius climbed onto these crates and stuck his head into the hole.

"What do you see?" I asked, breathing fast partly from the sprint from Doc's office, but mostly out of fear for Natalie. The place smelled the same as before—stale cardboard, damp cement, and a hint of rot.

He leaned in farther, calling out to us, "The camera is still here. One of the cords was loose."

"What about Natalie?" Doc asked, not winded at all.

"She's over here," someone said from behind me. It was a voice that I knew all too well after months of putting up with his bullshit.

I whirled around. Ray Underhill, the biggest horse's ass in all the kingdom, stood a short distance down the hall in a doorway.

Actually, it was *the* doorway. The one that led into the storage room where I'd faced off with the *lidérc* not so long ago ... and almost lost everything.

CHAPTER EIGHTEEN

L et me get this straight, Ray," I said a short time later after picking my jaw up off the floor. "You were just wandering around in an underground tunnel and happened to hear Natalie's voice?"

"I think so," Ray said, although he didn't look like he was certain of his answer.

Hell, for a moment when we'd first joined him and Natalie in the storage room, he seemed foggy, barely certain of his own name, let alone why he was standing in the courthouse basement. But since then, he'd mentally woken up and shaken off some of his confusion. Woken from what, though, I wondered. Had he hit his head recently?

Normally, Ray Underhill had an ultra-polished exterior, from his fake tan to his bleached white teeth and slicked-back brown hair without a single hint of gray to be seen in spite of his fifty-plus years. He was like an avocado that looked perfectly ripe on the outside but was mushy and rotten under the stiff skin.

Today, however, Ray's outer shell showed signs of bruising and rough handling, from his hair that laid flat on his head, matted and dull, to the muddy soles of his name-brand leather boots. His skin appeared paler than I'd ever seen it. Age spots showed on his face above the scruffy start of a beard, and there was a sag in his jowls that matched his drooping shoulders. He looked defeated, his glossy veneer worn through in spots. Confused with a touch of madness that peeked out through his icy-blue eyes as his gaze darted here and there.

"How did you find your way inside the tunnel?" Doc asked, carrying over the lone chair in the room for Ray to sit in before he fell down.

"He told me he doesn't know," Natalie answered from where she was leaning against the wall near the doorway, her arms crossed. She still had dirt smudges on her face, along with dried blood smeared on her forehead, but she was beautifully alive and breathing. "He came walking out of the darkness without even a flashlight in his hand. How bizarre is that? It's pitch black in there."

Ray lowered his wobbly body into the chair, which happened to be the same one I'd sat in weeks ago while trying to fight off the *lidérc*. Being back in this room gave me the creepy-crawlies, making my feet itch to run for higher ground, far away from that hole in the wall and all that had gone down in and around it.

Doc moved a short distance away from Ray, shouldering up next to a pyramid of slumped file boxes with several cardboard tubes resting against them. "The closet door in Jane's old office is still stuck closed, right?" He looked to Natalie and then me for an answer.

Cornelius had returned to the hole in the wall to check on his fancy camera again and the attached remote viewer. That left the three of us to figure out the mystery behind Ray's sudden appearance in the tunnel, which had two known forks—one that led to the Hellhole and the other down into the deeper dark.

I shrugged. "As far as I know, but I didn't go in there today. The outer office door was closed when I walked by it each time. I was only at work for a short while before my appointment this morning, and then I came over to have lunch with you right after the clients left."

"Corny and I checked the monitors in his apartment when we returned from taking the clock around," Natalie said. "The door was still shut from what we could tell, but neither of us thought to double-check it."

"Ray could have snuck in the back door while Mona and I were both out showing houses. Ben was there alone for hours with the front and back doors unlocked. If Ray were watching, he could have gone in when Ben went to the bathroom or he was on a phone call."

"Ray," Natalie said. "Did you sneak into Jane's old office this morning and go down through the trap door in the closet floor?"

His brow lined as he stared down at his clasped hands, which were trembling. "No. At least I don't think so. I don't remember going to Calamity Jane's at all."

"What do you remember?" Doc asked.

Ray let out a shaky sigh. He looked frail under the fluorescent light, his cheeks gaunt under his beard stubble. His paranoia of late about someone stalking him, for which he'd repeatedly blamed me, seemed to be eating him alive from the inside out.

"I remember going to Mudder Brothers," he answered.

Mudder Brothers Funeral Parlor, huh? That was where I'd found Ray one terrifying August evening strapped to an autopsy table on the verge of being dissected. We both undoubtedly shared nightmares about that night—him about being nearly dissected into bloody Ray pieces, me about finding him naked as a plucked goose in a chilled room that gave off an odor of formaldehyde and death. Not to mention the decapitation part of the show starring Ray's partner in crate-moving crime. I still winced at the memory.

So, why would Ray go back there at all? Especially when the place was closed up at the moment?

"Eddie is gone for a conference all week," I told Ray.

"I know that, Blondie," he said with a snide lip curl.

Ahh, there was that condescending prick that I knew and loathed. His earlier confusion seemed to be wearing off more and more. "Then why did you go?"

He peered up at me with red-rimmed eyes. "You remember the note I left you?"

"The supposedly anonymous one that said I'd screwed things up and you were being followed because of me?"

His eyes narrowed. "Yeah, that one."

"Let's see, that particular time you blamed me for running my mouth about something, of which you didn't specify and that could be anything considering all of the people I talk to on a daily basis, so next time you write an accusatory note, try to be more clear."

Natalie snort-laughed. "Snap!"

Ray's glare hardened, his cheeks turning a ruddy pink.

"Oh, and you said that if I didn't fix whatever wrong I'd supposedly done," I continued, "you'd tell some mysterious 'them' the truth. I don't know which truth you meant, but you seemed to think that this would make me quake in my boots." I glared back. "It doesn't."

He pointed at me, snarling. "Because of you, Blondie, I'm in this mess! No job. I can't sleep. I keep forgetting things. And someone is following me, watching every damn thing I do."

"Ray," Natalie said, still holding her spot by the door. "Violet has no time to deal with your demons with all that's on her plate now."

Hoo boy! Wasn't that the truth!

"I was fine before you came to town," he grumbled, hating me out loud with his eyes. "I had everyone in the palm of my hand, including Jane."

He never had Jane. Actually, he'd had her carnally right before her death, but according to Jane, that had been a weak moment when she'd run low on self-confidence thanks to an ugly, drawn-out divorce from ex-husband number 3.

"You have a major screw loose that connects your brain to reality, Ray," I said, frowning down at the man who used to be the self-proclaimed king of real estate. Oh, how the high and mighty fall. "At what point are you going to tighten things up north of your chin and realize that you've fallen down into this well of self-pity by tripping over your own gargantuan ego."

"No!" He stood up from the chair, his fists clenched. "It's all your fault, you bitch!"

Doc stepped between us. "Calm down, Ray. Violet hasn't done anything to draw attention to you." He glanced over his shoulder at me. "Maybe you should take a different tack, Tiger. Something has obviously knocked him off course lately. What we need to figure out right now is if the sources of his fears are internal or external."

I stepped back, putting some much-needed space between the arrogant ape and me. Ray settled into the chair, looking away from me as he huffed out his anger.

"Ray," Doc said calmly. "Why were you at Mudder Brothers today?"

Ray sniffed, wiping his nose with the back of his leather coat sleeve. "I was going to see if I could find something."

"Find what?" Natalie asked, moving next to Doc.

"Something I remembered George Mudder messing with once. Something in that room full of all those butchering tools."

He must be talking about the museum room in the basement where George and Eddie kept an assortment of macabre, antique mortician tools, including shears, knives, pinchers, drills, handsaws, and more. There had even been an amputation kit from the Civil

War era in there full of crude tools used on those poor soldiers in the battlefield.

"What was it George was messing with?" Natalie continued her interrogation. She must be taking lessons from Cooper.

Was it the huge, bone-cutting scissors I'd grabbed from the wall in that room and jammed into the back of the white-haired Juggernaut, who'd been on the verge of slicing Doc into ribbons? I'd always remember that first kill. At the time, I'd hoped it would be my last, but the joke was on me.

"There was a bookcase in there," Ray said, staring down at his hands again. "A big oak one full of journals and ledgers George had collected over the years from other morticians. Records of autopsies dating well over a century ago, back when unauthorized experiments weren't scrutinized closely, according to him. Some even contained drawings and pictures that were really gross. George had such a morbid curiosity about death."

Ray sat back, taking a breath, and then scowled up at Doc. "One night, I showed up at the funeral parlor when Eddie was out of town. I was supposed to pick up a shipment from an abandoned shack near Slagton per George's instructions, but I'd gotten a flat tire on the way home from work and was running late, so I'd decided to skip the pickup until the next day. I swung by the funeral parlor to let George know about the delay in person, because he wasn't answering his phone."

Natalie and I exchanged knowing looks. We'd spied on Ray and George one night together, watching them unload a crate that when opened had made George visibly upset and Ray get all threatening toward the funeral director. She and I had also sneaked into Mudder Brothers' side room more than once, finding a crate containing bottles of mead the last time. I wanted to ask Ray what else had been in the shipments and if all the crates were coming from Slagton, but that could wait.

After my experiences last month out in Slagton, it wasn't much of a surprise to find out some of the goods had come from the old mining town, which Doc had theorized was a stage stop for the *others* traveling to and from our world.

"I entered through the back doors that night, the ones where they move the bodies and coffins in and out." Ray's focus returned to his hands, which were once again trembling. "I was heading toward George's office when I heard a scraping sound coming from the antiques room along with the sound of voices. I knew Eddie was gone, so I looked through the doorway and saw one of the big white-haired freaks disappear behind the bookcase, which was pulled out from the wall."

Doc turned my way, his mouth drawn thin. I nodded, on track with him. That so-called white-haired freak had to be the Juggernaut I'd killed with the big scissors. Or maybe Mr. Black.

"The phone rang in George's office about then," Ray continued. "I hid around the corner as he went to answer it. While he was out of the way, I snuck inside and took a peek behind the bookcase." He shook his head, his face crisscrossed with wrinkles from his forehead to his jowls. "That was where I screwed up. I should have known better, but after months of moving crates that I was instructed not to open at any cost, curiosity got the best of me."

"What was behind the bookcase, Ray?" Natalie asked.

"There was a heavy steel door in the wall. Like one you'd see on a safe, only without a combination lock. It had a keyhole. A skeleton key was sticking out of it."

Ah, hell. Not another secret door. They always led to trouble. Why couldn't a hidden door just once lead to a pot of gold?

"The door was partly open, enough that I could see inside." Ray covered his face with his hands. "But it was so dark. And it stank, like spoiled milk and rancid dirt."

I gulped. Those were the same smells I'd noticed coming from the Hellhole. "Was there anything on the wall next to the door?" I asked. "A diamond-shaped drawing of some sort?"

"Some kind of cryptic symbol?" Natalie added.

"I don't remember. I wasn't there very long because I heard the sound of someone coming toward me from the darkness and I was afraid it was the big freak on his way back." He dragged his fingers down his face. "I ran out the door and down the hall. But I think George saw me. No, I'm sure he saw me, because the next night when I brought the crate to him, he asked if I'd been around the prior night, and I lied. I said I hadn't. But I could see in his eyes that he didn't believe me."

Ray's knees started to bounce. "I also saw that he was scared. I didn't understand why right then, but I figured it out the next time I saw the white-haired freak. He looked at me differently after that.

Like he knew I'd peeked into that tunnel and he was going to enjoy making me pay for my curiosity."

Ray's focus shifted my way, his eyes narrowed into thin slits. "That's why I told you to keep your nose out of my business, Blondie."

I ignored his sneer. "So, that's why the white-haired Juggernaut was going to slice you to pieces the night I showed up in the autopsy room, wasn't it?"

He nodded. "I'd seen too much, or so he thought—that door and what was on the other side. Only I hadn't, really."

I thought back to that time, back when Mr. Black had also been prowling around Mudder Brothers while pretending to work with the Juggernaut. Why hadn't he mentioned something about a hidden door to me? Maybe he didn't know about it. Then again, maybe he did and he didn't figure I needed to be in the know about that. Either way, I had a feeling that now I was going to have to see this door and find out where it led.

"I tried to tell the son of a bitch while he was strapping me to that fucking table that I hadn't seen anything. I swore over and over I'd keep quiet about the door, and I'd never go in that room again. That he could trust me. George told him the same. He begged for my life." Ray closed his eyes, his face crumpling. "But that bastard didn't care. I needed to die, and he was going to enjoy making it happen slowly."

"I recall hearing bits of that," I said, looking from Ray to Doc and then Natalie. "I remember George pleading on Ray's behalf right before …" I trailed off. My eyes welled with tears about what had come next. "George was a good man. He may have gotten into something he shouldn't have with the *others*, but he didn't deserve the punishment the Juggernaut handed down."

Doc reached over and squeezed my shoulder.

"You've really fucked things up around here, Blondie," Ray said, glaring, apparently back to blaming me for his own screwups. "You have the hornets all riled up and they're sting-happy. They're coming for me now. And they're coming for you, too."

Gee whillikers, as if that were breaking news in my world. But Ray didn't need to hear anything about me and the hand-me-down abilities that came with my family's DNA. Him knowing my "Spooky Parker" nickname was enough.

"Ray," Doc said, drawing the blowhard's attention his way. "Did you actually go into Mudder Brothers tonight?"

"Yeah."

"You broke in?" Natalie asked. "How did you get past Eddie's alarm?"

"I didn't break in. I still have a key and the code George gave me. Eddie hasn't changed it yet."

"Did you go down into that antiquities room with the intention of accessing the secret door?" Doc asked.

Ray nodded, but then his face tightened in a spasm. "I don't remember anything after standing in front of the bookcase, though, at least not until I heard Natalie's voice in the dark."

Cornelius dashed into the room at that moment, skidding to a stop next to me. His cornflower blue eyes were big and bright with excitement. "There's a side tunnel!"

"Yeah, I know," I said, noticing a cobweb in his black hair. "Don't you remember I told you about it before?" Why was his coat streaked with cobwebs, too? And swaths of dust? "It branches off to the right … no, to the left if you're entering the tunnel from here. The corbel vaulted beams holding up the ceiling don't follow that side tunnel down, though. It changes to old timber beams. At least as far as I could see."

"That's not the one I'm talking about." He glanced at Doc and Natalie, then back at me, his usually pale cheeks clearly flushed. "There's another tunnel. It's hard to see because of the rocks and shadows. The entrance is located in a hollow, nothing more than a tight passage that blends in with the surrounding rock. You probably passed it on prior visits without even realizing it's there."

"How do you know that?" I pointed at the radar gun–like apparatus in his hand. "Can you see that on your thermal thingamajiggie?"

"Of course not, Violet. Rock and air do not show up on a thermal radar." His smile widened, almost frighteningly so. "I went inside the tunnel and found the passageway while following that one's tracks in the dirt." He pointed at Ray. "Although there was a place near the fork where it appeared he traversed deeper into the other tunnel you mentioned."

"You went inside!" I wasn't asking, more like affirming that Cornelius's brain had temporarily flown the coop.

"Hot damn!" Natalie patted Cornelius on the back. "That's one hell of a set of snowballs on you, Captain Cornelius. I was shaky just being inside the hole in the wall, having heard Violet's horror stories."

"How far up this other tunnel did you follow Ray's footprints?" Doc asked.

"You went inside," I said again, shaking my head in disbelief.

"Can someone nudge Violet," Natalie said. "The needle on her record seems to be stuck in a groove."

I waved off her joke. "You guys have no idea what nightmares might be lurking in that place, waiting to grab you and tear you to pieces. But I do!" And they still haunted me when I was alone in the dark.

"A white hound," Ray said from behind me.

We all turned toward him.

"What did you say?" Natalie asked.

"I saw it!"

I stepped closer to Ray. "What are you talking about?"

He pointed toward the door. "I remember now. It wasn't Natalie who woke me up from the trance, or whatever it was when I went in through the door at Mudder Brothers. There were two bright orbs ahead in the dark. Glowing. I went toward them, deeper, and found a white hound waiting there."

"You saw an actual white furred hound of some kind in the passageway that went deeper into the earth?" Doc recapped, as if he were getting Ray's story straight for the record.

"Uh-huh. The glowing orbs were its eyes. It had a short snout. And long silvery-white fur on its shoulders, arms, and down its back. Big claws, too." He held out his hands as an example. "And teeth." He shivered. "Pointy teeth."

"That sounds like a strong candidate for the Hellhound title to me," Doc said, frowning my way.

I frowned back. The Hellhound was in the tunnel. Well, that explained why the clock hands were spinning above the Hellhole and nowhere else around town. It must be waiting at the gate.

"It was big. Taller than me." Ray nodded hard, his jowls shaking. "This sounds crazy, but I swear it's true. The thing was standing up on two legs when I got there, waiting for me. And for some reason, I wasn't afraid of it."

Maybe it had put some sort of spell on him. A trick it used to lure in its victims.

"Ray, are you sure this wasn't something you dreamed up while you were in your weird trance state?" Natalie asked.

"I'm mostly sure. It even talked to me in my head." Ray looked around at each of us, his expression almost manic. "Raspy like with some sort of accent, but I could understand it. I know that sounds really crazy, but it's true. I swear."

I rested my hand on my chest, feeling my heart rock and roll under my palm. "Maybe not *really* crazy," I murmured.

He perked up. "Oh, and I remember what the hound said, too."

Cornelius leaned closer. "That it was going to blow your house down?"

I would have chuckled, like Natalie, if I weren't so anxious to hear what Ray had to say next.

"It wanted me to give a message to someone with a weird name," Ray continued, his forehead forming into a series of V's. "It had this gargled sound to it. Like a sharfer. Maybe sharkfer. No, sharkfrick-something."

I crossed my arms. "Was it *Scharfrichter*?" I asked, using plenty of guttural stress when I spoke my official title.

"I think that's it!" Ray looked from me to Doc and then back, his eyes bright, clearer than they'd been since we'd first arrived to find him here with Natalie.

"What was the message?" Doc asked, but his focus was on me instead of Ray.

I braced myself for the usual threat on my life or worse, on my kids' lives.

Ray licked his lips. "It said that the myth is not true." He began pacing in front of the chair while shaking his head. "There was something else. Something about someone named …" He snapped his fingers. "Ayla. That was it."

"Ayla," I repeated.

I only knew of one Ayla. She was an ancestor of mine who'd lived back before the dark ages. Her killing deeds had been written about in one of our family history books. Fortunately for her, she was one of the few in the family *Scharfrichter* line who made it to old age.

I moved closer to Doc, turning my back to Ray who'd returned to pacing and muttering while tugging at his hair. "You remember that name?"

"Of course. I would've liked to watch Ayla in action. She must have been a clever fighter to live so long, like someone else I know."

"Or maybe she was just this side of deranged," I jested. "Do you really think it could be the same Ayla?"

"Yeah, considering these circumstances."

I took a deep breath. "You know what this means, don't you?"

"What does it mean?" Natalie asked, joining our huddle. "I don't remember who Ayla is."

That was because Natalie had been down visiting her cousins in Arizona over New Year's Eve, when we'd learned about this particular ancestor.

Cornelius leaned into our group. "Ayla is one of Violet's predecessors who mated with Charan the Basque, a Summoner, and produced many babies."

Wow, he'd been paying close attention that night.

Natalie's eyebrows rose. "How many babies are we talking about?"

"Too many," I said, cringing. "Three sets of fraternal twins plus two more boys."

"Damn." Natalie let out a low whistle. "You and Doc had better get busy."

I threatened to pop her in the nose.

"Ayla was both very deadly and extremely fertile," Cornelius whispered. "And there is something about that combination that spikes my testosterone level."

"Hear, hear," Doc said, giving me a wink.

"So, what does this Ayla business mean?" Natalie returned to her original question.

Doc looked toward the doorway and shook his head. "It means Violet is going into that tunnel again."

Oh, not just me this time.

I locked onto Doc's wrist. "Yes, *we* are."

CHAPTER NINETEEN

We decided to delay our trip into the Hellhole tunnel until the evening for several reasons.

For starters, I had no mace or bat or club of any kind on me, and I refused to go into the tunnel with nothing more than my sharp tongue and killer wit. Of course, Prudence would have chastised me for this decision and called me a clodpoll, a word that I'd since looked up in the dictionary. Foolish blockhead or not, I liked breathing oxygen, so sticks and stones might break my bones but a tunnel monster was not going to slay me today. At least not if I could help it.

In addition to my lack of something solid and deadly to swing in the dark, Doc had a late afternoon appointment for which he needed to do some prep.

"Money before monsters," I said, happy to put off entering that hole in the wall for a reason other than my current level of lily-livered-ness. Was that even a word?

How on earth Doc was going to be able to talk about putting away tax-sheltered dollars and maximizing return on investments without staring off into space and picturing what the representative of the Hellhound clock might look like in person was beyond me. But if anyone could pull it off, the Oracle could.

There was one thing, though, about this whole Ray situation that had me hesitating going into the tunnel at all. While Doc, Natalie, Cornelius, and I all agreed that Ray's tale about whatever was waiting for a *Scharfrichter* in the dark, along with the mention of my ancestor's name, were probably *not* just coincidences, there was a troubling snag in the tale Ray had woven: Why had he blacked out between the entrance to the tunnel in Mudder Brothers Funeral Parlor and the location of this "white hound"? If we were to follow his path, starting at Mudder Brothers, would we black out as well, making us vulnerable to whatever waited down there?

The four of us decided to relocate to Doc's office and come up with some sort of plan of action before Doc had to prep for his client. We invited Ray to join us so we could pick his brain a little more, thinking maybe he'd be able to focus better away from the hole in the wall, but he'd shifted back into asshole mode and started accusing me of drugging him and sending him into the tunnel.

There was no reasoning with Ray's idiocy, and because I had left my mace at home, beating sense into him wasn't an option. Although Natalie and I both voted that it should be one, if we could find something hard enough to make the beating count.

In the end, Doc sent Ray on his way down the sidewalk without further interrogation while I waved at the jerk's back … with my middle finger due to his last comment about my hair color affecting my intelligence. Jeez, some clodpolls never changed.

Over at Doc's office, the four of us put our heads together once again and decided it was time to call in for backup, aka Cooper. After working through the night, it took Mr. Detective a moment to not only wake up, but to catch up, which he did by listening to our recap in between spouting his usual colorful expletives.

Doc had a theory that Ray's blackout might be somehow tied to the invisible skirmish in Jerry's office that we'd witnessed through Cornelius's video cameras on Tuesday. That seemed a bit of a reach to Natalie and me, but Cornelius weighed in on Doc's side of the scale. The chances of all of this paranormal activity happening within such a small radius seemed much more than a coincidence to him.

"Have you considered that this white hound creature might be playing a trick on Parker?" Cooper asked through Doc's speakerphone. "Setting a trap for her?"

"Yes, we did," I said. "That was why we didn't want to go in there until I was properly weaponized." I flexed my arm muscles for Natalie's and Doc's benefit, earning grins back from both of them. Cornelius was too busy staring down at his remote viewing gadget again while pressing more buttons to notice my clowning.

"I don't think that word can be used that way, babe," Natalie said, still chuckling.

"Who died and elected you Dictionary Deputy?"

"More important," Cooper said tersely from the speaker, "What in the hell were you thinking by going into that hole in the wall, Nat? That was clearly a risk not worth taking in this fight. Not even for your best friend. You're not immortal, you know."

In a blink, Natalie's cheeks turned bright red and her eyes narrowed into a shootout-at-high-noon, hard squint. Cooper had not just gotten her dander up, but sent it flying high where it was now circling in for the kill.

Crud. Was this really the hill Cooper wanted to die on?

"Neither are you, Coop," she snapped. "And fuck you for your lack of faith in my ability and thinking that you are more bulletproof than anyone else on this team just because you have multiple guns. I hope the next bullet that flies your way hits you in the ass!"

She reached down and punched the button to end the call. "That damned man thinks I'm going to just sit home and knit hot pads while he runs around hunting monsters." She blew out a breath and forced a smile onto her cheeks for Doc and me before turning toward Cornelius. "The cards were right, Corny."

What cards was she talking about? Cornelius's tarot deck?

"As they often tend to be," Cornelius said, barely sparing her a glance while dinking around with his remote viewer.

"Are you okay?" I asked her.

"Yes." She grimaced. "Wait, I change my answer to 'No.' That bossy man makes my fangs itch."

"Welcome to the club," I said, giving her a sideways hug. "We have monogrammed toothbrushes."

Natalie frowned in Doc's direction. "Sorry for that public display of ass-chewing. Since the four of us have agreed to wait until this evening to go into the tunnel again, I'm going to run home, wash the cobwebs out of my hair, and try to cool down before I go nuclear."

"Do you want a ride home?" Doc asked.

"No, thanks. I'm literally going to run outside in the freezing cold wind for the few blocks between here and there to chill the hell out."

Muttering under her breath, she took off out the door.

"What did she mean about the cards being right?" I asked Cornelius.

He looked up. "She wanted to have a reading this morning, so she asked the question and I drew cards for her."

"What was the question?" Doc asked.

He shrugged. "Something about how her relationship would progress with the bristly detective."

When he focused back on his remote viewer without further explanation, I grabbed it away from him. "And? What five cards did you pull?"

"I only drew three—a simple three-card lineup for past, present, and future." He made a pained face. When he continued, I realized he was just thinking. "There'd been the Nine of Swords for the past, showing that she is feeling oppressed. Then the Four of Cups for the present, which signified her boredom and disgruntled feelings about the current situation. And finally the Three of Swords for the future, which predicted a quarrel and potential misery due to separation."

"Bing, bang, boom," I said, watching through the front window as she jogged away.

"I reshuffled then and did another drawing." His cornflower blue eyes landed on me. "This time for you."

"Great. Let me guess. The Tower card has returned for another shitstorm."

"Actually, no."

Doc leaned against his desk, pulling me back against him. "What question did you ask for Violet?"

"What might happen if she went into the tunnel today to figure out why the clock keeps spinning."

"What cards did I get this time? The three cards representing sunshine, happiness, and big lollipops for all?"

Cornelius's cockeyed grin appeared. "Not quite. I drew five cards, returning to the Cross of Truth spread for you. No need to vary the method, I figured."

"And what say the tarot gods?"

"The two most important and relevant to a trip into the tunnel had to do with challenges and outcome," Cornelius said. "They were the Hanged Man and the High Priestess, respectfully."

"Hanged Man?"

"Yes. In short, the card can indicate self-sacrifice and seeing a situation from a different perspective."

"A hanging man shows this?"

"Remember, he is hanging voluntarily."

I frowned up at Doc. "Who hangs voluntarily?"

"What does the other card indicate?" he asked Cornelius.

"You're buying into this?" I asked, a little surprised, although knowing some of his experiences with the supernatural, I shouldn't have been.

"You don't?"

I shrugged. "Depends on the hour and how deep the crap is at that moment."

Doc smiled. "Good answer." He turned back to Cornelius. "What did the other card represent?"

"The High Priestess shows that there may be secrets to be revealed and mysteries to be solved." He focused on me. Actually, he was staring at the middle of my forehead. "Violet may need to focus outward through her third eye to see that there is more depth and complexity to a matter than she'd previously believed."

"What if my third eye is itchy and crusty with conjunctivitis?" I half joked, but sort of serious.

"Then you should follow your intuition and trust your instincts tonight when you traverse the Hellhole tunnel to find what awaits you there."

"Yeah, about doing that tonight …"

"Affirmative!"

"What?"

Cornelius grabbed his remote viewer back from me. "I must go prepare."

"Are you going to clean out your chakras again?" I asked.

"Of course not, Violet. The veil between is far too opaque for that today."

What veil was he talking about? More important, "Between what?"

"And *when!*" he added, instead of answering. "I need to charge all camera batteries, make sure the monitors are online, test that my devices are ready to record, and thaw a T-bone." After a pat on my head, he left us.

"At least you didn't get the Tower card again," Doc said, chuckling.

"Yeah, that kind of fell on Natalie and Cooper today." I settled back into his arms, enjoying being cocooned for the moment while I watched traffic roll past outside his front window. "How about we wait until next week to go into the tunnel? Or maybe even next month?"

He dropped a kiss on my temple. "I'll be there with you tonight, Killer. Don't forget to try to contact Ray to see if he'll give you that extra key and the code into Mudder Brothers. And ask nicely even if he is an ass. I'd really like to check out that tunnel as soon as possible."

I didn't look forward to asking Ray for help. He'd probably just whine some more about how I'd screwed up his life. "I'd rather we send Ray in again alone with a video camera strapped to his head for our viewing pleasure while we sit up in Cornelius's place, watching as we eat T-bone steaks."

My phone rang. "It's Ben," I said after glancing down at the screen. "I'd better take it in case Ray wandered over there and tattled to his nephew about his misadventure down in the tunnel underneath Calamity Jane's."

I answered the call. Thankfully, it was only a request for me to come babysit the office while he took a walk-in client around town. Mona had left to meet another real estate agent from Hill City to talk about some properties a couple of buyers down that way might like to check out.

After a quick kiss good-bye, I left Doc to prepare for his client and returned to Calamity Jane's.

For much of the afternoon, I found myself struggling to stay focused on real estate. After all, way down under my feet something was waiting for me to come say "Howdy." Something that undoubtedly had the usual *other* deadly accouterments.

A while later, Mona returned from her meeting and proceeded to watch me over the top of her reading glasses as I fiddled and doodled in between sighing and knuckle chewing. However, since I continued to assure her that everything was "just fine" each time she leaned on me to spill my guts about what was bothering me, she didn't act surprised when I told her I was leaving early to go home and spend some time with my kids. Although she did make me promise to call her if everything wasn't "just fine" and I needed her help.

Instead of reaching out to Ray on the way home, I called Eddie Mudder, expecting to land in his voicemail box. Surprisingly, he answered.

"Eddie, I have a big favor to ask."

He was all ears. And then he was shocked into silence to learn about the tunnel under his place of business. So much so that I thought we'd lost signal for a few seconds.

Eddie proceeded to tell me that George had said there was no key to that door behind the bookcase. That it was just an old empty safe. George had blocked it with the bookcase because it was supposedly useless.

I wasn't sure how deep into this world of *others* that Eddie was at this time, or how much his brother had been mixed up in it all, so I tried to be as vague as possible about why we wanted to go into the tunnel. He bought that Ray knew about the tunnel thanks to George, and that we'd figured out it led to Calamity Jane Realty and wanted to explore it out of curiosity. His surprise that Ray knew of a skeleton key for the door seemed genuine.

Poor Eddie. So much had been happening right under his nose. Then again, knowing George's fate, maybe Eddie being in the dark was a blessing.

Eddie told me that he wouldn't be home for a few more days. However, he was happy to let me know where he kept a spare key and the code to the alarm, which saved me having to call Ray and put up with more of his insults in order to get into the funeral parlor tonight.

I wrapped up the call with one last request—would he try to get hold of Mr. Black again to set up a meeting with me? He agreed and told me to be careful with that heavy, old bookcase. He didn't want it to fall on anyone.

Ha! If only the bookcase were the true danger we were facing tonight.

With nothing else to do before our journey into the tunnel but fill in Aunt Zoe on my day, I parked in the driveway and went inside to grab a drink. The stronger the better.

Through the kitchen window, I saw the kids building a snow fort in the backyard while Aunt Zoe watched them from the doorway of her glass workshop. I skipped the drink and slipped out the door, kissing Addy and Layne on their cold red cheeks as I passed, refusing to let Rooster kiss me when I reached down to pat him on the head. Then I joined Aunt Zoe and we moved inside her workshop, where I filled her ears with tunnel tales.

When I was finished, she stared out the window at the kids, who now had Elvis the chicken standing guard while it wore one of the sweaters my mother had knitted for the dang bird. Rooster was running around the fort in circles, yipping every time he passed Elvis, who fluffed her wings and squawked at him.

"What do you think?" I asked Aunt Zoe.

She blew out a breath and turned to me with a small scowl lining her cheeks and forehead. "I think we need Reid to come to supper."

"What? Why?"

"Because he told me last night that when I need him, he'd be here for me, and right now we *need* someone to stay with the kids this evening."

I half-laughed, half-scoffed. "I think he meant another kind of need. The hot and breathy kind."

"If so, then he shouldn't have been so vague," she said with a wink.

"What about Harvey? He might be able to hang out here with the kids for a couple of hours. Or maybe Natalie?" I was being optimistic that we would go into the tunnel and come back out without hitting any snags. Probably foolishly so, but it was the only way I could charge forth instead of hiding in the closet next to Elvis.

"Harvey needs to come with us into the tunnel in case we need Prudence's eyes on this situation, so you should probably give Zelda a call and have her put Prudence on alert."

"How does seeing through Harvey's eyes even work for Prudence?"

Aunt Zoe shrugged. "You should ask her next time you see her."

"Or not. She'll probably poke me in the eye as part of the explanation."

"You'll have to wear my safety goggles to her lesson," she said, grinning at my grumbling curses about Prudence's style of schooling. "As for Natalie, she needs to be with Cornelius at his place, watching his monitors in case anything else tries to come through Jerry's office or the courthouse tunnel to get a jump on you by surprise."

"Good thinking. Where are you going to be?"

"With you." She crossed her arms. "I want to see whatever it is making those damned clock hands spin."

CHAPTER TWENTY

Walking around a dark funeral parlor at night was right up there with tiptoeing through a graveyard. There might not have been any dead bodies laid out upstairs in the viewing parlor or attached to tubes down in the autopsy room, but the ghosts of the dead probably roamed the halls here. It certainly felt like they were. I'd have to ask Cooper to be certain of that, though, since he was the only one of us who could see ghosts, but he was being a bristly badger at the moment, so I bit my tongue.

"Parker, would you move your ass a little faster? Some of us have to be back to work in the morning."

What was he talking about? We all had to be back to work, except for Harvey, and he probably had a hot date planned for later tonight.

"Nobody invited you along tonight, Cooper," I said as I followed Doc and Aunt Zoe down the stairs to the basement level.

"That's not true, Killer," Doc said, holding the door at the bottom for us.

"Okay, make that I was strong-armed by the rest of the team into inviting you to join us, so quit barking at me. It's not my fault you're in the doghouse with your girlfriend right now. I tried to warn you, but you wouldn't listen." I pulled a walkie-talkie from my pocket. "Natalie," I said into the speaker. "Tell your snarly boyfriend to stop barking at me. Over."

Harvey guffawed from the rear of our five-person train. "The law dog is in the doghouse."

"Zip it, Uncle Willis." Cooper poked me between the shoulder blades. "You, too, Parker. And leave Nat out of this."

"Leaving her out of things is what got you into hot water with her," I said, slipping past Doc into the basement hallway. "Haven't you learned your lesson yet?"

"Coop, don't take this out on Violet," Natalie's voice came through both the walkie-talkie in my hand and the one strapped to Cooper's belt. "She's not the one trying to keep me handcuffed to the bed day and night. Over."

"Kinky," I said, snickering along with Harvey as Doc closed the stairwell door behind us.

"Which way to the room with the hidden door?" Aunt Zoe asked, staring down the long hall that ended at the autopsy room on the left and the exit doors on the right.

The room we were looking for was the other way.

I aimed the pointy end of my mace in the direction of the room full of mortuary antiquities. "Follow me."

I led the way, pausing in the doorway to hit the lights before threading through the macabre exhibits the Mudder brothers and their ancestors had accumulated over the years. Just the sight of some of them made me shiver. Other pieces made me wince. Eddie really should move this stuff to a local museum so that others could learn about the history of their profession, even if the tales of how things were done way back when were often gruesome. It probably would be a big attraction come Halloween.

The air smelled of dust and old books, along with a hint of formaldehyde. It could have been worse, I figured, considering the messy work Eddie did just down the hall.

"I'm killing the lights," Cooper said, flicking them off. "Keep your flashlight beams down. The station knows that Eddie is gone and there are officers doing periodic drive-bys. We don't need anyone dropping in to see what we're up to in here."

Aunt Zoe turned on her flashlight, lighting up the floor in front of us.

The bookcase that usually blocked the entrance to the tunnel was pulled away from the wall thanks to Ray. The door behind it was closed, but the skeleton key was still in it, exactly where Ray said he'd left it before blacking out.

I continued to have my doubts about Ray's story and him somehow magically ending up in the tunnel. He could be leading us into a trap as payback for me still having a job at Calamity Jane

Realty, even though he'd hosed himself when it came to working there.

Aunt Zoe focused her flashlight on the skeleton key. "Well, at least that's some good luck."

"Is it, though?" I asked wryly, stepping aside so Doc and Cooper could take a closer look.

"Hmm. There's no sigil here," she said, shining her light around the frame of the door. "At least none visible."

I searched the wall, too. "They can be invisible?" If that were the case, this was going to make my job catching the imp even harder.

She shrugged. "It's possible, depending on what was used to make the sigil."

One tug by Doc and the steel door swung wide without a single creak.

"George must have been keeping the hinges oiled," Cooper said, his brow crisscrossed with frown lines. I had a feeling those lines had as much to do with Natalie as the tunnel we were about to enter.

I almost felt sorry for Cooper. But if he wanted to date a homebody who would wait on him hand and foot and never take dares, he shouldn't have set his sights on Natalie.

"George or someone else," Doc said, shining his flashlight into the dark mouth of the tunnel.

I thought back to the time after George was killed when I'd first learned that the law dog knew about Ray running shipments to and fro. "Cooper, you knew about the crates that George had Ray transporting, but did you have any idea where George was getting the stuff?"

He and his frown lines turned my way. Before he could say a word, I added, "And don't give me that police business bullshit. Not while we're standing here waiting to go into this freaking tunnel that's probably overrun with spiders and rats and other sharp-toothed pests."

Harvey harrumphed from behind Doc. "And hair-raisin' critters that'll send us runnin' back here with our tails between our legs."

"Like I said, spiders and rats."

"And five-inch-long centipedes," Aunt Zoe said. When I scowled at her, she shrugged. "What? I thought we were listing things we found unpleasant."

"If that were the case, I should have added Cooper's attitude tonight to the list."

"Parker," Cooper said with a definite huff. "I was going to answer your damned question if you'd have given me a chance. In the future, if you're going to interrogate someone, you need to keep your big mouth shut long enough for them to reply."

"Now is your chance." I mimed zipping my lips.

"No, I hadn't figured out yet where George was getting the items he was moving. Or who was supplying them." He thumbed toward the tunnel. "Maybe I'll know more after tonight."

"Coop's feelin' ornery," Harvey said, sidling up next to me. "You best duck if he pulls out his Colt. Bessie and I will have your back."

"There will be no shooting in a rock-lined tunnel," I said, glaring at both of them in turn, since Harvey had refused to come unless he could bring his shotgun along, and Cooper wouldn't listen to reason about packing heat.

"Violet Lynn." Aunt Zoe took me by the wrist. "Quit delaying the inevitable." She stooped as she walked through the entryway, pulling me along behind her.

I aimed my mace at Cooper as I passed him. "Maybe *we* will know more about those shipments after tonight. We're a team now, remember?"

His eyes narrowed, but he nodded while raising his walkie-talkie to his mouth. "We're heading inside," he said into the microphone. "Switch to breadcrumb mode. Over."

"10-4," Natalie said. "Corny says there's no sign of visitors under the courthouse, and Jerry's office appears to be clear. Over."

"Gotcha," Cooper said as he waited for his uncle to step inside the tunnel. "We'll check in via the camera at the other end. Over."

"Stay safe, law dog. Over." Natalie's voice crackled on that last word as Cooper pulled the door mostly closed behind us, leaving it open a sliver as an escape route.

Then we were in the dark.

Make that mostly in the dark, since Aunt Zoe, Doc, and Cooper had their flashlights on. Per the plan for tonight's underground escapade, Harvey and I were to hold off using our lights in order to save battery power in case things went sideways down here. In my opinion, things were already sideways. I had my fingers crossed that this trip didn't end with me upside down. Or worse, reenacting the

Hanged Man card Corny had pulled earlier from his tarot deck.

"Well," I said in a low voice, breathing in cool, musty air as I peered ahead into the darkness awaiting us. "As secret underground tunnels go, this one seems fair to middling. Roomy with a tall ceiling and enough width to walk two side-by-side. And as a bonus, the temperature will stay the same year around."

Doc chuckled from behind me. "Nice sales pitch, Agent Parker. I'm interested, but is it move-in ready?"

"It comes unfurnished, Mr. Nyce, and short one curly-haired blonde."

"I'll pass then. The blonde is the deal breaker."

"I'll take it," Cooper said. "Blondes give me heartburn."

I rolled my eyes. "Of course you would want it, Detective. It's a big, bulletproof safe room."

"It would make a great man-cave," Aunt Zoe whispered. "Except for the occasional visit from a deadly *other* or two."

"A lonely, one-man cave for Coop," Harvey said from the back. "At least until you get out of hot water with your woman."

"She's not *my* woman," Cooper said. "She's her own woman. Nat doesn't like possessive pronouns."

"Or possessive boyfriends who think they can run her life," I added, thinking of a few of the men in her past who'd gotten the boot.

"Just shut up and lead, Parker," he said, sounding more tired than annoyed.

I did lead us farther along, but I wasn't ready to shut up yet. "What did you mean by 'breadcrumb mode,' Cooper?" I asked over my shoulder.

"It means we're on our own until we reach Cornelius's camera at the courthouse," he explained.

"I'd rather he meant banana-bread mode," Harvey said from the back of the line. "I could use some sugar to settle my nerves."

"Are you talking about your girlfriend again, Willis?" Aunt Zoe teased.

Something was dripping up ahead. I could hear the *plink, plink, plink* of it hitting the ground. "I hope that's water I hear and not somebody's blood."

"Are you practicing for another haunted house tour at work tomorrow, Killer?"

"Not on purpose."

"Let's go see." Aunt Zoe still held my wrist and pulled me along with her.

The path dipped downward. Guessing by the aboveground distance between Mudder Brothers and the courthouse, we had about two city blocks to travel. But that was if the tunnel went in a straight line. Without a compass, which I didn't think to bring and might not even work underground, we wouldn't know which way we were heading after any bends in the route.

No sooner than I'd thought that, I noticed a bend up ahead turning to the left. Water dripped through a crack overhead, plinking onto the rocks below. Turned out it wasn't blood after all, thankfully.

For the next several seconds, the crunch of our boot soles on the stone floor layered with years of grit, along with the swish of our clothing, were the only sounds outside of our breaths and the blood pounding in my ears.

Besides the fact that I had no idea what I might be facing up ahead in the dark, I wasn't a big fan of playing earthworm deep in the earth. Not even if the ceiling in this tunnel was tall enough for Doc to stand upright. Being stuck in a cave-in was the mother of all my nightmares.

I gripped my mace tighter, holding it partway in front of me. The sooner we found this damned Hellhound creature, the sooner I could go back home, lock all the doors, and cuddle with Doc and my kids. And Rooster. Elvis, too. But I was drawing the line at Bogart the cat, whom I was still miffed at for shunning me yesterday when I needed her to listen to my woes for a little longer.

"I'd rather be freezing my ass off chasing an imp right now," I whispered.

Aunt Zoe shined the flashlight from side to side for a moment before returning the beam forward. "I'd rather be watching that show about Hessian soldiers with Layne."

I glanced her way. "You already watched it once."

"Yeah, well you've already chased the imp, too."

"Unsuccessfully," Cooper added dryly. "Several times."

"Bite me, Cooper." To Aunt Zoe, I said, "Don't you mean you'd rather be sitting on the couch next to Reid while watching the show?"

"Rest your lips, baby girl."

"Personally," Doc said, "I'd rather be sitting on the couch with Reid watching the Hessians right now. Hell, I might even be willing to hold his hand instead of this old bat of Violet's if it meant not being in this place."

I giggled, in spite of the fact that we were dipping lower yet and the walls were narrowing, making a two-by-two walk tight.

"I'd rather be at Junie's," Harvey said.

"Don't even think about saying anything more about my old English teacher," Cooper said to his uncle. "Clothed or not."

"What? I can't help it if I'm hot for teacher."

Cooper groaned. "Now you've gone and ruined a great Van Halen song for me."

"How'd your date go last night, Harvey?" Doc asked.

Aunt Zoe glanced over her shoulder. "Did Prudence show up for a round of naked Twister?"

"I don't think so. Then again, I don't think I'll know when she's in my noggin or not. It's downright disturbin'." Harvey grunted. "Didn't matter if she was there or not, though. I kept it PG all night. Even slept on Junie's couch. I told her I was feelin' a bit down in the joints so she wouldn't take my lack of lovin' to heart."

The tunnel angled to the left, dipping down even more. A short way farther, the walls began to sparkle with veins and pockets of greenish-aquamarine colored crystals, especially in the right wall. Aunt Zoe slowed, shining her light on the display. I stopped completely.

"Melanterite." Harvey answered my unasked question. Maybe Prudence was reaching out to my mind now, too. "It's common in many of the mines around here due to the humidity seeping inside."

"It's pretty," I said.

"Sure is, Sparky, but take it out in the sunlight and it'll crumble into fine powder."

"Really?"

"I remember seeing some of this in a copper mine in Colorado," Doc said. "It's like a crust in some old mines, if I remember right. It can even form into stalactites." He glanced at Harvey. "Seems like I read that it's a secondary mineral associated with the weathering of pyrite."

"Fool's gold," Cooper said under his breath, giving the common name for pyrite.

I knew all about fool's gold thanks to the tourist shops around town. But this melanterite was new for me. Then again, I didn't hang out in mines given the option.

"That's right, Doc," Harvey said, moving closer to the wall. "It's purty to look at, but only from inside the mine." He stumbled on a slightly raised stone in the floor, but caught himself. "Seems odd to have it down this far, though. Makes me wonder if there's an adit leading to the outside somewhere around here."

We continued on, rounding another bend only to come to a fork in the road.

I looked at Aunt Zoe, then Doc. "Which way?"

Doc slipped past us, shining his light on the ground down one fork and then the other. "There are fresh boot prints heading this way," he said, motioning to the right.

Oh yeah, Ray had been wearing his fancy boots.

Since the left fork dipped down even more, I was happy to take the right, which climbed shortly after the turn.

We traveled for a few minutes in silence. The weight of the earth over my head seemed to press down on me the farther we traversed. It couldn't be that much longer until we hit the Hellhole tunnel, could it?

After rounding another bend to the right, the back of my neck started to prickle. Then bristle. It was as if static electricity were hovering just above my skin. The sensation spread south over my shoulders, shivering down my arms until my fingers tingled. I downshifted, catching Aunt Zoe's arm and pulling her behind me.

"There's something up there," I said loud enough for all to hear. I didn't bother whispering. I was pretty sure that whatever it was already knew we were here.

Doc squeezed up next to me.

Farther ahead, a bright bluish light flickered into view down near the floor.

Adrenaline pumped through my body, turning up the heat all over. I continued along more quickly than before, my legs feeling strong and steady, ready to carry me into battle. My breathing slowed and deepened. I gripped the mace tighter, with purpose now, ready to start swinging.

"Violet, slow down," Aunt Zoe said from behind me, tugging on my coat.

I shook my head. "Stay back."

Doc kept pace with me. "Can you see it?"

"Somewhat." I glanced his way. "You can't?"

"Just the blue light."

I could clearly make out the outline of a hulking shadow. "It's as tall as you. Maybe taller. It sees us coming."

"You can see that much?" Cooper asked.

"I can tell that it's waiting for us."

"You're practically running into battle, Parker," Cooper said, jogging up behind me. "Maybe we should slow down and get a feel for the situation from a safe distance."

"I already have a feel," I said, holding out my mace to lead the way. "And remember, Cooper, if you shoot me by accident tonight, I'll come back to haunt you every hour of every day wearing something bright pink with flowers along with my scary clown grin."

"I can see the creature now," Doc said quietly. He aimed the flashlight beam down the tunnel, lighting up the beast. "Damn, it's big."

It actually stood several inches taller than Doc, judging from how close its head was to the ceiling.

"And wide," Cooper whispered. "Look at those shoulders. Is that white fur all over it?"

"Looks more silver to me," Aunt Zoe said from a little farther back. "But that could be the blue flare at its feet altering the color of the fur."

The creature was not quite as Ray had described it. For one thing, it was bigger both in height and breadth. And while Ray had mentioned its luminous eyes, which glowed like pearls in the dark, he'd left out its large pointy ears that stuck up through a long, thick swash of silver hair. In the bright flashlight beam, the pelt of fur around its shoulders and down its back looked more white than silver. The tunic beneath was black, along with the fur-lined boots below.

This had to be our Hellhound. Although it wasn't as terrifying to look at as I'd expected based on the carving on the clock.

I sniffed the air, expecting something putrid, like rotting meat or fetid milk, or worse. This creature couldn't stink any worse than a *Nachzehrer* and its decayed flesh, could it? Instead, I smelled ... I inhaled again. Weird. I smelled Rooster, after he'd come in from playing in the woods behind Aunt Zoe's house. A slight whiff of canine mixed with pine tree and an earthy smell. That last bit might be due to the mine we were standing in, though.

"Der Scharfrichter." It spoke clearly in a voice that was feminine yet raspy. Ray was right about that part. "I bid you to take pause." Her tone was low and serious, but not menacing. Her accent was exotic, unrecognizable to my ears.

I did as asked, keeping my mace gripped tightly just in case. My arms itched to swing, though. The urge to kill pulsed inside of me.

Doc gripped my shoulder, holding me in place. He must have

picked up on my natural instinct to execute first, ask questions never.

"I have been waiting for your arrival for some time now," the Hellhound said.

That might explain the clock hands continually spinning. "Why?"

"I have been summoned."

"By whom?" I hadn't somehow summoned it, had I? No, but I did have a Summoner for a son. Oh, fuck.

"Not whom, rather what." She tipped her head slightly, giving us a clearer view in the flashlight beam of her strong cheekbones and jawline, heart-shaped face, and long straight nose. "If you will rein in your weapon, I will explain."

"Okay." I lowered my mace. "I'm listening."

"Not that weapon. The one behind you."

Since Doc and his bat were standing next to me, she must have meant Cooper. I looked around at him, expecting to see his .45 Colt aimed and ready to fire, but his handgun was still in his holster. Although his hand was flexing near it.

Aunt Zoe held the hag stone pendant in her hand, but not out like a weapon. She was looking through the hole at the Hellhound. Maybe it was more than merely a stone with a hole in it after all.

"You mean the hag stone?" I asked.

"I am referring to the other *Scharfrichter* in your party."

She lifted her face and sniffed the air, her nose elongating along with her mouth, thickening into a snout for a brief moment. The sight reminded me of Mr. Black and the Juggernaut.

"Did you think I would not recognize the scent of *le bourreau* from our past clashes near the Seine and on the banks of the Rhine?"

I had no idea what word she'd said after "scent," but I did know the Seine and the Rhine were rivers in France. That could only mean …

"I never forget the smell of my enemy," she continued. "And this one is trying to hide in plain sight."

I looked at Harvey, noticing the lift of his chin and slight drag of his foot as he stepped closer. "Prudence?"

His eyes shifted to me, narrowing. "Are you going to stand here and play guessing games with that *mardagayl*, you clodpoll?" he asked me in the ghost's usual haughty tone. "Or kill the filthy beast and be done with this menace?"

CHAPTER TWENTY-ONE

Did you say *mardagayl*, Prudence?" Doc asked, sounding like that word meant something to him.

"Clodpoll?" I spared a quick glare at the uppity ghost, or rather Harvey. "Seriously, Prudence? In front of a stranger?" I sighed loudly, my focus returning to the Hellhound. "I swear, Aunt Zoe, if we're going to keep including Prudence on the team, someone needs to school her on how to present a unified front."

"Give her some leeway, Violet," Aunt Zoe said. "It's probably not easy for her, being dead and all."

Prudence scoffed. "I can kill better while dead than the clodpoll can alive."

I shook my head. "Jesus, Prudence. Has everything always been a competition with you?"

"Yes," the *mardagayl* answered for the ghost. "She measures her self-worth by the amount of kill marks on her scabbard."

"Don't forget her collection of teeth," Cooper said.

The *mardagayl* snickered. "You are still up to your old scrying tricks, I see."

Old scrying tricks? How long ago had these two known each other? Prudence was long dead.

Aunt Zoe cleared her throat, squeezing forward between Doc and me. "So, is *mardagayl* the name you go by, or is it your ethnicity?"

"Or your occupation?" Cooper asked. "Like these two pain-in-the-ass *Scharfrichters*?"

"You're funny, law dog," I said. "But don't quit your day job."

"*Mardagayl* is one of the many names my kind have been given over time," the stranger said, still eyeing Harvey warily.

"*Mardagayl,*" Doc repeated, "as in the mythical women from Armenian lore who are condemned to spend seven years in wolf form due to committing deadly sins?"

I took my eyes off the prize to gape at him. "How do you know so many myths?"

"I like to read, Killer." He shrugged. "And I have a degree in mythology and occultism."

No shit. All this time I thought his degree was in finance.

"That is one of the myths," the *mardagayl* told him. "But myths are rarely truths."

"Is there anything more to the myth, Nyce?" Cooper asked. "Or is it simply a way to keep Armenian women toeing the line?"

Doc rubbed his forehead. "If memory serves me right, these condemned women have to wear a wolf skin every night for the seven years, which causes them to crave human flesh."

"The flesh of children in particular," Aunt Zoe added, nodding. "I remember this one, too. A *mardagayl* will first devour her own offspring and then the children of strangers."

"Yessss," the *mardagayl* said, her lips pulling back into a pointy-toothed snarl. "My craving for the little ones. Their flesh is so very tender."

"Child killer!" Harvey aimed Bessie at the *mardagayl*. "We must execute the vermin."

Cooper grabbed the shotgun and yanked it from his uncle's hands. "Stand down, Prudence. This is Violet's crime scene."

"Is any of that true?" I asked the *mardagayl*, tightening my grip on the mace. Friend or foe, I wasn't going to let my guard down entirely.

"I do like children," she said. "But not to eat." She pointed at Prudence, her fingernail a normal length, not a claw like Ray had mentioned. "Unlike this vile Executioner, I am fond of humans, both tall and tiny, and do not kill without reason."

"Filthy lycanthrope," Prudence shot back, spitting a mouthful of French words past a curled upper lip at the stranger.

"Rogue Slayer," the *mardagayl* shot back, her hackles visibly raising as her back hunched menacingly.

Oh, boy, this could go south fast.

"Enough!" I leaned my mace against the wall and stepped

between them with my arms raised. "This name calling is getting us nowhere." I turned to Harvey. "Prudence, please hold your tongue until I have a chance to speak with this—"

"Foul hound," she offered.

"This *individual* who seeks an audience with me."

Cooper scoffed. "You sound like a queen."

Doc picked up my mace, holding weapons in both hands now. "I prefer to think of Tish as a gothic princess."

Harvey glared at me. "If you foolishly lower your guard, *Scharfrichter*, the wolf will rip out your throat. I have witnessed her deceit firsthand."

Was that what had happened long ago near the Seine and Rhine rivers?

"Still with this untruth?" the *mardagayl* said, her tone filled with loathing. "After all these years, even in death, you will not see your own part in the tragedy. Can you not fathom why the hunters were sent for your head?"

For her head? Was she talking about bounty hunters?

"I was not at fault," Prudence snarled.

What had Prudence done back in France?

I shook off my questions about the ghost's past for now. "Listen, Prudence. I appreciate you having my back here, but I don't need …"

Harvey's body jerked to the right, and then he stumbled forward.

Cooper grabbed him by the scruff of his coat, holding his uncle upright. "You okay, Uncle Willis?"

"I feel more up than I do down." Harvey shook his head once, and then blinked several times. "I think ol' Prudy slammed the door on her way out. Sort of knocked the wind out of me."

I turned back to the *mardagayl*. "It appears my cohort has stepped away for the time being. Now, why are you waiting down here for me, and what was it that summoned you here?" My fingers were crossed it had nothing to do with Layne.

"The Balance was my summoner." She said the word "balance" as if it were a name. "It is why I reached out to you and waited for your presence."

Yeah, none of that made any sense to me. I looked at Doc to see if he and his mythology degree could figure that out. He frowned back, shaking his head.

"You reached out how?" Aunt Zoe asked.

"The *Scharfrichter* is a Timekeeper, yes?" At my nod, she said, "You have a talisman that was once mine."

I did? Did she mean her clock? Then it hit me. "Oh, you mean the hag stone pendant." I turned to Aunt Zoe, who already held out the pendant for the *mardagayl* to take.

"Keep it," she told Aunt Zoe. "That is for you, Timekeeper. You will need it."

"I will?" I took the pendant, looking down at the hag stone. "Is this something to do with your clock?"

"No, it is to do with your lack of vision."

Were we talking about seeing into the future or did this have to do with my supposedly plugged-up chakras?

"Unlike you," she continued, "I am able to see in the night. It is why my kind are great hunters. We are even as renowned as *der Scharfrichter* in some arenas. Although we do not have the other gifts bestowed to your breed."

"What gifts?" Doc asked.

"The ability to see through the deception of all creatures and view their true forms." She paused to sniff the air several times, checking behind her for a couple of seconds before focusing back on me. "The stone opens our vision to even the most secretive creatures. It was bequeathed to the previous Timekeeper to help her see that which she normally could not."

"Since I probably don't need it, are you sure you don't want it back?"

The *mardagayl* lifted a similar pendant from under the silvery white pelt draped around her neck. "I have my own. It helps me to hunt. And kill."

"Are you a bounty hunter?" Doc asked, stepping closer to me.

"At times." She stared at him for a moment, sniffing in his direction. "What is that scent? It is almost familiar."

Oh, hell. The last thing we needed was a hunter learning there was an Oracle in our midst. It was bad enough that Dominick knew. I shot Doc a quick warning look, nudging my head, trying to get him to back away from me.

He ignored me.

"Is that why you have been summoned? To hunt the *Scharfrichter*?" Aunt Zoe asked.

"I value my life too much to dare that hunt." She turned to me, her luminescent eyes glowing brighter. "I have come to warn her."

Another warning to add to my list? Criminy. She might as well get in line. "I have received many prophecies about my demise," I said. "Why would you want to help me?"

"I knew Ayla. Your distant relative. Have you been told of this *Scharfrichter*?"

I nodded. "I've heard stories of her successes." And her fertility. Eight babies, damn! That poor woman's womb.

"She saved my life once," the *mardagayl* said. "I made a promise to her then. If I were to live long enough to be of help to her line in the future, I would offer my services."

"So, you're here to warn me and help me?"

"I am here to help restore the Balance."

Apparently, one of the *mardagayl's* talents was to not answer a question directly.

"Did the guardian hire you?" Aunt Zoe asked.

The *mardagayl* sneered. "These guardians believe they have control over territories of their own making. That they can form a council to rule all. But they mistakenly believe they can maintain control. They are merely long-lived alchemists mixing different potions." Her ears twitched. She paused and stared back into the darkness again for a few seconds. "Nature will keep the Balance," she said, turning back to us. "I am one meager weight on the great scale. However, it is an imbalance that brought me here."

"What kind of imbalance?" Cooper asked, still holding onto his uncle's shoulder. Prudence must have really done a number on Harvey.

She looked at him for a moment, then focused on me. "Has the guardian told you of what lies beneath?"

"You mean down here in the tunnel?" I asked, indicating the ground. "Or in what's left of the gold mine in Lead?"

I had seen a model once of the full Homestake gold mine that spread deep and wide under Lead, Deadwood, and the surrounding area. It was impressive, considering how many men and how much time had gone into excavating the earth.

Wait, was this about the *Duzarx* that Prudence had seen leave the mine?

"No, below," the *mardagayl* said. "The humans dug too deep

before they stopped. Protective wards were set to hold back the menaces. Then the water filled all but the top, securing the area, acting as a shield along with the linked sigils. But now they have drained the water again and blasted away many of the sigils. The wards are beginning to fail. When this last line of defense crumbles, an imbalance as we have not seen since before my time will be upon us." She leaned forward, her face contorting into a wolf-like beast that was heart-stopping with its savagery. "Bloodshed is coming. Ruin will follow."

I cringed, glancing at Aunt Zoe. "Do you know what she's talking about?"

Aunt Zoe's eyebrows were drawn together. "No."

"Ms. Wolff spoke of something similar, remember?" Doc said to me. "I think her words were 'Carnage is coming.' And then she said something more along the lines of a bloodbath that hadn't been experienced in generations."

"That's right," Cooper said. He'd been there with me when Ms. Wolff had forced my hand into becoming a Timekeeper. "She mentioned that cages had been opened. That Parker's skills were not going to be enough to stop the wave of upheaval and ruin. I think that's how it went."

"You speak of the old Timekeeper." The *mardagayl* eased back, her face returning to its almost beautiful guise. "She was correct. There are those who want to see chaos spread once again and return us all to the age of dark wickedness."

Chaos? Dark wickedness? I had an idea where this was going. "You're talking about Kyrkozz, aren't you?"

The *mardagayl* tilted her head slightly, her luminous eyes narrowing. "How do you know of that fiend?"

"I've run into the orange-eyed bastard a couple of times, but we're not the best of pals. First, I refused to let his minions use my womb to make a Hell baby. Then he was rude and spit on me. Most recently, though, I ran into him in the dark and had to blast him out of my way."

"You have traveled in the dark?" Her focus shifted to Doc. She sniffed again. "Ah, now I understand your scent."

And the Oracle was out of the bag. Damn it.

"You have one of the Ancients by your side," she said, returning to me. "Kyrkozz will surely come for you now."

"And here I was hoping we could avoid a fourth play date together." My joke fell flat with her. Kyrkozz had a way of bringing down a room.

"We must prepare, *Scharfrichter*," the *mardagayl* said.

"For Kyrkozz to return and try to kill me again?"

"No. From the tales I have heard, that is not his method. He will first send his horde."

"Oh, great," Cooper grumbled. "A horde in Deadwood. That's going to cause some crowd control problems."

"What horde?" Doc asked.

She tapped her boot on the ground. "Those below us, from deep down. Those who the guardians believe are caged for eternity. The very pests and thorns that have plagued the living for eons. Kyrkozz is now setting them free to come forth and put an end to life as we know it."

Fuckity fuck. Wasn't that just my luck?

I frowned at Doc. "Is there a tarot card worse than the Tower? Because I think I've been dealt the shittiest one of all."

The *mardagayl* pointed at me. "You must watch the clock for my signal."

"You mean the one that's been spinning for days now?"

She nodded. "Do you know how to tell if I am slain?"

"Not really."

"Did the previous Timekeeper not teach you?"

I squirmed at my part in the truth. "I saw her off pretty quickly after she handed over the role, so no."

"I will share what I know. The clock hands spin when a traveler is physically close to their clock. As long as my clock continues to spin, you will know I am down here watching the gate to keep any creature freed from making it to the surface."

"And if your clock stops?" Doc asked.

"I may have to travel elsewhere for a time. If so, another will take my place here." She looked behind her for a moment, her ears twitching again. "If all clock hands point straight up," she continued, her attention once again on us, "that means the traveler has perished and the clock has stopped for good."

"Only when the clock stops will your time be at an end." Doc said to me, "That's what was written on the inside of the drawer in Ms. Wolff's apartment."

"The Timekeeper's mantra," the *mardagayl* said with a nod. "Let us hope I can hold the line here and my clock continues to move through time."

"Hold for how long, though?" Cooper asked.

"Until the *Scharfrichter* stops Kyrkozz for good and we can return the Balance."

Harvey guffawed. "Oh, just until that happens."

A strangled laugh escaped before I could stop it. I covered my mouth, staring wide-eyed at my aunt. Her worried gaze made my gut clench. I saw doubt there. I couldn't blame her for it, because I felt it myself.

"I must return to my station." The *mardagayl* started to leave, but then paused. "One more thing in regards to the human I charged with delivering my message to you."

She must mean Ray. "What about him?" I asked.

"He is not alone."

Oh, come on! How many times was I going to hear that without any additional explanation?

"What does that mean?" Cooper beat me to the punch.

She touched her nose. "I smelled a sorcerer on him." She held up her hand in a frozen wave. "I do hope you find Kyrkozz before it is too late, *Scharfrichter*. While I have aged through many cycles of life, I would like to live in peace longer and possibly have a child of my own."

CHAPTER TWENTY-TWO

We made it back to Aunt Zoe's without running into anyone or anything more in the tunnel, although we did pause to debate if we should explore the other fork in the tunnel we'd found between Mudder Brothers and the Hellhole-to-courthouse tunnel.

Harvey and I weren't up for further adventures at that point, both due to *Scharfrichter* woes. He was worn out from whatever Prudence had done to him, and I had too much weighing on my mind after the bomb the *mardagayl* had dropped about Kyrkozz and the cages. I needed to process what I'd learned, and the safety and comfort of Aunt Zoe's kitchen called to me, along with some freshly baked molasses cookies.

Unfortunately, I had to settle for store-bought chocolate chip cookies from the pantry this time, because Cornelius beat me to the Betty Boop cookie jar. He and Natalie were waiting for us at Aunt Zoe's when we arrived home, standing on the porch along with Reid. Natalie even gave Cooper a lingering kiss, but then punched him in the shoulder before following me inside.

I detoured upstairs to check on the kids first thing, finding them safely tucked into bed and sleeping away while Rooster played guard dog in the hall between their bedroom doors. After watching each child for several seconds, I dropped a whisper-soft kiss on their foreheads, pausing on the way to my bedroom to scratch Rooster behind the ears.

By the time I'd changed into some yoga pants and a baggy sweatshirt and returned to the kitchen, the retelling of our trek into the tunnel had already begun. I grabbed a beer and joined everyone at the table. Natalie and Cornelius hung on our every word as we told the tale of the *mardagayl*. Reid listened in, too, but since much of this recent tunnel business was news to him, he had to have Aunt Zoe give him further explanation on the side at times.

After we all shared what we could remember, the others around the table took turns theorizing about the *mardagayl's* and Prudence's shared past. This was preferable to addressing the elephant in the room—Kyrkozz and his horde. But I couldn't stop thinking about the orange-eyed bastard. I sipped on my beer and tried not to frown too much, hiding behind what I hoped was a rock-solid poker face.

Good grief, this was too much. I didn't know if I was up to the task set before me. Ms. Wolff had made a big mistake turning me into a Timekeeper. I wanted to pretend none of what I'd learned tonight was real as I gazed around the table at those I loved. To keep my head in the sand. To sit up in life's bleachers and enjoy watching my children grow up without worrying about them being hurt or worse every waking moment.

When I finished my beer, Doc offered to grab another one for me, or something stronger, but I shook my head. As nice as it would be to numb the edges of my real-life nightmares with tequila or some other hard liquor, I needed to keep my thoughts clear. I had to try to make sense of all this craziness before I headed off to work again in the morning, or Jerry would think I was getting back into my zombie character role for the final episode of *Paranormal Realty* on Sunday. Not to mention I had some more clients lined up for tomorrow at noon.

I was pretty sure I did my best to hold my chin up through the rest of the evening, reacting to the conversation appropriately so that nobody could see that I was shaking in my slippers under the table.

Eventually, everyone went their separate ways, including Natalie and Cooper. Part of me wondered how much more snarled that knot would become thanks to Cooper's inflexibility when it came to Natalie's safety, and her determination to make him recognize her independence and strength. But that wasn't my problem tonight, so I shrugged it off.

After Doc went upstairs to trim his beard and shower, Aunt Zoe offered to drive Reid home since his pickup was still out of commission. I took my leave and escaped to my bedroom closet. Elvis wasn't there this time. She'd been put to bed down in her basement cage, so the closet was all mine tonight outside of a few feathers.

I shoved my shoes aside and closed the doors, blocking out the world. Folding my legs into my chest, I rested my forehead on my kneecaps and let out a sigh of relief.

This was all so fucked up. How was I supposed to wrap my mind around it all and still walk out the front door each morning and go to work selling stupid real estate? There were real monsters in the world, not just greedy assholes with big egos. The kind that hunted humans—and the local *Scharfrichter*. Monsters that tore flesh from bones and thrived on chaos.

I sat in the quiet dark, waiting for tears to come and wash away some of the tension and stress locking up my muscles, but they didn't.

Maybe it was because something was jabbing me in the hip. I glanced down. It was the toe of my red suede clog. I tossed it to the other end of the closet, where it hit the wall with a clunk before landing on the other shoes.

I settled back into my shit-was-about-to-hit-the-fan position. But still no tears flowed.

What the hell? Throughout the evening, I'd been slowly suffocating under the weight of the terrifying tasks ahead of me. My breathing had been shallow thanks to the tightness in my chest, my neck had grown stiff from holding up my chin, my cheeks hurt from trying to keep smiling, and my back ached from sitting upright instead of curling into a ball. Surely there were some much-needed tears of frustration and fear to release, but my eyes remained dry.

Perhaps I needed to take a page from Cornelius's book and try meditating. Remembering him spread out on his table, I decided to give that a shot. I opened the closet doors and tossed out all my flats, heels, sandals, mules, and random pieces of fallen clothing. Before shutting myself in the closet again, I grabbed the spare quilt off my chair.

With the doors closed, I pushed Doc's few pairs of shoes down to the other end of the closet, spread out the blanket, and lay flat on my back. Nope, the floor was too hard under my head even with the quilt cushion. I needed a pillow. I tugged down one of my old terry cloth robes, dodging the hanger that came down with it, and rolled it into a sausage. There, I thought, putting it under my head. That should do it.

I closed my eyes and shoved aside the scene in the tunnel with the *mardagayl*, blocking out her warning. I needed to focus on something else. Something soothing. A color would do. Maybe pink again. No, wait. Yellow, like the sun and happy faces and the beautiful center of a white daisy.

I had no idea what Cornelius would say about putting all of my mental money on yellow, but thinking about it already seemed to ease my anxieties and brighten up the shadow-filled corners of my mind.

Yellowwwww.

I sank even deeper into the joyful color, humming along with Bobby McFerrin in my head to "Don't Worry, Be Happy."

After a few deep inhales and exhales, the weight on my chest lifted.

A few more slow breaths and my shoulders relaxed.

Next came my lower back, the muscles loosening, my spine resting all the way onto the floor.

Yellowwwww, I thought with each breath in, humming on the exhale, seeing the color behind my closed eyelids.

I started smelling something sweet on the inhales.

I took another deep breath. It smelled like cookies.

That was odd. I inhaled again, picking up a whiff of chocolate, too.

What the …?

I opened my eyes and stared up at an actual cookie.

Hot diggity dog! Had I conjured that?

"Hello, Sleeping Beauty," Doc said, leaning over me.

I turned my head to find him kneeling on the floor just outside the open closet door, holding a cookie near my nose. Wow, I hadn't even heard him open the door. That color meditation business really worked—or my exhaustion had caught up with me and knocked me out for a short stint.

He raised a steaming coffee mug and smiled down at me. "I'm hoping to tempt you out of the closet with some cookies and hot chocolate."

A cookie sounded lovely, the world outside of my closet, not so much yet.

I sat up and turned, leaning back against the wall under my

hanging shirts. I patted the blanket next to me. "How about you come in here and join me instead."

One dark eyebrow raised. "In the closet?"

I nodded.

"With the cookies?"

"And the hot chocolate." I reached for the steaming mug, taking it and the cookie from his hand.

He looked back at the bed, then shrugged and grabbed the small bowl of cookies he had sitting on the floor next to him. After pushing my shirts aside to make more room for his head, he crawled in next to me and stretched his long legs out into the bedroom.

"You good?" he asked after picking up a cookie for himself since I'd pretty much demolished the one he'd used to wake me from my happy place in Yellow Zen.

"I'm better now." I held up the cookie. "Especially since you're here with cookies. Thanks for waking me, Prince Charming."

"Sleeping Beauty's hero isn't named Prince Charming," he said. "It varies depending on the version of the fairy tale."

"How would you know that?"

"Mythology and occultism, remember? Those are some of the more basic tales in my repertoire." He smiled my way. "When I came back from showering and saw all of your shoes out there on the floor, I figured you were in here and could use some sugar." He took a bite of his cookie, chewing in silence as I sipped the hot chocolate.

"You even added a couple of marshmallows," I said.

"After tonight's fun in the tunnel, marshmallows were a must." He shifted closer to me so our shoulders were touching. "You want to talk about it, Killer?"

"What's to say? The *mardagayl* pretty much spread it all out in front of us, and none of it looked like a skip through the tulips." I sighed. "I have so many questions swirling around in my head, but there are no answers."

He grabbed two more cookies, handing one to me. "I have a feeling we'll have to find the answers in time."

"Ha!" I shoulder bumped him. "That was a clever Timekeeping pun."

"I have a lot more where that came from, sweetheart." He looked over at me and then higher. "Hold still, you have a chicken feather in your hair."

I waited for him to pluck it free, and then took another sip of hot chocolate. "I think I need to get more clocks from Ms. Wolff's apartment."

"Yep." He took the mug from me. "We'll have to see if Coop can help with that somehow, but Detective Hawke is going to make it tough."

I guffawed. "What's new? He thrives on being a thorn in my side."

He sipped on the hot chocolate, then handed it back to me. "What do you think of what Prudence said about the *mardagayl*? You were pretty quiet downstairs when we were talking about that."

"Like Aunt Zoe said, I have a feeling something happened between them back in France when Prudence was alive." I pondered that for a moment. "How trippy is it that we're dealing with *other* beings who have been alive long enough to know Prudence then?" I shook my head. "Hell, long enough to know Ayla, my great-times-ten generations—or more—ancestor. It's hard to wrap my mind around that."

"Same here." He nudged my knee with his. "Any ideas on how we are going to find this sorcerer?"

"If it's a ghost, maybe we can draw it in with Cornelius and his pied piper routine, and then use Cooper's abilities to see what it looks like. But I don't know what to do with it after that."

"What would it want with Ray, though?"

"What would anything want with that horse's patootie?"

Doc chuckled.

I ate the last bit of cookie and washed it down with hot chocolate. I held out the mug toward him. "You want anymore?"

"No. You finish it."

I swallowed the last of the sweet drink and set the mug aside, brushing the crumbs off my yoga pants. "I think Aunt Zoe is softening toward Reid."

"Good. He's really nuts about her."

I leaned my head on Doc's shoulder, taking his hand in mine. "Natalie and Cooper are going to need to find an agreeable middle ground if they're going to stay together."

"It will be awkward again for everyone if they don't."

I scoffed lightly. "Even more so than before."

He leaned closer and kissed my forehead, sending a shiver of warmth down through me. "Your son wants me to find him some books on Hessian soldiers."

"Did you see that Addy is sleeping with my old softball bat like it's a teddy bear? The one she painted with peace symbols."

He nodded. "Your kids are awesome."

"Yeah," I said, smiling. They were. That was why I needed to do whatever I had to, no matter the cost to me, in order to protect them. And I would.

Perhaps it was the color yellow that was making me feel more optimistic at the moment; or the sugar from the cookies and hot chocolate. Or it could be the vibe Doc was giving off. Whatever the reason, I had a feeling that maybe—just maybe—we might make it through this hellish mess and out the other side if he and I stuck together.

I glanced down at our entwined hands, thinking about the "together" part. Pulling my hand free, I lifted his arm and wrapped it around me. "Hey, Gomez?"

"Yeah?"

"Thanks for helping to silence my demons tonight."

He pulled me closer. "Tish, how long has it been since we …" He tipped my chin up so he could stare into my eyes. "Waltzed?"

"Too long," I whispered and then turned fully toward him. "Hurry up and kiss me before a kid or a chicken or an aunt interrupts us."

He lowered his mouth to mine, taking his time with my lips. "You taste sweet and chocolaty, Boots." He dipped down for seconds.

The yellow flowing inside of me burned brighter, heating me from the inside out, making me want more.

More heat.

More pleasure.

More Doc.

I pulled away and moved so that I was straddling his lap. I lifted off my sweatshirt, tossing it behind us into the bedroom.

He smiled at me, looking very handsome and prince-like. "Is this leading somewhere?"

"Yep."

"Like to the soft mattress on our bed?"

"Nope." I pulled off my camisole next, baring all from the waist up. "We're having closet-floor sex."

His gaze got stuck below my chin. "We are?"

I nodded, reaching for his shirt. "I want you now. Here. In my new sanctuary."

"I thought this was Elvis's place." He didn't fight me as I helped him off with his shirt.

"We share it now." I slid my palms over the soft beard lining his jaw, cupping his face in my hands as I stared down at him. This man was mine. Damn. "I'm so in love with you, Doc."

His eyes turned all dark and dreamy. "Okay, you win. We'll have closet-floor sex. But if we're going to continue to have sex in here in the future, we need to get some plush carpet to save my knees and your tailbone. Or vice versa."

I leaned in for a kiss, feeling the yellow radiance that was still warming me on the inside spread and glow brighter. My hips moved against his, slowly at first, but then faster with his help.

"Close the door," I said while kissing my way down the side of his neck.

"It's going to be a tight fit."

"Isn't that the way you like it?"

A groan came from deep in his chest. He hitched me closer and shifted sideways, tucking his legs inside so he could close the door.

In the darkness, we wriggled free of what was left of our clothing, helping each other in between moans and chuckles and a cramp or two. Finally, we made it to skin on skin, and then the laughter faded.

"Top or bottom?" he whispered.

"Top," I said, moving over him. My elbow hit the door, rattling it. I shifted and my knee connected with the wall.

Doc moved to the side to give me more room. "You okay?"

"I will be in a second." I settled onto him, moaning as I took all of him.

The light seeping in under the door lit the space enough so I could see the side of his face as he stared up at me. "This is crazy, Boots," he said, his hands spanning my hips as I moved over him. "The bed has a lot more room."

"I know, but this is better." At least it was right now, when I needed him, and I needed to feel safe.

I reached down and ran my finger down the center of his chest, my love welling clear up and out, overflowing with that warm yellow sunshine I'd felt earlier while melting away my fears and worries. As a matter of fact, all of my anxieties seemed to have been blasted out by the yellow light, making me feel like I could shine bright enough to burn away all of my doubts.

Then again, maybe it was simply great sex.

I closed my eyes, embracing the rush of yellow light flooding through me as he moved just right.

"Kiss me," he ordered in between quickened breaths.

I leaned down, brushing my body over his in the process. He groaned my name, moving faster now. My mouth toyed with his, my lips skimming, my teeth nibbling, before deepening the kiss.

Then there was only whispered sweet nothings and cries of pleasure as my body let go of it all. Everything but him.

"It's your turn," I said when I caught my breath, nibbling his earlobe, which was one of his hot spots.

"Yesssss," he groaned.

I scraped my nails down his chest, and that was all it took for him to follow me over the edge, shuddering for several seconds.

When he stilled, I leaned forward onto my hands, staring down at him in the dim light.

His pure smile tickled me clear to my toes. He reached up and caressed my cheek. "How are your knees?" he whispered.

Who cared about my knees? God, I loved this man. Our remaining time together might be shorter than ever according to the *mardagayl*. What was I doing wasting it on silly doubts?

"Doc, I think I want you to carry me over the threshold."

His hand froze against my cheek. His eyes widened.

Several seconds of very pregnant silence passed agonizingly slowly.

"What did you say?" he asked, no longer whispering.

My heartbeat started pounding in my ears. Oh shit, what had I just said? Apparently, the color yellow had made me love drunk.

I opened my mouth to repeat my words, or maybe deny them, but then closed my lips and gulped, my throat suddenly super dry.

He pushed himself up on one elbow, his face close to mine. "Violet, what did you just say?"

I sat upright, pulling away, the shadows growing in my mind again. "I … I might have spoken out of turn."

"No." He caught my wrist, pulling me back. "You don't get to run away."

"I wasn't going to run away." I grimaced. "I was just going to slink out of here and lock myself in the bathroom until I can get rid of the yellow and think straight."

He tugged me on top of him and rolled, doing some maneuver in the tight space that left me pinned under him in the corner between the wall and the floor.

"Violet." He stared down at me, his expression dead serious. "What did you say to me?"

"I think you know what I said," I whispered.

"Honestly, I'm afraid I might have fantasized part of it after that amazing closet-floor sex." His dark gaze held steady on mine. "I'd like to hear it again, please."

I took a steadying breath and prepared to explain myself, although with his weight partially on me, it wasn't easy. Then again, this explanation wasn't going to be either.

"You see, Doc, I've been breathing the color yellow since I came into the closet tonight."

His brow creased, but he held his tongue, clearly waiting for me to continue.

"And I'm not sure what that color has in it, but it seems to have possibly interfered with my ability to contain my more amorous emotions."

"The color yellow has done this?"

I nodded, licking my extremely dry lips. "It's a dangerous color. I mean, look how it's used on traffic warning signs."

He nodded slowly, his eyes narrowing. "I think that the only warning here is for me."

I frowned. "What do you mean?"

"I need to be warned—and reminded—that you are a big chicken."

"If this is about facing off with Kyrkozz, you're right, I'm freaking the hell out." I was deflecting, and I was pretty sure we both knew it.

He slid off to the side onto his elbow, resting his head on his hand, back to the door, but kept one leg over me to hold me in place.

"This 'color yellow' excuse isn't about any of the madness outside of this closet." He tapped me lightly on the sternum. "It's about you protecting the beating organ in here."

"So, you're saying I'm a chicken with my heart?"

"Exactly." He drew a line down to my stomach, his gaze following his finger. "Violet, you know I love you."

"Yes." I had no doubts about that.

He looked up at me again, staring while his finger drew circles around my navel. "And I love your kids."

My eyes watered a little at hearing him say that, but I swallowed the lump in my throat and replied with an intelligent-sounding, "Uh huh."

He stared at me, his hand moving down over my hip. "Did you or did you not just say you wanted to get married?"

My breath caught.

There it was, the M-word, flipping and flopping out there between us.

I weighed how to answer that. Would the truth make him cringe or smile? It had to be the latter, didn't it?

Reaching up, I tenderly touched his cheek, letting his beard tickle my palm.

He didn't pull away.

"I've never been married," I whispered.

"Me either."

I grimaced. "It scares me."

He caught my hand, moving it to his lips where he softly kissed my palm before releasing it. "We've faced far scarier things together."

Together. That was true. But … "I have kids."

He chuckled. "I know. And several pets."

"This might scare them, too. Especially Elvis."

The love shining in his gaze warmed me more than the color yellow. "We could ease them into it."

My heart returned to my throat, thumping loud enough to be heard clear over in Wyoming.

"Doc," I said, pausing to swallow the panicking organ back down where it belonged so I could take a deep breath. Then I jumped. "Will you marry all of us?"

CHAPTER TWENTY-THREE

Friday, February 1st

Calamity Jane Realty was hopping this morning.
And so was I!
Doc had said, "Yes," with one condition—we move out of the closet and onto the bed to seal the deal.

So we had, and the sealing process had been sweet and tender, and then hot and rough. Through most of it, I couldn't stop smiling wide. I'd probably looked like a deranged clown. It was a wonder Doc hadn't needed to cover my face with a pillow in order to get the job done.

Come morning light, we'd agreed that it was best to keep the whole concept of marriage to ourselves for the time being so that we could decide when it was best to let the kids in on it. They should be the first to learn of the nuptial news, since they were the most affected by it.

In the meantime, though, I was engaged for the first time in my life! I wanted to dance and sing and hop around both at home and at work. Hell, throughout the town.

But I didn't.

After Doc had left for the Rec Center, I'd hid my big smile behind toast and coffee, so Aunt Zoe didn't see it. Lucky for me, the kids had been slow to wake this morning and I'd managed to skip out of there before they woke up and came down for a no-school breakfast feast thanks to Harvey, who'd shown up as I was hurrying out the door.

I had no idea how I was going to keep everyone from figuring out that the M-word was no longer a forbidden topic around Doc. However, after a stop in the bathroom upon entering Calamity Jane Realty in order to practice my serious face, I was pretty sure I could pull this off … for now.

Mona had two clients corraled at her desk when I arrived at mine. She was too busy to spare me more than a glance. Whew!

Ben also had a client sitting next to him as he scrolled through listings on his computer monitor. He waved without looking my way. Double whew!

Jerry's desk was cleared off, which usually meant he was out of the office. I'd have to ask Mona later where he was this morning. My fingers were crossed it had nothing to do with marketing efforts.

I'd no sooner settled in behind my monitor when the front door opened and in walked an older couple without an appointment interested in checking out some houses around town.

Toot toot! Today was off to a winning start.

I spent the next couple of hours driving the nice folks here and there while telling them about Deadwood's ghosts. As we skip-a-dee-doo-dahed around town, I was singing along with good ol' Donna Fargo under my breath about being the happiest girl in the whole damned USA.

A little before noon, I was back at my desk waiting for my next appointment. The couple from this morning were coming back next week to check out some more homes in the area, including Lead and Central City.

Mona and Ben were both out of the office, taking their clients around to look at available properties. I had to admit, Jerry's decision to have us on the *Paranormal Realty* television show seemed to have given us a good boost in the midst of what was usually the slower season for real estate in the Black Hills.

I grabbed a coffee and returned to my desk. After a late night consummating my secret engagement, I needed a boost of energy to keep going. Although the clown smile was still quick to fill my cheeks, I closed my eyes and practiced not smiling while I waited for my next appointment to arrive.

My cell phone rang, interrupting my mini-meditation. The eerie tone told it was Cornelius, my eye in the sky.

I stared up at one of his cameras in the corner as I answered the call. "Hello, Corny! Are the tarot gods shining down on me today?"

Silence came from the other end for a few beats, and then he cleared his throat. "Violet, that's an alarming smile."

Oops. It was back.

I tried to flatten out my lips. "Sorry. I'm a little tired and overcompensating with caffeine. What's going on?"

"We have a situation in Jerry's office."

I turned in my chair and peered down the hallway toward his office door. "What do you mean?"

"The door is open."

The door to Jerry's office was closed, same as it had been all morning. "Are you sure?" I stood, moving to get a better look at the office door. "The room is still closed up as far as I can tell."

"I'm talking about the closet door."

Skirrrrch. The imaginary singing bluebirds that had been circling my head all morning fell to the ground dead.

I turned on the fluorescent lights overhead and walked down the hallway. In the quiet, empty office, my boots clunked extra loud on the old hardwood floor. The boards underfoot groaned when I pulled up right in front of the office door.

I started to reach for the doorknob, but then stopped and looked up at the camera positioned in the corner above the back door. "Cornelius, can you see me?" I said into my cell phone.

"Yes."

"Is there anything moving on the other side of this door?"

"I don't think so." I could hear his fingers tapping on his keyboard. "No, it's all quiet in there."

"I'm going to see if the door will …" Before I'd even finished, the door opened a sliver on its own.

Goosebumps raced up my arms, sending shivers down my back.

"Did you see that?" I whispered into my phone.

I heard paper rustling on his end of the line. "No, what?" he mumbled, sounding like his mouth was full.

"Are you eating right now?" I asked.

He grunted. "I'm hungry. You know how I get if my blood sugar dips too low."

I growled. "Yeah, I do." I pushed open the door the rest of the way.

Of course the hinges creaked.

"That sounded spooky," Cornelius said through a mouthful of

whatever.

"I know. You should be experiencing this live."

"Actually, I sort of am."

No, he sort of wasn't. "Shut up and eat, Cornelius."

I reached into the semi-dark office and turned on the lights.

They didn't work.

I turned them off and on again.

Nothing.

"The lights aren't working," I told him.

"I can see that. Go open the blinds."

I looked across the room at the window and then over at the closet door. It was open several inches. Darkness filled the crack.

"Uh, that will require me to walk past the closet door."

"You think the boogeyman is waiting inside to grab you?"

"Well, I didn't until now!"

"Hold on," he said.

Over in the corner of the ceiling, his camera made an electronic humming sound and turned to the right.

"I'm focusing in on the closet," he said.

"And?"

"And …" The camera stopped making noise. "It's too dark for me to see inside. Can you shine your phone's flashlight in there?"

"No, Cornelius. That would require me to stand in front of the closet door, and now I'm worried about the boogeyman."

I looked around the office. Everything seemed fine. Quiet. Ghost free.

"Hmm. Maybe you could—" He stopped. Or the phone call cut out.

I checked. No, it said the call was still going. "I could what? Cornelius?"

"The camera went black," he said. "Can you see a red light shining below the lens?"

I took a step into the room to see for sure. "No. It's dark. Is there something you want me to do with it?"

"Violet," he said very quietly.

"Yeah?" I said quietly back.

"There's someone standing behind you in the hallway."

I gasped and whirled, backing several steps farther into Jerry's office.

There was nobody there.

"I don't see anyone," I whispered.

To my right, something slowly *creeeaaaked*.

Cringing, I looked over at the closet door, watching as it opened wide.

"Oh, shit," I said into the phone, my heart skipping several beats in a panic. "Are you seeing this, Cornelius?"

"Of course not. My camera in there is dead, remember?"

I might be too in a few minutes.

"Then maybe you should get your ass down here!"

No sooner had I finished speaking, the door to Jerry's office slammed shut.

"Fuck me," I said and rushed over to the door.

It wouldn't budge.

I pocketed my phone and braced my foot against the wall next to the door, tugging on the doorknob. "Come on, damn it!"

Nope. The sucker was stuck tight.

I stopped pulling and got out my phone. "Cornelius, are you still there?"

Nothing.

I looked down at the screen. It was black. I pushed several buttons, but the phone stayed dark.

"And then there was one." I lowered the phone, frowning at the empty desk across the room. "Here we go again."

I looked around for something to swing in case the boogeyman came flying out of the closet at me.

"Listen, Killer," I heard Doc say loud and clear.

I froze. Where had that come from? "Doc?"

Silence.

From the closet, I heard a scratching sound.

What was that? A mouse? A rat? Maybe something bigger? Or maybe something … deadlier?

I licked my lips, squinting into the shadows. "Who's there?" I asked, my voice croaky.

"I know you are hell on wheels," said the voice from the closet. "But ghosts are my specialty."

Yep, that was Doc's voice all right, only there was a scratchy echo to it, like it was from an old record player.

"Jane?" I called out, hopeful she was in the room with me. "Is this your game?"

Silence once again.

Fudge, I could really use Cooper right about now. For all I knew, there was a ghost standing right in front of me touching me with its wispy finger. Or off to my side. Or even behind me.

I pressed back against the office door, searching the shadowed corners for movement before focusing again on the open closet door.

"Violet," Doc called out from the closet.

Damn, it really sounded like him that time. "What?"

"Come here."

Nope. No way. Huh uh. I wasn't falling for that trick again. The *lidérc* had taught me a lesson the last time.

"I'd rather not," I told the closet voice.

Great balls of fire! Where was Cornelius? He should be here by now.

"Jane?" I called again, louder. "If you are in here with me, please let me know."

The scratching noise was back, only this time it sounded louder. Closer.

Movement on the desk across the room drew my eye. There was a long thin blade digging into the top of the desk. I leaned forward a step. Was that a knife? No, it was a letter opener. Someone was trying to communicate. Maybe Jane was here with me after all.

"What are you writing?" I asked, not expecting an answer.

"Violet," Doc's voice said again, sounding louder, like he was standing in the room with me.

I reached behind me, sneakily trying the doorknob again. Nope. It was still stuck, same as me.

"The one that I love," Doc's voice said.

Only that wasn't Doc's line.

"Shit fire and save the matches," I whispered.

Not this again. Not the ghost of Wilda Hessler back for more good times with her freaky-ass clown doll.

I stared toward the closet, cringing, waiting for that half-burnt little clown doll to come walking out of the dark, stiff-legged with half a creepy smile, while the damned changeling operated it by invisible strings.

Suddenly there was a sharp pain in my head. I stumbled to the side, reaching for the doorknob behind me and missing. The pain spread, turning into a squeezing pressure, feeling like several fingers trying to burrow into my skull.

"The one that I love," a voice whispered in my ear. It wasn't Doc, though. Not this time. It was gruffer.

The vice-like grip squeezing my head tightened even more. A wave of nausea roiled up from my stomach. I bent over, dry heaving.

The pressure increased. Something was trying to get into my head. I swallowed the bile starting to come up my throat, and then cupped my hand over my ears and pictured a candle flame. It flickered for a moment before burning bright.

The pressure eased, but not much.

I inhaled through another round of queasiness and then stood upright. In my mind's eye, I spun around with the candle flame several times, surrounding myself with a circle of fire.

Then I noticed a cloaked figure standing on the other side of the flame. I spun again and again, watching for it every time I came around. There was no face under the hood that I could see.

"The one that I love," the figure said. Long, pale fingers reached through the fire toward me, turning the flames around it bright green.

"No!" I screamed and threw the candle at it.

The candle fell to the ground at its feet. In a blink, bright green flames engulfed the cloak, hissing and sizzling as they climbed upward.

The figure shrieked and flew off into the darkness, green flames and all.

I opened my eyes and the pressure was gone.

A loud shriek filled the room, and then Jerry's desk skidded across the wood floor toward me. I jumped to the side, pressing into the wall next to the door. The desk stopped a couple of feet in front of me.

"What do you want?" I yelled.

"What do you want?" a voice repeated from the shadows in the closet. This time the voice sounded like mine, frustration and fear included.

What in the ever-loving hell was going on here?

I leaned over to look at what had been carved on the top of the desk. The three words I saw sent shivers down my spine:

JANE IS DEAD

"I know she's dead," I said, focusing back on the open closet. "And I also know you aren't really Wilda Hessler. You're her sister. The changeling." Although whatever it was I'd seen cloaked in my mind had been taller than a child changeling should have been.

Something clattered on the floor across the room. It was the letter opener. It lay on the floorboards, trembling.

"What are you doing here, dammit?" I asked.

The letter opener lifted and arrowed toward me.

I ducked behind the desk.

The blade hit the wall over my head. I gaped up at the piece of metal sticking out of the drywall.

Jesus! I peeked over the top of the desk. My gaze darted around the room, searching for any movement.

Something thudded in the closet.

I froze. I knew that sound. It was the trapdoor in the floor opening, clearing a path to the Hellhole.

That was it! I'd had enough of this bullshit. I took a deep breath, funneling my thoughts and emotions toward one purpose. It was time to stop running and start killing.

A blast of heat and energy surged down my arms to my fingers, making them tingle. I rose, reaching for the letter opener. If something was coming up through the trapdoor, I was going to jam the piece of metal into its goddamned eye. And then carve a smile into its freaking throat!

The letter opener pulled free with a hard tug. I eased around the desk, taking a step toward the open closet.

The shadows inside seemed to ripple.

I took another …

"Parker!" Cooper called, pounding on the office door.

I squawked and whirled. I could see a dark form on the other side of the frosted glass.

"Open the door!" he said, sounding very cop-like.

A door slammed behind me.

I turned again. The closet door was now shut.

The office door behind me opened, banging into Jerry's desk.

Cooper shouldered the door, leaning into it, moving the desk several inches. "What the hell is going on in here?" he said in a loud whisper.

I leaned over and shoved the desk, sliding it completely out of the way. The thing was heavy, giving me an idea of the strength of my invisible foe.

He started into the room, but I put my hand on his chest and shoved him back out into the hall, following him.

"What are you doing, Parker?" he asked quietly, blocking the path to the front room as I pulled the door shut behind us.

"Getting the hell out of there," I whispered back, wondering why we were whispering.

Cooper frowned at the closed door and then back at me. "What happened?" The furrows on his forehead deepened as he searched my face. "You look like you saw a ghost."

"That's your job." I blew out a breath. "I saw something else. I think we saw Jane battling the changeling on camera the other day."

"You mean Wilda Hessler's sister?"

I nodded and then shrugged. "Or maybe Mrs. Hessler and her parasitic ghoul."

He thumbed toward Jerry's office. "In there?"

"Yeah. I think it came from down in the Hellhole."

"You got to be fucking kidding me."

"Does this face look like I'm fucking kidding?" I folded my arms tight into my chest. "At first I was sure it was a ghost, but then it tried to pull some bullshit on me."

"You couldn't see anything?"

"Nothing but the closet door opening wider and the desk sliding across the floor right toward me." I held up the letter opener. "And this. It flew across the room and impaled the wall right where I was standing a second before."

"Jesus Christ, Parker."

"I know." I shuddered. "Worst of all, it called for me from the dark closet."

"It knew your name?"

"Yeah, but it used Doc's voice to try to reel me in."

"You're shitting me." He wiped his brow. "That's like what Cornelius and you heard in the basement of his hotel a couple of weeks ago."

"Exactly." I was debating on telling him about the cloaked figure on the other side of the flames, but the rumble of voices out front caught my ear. I peeked around Cooper's shoulder. "Who's out there?"

"Cornelius and some people who said they were here for their appointment."

"Oh, hell. I forgot all about them." I frowned up at him. "What are you doing here anyway?"

"Cornelius called me. He said he couldn't get in either of the doors because they wouldn't budge, and he thought I might have a way to get in since I'm a cop."

"Do you have some sort of master key?"

"There is no master key, Parker." He huffed. "But there is a baton that will break glass, if needed. Lucky for your boss, it wasn't needed."

"What do you mean?"

"By the time I got here, the front door magically opened."

"How in the …"

"I don't know. What I do know is that if you're going to take these people out looking at houses, you need to slap some pink into your cheeks and put on a smile."

I thought about Doc's and my secret and smiled.

He recoiled. "That's too creepy. Bring it down about two hundred watts."

I did and patted my cheeks. "How's this?"

"Good," he said, still frowning like it wasn't. "You want me to tell Nyce about this closet door deal?"

"Yes. But he's at a client's right now. Whatever you do, don't let him go in there. It's too risky. It mimicked my voice, too. We need to come up with a plan that includes some sort of protective metaphysical bubble around us."

"Okay. Go." He pointed toward the front. "Sell some houses."

"Right." Whatever was in that closet had the door shut and probably stuck tight again.

I took a deep breath, thought about the color magenta, which I'd read about on my phone before all hell broke loose in Jerry's office. That color was supposed to help with easing anxiety-triggering thoughts and letting go of the past.

Slapping on what I hoped was a not-so-scary smile, I headed out to greet my clients. Cornelius watched me approach with a worried brow, but kept quiet. He stepped back as I took over, giving me a thumbs-up and joining Cooper down by Jerry's office door. They whispered and waited at the end of the hall until my clients and I headed out through the door to the parking lot, sticking around as I locked up the office before disappearing up the stairs to Cornelius's apartment.

I turned to the happy couple who were considering retiring in the area. "How do you two feel about driving separately and following me around town? I need to ..." I paused, trying to think of an excuse besides the truth, which was to call my best friend and have her talk me off the ledge after what had just happened. "I need to make some quick phone calls via speakerphone to check on availability."

Thankfully, they agreed. I saw them to their sedan.

Back at my SUV, I slid behind the wheel, closed the door, and roared like a lion. When I finished being the king of the jungle, I started singing about being the happiest girl again and headed out of the parking lot to sell some real estate.

CHAPTER TWENTY-FOUR

Later that afternoon ...

Where are we going, Sparky?" Harvey climbed into my SUV, closing the door behind him.

I took a gander in his direction, which turned into a stare. He looked worn around the edges with his trapper hat jammed on crookedly. Sad faced, too, like the cheese had fallen off his cracker. I leaned closer and sniffed. He smelled like he'd been baking.

He turned my way and scowled. "You tryin' to stare a hole through me?"

"Why do you smell like fresh-baked bread?"

Harvey once told me that he liked to bake bread when he was feeling down and out. It reminded him of his momma, who used to make a loaf to cheer him up when he was a kid.

"Because I just made a loaf of sourdough potato rosemary."

The sound of that alone inspired some drooling. "But why are you baking bread in the middle of the day?"

"It's not the middle. It's almost evenin'. What are you, the bread police?"

"Is the bread for you or Junie?"

His gaze narrowed. "Why are you all up in my loaf?"

"Because I'm a caring person."

He snorted. "Nah, you're just being Miss Nosy Parker." He crossed his arms. "Now, are you gonna tell me where we're headin' or not?"

"You're also being cranky, like your nephew. Did you sleep on the wrong side of an old flame's bed last night?"

"I slept in my own bed, thank you very much." He raised his chin. "I think I'm gonna take a break from the pretty birds and enjoy the bachelor life for a while."

I had a feeling that Prudence had something to do with that decision.

"We're heading to Lead," I told him as I backed out of Doc's driveway.

"What for?" He grinned. "You wanna get more honey for our imp trap?"

"We don't have an imp trap yet." I took off down the road.

"Maybe we should spend some time this weekend buildin' one, then. That critter ain't gonna go away anytime soon unless we make it."

He was most likely right about that, but the imp was the last thing on my mind today. "We're going to Lead to pay a visit to Zelda and Prudence."

"Nope!" He reached for the door handle even though I was rolling along.

I locked the door. "Yep."

"No way." He unlocked it.

I locked it again. "I can do this all the way to Prudence's place," I said, my finger hovering over the lock button.

He scowled at me, but eased back into the seat. "Why do we need to go see ol' Prudy?"

"I need to ask her if she knows about the cages the *mardagayl* told us about. We're going while Zelda is there because I don't want Prudence using you as a microphone. I need your ears there to listen along with me, so we can share everything we learn with the rest of the team."

I suspected Prudence might have heard something about these cages before due to some of the comments she'd made in the past about impending doom, but then again she could just be a Debbie Downer in general. Hell, after the bruisings I'd taken from her over the last few months, I'd borrow money on that likelihood.

Harvey harrumphed, scowling out the windshield.

"Also, I was thinking about this *Duzarx* that has Prudence all worked up." After dealing with an invisible jackass in Jerry's office and the frustrations left in its wake, I decided it might be time to tackle my cohort's list of things to kill.

"Prudy gets worked up easily." He snorted. "She's so contrary that she'd float upstream."

I wouldn't argue with that. "I wonder if the *Duzarx* is one of the creatures from these cages. Prudence said she'd seen it come out from an opening in a wall of the Open Cut."

"What's that even matter, Sparky? It either has to be killed or not. And accordin' to Prudy, you need to take it out."

"Yeah, well I'm learning that Prudence thinks just about everyone and everything should be executed, including Cornelius. Had I killed the *mardagayl*—or tried to—we wouldn't have a clue how deep in shit we're about to be standing."

"I'm thinkin' it's time to stock up on shotgun shells for Bessie," he said.

I nodded as we passed the turnoff to Strawberry Hill. "I need to try to get a handle on the level of threat that we're talking about here. I mean, are these things being freed from their cages going to be easier kills, like the chimera we dealt with in Slagton? Or as deadly as the *lidérc*?"

"Those mutant griffins were plenty troublesome, if ya ask me."

"Only because they hunted in packs. One on one, they weren't anything worse than a couple of rabid dogs."

He cocked his head as he looked at me. "Who are you and what have you done with Sparky?"

"I'm still me."

He snorted. "You sound more like Prudy, ready to throw a punch before the 'howdies' are even over. Why are you all puffed up this afternoon?"

I wasn't puffed up. Or was I? I checked the rearview mirror, seeing the same curly-haired woman as always. I stuck out my tongue, wiggled my nose, and flexed my brow muscles. Everything looked and worked the same as before.

"Is it because you had a run-in with a ghostie in Jerry's office earlier?" he asked.

"You heard about that already, huh?"

"Of course. Word travels quick as greased lightnin' around these parts."

"Let me guess, Natalie called you."

She'd been fired up after I told her on the phone about my battle with the closet phantom, ready to rush the Hellhole with torches and pitchforks. I doused her angry mob fantasy when I reminded her that neither she nor I could see ghosts. We'd need a certain detective with us. That spurred several curses about Cooper's "stubborn-but-sexy ass." The conversation went downhill from there, spiraling into her listing his other parts that she found hot, until I told her a meteorite was about to crash into me so I had to go.

"It wasn't Nat," Harvey said.

I weaved my way up toward Lead. "Was it Doc then?"

Doc had texted me while I was in the midst of showing a house behind the hospital to my clients, making sure I was doing okay after getting a phone call from Cornelius about my troubles in Jerry's office. Cooper must have gotten busy with his "police business" and had Corny call. I'd sent Doc back a smiley face, since my own grin was still malfunctioning, and I'd written that we'd catch up later.

"No. Yer stallion was busy all afternoon fiddlin' with numbers."

"So, Cornelius called you, too."

"Bzzzt. Wrong again."

"That leaves Aunt Zoe." Natalie or Cornelius must have phoned my aunt to tell her about my lunchtime play date.

"You forgot about Coop."

"Cooper called and told you?"

"Sure thing." He smirked in my direction. "That boy worries about you."

I wasn't buying that. Not completely. He probably worried about what sort of destruction I was going to accidentally leave in my wake. "I think your pants are on fire, old man."

"Maybe a little. Coop probably worries about you when he's not busy cursin' you, but today he was frettin' about me. When he called to check in, he told me about the monkey business in your office." He scratched his beard. "Maybe Bessie and I should start sharin' your desk at work so we can keep a closer eye on you."

"Or you could move in with Cornelius and cut a hole through the floor to watch me from above," I joked.

"Hey, that there ain't a bad idea. We could put in an upside-down periscope."

Oh, Lord. What had I done?

My cell phone rang, playing an eerie tone.

Harvey grabbed it from the seat before I could. "It's Corny." He answered the call for me. "Plush Touch Massage Parlor," he said in a high, girlie voice. "If yer looking for rubs in all the wrong places, you called the right hands."

I gaped at him. "What the hell?"

He ignored me, listening for a moment. "Corny wants to know if you'll massage his hallux valgus, too."

I cringed. "His what?"

"His bunion," Harvey said.

"Oh. How do you know that?"

"Because I'm old and smart."

"Well, one out of two isn't bad," I joked with a grin. I grabbed the phone from Harvey, tapping the speakerphone button. "It's Violet. What's going on?"

"Well, I have a rather painful bunion on my big toe."

"I'm not talking bunions with you. Why did you call?"

"To talk tarot cards, but I'd rather talk about feet. Did you know that you can actually make cheese with the bacteria in foot sweat?"

I gagged out loud. "I'm not talking anything foot-related with you today. Let's stay focused on tarot cards."

"Fine, your loss," Cornelius said. "You remember earlier when you asked me what the tarot gods had in store for you today?"

"Sure." That was right before all of the spooky shit had gone down in Jerry's office.

"I have news on that front."

"Do I want to hear it, though?"

"Do you like death?"

I grimaced at my phone. "What kind of a question is that? Of course I don't like death. Who likes death?"

"Well, Eddie Mudder, for one," Harvey said. "He makes his money off death."

My grimace merged with a scowl that I aimed at him. "That was a rhetorical question."

"You look like you bit into some foot cheese," Harvey said with a chuckle. "Hey Corny, what's Sparky likin' death have to do with your tarot cards?"

"I drew a Two of Wands for matters that will be helpful in clearing her third eye to better see what she can't with her regular two."

Harvey and I exchanged shrugs.

"What's that mean?" I asked.

A sigh came through the phone. "Violet, you really should learn the major and minor arcana of the tarot."

"Yeah, but you're so good at it, and I'm a little busy running for my life these days."

"Excuses hinder success," Cornelius proclaimed.

I growled. "Just tell me about the dang Two of Wands."

"Fine. The card speaks of a possible partnership."

"It must be referring to Doc," I said, without thinking about Harvey sitting right next to me and how I was supposed to keep my big mouth shut about being engaged. I winced, glancing over at him. "Doc keeps preaching about us being partners in hunting *others*," I explained, crossing my toes he'd buy that. "So, that must be the partnership the card is talking about."

He eyed me. "Why's your nose twitchin', Sparky?"

"Because you smell like bread and I'm hungry."

He pursed his lips, but then nodded. "What other cards did she get, Corny?"

"The Lovers card for her current desires."

Oh, Lord! The tarot gods needed to shush.

My cheeks warmed under Harvey's persistent stare. "Like that's news to anyone," I said, scoffing a little too loud. "What is it you're always saying, Harvey? That I'm like a heifer in heat around Doc?"

Harvey lifted one bushy eyebrow. "Hmm. Give us the next one, Corny?"

"The Ace of Pentacles came up as your outcome, which is very curious."

"Curious why?" I asked, keeping my eyes glued to the road to avoid Harvey's prying gaze.

"It often indicates the start of a successful venture. Or a gift. Or both. Have you recently received a gift from anyone, Violet?"

A gift? Was Doc's acceptance of my proposal a gift? Or could the news from the *mardagayl* be considered a gift? Maybe it was referring to the clients from today who showed a legitimate interest in buying something and not merely hearing the ghost stories that went with a house.

"Didn't you mention something about death?" Harvey asked as we passed the road up to the Sugarloaf Building.

"Yes, Death was the challenge for Violet."

I snorted. "Not dying is the challenge."

"You're thinking of Death incorrectly," Cornelius said. "In this case, it refers to a transformation or a significant change in your situation or outlook."

Maybe it was referring to the death of my life as a single mother, transforming me into half of a happy couple. I liked that. I liked it a whole damned lot.

"Why are you smiling like that?" Harvey asked.

Oops! I tried to frown. "Like what?"

"Now you look like you're trying not to pass gas." Harvey snickered. "Sparky, is there somethin' you want to tell Corny and me about your take on the meanin' behind these cards?"

"No!" I shouted.

"Whoa!" Harvey held up his hands. "No need to go all curly wolf on me."

Gah! This keeping secrets business was a pain in the ass.

"I mean, no, there's nothing I can think of that I need to tell you."

He didn't look like he believed me.

I stared straight ahead. "Maybe the Death card is referring to the *mardagayl* and what she revealed about the cages below. That has certainly changed my view of Deadwood and how I fit into things here."

"Oddly," Cornelius said, "the Five of Pentacles was in the present position in the spread."

"What's odd about that?" I asked.

"That card sometimes means you might experience temporary hardship and need to guard against loss."

"That seems on target. You know what happened in Jerry's office this morning. I was on guard for the potential loss of my life the whole time."

"It is peculiar when considering the other cards drawn and how the energies merge. Something isn't adding up."

Since they were just cards, I wasn't going to spend the rest of the day worrying about them.

"At least I didn't get the Tower card again," I said, slowing as a Lead cop car passed us heading the other way. "I don't need anything else tipping over onto my head. The sky fell plenty yesterday."

"Speaking of your old boss," Cornelius said.

"We weren't, were we?" I glanced at Harvey, who shrugged.

Although, after that message carved into the desk, I was worried about Jane. I'd gotten used to knowing her ghost was hanging around the office, watching over us. If she wasn't there, where was she?

"I reviewed the video from earlier and have a question."

"What?"

"Did you happen to see a hooded figure at any time?"

Green flames flared in my memory. I tried not to react outwardly to his question, since I had an eagle-eyed audience at the moment. I hadn't told Natalie about that part of my ghostly encounter, because I wanted to tell Doc about it in person first and see what he thought it meant.

"Why do you ask that?"

"You remember when I told you there was someone in the hallway?"

"Of course." I'd almost peed my pants at the time.

"The visitor wore a cloak with a hood, hiding any facial features."

I gulped. It had to be the same one I'd seen in the dark, didn't it?

"Did it have a scythe?" Harvey asked. When I looked at him, he said, "Maybe the Timekeeper ran into the Grim Reaper. That'd explain the Death card." He grinned. "Hey, we should call you a TimeReaper!"

I just stared at him.

"Get it, Sparky? A Timekeeper plus a Grim Reaper?"

I shook my head at him. "That's dopey."

He looked miffed at my response. "Yeah, well you should watch the road more when you drive."

"I like the sound of it," Cornelius chimed in.

"Listen, you two, it was not the Grim Reaper," I said as we rolled by the visitor center in front of the Open Cut. "It's probably just a coincidence that—"

A block ahead, I saw the imp race across Main Street. If I'd blinked, I'd have missed it.

I gasped and pointed. "The imp!"

Harvey sat forward. "Where?"

"There!" I made a left onto Siever Street, hitting the gas as the little bastard crossed Julius Street and raced up the road.

"Jeez, girl!" Harvey gripped the dashboard. "Slow down before you make that Death card come true."

"I'm going to hit that damned imp if I can help it." I halfway slowed for the stop sign at Julius Street, making sure the coast was clear before gunning it.

Up ahead, the imp glanced back, letting out a screech so loud I could hear it through the closed windows, and then it dashed into a parking lot.

"There!" I pointed again, forgetting that Harvey couldn't see it. "The bastard is heading for the old middle school."

I followed it into the lot, slamming on my brakes in front of the old building and shifting into park.

"Ah hell," Harvey groaned, staring out the windshield. "Don't make me go into that prison again."

"Fine. Stay here, you big wimpy bodyguard."

"There's no need to go spittin' poison, Sparky."

I grabbed my phone. "Cornelius, we have to go."

"Violet," he said. "Based on the tarot cards, this might be a bad idea."

"They're only cards. I'm going to change my destiny today. Over!" I ended the call and pocketed my phone.

"That's not a walkie-talkie," Harvey said.

"We need to work on limiting your sidekick sassiness. Now grab my mace and let's go." I opened my car door and leaned out.

The imp was tugging on the double red doors that were chained shut today.

"I see you!" I yelled at the imp.

It glanced back at me and shrieked.

"Got you, sucker." I hopped out onto the ground and took off after the imp, which was trying to squeeze its head through the narrow opening between the two chained doors.

I pulled off my coat, figuring I'd wrap the thing up like a cat in a blanket and then knock it out with a solid thump on the head. But before I could grab it, the imp squeezed through the crack. It hissed at me when I tugged on the doors and rattled the chain. Through the opening, I watched it race off into the shadows.

"Damn it!" I turned around as Harvey jogged up next to me.

"The little shit made it through the doors."

Harvey huffed, his breath steaming in the cold air as he checked out the chain and then peered through the crack between the doors.

"Here," he said, handing me my mace. "Put on your coat and follow me."

I stared after him as he took off, heading across what appeared to be the old playground next to the school. "Where are you going?" I called out.

"Come on, TimeReaper! I know another way inside this prison."

CHAPTER TWENTY-FIVE

T his might have been a bad idea," I whispered a few minutes later.

"Too late, Sparky."

Harvey was using my phone's flashlight to lead us through a nearly pitch-black, underground walkway between the old school and an annex building on the other side of the playground, where he'd used his ever-handy screwdriver to break in through a side door.

According to Harvey, the annex had been constructed decades after the old school to add more prisoner cells, aka classrooms. The two structures were connected via the wide walkway so that kids didn't have to go outside to reach the cafeteria, which was located through some doors a few steps behind us in the basement of the annex.

"Why put a cafeteria in the basement of a building? That seems like a gloomy place to eat." Cool and clammy, too. I glanced behind me into the dark, listening for something else moving around down here besides us. "And spooky."

He sniffed. "Like a haunted prison, right?"

Before I could agree, a fat rat scurried across the floor in front of us, ducking under a pile of haphazardly stacked school desks and chairs on our left. I recoiled. That explained why I could smell urine along with the musty odor of damp concrete and rot. At least I hoped it was from the rats. My grip tightened on my mace as I peered into the dark nooks and crannies near the base of the clutter. Was there anything else living in the pile besides Mr. Rat?

"That critter looked fat and happy," Harvey said. "Makes ya

wonder if someone is feedin' them."

"And if someone is eating them."

We both shuddered and tiptoed onward without talking for a few seconds. The wall on our left had a colorful mural painted on it with different flags that were all connected in a long string. In the center were big overlapping circles and a torch, but the paint had chipped in some spots and been scraped away in other places, turning a happy scene into something eerie.

"Oh," I said, putting it together. "It's the five Olympic rings with the lit torch."

"They painted that after my time in this joint. When I was here, it was just flat yellow to try and cheer us up about spendin' day after day learnin' fractions and diagrammin' sentences."

Something creaked behind us in the pile. I heard something scuttle across the concrete floor. I really hoped that was the rat.

Ahead, a mound of debris blocked most of our path. It looked like the ceiling had caved in, but there were only concrete beams overhead, so nothing to fall. Upon closer inspection, the rubble contained broken wooden shelves and bookcases, chunks of flooring, pieces of chalkboard, and a couple of interior doors thrown on top of it all. Someone must have dumped it all there for a reason.

"You think this mess is supposed to block the path of any trespassers?" I whispered.

"Probably. It looks to me like there's a route through to the right of the logjam." He led us in that direction. "Watch where you step, Sparky. I see some rusty nails sticking out of several boards."

We weaved through the potential tetanus hazards and crunched as quietly as possible over the shattered pieces of glass. As soon as we were past the barricade, Harvey raised the light, trying to see what waited for us ahead. The sight of someone standing in a doorway on my right made me gasp. Then I realized it wasn't a person, just an Army poster with Uncle Sam on it.

"Hey, I know that poster," I whispered.

"Me, too. Like I said, I'm old."

"No, I mean I remember it from when I was in here with Doc a few days ago." I pointed in front of us. "Shine the light that way. There should be stairs."

"I know there are stairs there, Sparky. I remember fallin' down them once in my rush to get some grub. They were havin' grilled cheese sandwiches and tomato soup that day." He chuckled. "That was back when my bones were made of rubber. Now I splinter instead of bounce."

He shined the light up the stairs. Closed double wooden doors waited at the top of the steps. Several of the glass panes were broken out. Yep, those were the same doors Doc and I had peered through before deciding to head in the other direction.

I picked up the pace, climbing the steps beside Harvey instead of bringing up the rear. I was ready to be out of this rat-infested dungeon and return to the aboveground part of the schoolhouse of horrors tour.

We were almost to the top of the stairs when a loud crash rang out from the other side of the doors. Streaks of daylight shined through the panes above us, brightening the stairwell.

Harvey froze.

So did I for a second, but then a bolt of energy crackled from my head to my toes. My drive to kill kicked into gear, tickling my need to knock something to kingdom come. I sniffed the air, smelling rancid meat. Yeah, that definitely wasn't human.

"Was that the imp leavin'?" Harvey asked, barely at a whisper. He stuffed my phone inside his jacket to hide the flashlight.

"No. Something just joined us."

Clack, clack, clack, clack.

That sounded like claws on the tile floor in the entry hallway. Probably nice and sharp, too.

Whatever had entered the school was coming our way.

Harvey held his index finger to his lips, tugging me to the side of the stairs into the shadows. He motioned for me to drop lower and put our backs against the wall.

One of his knees popped as he squatted next to me. We both winced, exchanging cringes. I gripped the mace with both hands, praying that whatever was up there hadn't heard the pop because we weren't in the best position to defend ourselves at the moment. I didn't relish repeating Harvey's tumble down the concrete steps in the midst of fighting for my life. I'd probably splinter, too.

A snuffling sound came through the empty panes in the wood doors. It was followed by more clacking on the tiles, and then a deep rumbling growl that was so loud I could swear the thing was crouching right next to us.

I stared up at the doors, waiting for them to slam open. For something with gnarly claws and teeth to crash down the stairs on top of us.

A shadow blocked the daylight coming through.

I pressed my back harder into the wall, trying to think of a way out of this trap that we'd stumbled into because of the damned imp.

A thump came from the other side of the double doors. Then another. Not a knock, more like a shoulder bump.

Oh, hell. Was it trying to push through to get us?

Another thump, followed by a wet, sticky, gurgling-snuffle, like drool sucked through teeth.

I gagged a little.

If I remembered right, the doors had handles on the other side, so the creature would need to pull them open or crash through. Hey, that could give me the advantage I needed to spring on it with my mace already swinging.

I stood.

Harvey looked up at me, shaking his head.

I nodded, pointing at the doors, pretending to swing.

There was another thump. This time louder, more violent. The doors rattled.

He scowled, pointed at me, and circled his finger next to his head.

I wasn't crazy. I needed to get the jump on whatever was up there rather than the other way around.

Still pressing against the wall, I took a step up, quieter than the rats below us.

A loud screech rang out from the other side of the doors, making me slide back down in surprise.

I knew that screech. It was the imp.

A guttural howl followed. I covered my ears, cringing. *That* wasn't the imp.

Whatever it was, the thing was close. It had to be our snuffling pal on the other side of the doors.

When I lowered my hands, I heard the pounding racket of something clambering up the stairs in the old school.

I popped up in time to catch sight of a white, furry haunch before it disappeared from view.

"Oh, fuck," I whispered.

Harvey stood next to me. "What in the hell was that?"

"That is a Bone Cruncher."

Harvey hadn't been in the cemetery behind his barn the night I'd fought the other one.

"You mean a white grizzly?" He used the name given to the beasts in the legends that had been passed down through generations in the Black Hills.

"One and the same."

He looked at my mace. "You really think you can kill that sucker if it comes for us? It looked big as a wagonload."

"I'll certainly try. Thanks for the boost of confidence, though," I said with a sideways glare.

Another screech rang out from somewhere in the building, followed by a crash and a thundering boom.

"It must be chasin' the imp around up there," Harvey said. "Listen to that thing pound the floor. It's a wonder it doesn't fall clear through."

"Yeah, I have a feeling they're not just rough housing for fun."

We hurried up the last few steps and pushed open one of the doors. The hinges didn't make a sound. Someone had to be keeping them greased.

I walked out onto the tile floor. There was a jangling sound coming from my right. I glanced over. One of the outside doors was open wide, while the other swayed softly in the breeze with a broken chain dragging on the concrete below. The Bone Cruncher had made short work of that barrier.

Boom! The ceiling shook overhead. Small pieces of plaster and dust rained down on our heads.

A shriek echoed down the stairwell in front of us. Part of me wanted to run far, far away, but the Executioner in me held steady.

"We should skedaddle, Sparky."

I bristled at the shrilled cries coming from the imp. That thing was so tiny compared to the Bone Cruncher, which had been hanging around in the exact spot I was now standing a mere minute ago. Talk about a close call. Much longer and it would have sniffed out our hiding spot. At least it'd certainly sounded that way. Did it know the smell of a *Scharfrichter*? The other one I'd killed had.

"What are you waitin' for, girl? Let's go before that thing comes back lookin' for some dessert."

"Wait a second."

There was something about the imp's actions that had me hesitating. When the Bone Cruncher was nearly upon us, the imp's shriek had been loud and clear. The little shit had probably been standing on the stairs that were in front of me.

That shriek had lured the Bone Cruncher away and saved our asses. Could that have been a coincidence? Or was there something else besides the big stinky furball in the building with us that had spurred the imp to cry out?

Maybe the imp had been coming downstairs to escape outside, it had seen the ugly brute, and then shrieked in surprise and run back upstairs.

No. It had to have heard the sound of the outside doors crashing open, same as us.

"Sparky, let's go!" Harvey reached for my arm.

I pulled away. "I can't."

"Did your legs turn to puddin'? 'Cause I can carry you out, if so."

"My legs are fine." I sighed, thumbing toward the door. "Wait for me in the car."

"Why? Where are you goin'?"

"I need to help that damned imp, and I don't want to worry about you getting hurt during the fight."

He did a double take, and then looked at me like a third eye had grown between my other two. "You're gonna go help the imp?"

"Yep."

"Why on earth would you do that? The white grizzly is saving you a headache."

"True, but that is a deadly predator, not to mention probably carrying a grudge against me for killing the other one." Mr. Black had told me before that Bone Crunchers hunt in pairs, so I was assuming this was the other half of the problem. "That imp is just a pain in the ass. It doesn't want to kill anyone."

On top of that, the imp might have helped us on purpose. Why it would do that, though, was beyond me. Could be it had something to do with the Balance that the *mardagayl* had talked about last night.

His bushy brows pinched together. "You're not thinkin' this all the way through."

"Maybe not, but my gut tells me that I need to go upstairs and do my job."

Another boom rumbled overhead, sending down a cascade of dust and plaster over near the shadow-filled restroom. A squeal of terror from the imp struck a sympathetic chord in me.

I gritted my teeth. Enough was enough. I wanted to see blood—Bone Cruncher blood.

"I have to go, Harvey. Once you're safe in the vehicle, send a text to the group for backup. If I can't kill the big asshole, maybe I can hold it off until more help arrives."

I took off up the stairs, trying to hurry while stepping lightly. If I could sneak up on the beast, I might have a chance at landing a few solid hits.

After three short flights with ninety degree turns in between, I was at the top. In front of me were two doors opened wide. I eased closer, peeking inside.

I'd found the auditorium Doc had predicted would be in the building, but there was no sign of the imp or the Bone Cruncher.

The huge room was slightly tilted with a stage at one end and five rows of wooden theater seats still secured to the floor at the other. In the middle of the seats, an aluminum ladder was extended all of the way up to the ceiling, poking through a trap door at the top. The place smelled like dust and old varnish.

All the windows along the side walls were tall and boarded over, except for the one closest to the stage. Daylight spilled into the room through the multiple panes of glass, illuminating the stage and the small room to the right of it. The room on the left side of the stage was full of shadows, but I could see steps just inside the doorway.

On stage, a faded backdrop painted with a flower-covered hillside undulated, as if something had been moving behind it recently. I took a step in that direction.

A long, shrill shriek echoed throughout the room, making me cringe. Jeez, the imp had a big set of lungs in that small body. That or the acoustics in the room were excellent.

I took another step toward the stage. I was pretty sure the imp might be back behind the painted backdrop or the tattered velvet curtain on the left that was partially closed. Or maybe it was in the shadow-filled room with the stairs on the left.

"Sparky," Harvey whispered behind me.

I looked around. He stood in the auditorium doorway, waving

for me to come back to him.

I hurried over. "What are you doing up here?"

He held up a broken two-by-four board about three feet long with several rusty nails sticking out of it. "Playin' bodyguard."

"You were supposed to go call for backup."

"My phone is locked in your rig."

"What? I didn't lock it."

"I know. I did on the way out. What? It was an accident."

"So use my phone."

He held it up. "I don't know your password." He pocketed the phone again. "Now let's go kill that bone-eatin' son of a bitch."

Oh fudge nuggets! Cooper was going to kill me.

"Fine. Come on." I started toward the stage again, but Harvey grabbed me by the arm and turned me toward the rows of theater seats.

"They're back through that door in the old library room."

"How can you tell?"

He sighed and shook his head. "How many times do I have to tell you that I served years in this prison?"

"Right. Let's go, inmate."

But before I'd taken two steps in that direction, the imp ran out from the doorway behind the seats on the far side of the room. It stopped long enough to slam the door in its wake and then took off toward the stage, scrambling along on all fours. But it had a definite limp. And I could see a streak of what might be blood along its flank.

I stood frozen, watching it scamper-limp-run.

The imp glanced my way as it crossed the auditorium, but didn't stop to stare back. It was halfway to the stage when the Bone Cruncher crashed through the door after it, sending pieces of wood and glass flying.

This one looked just as ugly as the other one. There was a reason they'd been called white grizzlies, and this one lived up to the size hype. It loped on all fours after the imp with an open-mouthed snarl that showed off its sharp teeth and black tongue. Tufts of white fur covered the beast from its hideous head to its thick tail. The claws were retracted as it chased, but they were still long enough to clack on the wooden floor as it hounded the imp.

Harvey was right to wonder if my mace would do any damage to that frightful beast.

No sooner had I thought that, the thing bellowed another guttural howl that practically rocked me on my heels. Its teeth gnashed, drool flying as it whipped its head back and forth.

The imp charged through the open doorway on the right side of the stage. I watched it slam into the wall and fall down, but then push back up and race out of sight. I looked at the stage, expecting to see it there, but I didn't.

The Bone Cruncher pursued, slipping on a torn piece of the velvet curtain lying on the floor in front of the stage. It slid sideways and collided with the door frame, taking off part of the jamb in the process. Then the thing righted itself with a grunt and scrambled into the room after the imp, disappearing from view, too.

"That Bone Cruncher didn't even see us," Harvey whispered.

"His milky eyes were on the imp the whole time. It's all about the kill."

The imp squealed from somewhere up near the stage, but it sounded quieter, muffled. The growl and snarl that came from the side room was louder by far.

"Come on," I told Harvey and headed for the side room with my mace half-cocked and ready to start bashing.

"Maybe we should wait," he whisper-called over the commotion.

But I kept going, slowing as I neared the side room. The Bone Cruncher's growls and grunts sent chills down my spine. I knew bloodlust when I heard it. I peeked through the doorway, wincing in anticipation of finding the bully in the act of tearing the imp apart limb by limb.

The first thing I saw was a rusted wall radiator keeled over on the floor across a small room slightly bigger than Aunt Zoe's bathroom. A couple of rusted pipes lay on top of it, as if someone had made a point of keeping the dead radiator and all its parts together. The wooden floorboards around it had seen better days. They were warped and half torn up, leaving long narrow holes in the floor.

The grunting and snarling continued right on the other side of the wall.

My breathing slowed. A feeling of calm spread through my muscles, cooling everywhere except for my hands, which burned like they'd been frostbitten. I choked up on the mace, my grip strong, and made sure the spikes were aimed to do the most damage.

I took another step forward, peeking around the broken door frame.

In the near corner of the room was a miniature door in the wall. It was a dog door–sized entrance to the space under the stage. Sticking out of the small doorway was the Bone Cruncher's body. Its head and left arm were jammed inside the frame. Meanwhile, its back legs were clawing at the warped floorboards, tearing into the rotted wood as it tried to push and squeeze through the small doorway.

Another muffled screech came from the other side of the wall, trailed by a frightened-sounding hiss.

I stared down at the Bone Cruncher, which was oblivious of my presence at the moment. Then I looked at my mace, running that scenario in my head. A few good hits to the torso, but probably nothing fatal. Nope, no good. I needed a Plan B.

I glanced over at the dead radiator and its rusty pipes. That just might do.

I heard the rustle of clothes behind me. Harvey moved in close. I held my mace out for him to take and then put my index finger to my lips. He frowned but took the weapon from me.

The imp squealed again.

The Bone Cruncher pressed its shoulders harder against the small door frame. I heard a *crack*, and then the upper part of the frame splintered.

Stepping carefully around the beast's feet and claws, I grabbed a pipe from the radiator pile. One end was ragged and sharp, like something had torn the metal pipe in half. What in the hell could do that?

Never mind. That didn't matter at the moment. This pipe would work perfectly—I hoped.

I stepped closer to the Bone Cruncher's torso. The warped floorboards under my boots creaked loudly in the small room.

Well, shit.

The Bone Cruncher stilled. A growly huff came from the other side of the wall.

"*Scharfrichter* kill!" came a high-pitched, muffled yell through the wall.

That sounded like the imp. It must still be alive in there.

Keeping a firm grip, I lifted the piece of pipe, clenched my teeth, and drove the metal straight down through the Bone Cruncher's midsection.

It yowled loud enough to shake the rafters. When it finished, it scrambled backward out of the small doorway.

"Sparky, catch!" Harvey shouted, tossing my mace.

I caught it right as the Bone Cruncher's head came into view. "Pick on someone your own size!" I yelled and swung the mace hard.

It slammed into its skull. The crunch of bones breaking filled the small room.

The beast groaned, teetering like it was punch drunk.

But then it shook its head and turned toward me, baring its black gums and long teeth.

I swung again, nailing it across the side of its face this time.

Pieces of teeth flew into the wall, along with a splash of blood.

It tried to rise up onto its hind feet, growling bubbles of slobbery goo at me, its milky eyes rolling around in its big head. The beast teetered and stumbled. It took a clumsy swing at me, claws extended, but I dodged it easily. It tried to stand again, wobbling halfway upright.

I couldn't let it have the advantage of height.

"Say good night, Gracie," I said, same as I had the last time I killed one of these assholes. Then I swung once more, delivering a hard hit upward into its jaw.

Blood and bits of teeth splattered the walls and ceiling. Part of its black tongue plopped onto the floor at my feet. Then the Bone Cruncher's head fell back, followed by the rest of its body, crashing down onto the rotted boards. The weight of its own bulk jammed the metal pipe clear through, finishing the job for me.

"Good night," Harvey said Gracie Allen's line, peering around the door frame at the dying menace.

After one last gurgling growl, the Bone Cruncher gave up the ghost. Actually, I wasn't sure if a creature like this had a ghost. God, I hoped not. If so, that would be Cooper's problem.

"What are you doing out there?" I asked Harvey.

He looked at me. "Trying not to get wet."

I sniffed and wiped at the sweat running down my cheek. Only it wasn't sweat. I stared down at the smear of bloody goo on my palm and fingers. My stomach heaved. "Oh gross," I said, stifling a retch at the rancid smell coming from my hand. "Please tell me this isn't in my hair, too."

He made a puckered face. "Well, you do tend to set the woods on fire when you start swingin'."

I looked down at several streaks of the Bone Cruncher's blood on my coat. "Damn it, this is my good coat, too." It was the one Doc had bought me for Christmas. I hoped the dry cleaner could get this blood out and not ask too many questions in the process.

Harvey nudged the Bone Cruncher with his two-by-four. "You want to do something with this ugly critter? Take it to Coop, maybe?"

"No, let's get out of here before it liquefies into nasty tar-slop and stinks up the whole place."

Harvey grimaced. "It'll do that?"

"The one I killed behind your barn did."

"Oh yeah, I forgot." He hurried toward the auditorium exit with me following, but then stopped halfway there and looked back. "Aren't you gonna get the imp while it's trapped under the stage?"

"Not today." I grabbed his arm and pulled him along through the exit toward the stairs. "One execution is enough. Besides, Masterson might show up at any moment, and I don't want to listen to him whine about where his stupid *lidérc* is."

We hurried down the steps and out the front doors.

"You still want to go see ol' Prudy?" Harvey asked as we climbed inside my rig. "Ah, damn, you should have grabbed a tooth for her before you knocked that ugly critter into next month."

I started the engine. "Prudence can get her own damned Bone Cruncher tooth. I want to go home and scrub off this disgusting stuff and then hug my kids."

And my fiancé, I thought with a flutter of happiness as I shifted into drive.

As I rolled through a pothole on my way out of the lot, I thought I heard something clunk in the back end.

"Did you hear that?" I asked Harvey.

He shook his head. "My ears are still ringin' from all of the commotion up there."

Huh. Maybe I'd have Doc check that out later.

Harvey stared over at me long enough that I began to twitch.

"What?" I asked, glancing in the rearview mirror, recoiling at the sight of streaks of blood on my face. "I know I'm a mess, but at least you can't see my imp scratches with this new look."

"You just killed a white grizzly, Sparky."

"Yeah." That hadn't been written down in my planner. Good thing I'd left some time open for random executions.

He snapped his fingers. "Just like that. Easy peasy."

"Well, the imp had it distracted. I simply took advantage of an opportunity."

He snorted. "I hope ol' Prudy and her high-ridin' britches was watchin' you from behind my eyes that time."

"If so, she'd probably point out all of the things I did wrong and tell me I took too long to kill it."

"Most likely. I still think you should've grabbed her a tooth, though."

I smirked at Harvey. "I guess it was a good thing I got the Death card today after all."

CHAPTER TWENTY-SIX

Don't take this personally, Sparky," Harvey said as we cruised along Aunt Zoe's street a few minutes later. "But you're starting to smell like bad meat a half-mile off."

The streetlights glowed in the early evening twilight. The neighborhood looked cozy and serene, like there weren't monsters lurking underground, waiting to be freed to run amok and create chaos.

"I think I need a new job," I told him, rolling into Aunt Zoe's driveway. "This one really stinks."

Harvey chuckled, and then turned in his seat. "Hey, Coop's pulling up. Good thing, because it's his night to cook supper and I'm havin' some downright serious miss-meal cramps."

As we climbed out of my SUV, Cooper parked at the curb. "Uncle Willis," he called out, heading around to his passenger-side door. "Come over here and help me carry this food inside."

"What you got there, Coop?" Harvey asked, hurrying over to his nephew.

"Chinese takeout," I heard as I crunched along the salted sidewalk toward the front porch.

A squeal of laughter rang out in the cold, still air. I knew that laugh. Addy must be playing in the snow in the backyard. A battle cry followed—and that came from Layne.

I shook my head. That dang documentary on Hessian soldiers had really made an impact on him. Then again, anything with soldiers and weapons these days stuck to his brain like glue. I had to wonder if this hunger to learn everything he could about battle techniques and armaments had anything to do with being a Summoner who would possibly need to fight for his survival in the future, or if it was just an adventurous-kid thing.

I waited for Harvey and Cooper at the edge of the porch light's reach near the bottom step. "No pizza," I said when they neared with Cooper leading the way. "You're leveling up, Detective."

"Well, it's not gourmet fish stick nachos, but I'm trying," he said with a smartass grin. He stopped when he got close enough to take a good look at me. "What's on your face and coat?"

"White grizzly blood," Harvey answered for me.

Cooper's eyebrows crinkled. "Seriously?"

I nodded. "Unfortunately."

"Sparky kicked the bastard's butt until its teeth fell out," Harvey told his nephew, his smile beaming plenty enough for the two of us. "And then she made a shish kabob out of it with a lead pipe. The big ugly cuss is too dead to even skin now."

"Jesus, Parker." Cooper shook his head.

"It wasn't my fault," I said, holding my hands up. "The Bone Cruncher started it."

"Well, that explains the call-in I heard about earlier this afternoon. A guy up in Lead claimed he'd seen a white bear running through his backyard. Lucky for us, he'd been drinking to celebrate the end of his work week, so everyone figured it was a six-pack inspiration."

"Well, that should be the end of the white bear reports for the time being," I said. Although all three of us knew there could be more to come, at least according to the *mardagayl*'s doomy dispatch.

Cooper sniffed, leaning closer to me. "Is that rancid meat smell coming from you, or are you trying out some new perfume?"

"You're funny, Cooper. And I'm not just talking about your face." I started up the steps, asking over my shoulder, "Is Natalie coming, or is she avoiding you tonight?"

He grunted. "She's coming. She texted me earlier and told me what I was bringing for supper, and then she called in the order to make sure I didn't screw it up."

I laughed. "That explains why you're here early."

"She warned me not to be late, or I'd pay for it later."

"At least there might be a 'later' for you," I said, holding the screen door for him. "Unless you really bugger things up during supper with your mother hen act again."

"Shut up, Parker."

"Cluck, cluck, cluck," I shot back, chuckling.

"Hoo-wee," Harvey said. "Who'd have ever thought we'd see the day when Coop would let a woman run roughshod over him."

Cooper pushed open the front door, stepping back to let Harvey pass. "Get your ass inside, Uncle Willis."

Harvey was still snickering and ribbing Cooper as they headed for the kitchen.

I detoured upstairs, grabbed some clean clothes, and locked myself in the bathroom. The sight in the mirror made me wince. Ugh. Killing sure didn't look good on me. I sniffed my coat and gagged a little. It smelled even worse.

I took it off and hung it on the hook behind the door, tossing my robe hanging there onto the bathroom counter. I spent the next several minutes trying to daub and brush off what I could of the Bone Cruncher's blood with a cleaning rag from under the sink. Crud, I hoped I wouldn't have to burn my Christmas present from Doc. At this rate, I was going to have to start carrying a hazmat suit in my rig to save on new-coat costs.

With a growl, I tossed the rag in the trash can and stripped off my clothes. Hot water did wonders for my frustration about the coat. By the time I'd finished scrubbing and rinsing, I was back to smiling about the new secret Doc and I shared.

I pulled back the shower curtain and yelped in surprise at the sight of Doc sitting partway on the bathroom counter with one foot dangling above the floor.

"Damn," he said, getting an eyeful of steamed pink skin.

"How did you get in here? I locked the door."

I tried to play it cool and siren-like as I reached for the towel hanging outside the shower, but it was freaking cold in the bathroom in spite of the warm steamy air. I didn't waste time posing in the raw for him and wrapped the towel around my middle while my knees shivered.

"I told you before I'd find my way to you through a locked bathroom door." He grabbed my robe from the counter and held it out for me to stick my arms through. "Come here, my beautiful fiancée, and tell me all about your latest kill."

I slid into the warm robe. Then I turned around and dropped

the towel, sliding my arms around his neck. His eyes were level with mine since he was still sitting on the counter. So were his lips. I took advantage of our situation, trying not to smile like a mad clown during my kisses, or when his hands slipped inside of my robe and heated me up and down.

Too soon, the sound of pounding footfalls coming up the stairs interrupted our fun. It was only a matter of time before a kid knocked on the door, so I stepped back. While I got dressed, combed through my curls, and touched up my war wounds with coverup, I gave Doc a quick replay of what had happened inside of the old school. I ended my tale of blood and gore with the weird *clunk* I'd heard when I'd hit the pothole on the way out of the school's parking lot.

Doc stared at me with two vertical lines above the bridge of his nose that ran perpendicular to the multiple horizontal lines across his forehead. "So you think the Bone Cruncher might have been set free from one of the cages the *mardagayl* warned us about?" he asked, watching me apply a layer of gloss to my lips.

I lowered the lip brush, surprised. "I thought the first thing you were going to say was that I shouldn't have gone after the Bone Cruncher on my own."

He shrugged. "It was dangerous, but you're a *Scharfrichter*. You've slain one of them before, so you knew where to aim for the kill shot." He caught my hand and pulled me closer. "Besides, it's madness for a sheep to talk of peace with a wolf."

"I think you have me confused with the *mardagayl*."

"That's a quote that sort of applies here." He leaned forward and kissed me, taking his time from start to finish. He groaned when he pulled back. "Cherry-flavored. You did that on purpose, Tish."

I winked at him and returned to the mirror, adding a little more gloss. "How about we do some sweaty naked monkey dancing after we shut off the lights, Gomez?"

Someone pounded on the door.

Doc crossed his arms. "Tempting. Will there be biting involved?"

"Probably, along with panting, grunting, and lip smacking. Maybe even a whoop or two."

"Mom!" Layne hollered from the other side of the door. "Quit hogging the bathroom!"

Chuckling, Doc stood and dropped a kiss on my forehead. "It's a date, Queen Kong." Then he went to the door and pulled it open. "Layne, guess what book came in the mail today?"

My son gasped. "The one about the Maya gods?"

"Yep. You want to see it?" Doc headed toward the stairs with my son bouncing along behind him.

"Yes! Yes! Yes! Does it have lots of pictures?"

I didn't hear Doc's reply as they headed downstairs.

Apparently, the Maya ranked higher than the need to pee in Layne's world.

The doorbell rang as I came down the stairs a few minutes later.

"I'll get it," I called out and opened the door.

Reid stood on the other side of the threshold in a flannel coat and stocking cap. He held a couple of bottles of wine in one hand and a two-liter of root beer soda in the other. "Hey, Sparky. Thanks for opening the door."

I pushed the screen door wide and then stepped back to give him room to pass. "Does Aunt Zoe know you're coming?"

"Zo called and invited me over."

I smiled. "Glad to hear it." I closed the door. "Reid's here with drinks," I hollered, figuring I'd give my aunt a warning in case she was in the kitchen with the others. To Reid I said, "You can go ahead. I need to take care of something."

I detoured into the living room where Addy was just starting *The Jungle Book*, one of her favorite old cartoons. Layne sat on the couch beside her, engrossed in a thick book with pictures of Maya ruins. I squeezed in between them for several minutes, loving them silently without pestering them. Well, at least not pestering them too much.

"Mom," Addy said, pushing me away. "That's enough snuggles and kisses. I'm watching my show."

Layne endured a few more cuddles, bless his momma's boy heart, and then asked if he and Addy could have supper on TV trays in the living room. Since I wanted to talk about things they didn't need to hear, I praised his idea and helped him set up the trays, telling them both I'd bring their food if they'd sit tight.

When I joined the adults in the kitchen, Cornelius, Doc, Harvey, and Aunt Zoe were already settled in at the table. Reid was pouring and handing out drinks while Cooper and Natalie set out the plates, silverware, chopsticks, a big bowl of sticky rice, and various boxes of

Chinese food.

"Hey, Cornelius," I said, grabbing some plates for the kids. "What was the birthday gift my mom gave you?" I'd dropped off the present at his place a few days ago.

"How should I know?" he said, sipping from a glass of what looked like root beer.

"You haven't opened it?"

"Of course not. It is a common superstition that opening a gift before the official date will bring a year of bad luck." He scoffed. "With the way things have been going here in Deadwood, I do not believe we need to encourage further misfortune."

"Damned straight," Natalie said.

I quickly dished up plates for the kids, which Doc helped me deliver. We came back and took our seats as Reid carried two glasses of red wine to the table and sat next to Aunt Zoe, who looked beautiful and bohemian in her embroidered sapphire top and loose, wavy hair.

Aunt Zoe thanked him for her glass of wine with a smile that didn't seem forced for once and then turned to me. "I heard about what happened in Jerry's office and with the Bone Cruncher. You doing okay?"

"I'm good, I guess. All in a day's work, right?" I didn't quite feel that in my bones, but this was my life now. I was doing my best to accept it without having to hide in my closet daily along with Elvis.

Aunt Zoe nodded, her forehead tightening. "I've been thinking about the sorcerer."

"The one supposedly attached to Ray?" I asked.

She nodded. "You know how there is a sigil down in the Hellhole, as well as one on the wall next to the entrance in the basement of the courthouse?"

Doc and the others were listening now, too. "You think they're linked to the sorcerer?" he asked.

"Well, if it has attached itself to Ray, and he was able to move about in the tunnels, including exiting into the courthouse basement when he came upon Natalie, maybe the sorcerer is the one who made those sigils."

"An invisible ghost sorcerer," Natalie said, holding the bowl of rice as she scooped some onto her plate. "Do we know for sure if this sorcerer is good or bad? We thought the Hellhound would be terrible, but it turns out she's on our side."

"Nyce," Cooper said, taking the bowl of rice from Natalie. "Didn't you say there was a discrepancy between Underhill's description of the *mardagayl* and what we saw down in the tunnel?"

Doc nodded. "Ray mentioned big claws and pointy teeth, but her teeth and fingernails looked normal to me."

"Yeah, same here, but if the sorcerer was attached to Underhill, that might have spurred an instinctive reaction from the *mardagayl*."

"Bringing out its claws and sharp teeth," Natalie said, nodding. "So, the sorcerer is most likely an enemy. But why didn't the *mardagayl* attack Ray?"

"It could be," Cornelius said while plucking some egg rolls from a carton with his chopsticks, "that the *mardagayl* somehow exorcised the sorcerer from Ray for the time being."

Harvey pointed for me to hand him the soy sauce. "That would explain why he was confused as a turkey with a train ticket about how he'd landed in that tunnel when you-uns first showed up."

I handed the bottle to him. "So, we add a sorcerer to my catch-and-possibly-kill list." I had a feeling I would fail miserably at that without the help of at least half of those sitting at the table with me.

"*Our* list," Doc said, handing me the container with sesame beef, one of my favorites.

"Along with the *Duzarx*," Harvey added, setting the soy sauce back in the middle of the table.

I frowned at him. "Are you saying that, or is Prudence?"

"Hard to tell. Sounded like someone who knows enough not to pee on an electric fence, so it was probably me." He shrugged. "I think."

Cornelius forked some vegetable lo mein next to his egg rolls. "Let us not forget about the changeling and the parasitic ghoul attached to the Hessler woman." He glanced over at me. "I have a suspicion that the entity in Jerry's office with you earlier today was most likely one or the other."

"Or it was the sorcerer," Aunt Zoe said. When I looked at her, she shrugged. "A sorcerer would certainly have the strength to move a heavy desk around and mimic voices, even after death."

"True," Cornelius said, frowning. "Of the three, I'd prefer the changeling."

"Why?" Natalie asked.

"Well, anything parasitic makes my skin crawl, especially if I can't see it. As for the other, my grandmother used to talk about dead sorcerers being able to draw strength from vulnerable spirits."

"This is so fucked up," Cooper said, shaking his head while plucking pieces of orange chicken from the box.

Doc offered me vegetable fried rice. "Has anyone considered that the sorcerer is the parasitic ghoul that I brought through the door when we had the séance in Hesslers' root cellar?"

"As in one and the same," Cornelius said. "Interesting."

"*We* brought through," I said to Doc, dishing up the fried rice. "I was part of that, too, don't forget."

"We all were, except for Zoe and Reid," Natalie said. She squeezed Cooper's forearm. "This lucky law dog ended up with the door prize, though."

I winced at the glare Cooper aimed at me across the table. That was the night that he'd come up behind me to help in the midst of all hell breaking loose and was accidentally blasted open, allowing him from then on to see ghosts in all of their sometimes gruesome glory.

He huffed, but then shrugged. "I guess it's better to be able to see this shit going down around us than to be in the dark."

Natalie shoulder bumped him. "See, reading that book on paranormal stuff was a good thing." She scooped up some sesame beef and dumped it on her rice. "I wish I could see a little more, too."

Cooper's upper lip curled. "It's no treat, believe me." He shoulder bumped her back. "But in the meantime, maybe you could help me figure out how to handle it better."

I paused, exchanging a wide-eyed look with Natalie.

She nodded as she broke apart her wooden chopsticks. "It's a deal, Hot Cop."

"I have a question, Sparky," Reid said, taking a break from spooning some hot and sour soup into his bowl. "Why did you let the imp go at the old school?"

Aunt Zoe must have filled him in while I was snuggling with the kids. "I thought you guys were looking for those sigils in the Sugarloaf Building so you could catch it again."

"You had it right there," Cooper said. "Trapped under the stage, even. What were you thinking, walking away? Now we have to keep dealing with it breaking and entering around Lead."

I paused at the sound of the kids' laughter from the other room, wondering how much time we had until one of them came running in for more rice or a fortune cookie.

I shrugged. "I just couldn't do it. Especially after it most likely saved Harvey and me by luring the Bone Cruncher away." I reached across Doc and grabbed an egg roll from the carton. "I promise I'll catch the thing soon, Cooper, but I'll be honest—I feel bad about killing it now, claw-happy little bastard or not."

"It doesn't like bein' in a cage," Harvey reminded me.

"Yeah, I know." I pointed a chopstick at Cooper. "In the meantime, we have to figure out how to get more clocks from Ms. Wolff's place without making Hawke foam at the mouth."

"That's impossible." Cooper shook his head. "He has those clocks inventoried and has patrols monitoring the building. Getting in and out would be like tiptoeing through a mine field."

"Yeah, but I need those clocks. You heard the *mardagayl's* warning. I have to try to keep track of where all of the players are in this game."

"Maybe Mr. Black will have some ideas on how to get around Hawke when you meet with him," Aunt Zoe said.

Harvey squinted across the table at me while chewing on an egg roll. "Maybe we can fill the place with decoys. Like the clock version of duck huntin', you know."

"Not a bad idea," I said, "but where are we going to find a bunch of decoy Black Forest clocks?"

"We need to get him to move out of that apartment," Natalie said. "Or at least relocate for a while."

"We could try to spook him out with ghostly sounds and funhouse tricks," Cornelius suggested, looking around the table. "Where's the molasses syrup?"

"For what?" I asked.

"My egg rolls, of course."

While I made a face, Aunt Zoe got up to grab the syrup.

"That's not a bad idea, Corny," Natalie said. "I could sneak inside Ms. Wolff's apartment while Hawke is at work and install a few sinister decorations."

Cooper scowled at Natalie. "I don't think—" He stopped at her narrow-eyed glare and swallowed. "I mean, I don't think molasses on egg rolls seems palatable," he continued in a hesitant voice, focusing on his plate. "But since I haven't tried it, I could be wrong." He took a bite of orange chicken and chewed slowly, glancing in her direction a couple of times.

Natalie grinned. "That's better. How about I show you a trick I learned with molasses later tonight?"

His glance turned into a smoldering stare.

Doc nudged my arm. "Any word from Eddie on a meeting time or place with Mr. Black?"

I shook my head. "Between him and Masterson, I'm waiting for my phone to ring."

"Masterson?" Natalie asked. "Why? Because of his precious *lidérc*?"

"That and the Bone Cruncher. At some point, he's going to see that black stain left behind in that room next to the stage and figure out I killed something there." I swallowed a drink of ice water. "I doubt he'll be happy with me trespassing in one of his buildings, especially since I'm relatively sure he's housing *others* in that old school."

"I wonder if the sorcerer shadowing Ray is connected to the imp at all," Aunt Zoe said.

"The same sorcerer that could be latched onto Mrs. Hessler?" I asked.

She nodded, reaching for her wine glass.

Harvey cleared his throat. "Ol' Prudy seemed to think the imp drawin' sigils meant it could know sorcery, remember, Sparky?"

"Yeah," I said. "But that connection seems like a reach to me."

"It's possible, certainly," Aunt Zoe said. "Odder things have happened up here in the Hills."

I shook my head. "A sorcerer, an imp, a *Duzarx*, Kyrkozz, and who knows what else in between them all. I don't even know where to turn next."

Doc squeezed my leg under the table. "We'll figure it out together." He looked across at Cooper. "All of us. But not tonight." He took a sip from the glass of root beer that he'd told me Layne had poured to toast to the new Maya book. The kid must have gotten that toasting idea from our New Year's party.

Addy came flying into the room then, carrying my cell phone, which I'd purposely left upstairs on my bed.

"Mom, I heard your phone ringing when I went up to the bathroom, so I answered it." She held it out to me. "It's Aunt Susan."

I glared at my phone, but took it from Addy anyway. "How can I help you, Susan?" I asked, restraining my inner snarky bitch since my daughter was listening.

"Guess where I am?" my sister whispered.

I pasted a smile on my face for Addy's sake. "The dark side of the moon?" Oh, how I wished that were the case.

Susan sighed with an extra dose of drama. "I thought we were done playing these games."

"Fine." I heard the sound of a door creaking shut through the phone. "I don't know. Where are you?"

She tittered, sounding remarkably like an evil child doll possessed by a demon. "I'm doing reconnaissance in Rex's bedroom, and you'll never guess what I just found."

* * *

Saturday, February 2nd

I woke early the next morning to the sound of clucking out in the hallway.

After grabbing my cell phone and carefully getting out of bed so as not to wake Doc, I pulled on my robe and shooed Elvis down the dark stairwell. What was she doing out of the basement so early?

I tiptoed along the hallway to Layne's room. He lay sleeping under his comforter. Addy was snoozing away, too, my old softball bat leaning against her nightstand this morning instead of in bed with her.

Farther down the hall, Aunt Zoe's door was closed. I hesitated outside of it, debating on knocking, but it was only a little after five and she had enjoyed enough wine to probably sleep for a few more hours.

Now that I knew the kids were okay, I had a chicken to tend to.

I found Elvis roosting by the front door on top of my snow boots.

"Come on," I whispered, reaching for her but then stopping at the sight of something yellowish smeared on her white feathers. Was that pine pitch? No, not in the winter. "What did you get into, girl?"

Before I could touch her, she squawked and fluttered off toward the kitchen. I chased after her, shushing her the whole way to the basement door. She was going to wake up the whole dang house.

I followed her down the steps and gave her some chicken food. She seemed happy to go back into her cage.

"Get some sleep, dirty bird. Addy is going to be giving you a bath later."

The lights were on in the kitchen when I returned topside. Doc stood at the counter, prepping a pot of coffee in his pajama pants and a thermal shirt.

"Good morning, my big hunka hunka burnin' love," I said, joining him.

"I wondered where you went," he said, yawning while pulling me into his arms for a warm hug.

"Elvis was out of her cage." I wrapped my arms around his waist, shivering. "It's freezing down here this morning. It feels like someone left the back door open."

He pulled away a little, giving me a mock glare. "Don't even think about sticking your icy hands inside my shirt."

"Aww, but I thought you loved me." I started to inch my fingers under his hem, but he caught my hands and spun me around so I had my back to him while facing the window over the sink.

He nuzzled the side of my neck, his beard tickling me. "I do love you, ice princess."

I smiled, staring out the window into the backyard. The snow animals out there were visible in the pre-dawn gray light. The wind must have knocked the red stocking hat off the snowcat, though.

"What are you going to do about Susan?" Doc asked.

I leaned my head back against his shoulder. "I don't know if there's anything I can do. Even when we were kids, she wouldn't listen to me. It's only gotten worse with age."

"Do you think those old pictures Rex has of you warrant any concerns?"

That was what Susan had found, just a pack of pictures from when Rex and I were dating. I doubted it meant anything suspicious, just weird and borderline wacko. I wouldn't put it past him to keep them as some sort of trophy, the egotistical jerk that he was. There were probably pictures of other women he'd bedded stashed somewhere else in his things.

"No. The only concern I have is how to distance myself from Susan so that when she gets caught spying on Rex, he doesn't come to my door and follow through on his threat to tell the kids his role in their lives."

Doc turned me toward him, cupping my face. "Someday they're going to want to know who their father is."

"Yeah, but my fingers are crossed he's long gone by then, living on the other side of the planet, doing some super top-secret science project."

He smiled and kissed me. "I like the sound of that."

"In the meantime, *mon cher*, you and I have to figure out how to broach a much happier subject with them."

"I like the sound of that even more, *cara mia*." After another quick kiss, he let go of me and pulled a couple of coffee mugs from the cupboard.

My cell phone pinged. Who was messaging me this early on a Saturday morning?

I pulled it from my pocket. "It's Cornelius," I said aloud and tapped on the message.

The picture he'd sent made me groan.

"What is it?" Doc asked.

I held my phone out for him to see a picture of the Tower card.

"Stupid freaking tower," I said, pocketing my phone. "I'm not going to let that ruin my day. I have two legitimate appointments today, and then we're taking the kids out for dinner and bowling, right?"

"Right." He poured coffee into the cups. "I take it you want honey in yours, Tish."

I shook my head. "Why would you think that?"

He thumbed toward the kitchen table. "I figured you got those out."

I looked over. In my efforts to get Elvis back down into her cage in the dark, I'd walked right past the four bottles of honey sitting on the table, all but one missing their caps and mostly empty.

"Oh shit," I said, frowning at Doc. "Why is the honey out?"

The End ... for now

Ann Charles is a USA Today bestselling author who writes award-winning mysteries that are splashed with humor, romance, paranormal, and whatever else she feels like throwing into the mix. When she is not dabbling in fiction, arm-wrestling with her children, attempting to seduce her husband, or arguing with her sassy cats, she is daydreaming of lounging poolside at a fancy resort with a blended margarita in one hand and a great book in the other.

Facebook (Personal Page):
http://www.facebook.com/ann.charles.author

Facebook (Author Page):
http://www.facebook.com/pages/Ann-Charles/37302789804?ref=share

Instagram:
https://www.instagram.com/ann_charles

YouTube Channel:
https://www.youtube.com/user/AnnCharlesAuthor

Twitter (as Ann W. Charles):
http://twitter.com/AnnWCharles

Ann Charles Website:
http://www.anncharles.com

MORE BOOKS BY ANN

www.anncharles.com

The Deadwood Mystery Series

WINNER of the 2010 Daphne du Maurier Award for Excellence in Mystery/Suspense

WINNER of the 2011 Romance Writers of America® Golden Heart Award for Best Novel with Strong Romantic Elements

Welcome to Deadwood—the Ann Charles version. The world I have created is a blend of present day and past, of fiction and non-fiction. What's real and what isn't is for you to determine as the series develops, the characters evolve, and I write the stories line by line. I will tell you one thing about the series—it's going to run on for quite a while, and Violet Parker will have to hang on and persevere through the crazy adventures I have planned for her. Poor, poor Violet. It's a good thing she has a lot of gumption to keep her going!

The Deadwood Shorts Series

The Deadwood Shorts collection includes short stories featuring the characters of the Deadwood Mystery series. Each tale not only explains more of Violet's history, but also gives a little history of the other characters you know and love from the series. Rather than filling the main novels in the series with these short side stories, I've put them into a growing Deadwood Shorts collection for more reading fun.

The Deadwood Undertaker Series

From the bestselling, multiple award-winning, humorous Deadwood Mystery series comes a new herd of tales set in the same Deadwood stomping grounds, only back in the days when the Old West town was young.

The Jackrabbit Junction Mystery Series

Bestseller in Women Sleuth Mystery and Romantic Suspense

Welcome to the Dancing Winnebagos R.V. Park. Down here in Jackrabbit Junction, Arizona, Claire Morgan and her rabble-rousing sisters are really good at getting into trouble—BIG trouble (the land your butt in jail kind of trouble). This rowdy, laugh-aloud mystery series is packed with action, suspense, adventure, and relationship snafus. Full of colorful characters and twisted up plots, the stories of the Morgan sisters will keep you wondering what kind of a screwball mess they are going to land in next.

The Dig Site Mystery Series

Welcome to the jungle—the steamy Maya jungle that is, filled with ancient ruins, deadly secrets, and quirky characters. Quint Parker, renowned photojournalist (and lousy amateur detective), is in for a whirlwind of adventure and suspense as he and archaeologist Dr. Angélica García get tangled up in mysteries from the past and present in exotic dig sites. Loaded with action and laughs, along with all sorts of steamy heat, these books will keep you sweating along with the characters as they do their best to make it out of the jungle alive.

Made in the USA
Las Vegas, NV
31 October 2023

79948994R00204